ANCIENT TIDES ASHORE

MIKE ROBINSON

Black Rose Writing | Texas

ISBN: 978-1-68513-377-1
LIBRARY OF CONGRESS CONTROL NUMBER: 2023948135
PUBLISHED BY BLACK ROSE WRITING
www.blackrosewriting.com

Printed in the United States of America
Suggested Retail Price (SRP) $23.95

Ancient Tides Ashore is printed in Minion Pro

*As a planet-friendly publisher, Black Rose Writing does its best to eliminate unnecessary waste to reduce paper usage and energy costs, while never compromising the reading experience. As a result, the final word count vs. page count may not meet common expectations.

ANCIENT TIDES
ASHORE

I

Near the Hawaiian Islands
620 A.D.

1

A shape rose on the horizon, like a monstrous mouth seizing the sky's edge.

He thought: *The wayfinders have succeeded.*

The journey had been so long that Kaimi could not imagine it was land. Through the sail-bulging gusts of wind, the stillness, the hunger, the darkness, the burning sun, the aches racking his body, the destination had grown mythic: a thing which existed, but, much as the guiding stars, could never be touched.

Double-hulled outriggers cut over the hissing swells. Fashioned from sandalwood and blessed by sacrifice, the canoes had sustained well the journey of these thousands of miles. The prospect of the Great Voyage had filled many with dread, including Kaimi. For him, though, dread had been but a guest in a house of mourning. Akamu and Kaha'i were gone, after all. Home, whatever it was, whatever it was to become, was now windborne.

The swells were rising, another sign of land not far away. Salt-spray and headwinds chattered cold nonsense at them, as if urging them back in the direction from which they came. They would not return, however.

They would never return.

Kaimi's own oar had become a separable limb. Respites had been infrequent, and he had not slept well even if he was constantly tired. Food was highly controlled. The livestock, particularly the pigs and chickens, were dwindling, though in the last few days the nets had snared a hefty amount of fish and two turtles. Rations of yago, bananas, coconuts and yams still bloomed from the hulls' deeper crevices.

The Voyage had not gone untouched by death. Over these two months, two men and one woman had succumbed (though none from Kaimi's canoe), their bodies cast in hasty ceremony to the bottom of the world. To meet the jaws of creatures unseen.

"Our virgin world waits beyond the horizon," Chief Haunani had proclaimed. Kaimi did not understand how a man might be so resolute, so certain in the face of such doubt. Like much of the community, Chief Haunani had absorbed several generations of *kunlun* speculation and rumor about a northwesterly land known only by swell patterns and the golden plovers seen riding the wind.

Before his death, the Priest Iram himself had blessed the Voyage. "In this," he had said, "we will become embers escaping the fires of war. We will kindle a new hearth, in a new Garden of the gods."

Large sooty clouds loomed ahead, rain smudged across the distance. The sea took long heaving breaths. Kaimi tried to expel all ominous notions from his mind. They had weathered storms on the Voyage, sure, but all had been relatively small.

Though he would never voice it, Kaimi imagined a situation in which Nature allowed most, but not all, of their passage. The misfortune that had seen them off their home shores might have followed them, to deliver its final stroke in this hopeful stretch.

Chief Haunani shouted something about the Voyage nearing an end. About a final test. Kaimi could not hear most of his speech, drowned as it was by the silvered spray and winds.

Lightning splintered across the horizon, followed by grumbling thunder. The air muggy and electric.

Kaimi closed his eyes. This entire Voyage he'd not felt alone. Of course, in the strictest sense of the word, he wasn't. He sat in a boat of over a dozen people, which was just one of a dozen other canoes. But there was something ineffable that hovered close to him, and it had been growing steadily over the journey.

In dream-flashes, he considered they were rowing toward a softer edge of the world, where the hands of either the living or the dead might breach easier the wall dividing them, and find one another.

Rain pattered down, punishing. The sea grew mountainous. Kaimi and the others pushed harder, cresting the swells in foamy bursts of seawater, outriggers nosing down toward roiling valleys before rising again.

Darkness grew and the conch shells sounded, bellows barely audible in the storm.

All was soaked and lashed and stinging. Kaimi's eye sockets felt like they were packed with thistles. In all such howling pandemonium, there was, perhaps, a token of mercy: that his vision was necessarily restricted in the full scale of the storm.

•   •   •

Dawn broke over the world.

Still they rowed, the island much closer. With enough morning light, Kaimi could see the deep rich green of its valleys, the massive mountain rising into ghostly acres of clouds. His spirit lifted. The storm had passed.

The land grew clearer. High narrow hills, pristine darkness drunk on long wild epochs. Perhaps the land was not meant to be disturbed. Perhaps that was why the gods had placed it so remote: it was a piece of earth unwilling to join the rest. A *hale* of forsaken shadows.

They would have to find a suitable shore. Much of what faced them on this side of the island was a series of red precipitous cliffs. The sea hurled wave after crashing wave against the stone, as though attempting to collapse the land and reclaim it. Blurry rainbows appeared in the air, and were gone.

It was here Kaimi began to feel the tingling in his limbs. He wasn't sure what it was, but it did not impede his oarsmen duties and he easily ignored it.

They came across a small bay, a crescent of sand rimming a swollen jungle. Some of the trees leaned curiously out over the water.

At the terminus of one peninsula stood a large cone-like formation, dark lava rocks rising to almost a spearpoint.

Chief Haunani stood on the bow of his canoe, gesturing to the bay and declaring the Voyage nearly done. Conch shells bellowed, righting all men at attention, turning the fleet in unison.

Kaimi's stomach fluttered. He grew lightheaded.

"No," he muttered. "We cannot go there."

Makui, his younger brother and the oarsman before him, was the only one to hear Kaimi. He twisted around.

"What did you say?" Matiu asked, stern-eyed.

"Look!" someone shouted.

Once visible through the azure water, much of the ocean floor was now eclipsed by a massive school of gray-blue fish all streaming as one. Bigger fish flitted on the periphery.

Following their southerly direction, Kaimi saw just past the outermost canoes a series of dorsal fins piercing the surface. A pod of dolphins, moving away with the fish.

Not moving, Kaimi thought, with a random chill.

Escaping.

Orders came to drop the baskets, to take advantage of the sudden plentitude. Kaimi received a basket and a line and, alongside others, rose to deploy them. The school of fish split, shifting and regrouping. A few squirmed toward the basket, including one of the larger ones.

He closed his eyes, swallowed hard against dizziness unprecedented in all these thousands of miles of sea-travel. He loosened his grip on the basket and the line and sank into his seat.

The sun seemed bloated and oppressive. Makui's and others' queries into his wellbeing reached him as if from the ends of tunnels. He was transfixed by the fish. More tingles over his bones.

Then he was moving forward, and not by choice. The outrigger was tipping, *being tipped* by a strong and sudden force, and he fell and there was a splash and ocean-chill swept over him.

Fish broke past him. Through the tizzy of bubbles and commotion he saw other men and women floating there, flailing, kicking their way to surface where light was a gooey mess, where voices were as inarticulate as waves.

That had not been an ordinary swell. No. Nor had it been a wave. It had been some sort of *push*.

From something below.

Something alive.

The most obvious culprit was a whale. Many *kunlun* stories existed of the square-headed whale, specifically. Its bullishness. But wasn't that a creature of deeper waters?

Turning, he wasn't sure what he saw.

A shape drifted toward him, neither fish nor dolphin. He thought it a creature or part of the school of fish, but it was neither. Somehow it was both distinct and not, and it had a face and it was dark and it was old. Perhaps his own eyes were to blame, unaccustomed as they were to this alien constitution. Maybe that was why he was growing even dizzier.

A symbol flashed across his mind:

Hands grasped him, pulled him up. Dripping and disoriented, Kaimi managed to resituate himself into the canoe.

"Are you alright?" Makui said.

Kaimi breathed.

"What did you see, brother?" Makui asked.

Other bewildered looks prompted Kaimi to scour the water. Much of the school had gone. Coral reefs sat undisturbed but for small, foraging fish. The chop was calm.

There was nothing else.

Chief Haunani's canoe made its way over to Kaimi. Half his attention seemed to be on the sea at his feet.

"What was that?" Haunani asked.

No one could answer.

Makui said, "Kaimi does not think we should land here."

Kaimi kept his head down, water dripping from his brow and hair and lower lip. Chief Haunani's gaze, and all thought behind it, lay heavy over Kaimi. He expected to be reprimanded.

"I don't believe we should, either," said Haunani, with regret.

•　　•　　•

They pressed on. Gripping the oar, Kaimi watched the bay as it glided farther and farther from sight. The tingling held, but was not as severe as it had been. The dizziness lessened, too.

The creature—if it was *a creature—was so very … old.*

Older than old.

They rounded a dark finger of reef. The tingling left him, the dark and the cold replaced once more by warm wind and sun.

The bay was a bad spot, Kaimi reasoned, like mold on fruit or a diseased growth on skin. If they stayed away, their own spirits might remain unaffected.

Then—a voice just ahead. A cry.

They all saw her. Fingers pointed, heads whipped about. Some oarsmen and slaves even stood to get a better look.

With his view obscured by Makui and the bobbing of the double-hull, Kaimi could still make out the creature's head. It had extremely light skin and odd, yellowish hair, like the color of summer grass. She looked womanly. But if it—she—was a woman, she looked like none he had ever seen before.

While it was hard to see much below the surface, she appeared to be wearing a singular piece of black clothing. Her eyes were wide. Frightened and alone, she floated in the sea.

"Please! I need help!" she shouted, in a tongue no one could understand. "I don't know what's happened. *Please!*"

Her tears mixed with the seawater drenching her face and hair. Was she a lost spirit? A creature abandoned or injured? An omen? It disconcerted Kaimi that they should encounter her so soon after that rogue swell, and the dark shape drifting toward the bay.

There was supposed to be no one here, in this "virgin land".

The rowers shipped their oars, the canoes slowing. Her limbs pushing through the water, the gold-haired woman watched them with visible unease, like an animal unsure whether a stranger means harm.

2

Marilyn Toomey's earliest childhood memories were like visions glimpsed by someone drowning, her young consciousness periodically surfacing with hazy impressions of any given moment.

Until that one moment when Marilyn was barely four years old. The moment that seemed to jolt her faculties into higher working order.

The Osman wedding, between her mother's cousin Bethany and her beau Jon, proved one of the last big events her family would attend in the town of Byrneville, Oregon, before the move to Southern California. As the first of what would become five siblings, Marilyn had the distinction of being the only one at all privy to these "B.C." years, the life Before Children (well, the rest of them), and, most significantly, before the sprawling frenzy of Los Angeles.

One of the few bleary images from that day: Beth and Jon beaming before the congregation, clad in the white garb that snarky, non-Mormon Gentiles might dub "magic underwear." Sometimes Marilyn thought she recalled the *feeling* of the ceremony better than anything else. The air seethed with joyful sureness, but there was also a subtle note of fear.

The rest of the day rushed by in faces. The next thing she knew, she was standing in a patch of lakeside woods, surrounded by many of the same people from the wedding and from church, all of them towering as high as the trees. They smiled down at her, making her feel at once happy and uneasy.

"This *can't* be Marilyn!" cried her aunt Sarah, who'd traveled from Provo—then a million miles away—and whose finely-sculpted face blotted out the sun. "You're supposed to still be the little shriveled pink thing I was just *so tempted* to eat up with a knife and fork."

Caressing her rounded belly, Mom threw a dreamy glance at Marilyn. She said to Sarah, "Yes, Marilyn's going to be a big sister now. Like you! How do you like that?"

This event, held at Gordon Lake the day after the wedding, was a barbecue for the newly-married Osmans. The lake itself was a donut-shaped stretch of dusky water with a small, forested island in the middle.

Strange, unseen company lurked here—a Big Stranger, she thought—that no one in their eating and talking and hugging and picture-taking appeared to recognize.

"Marilyn," her mother called firmly at one point. "Come back here."

She didn't remember walking to the shore. The gravel bit at her bare soles, the water just inches away, glassy and still. Two years later, when she would see the ocean for the first time, the waves would frighten her in their noisy, aggressive reach. Right then, however, even Gordon Lake's tranquility unsettled her.

Why, though? And why had she walked to the edge of the water, as if ready to jump in? Usually she'd be too scared to do something like that without Mommy or Daddy. She felt an odd tingling in her body.

A thought came to her: *The Big Stranger wants to say hi.*

Her mother approached. Looming over Marilyn in her buttery floral dress, she seemed spun from daylight. She took her daughter firmly by the wrist and led her back to the crowd milling within the smoky shade of the grove.

"Don't go wandering off, Mary. It isn't safe."

As her mother led her away, she glanced back at the lake.

The day's imagery bled away again, leaving only residue of what followed. There was the food, the chicken that was really spicy. The imperious seven-year-old who for some reason muttered to her, "It's good you have blonde hair. Girls without it are ugly." Her father had made a toast during which everyone raised their red cups, and then some people put up a badminton net and there was a distant picture of the shuttlecock spinning through the air like some windblown flower and a man who dove for it amid laughter. Other grown-ups went away and re-emerged in swimsuits and started wading in the lake, arms raised as they shimmied one chilly inch at a time while their children dove in with huge, fountaining splashes.

Then, cutting through these pleasant memories: her mother's scream.

Confusion lingered. Mommy had *been* screaming. How long she'd been screaming, Marilyn didn't know.

Where am I? she thought. Her eyes squinted in the sun. She was really cold.

She saw water in front of her. A lot of water. A bird flew over her. Heart beating, she glanced slowly around.

She was floating out in the lake.

"Marilyn!" her mother cried from far away. "Oh my *God!*"

The grove and the barbecue now sat across a gulf of deep blue water. She panicked. Her family and her family's friends and everyone else had gathered at the shoreline and all the eyes were on her.

Those in the water poked their heads up and gasped. Some began swimming toward her. Garbled voices rang out across Gordon Lake.

How did I get out here?

At the shore, she saw her father embrace her mother. Marilyn picked up distant words like "911" and "trouble," and there was an explosive fluttering of frantic questions.

She was out in the middle of the lake, yes, but she wasn't moving or sinking because there was something hard beneath her. Something holding her up.

"...Marilyn! Honey...!"

"...can you wave to us...?"

"...are you *okay*...?"

Too scared to move, she began to cry.

The Big Stranger was all around her, though she couldn't directly see him. Did he want to punish her for some reason? No, he didn't. Of all things, Cookie Monster from *Sesame Street* popped into her head— a weird, funny creature, big and dumb but friendly in its way.

Still, she was terribly frightened. Still she cried.

Then, movement under her. Starting to move. For a brief second, she flashbacked to the elephant ride she'd taken with Mommy at the Portland Zoo.

The water rose fast up her hips, her belly.

She screamed.

"Holy shit!" someone shouted. It was one of the first times, if not *the* first time, she'd ever heard someone curse like that.

The Stranger kept moving, taking her down with him. Marilyn screamed until the water filled her mouth, turning everything inside her to ice. The world melted, all sounds muffled. Her muscles kicked back into gear and she flailed her arms, yet she couldn't swim and the water pinched everything in her closed.

—so cold—

Her eyes throbbed. She was shutting them tight. A tension was relieved in her private parts, a cloud of warmth passing over her. She'd peed. Bubbles streamed from her mouth and she imagined that it was her soul leaving. Her head squeezed from every side.

The terror had shaken her. Now, though, whether it was the cold or the quietness or the stillness, her senses appeared to settle down.

Her eyes sprang open. Through the murk moved a shape, growing larger and larger the longer she looked at it. It was long and it was gray and white, and it swayed back and forth like a snake. And she knew.

The Big Stranger.

Her chest seized. She sank down, down. What was that in front of her? If it was a fish, it was the biggest fish she had ever seen.

Would it swallow her? Chew her up?

No. I'm sorry, God. Please.

The Big Stranger was turning its gray-white body around and through the deepening dark she saw what could have only been some sort of face, but it was not a fish's face nor a snake's. Its eyes—swirling black, and heavy with something like loneliness and curiosity—were smarter than those animals but maybe not as smart as a person.

If the Earth itself were smart, if it knew what it was doing, she thought, it might have eyes like that.

Marilyn shut her eyes once more. She could sense her tender body powering down, switch after switch. She felt wrung. That her head and heart might explode.

She heard murmuring that sounded like her name. A presence enveloped her and swept her up, up toward the daylight. Death ceased its premature duties. Spirit flooded her veins again and soon there was a splash and a great glorious burst of breath and the sun's warmth and the crackling shouts from the shoreline.

"Marilyn?" said a voice.

She was coughing, huge convulsing rips up her throat. Snot filmed her whole chin. She tried to speak and thought she might throw up but instead just spit.

"It's okay, Marilyn, get it all out."

The voice belonged to Jon Osman, the groom. Her cousin. He'd been one of the grown-ups swimming in the lake and had been the first to see her and to reach her. Others bobbed nearby, hair all slick, eyes bulging.

Talking was hard, but after a few seconds she said, "Sorry."

"Sorry?" Jon said. He gave a wan smile. "Don't be sorry. I'm just glad you're alright."

He began towing her in, backstroking while propping her above the inky chop. The other swimmers made comforting gestures toward her.

"Did you see it?" Marilyn sputtered at one point.

"What, Marilyn?"

She coughed again. "The Big Stranger."

A voice nearby, from a teenage cousin named Tom. "What 'stranger,' Marilyn?"

"The big fish-snake," she said.

Tom snorted. "There's fish here?"

"'Course there's fish here," Jon said. "But not very big ones. And I don't know about snakes."

Marilyn was confused. How had no one, especially Jon, not seen something as huge as the Big Stranger? It was *there*. She'd been *sitting* on it. And somehow it had brought her out there, scaring her and scaring Mommy and everyone.

As best she could, she glanced farther out toward where she'd been. Maybe she would see it swimming away, like the whales on TV.

Nothing. The ripples had nearly smoothed over.

Marilyn came to recall every detail of the rest of that day. The wet embrace with her parents and the blotchy spot she left on her father's dockers. The wondrous relief. The hesitant questions she couldn't answer.

No one had any idea how she'd gotten out there. Jon mentioned something of her "big fish-snake," yet when she was pressed about it, Marilyn looked down, shrugged and acted confused. Because she was, of course. She was also beginning to understand that talking to grown-ups about it would only make *them* confused.

The smell of her mother's perfume clouded that afternoon and evening. Probably because her mother would hug her every chance she got. There was a heightened, almost electric warmth to her love. At one point, Marilyn was pressed against Mommy's belly and could feel the dull kicking of the baby that would come to be Shane, her first younger brother.

That night, she did not fall asleep for a while. She thought she could still feel the Big Stranger, tingling over some faraway horizon. As exhaustion finally washed over her, Marilyn imagined that perhaps she would get to see the Stranger again in her dreams. But then she fell into a deep sleep, and the dark brought nothing.

3

Years Later

Marilyn looked up. An ogre was staring at her.

By far, it was the most impressive creature she'd seen in this Grand Central Station of the weird and the wondrous, where gossamer-winged fairies rubbed elbows with Klingons and chalky-skinned vampires, where in one hand superheroes and wizards toted bags of merchandise while clutching in the other their hammers and staffs.

She sat alone in the food court, her rising pulse in step with the dull kicks of the baby stirring in her belly.

"Marilyn?"

Her name floated out from the colorful foot-traffic. She leaned forward, met eyes with the ogre. Unsure it was he talking to her, she threw glances to either side of her, toward the clustered Potterheads chowing down two tables over, then to the passing Vulcan couple.

She gave a hesitant smile. "Yes?"

The creature walked over, all six feet of hairless squeaking rubber and prosthetic. He held a staff topped with a plastic skull, which he leaned delicately against the table. He was close enough now that, through the costume's eye-holes, Marilyn could glimpse the light of the human eyes underneath.

"Hank?"

A muffled chuckle. "You got it!"

He struggled to pull out the other chair. Marilyn rose to assist, but he waved her away with a bulbous, green-warted hand.

"I got it," he said. "Sit down. You look like you're about to bust."

Half-grinning, she eased back into her seat. Hank sat down and removed his mask and set it beside the remains of her teriyaki rice bowl. The man's narrow face now regarded her from the comically disproportionate girth of his shoulders.

"Wow, it's been a while," he said. "You guys weren't here last year, right?"

Marilyn shook her head. "We haven't been since they moved *Realms* from LA to San Francisco, actually."

"Oh! Damn. So, what, three years or something?"

"Something like that. We figured we'd treat ourselves to a little getaway. See some old friends. Like you! It's good to see you, Hank."

"Well, you remembered my name. That's certainly a start."

Marilyn wasn't sure how to take that. Innocent irony or passive-aggressive jab? Even as she'd fully enjoyed these hectic days of the *Realms of Magic* Convention, the reunion with faces she and Joe had come to know almost exclusively through cons, social media or games like *Errowind Tales Online*, with their generally less-refined social graces, had reminded her why she tended to keep her distance.

Not that she herself was any better. Even now, one hardly needed Holmesian deduction to pick up on her agitation, that she was not someone used to dining solo. To being, well … stood up. By her husband, no less.

The baby kicked again, as if to remind her: *You're not alone.*

"That's a rockin' costume," Marilyn said. "You went all out. Is that real chainmail?"

"God, no. It's plastic. I couldn't hack that." He glanced about. "Joe with you?"

As frustrating and hurtful as Joe's absence was right now, it probably protected her from Hank's self-indulgent babbling. Like a lot of guys, he was always more the talker with Joe, who was never the enthusiastic recipient.

"I've been waiting on Joe for, let's see…the whole dang meal."

"Really? Is everything okay?"

"Oh, I'm sure. We're here for fun, but he's turned it into a bit of a business trip."

"He still at WaveSystems?"

Marilyn nodded. "Good memory. He's been meeting with some software and distribution folks. Write-offs, Marilyn, he says. Write-offs!" She made a gesture like one conceding a point. "Though he loves the work, too. Guess I can't fault him for that. *Too* much."

Marilyn formed a smile with this last sentence that she hoped came across as playful.

Hank frowned. "Seems like you can fault him for not showing up on time."

"That!" She raised her index finger. "That, yes, by God, I can fault him for."

"Congratulations, by the way." Hank pointed a long yellow nail at her stomach. "How far along?"

"Thank you. Due date is July 12th, so right around the corner."

Speaking the date aloud always gave her a brief, sinking fear, undiminished even with two children behind her. It was as though she expected to discover some new and unpleasant dimension to the process.

"Very cool. And this'll be number … two?"

She held up three fingers.

"Holy smokes! Well, that's great. Boy or girl?"

"This one's a boy. We've got another boy, Tommy, my oldest, and Tamara. So we seem to be rotating."

"They didn't join you here?"

"Nope. We left the li'l goblins back in Los Angeles. My brother and his girlfriend are watching them. We wanted a couple's retreat before, well, this next goblin makes his grand entrance."

"Love that *Realms* is your guys' idea of a retreat."

"Hey, we are who we are."

"Are you still playing *Magescape*?"

"No. I got sucked into ETO. *Errowind Tales.*"

"Ah. Yeah. I didn't think I'd seen you on lately."

"Sorry about that."

Sorry? For what? The apology had just slipped out.

Hank started to reply when a familiar face emerged from the crowds. He wore a shirt featuring a faded, old-school Dalek. His hands were in his pockets, his head down and he looked to be muttering to himself in frustration.

Seven years into their marriage, Marilyn might've felt confident she could tell when Joe's affected frustration was genuine and when it was theatrical, designed to excuse, or extract sympathy. In reading him now, though, she felt like a first-date novice.

"Well *hey* there!" she said, flatly.

Hank turned and extended an ogre's paw. "Joe! Long time no see, sir!"

Joe recoiled a bit. He shook Hank's hand, wearing a look of desperately not being in the mood which settled quickly enough into resigned courtesy. Hank didn't seem to notice.

"Good to see you, bud," Joe said. "Love the costume." He promptly went to Marilyn and kissed her scalp. "Mare, I'm so sorry. I got snagged by shop-talk, as you might imagine."

"I figured. Did you eat?"

Joe grabbed a chair from an empty table, scraped it over and sat down backwards. The pose made him look like a restless teenager, ready to leave at a moment's notice.

"Not really, no," he said. "They had some donuts and candy at the booth. That's it."

"Have *you* eaten?" she asked Hank.

Hank shook his head.

"Well! You two should totally grab some grub. I recommend the rice bowl place." Marilyn pushed herself up, taking her tray in hand. "I'm gonna head back to the hotel and nap for a bit."

"Whoa, wait. Marilyn…" Joe got up and put his hand on her elbow. "I'm sorry I was so late. I really am. But if some of these connections pan out, that could be really, really good. For the company *and* for us."

"I know. I totally get it."

She kept her tone neutral, enjoying the little-boy-lost look in Joe's eyes.

"I'm sorry," he said again.

"I know. It's okay." She smiled, and his anxiousness seemed to lessen. "Catch up with Hank. I believe he has a story about *Magescape* versus *Errowind Tales*?"

"Oh yeah," Hank said. "I've got *plenty* of those."

Joe's face fell. The silent gavel had fallen, the sentence given.

Marilyn walked away. She planned to head back to the hotel, where Joe would eventually catch up with her. Where she would embrace him and tell him that she understood and to not worry, that it wouldn't be a geek-out getaway if he didn't also geek out in his own ways, even if they didn't always include her.

•   •   •

Her destination was still the hotel when she left the convention floor, passing under the *Realms of Magic* banner near the large windowpanes facing downtown San Francisco. She was tired, for sure, and, submerged as she'd been this weekend in so much humanity, she craved true alone time. A space to hear her own thoughts. A space where, as Mom might've said, she could hear God's whispers.

But then, an urge rose in her: adventurous, rebellious, tugging her toward those unexplored streets and hills.

Arriving a day before the con, they'd done the requisite tours of Golden Gate Park and the Japanese garden and Fisherman's Wharf. All beautiful things, to be sure, whatever their cliché. Joe had then suggested Alcatraz, which, to Marilyn's relief, proved such a cliché that all ferries were booked that week. The Wharf was the closest she wanted to get to the water.

Now she teetered. Her tired, reasonable self, which she loosely nicknamed "Mom-Marilyn", threw out its arsenal of wild worries— *getting lost! getting run over! getting mugged!*—and with every step she took toward the pavement of those Great Outdoors, the more her fears and paranoias crowded themselves into a pesky din.

She held her stomach. The kick of life there. This calmed her, as she ventured outside and began to walk. Chill wind swept over her. Fog claimed the sky.

Actually, she thought, I should go back for my jacket.

But she ignored this last stab at an excuse and kept on. She made her way to the bottom of the hill, feeling as rejuvenated as she did naked and vulnerable.

She stopped, craned her neck up. Downtown's high-rises and skyscrapers leaned over her, as if ready to topple. Sunlight had won a few openings in the fog, throwing a melancholic, painterly glow over the city.

Marilyn took notice of the numerous tent communities bubbled across alleyways, empty lots or any other crevice offered by the unthinking bulk of so much silicon-powered progress. Not anyone's fault, Joe might remark. These people just needed purpose, inspiration, motivation. Yet there were so many of them, and the constant sightings wrung Marilyn's heart.

Under the yellow awning for a *Yolk Artisanal Cafe*, she stopped and uttered a prayer for the downtrodden and disenfranchised. As she spoke, she felt the graceful Life of the Divine radiate down her bones, brighten every molecule of her being.

Then she walked on, noting several landmarks along her journey to aid her way back. She wasn't sure where she was going, really, and the sheer freedom buoyed her spirits.

Yet there was no denying the tension in the air. It was pervasive. Unsettled. Marilyn had always felt like she could read personalities in things, in objects, places, even areas like whole cities. Most people felt at least a little of this. That was why they named their cars, why certain houses felt like "homes," why folks referred to New York or LA with feminine pronouns.

There was more, though. Often, non-living objects had one fixed energy—say, a bicycle ridden solely by its owner. Some, like public spaces, churned and changed constantly, susceptible to so many different flavors and textures.

A war of spirits, of ideals, rode the winds of San Francisco.

She crested another hill, her breathing labored. The metal sheet of the Pacific spread into view through the towers. Steady, murmuring static rose from what sounded like a few blocks over. Music boomed. The stirring of a crowd. Marilyn followed the noise through a tightening braid of foot and vehicle traffic.

Something was happening.

Prickly self-awareness filled Marilyn as she approached the source of the commotion. Costumes floated by her, but they were hardly Vulcans or ogres.

Skin, and more skin. Rainbow flags hovered, swirled. Young men, some with makeup, passed out literature or held out petitions or, in one case, distributed tiny free chapbooks of poetry. Some sported leather sex-dungeon-type getups, some women's clothing, some nothing but a thong or speedo though many of the latter were hairless and well-built. People embraced, groped, stood with hands in each other's back pockets.

Some of the more scantily clad people smiled at her, perhaps sensing with amusement that she'd gone astray, this young pregnant Mormon wife stumbling into what looked more and more like the Gay Pride Parade.

Marilyn edged cautiously toward the fringe of the crowd lining the parade, as all its floats and marchers and dancers and performers rolled by to the concussive music and cheers of so many.

She had met gay people, of course. Hard to avoid in Los Angeles, really, though she suspected some were just posers. Regardless, the actual, physical sight of men kissing men, or women pressing against women, was still alien to her. She stiffened.

Had God directed her here for a reason? For her own spiritual edification, maybe she was supposed to glimpse the lives these particular Gentiles had chosen for themselves. Whatever their questionable virtue.

She stood back from the thick of the crowds. On a street corner about a block away, people over-dressed in drab sweaters and dresses held up signs, some as colorful as the strokes of rainbow across the parade.

God Hates Fags.

God Watches & Judges. REPENT.

No Forgiveness Without Christ.

The LAKE OF FIRE Awaits!

No one seemed to be engaging the sign-wavers, though officers and squad cars lingered nearby.

Such a dreary waste of time, Marilyn thought, observing those protestors. They were like a hopeless island, sidelined by this cultural river charging onward. Charging in directions that, sure, she herself might not have agreed with, but which were useless to fight. God had ultimate control, after all.

Saddest of all were the children in that group. Their expressions were dull, perplexed, glimmering only when their parents acknowledged them.

Mom had once stuck signs in their hands, for events Marilyn now barely remembered. These days, her mother would occasionally encourage her to do the same with Tommy and Tamara, though Marilyn never would. It was bad enough she'd been pressured into attending some of those Prop 8 rallies when she was younger.

All at once, Marilyn sensed something rotten and wrong.

Then the explosion.

A high and piercing pop-*bang*, it threw everyone around her into startled confusion. Given all the antics and bodies present, it was hardly unthinkable someone might've crossed the line and broken out fireworks, or that a bus might've backfired.

A ripple of people pushed back toward her, murmurs heightening to chatter which heightened to calling and crying and shouting, and the voices and the agitation grew exponentially until screaming cut through all of it, and the harsh smell of smoke gave pointed edge to the unknowing anxiety which had halted the parade and which now unleashed a violent tremor of terror through the crowd.

Then the second bomb went off.

Marilyn felt as if she'd been immersed in a toxic liquid that had dissolved her every definition, bled her into this churning sea of emotion. Faces blurred past her. A terrible heat descended on the boulevard.

People screamed and shouted and rammed into her even as more people broke her fall. The baby, oh God the *baby*. She steadied herself, cupping her belly. She was the crude vessel now bearing invaluable cargo. She could lose a limb or even her life and it wouldn't matter, wouldn't matter so long as the baby made it safely into the life God intended for it.

Yet in watching the monstrous smoke loom over the city, she thought, *What world am I bringing him into?*

That she'd kept some distance from the crowds helped her head start, though not by much. Her pulse hammered. She'd never felt so simultaneously in tune with and detached from herself.

She stumbled. A passing elbow clipped her shoulder. Something came undone in her, too, but she had no idea what. In all the madness, she had only a flashing conceit: the re-opening of a scar.

There are more than just people here.

Painful twinges in her stomach, growing worse. *Baby's dying.* This was it. Marilyn fell to her knees, began to sob.

No, she thought, fully recognizing the pain. The baby wasn't dying.

It was coming.

II

Present Day

1

"That's…wow." The young Sister named Josephine leaned back, exhaled quickly. "That's incredible. I can't believe it."

The other Sister, Carly, sat with her potato-lumped fork halfway to her mouth. Her eyes were wide. "Your angel was working overtime that day. For sure."

"As was his." Marilyn leaned over and kissed the top of Troy's head, as he stabbed peas on his cartoon dinosaur plate. "The four-foot miracle, right here." She looked at Tamara and Tommy across from her, five and eight respectively, both born in merciful comfort in the depths of Cedars Sinai Hospital with loved ones clustered outside to welcome them. "But no less a miracle than you two. Just different. You know."

Periodically, Marilyn Toomey would forget she had three children. Not that she would forget *about* them, of course, just that the idea of children had been with her so long (even as far back as kindergarten, when Mom had made an offhand remark about grandkids) that the reality had become an expected business which absorbed the quirky, distinct miracles of Tommy, Tamara and Troy into the texture of daily life.

Only randomly would it hit her: *Three beings came* out *of me. Three individual spirits.*

Carly leaned forward. "So how did you make it to the hospital?"

Joe sat back, took a gulp of soda then glanced off toward the kitchen. Marilyn sensed discomfort in him whenever this topic arose. A checking-out.

"Thank God I wasn't trampled," she continued. "I did kind of click into ultimate mama-bear mode, where nothing mattered but the baby. The timing was horrific then, but, looking back, I think God was meeting that awful carnage with precious new life."

Josephine smiled. Carly's smile was more reserved, as if she found this whole notion cheesy. And yes, there was a whiff of cheese to the way she told it. And vanity.

"The contractions were getting worse, but they weren't as bad as I remembered them—"

"I'm guessing because there was so much going on around you, maybe?" Josephine ventured. "Like, an adrenaline rush?"

"Could be. I could move okay. I kept breathing in sweat and smoke…"

Toward the back of her mind, Marilyn was pleased with how rapt these two young missionary Sisters were, how rapt Tommy and Tamara were even though they'd heard the story often.

"In the craziness," she continued, "I felt a hand grab mine."

"Whose was it?"

"I…never saw him. Or her. But they led me to the very spot where two firetrucks pulled up. I had paramedics assisting me right away. I felt bad. I mean, I wasn't even injured…"

"You should *not* feel bad," Carly said. "You were going into labor."

"That's what I say," Joe noted. He glanced toward the front door. Something preoccupied him.

"That's true." Marilyn thought about the mysterious guide. She had felt all sorts of other things in those moments, most prominently a sense of things coming … undone. Like certain scars, once thought healed, had been torn open, certain sensitivities revealed.

Since the Parade Bombing, the world's secrets had scooted that much closer to her ear. She was convinced of this. Was convinced, too, that such feelings had mitigated any deeper trauma she might've otherwise sustained.

Carly rose from her seat. "I'm going to get more juice, if anyone wants anything."

"Could you get me another Sprite, please?" Joe asked.

"Sure." There was a brisk forthrightness about Carly's movements, an assumption of automatic welcome that, legit or not, irritated Marilyn.

"Again, that is amazing, Marilyn," Josephine said, munching her potatoes. "Seriously."

"We've talked way too much about me," she said. "Tell us about how things are going with you."

Apparently, neither Carly nor Josephine had known one another before being sent on missions to Southern California. Carly was from Ohio, Josephine from Florida. They'd not been dispatched to the most unique locales, unfortunately. One of Joe's friends had gone to Norway, and even Joe, for his mission, had at least gone to Alaska. Marilyn was envious of all of it—she'd never gone on a mission.

She'd dreaded this evening, even as she was privileged to host these dinners. The house was a mess, and she hadn't had the time to get everything sorted, so under every smile or kindly glance from either Sister, Marilyn imagined an ongoing stream of judgment: how trashy the living room looked, for one, full of hopelessly scattered kids' toys, how the front lawn needed weeding (heck, landscaping of any kind), how the bathtub needed bleaching.

Josephine lifted a bite of Cornish game hen to her mouth. "This is really good, by the way, Marilyn. Thank you so much."

"You're very welcome. I'm improving. Cooking is not a natural thing for me. Joe's actually much better than me."

"My problem is I just hate doing it," Joe said. "I like *having* cooked. Fruits of my labor and all. But after cooking up code all day? No way."

"My real specialty is drawing cephalopods," Marilyn said. She pointed to a framed pastel of a Kraken fighting Cthulhu. Completed two years ago, it was one of her favorites. The digital version now commanded thousands of DeviantArt and Insta likes.

The girls turned.

"Oh, that's cool," Carly said. "What did you say, though? Seth…?"

"Cephalopods? Octopuses and squid."

"Oh. Okay. Isn't it octopi?"

"Nope! That's a misconception."

Carly shrugged. Marilyn was stung by their lack of enthusiasm. I'm a good artist, she thought. Not Frazetta. But good. She had a hefty amount of DeviantArt followers, after all. And all stupid hentai jokes aside (and she'd heard plenty, mostly online), creepy tentacled things were darn fun to draw.

"My cousin went to art school in New York," Josephine said. "He doesn't really draw things, though, not like that. But he can. I think."

Marilyn held up her nose, affected her voice. "He's more the, dare I say, 'fine *aw*-tist type?'"

"I guess so. I haven't talked to him in a while. He left the faith, unfortunately, not long after moving."

"City like New York," Joe said, shaking his head, "can put your soul through a grinder."

"It wasn't so much the city, I don't think. It just pushed him over the edge. According to him, he'd been struggling for a while. Finally became a true apostate when he was back for winter break."

"Well, I'm sorry to hear that," Joe said.

"A prostate?" Tommy asked, with a devious, food-filled smile.

"Hey, not cool," Joe said. "You know better."

"What does that mean?" Tamara asked. "Apos…?"

"It means he fell behind," Marilyn said. "It's like if you got sick and stayed home from school, forever."

"Geez, don't say *that*," Joe said.

Tamara's eyes brightened. "That sounds fun!"

"To be sick all the time? That sounds fun?"

Chuckles around the table. Marilyn felt a shiver down her spine, had no idea why.

"I feel for you," Marilyn said to Josephine. "My younger brother Shane is also—"

"A militant atheist," Joe finished. He tapped his temple. "Talk about sick."

Marilyn resented Joe's dismissiveness. Shane wasn't sick. He was one of the smartest people she knew. He was just lost. Lost and angry. He'd let the toxic grit of the world penetrate his soul.

"I do think some people need a little time in the wilderness," Marilyn said. "If God laid out a straight shining path for everyone, what wisdom or achievement would really come from that?"

"That's true," Carly said. "And you certainly had your moment in the wilderness."

Marilyn nodded slowly. "We all pass in and out of it. Throughout our lives."

Carly turned to Joe. "Wise woman you married, Mr. Toomey."

"Don't I know it." Joe regarded her with an ambiguous expression, though she caught flickers of admiration that validated her.

"Sooo…" Joe began, in a sudden uptick in tone. "*I* have news."

"Uh oh," Carly said. "Sounds big."

"What's going on?" Marilyn asked.

"Well, today was my lucky day," Joe said. He leaned toward Marilyn, as if to impart a secret. "And by extension, it'll be ours, too."

"What is it, Dad?" Tommy asked.

Troy was the only one who seemed disengaged from the suspense. He looked dazed.

Joe cleared his throat. "So that call-in trivia contest that BlastFM does every Friday morning? I finally got through."

Marilyn snickered. "Oh really?"

"Did you answer everything right?" Tamara asked.

Joe finger-gunned his daughter, a gesture of *You're getting' ahead of me*. Marilyn grew excited. Best as she knew, that contest rotated prizes every week, everything from a wad of cash to Disneyland tickets to full-covered spa treatments. She hoped it was cash. They could use the money, though at the same time she didn't want to come off as materialistic to Josephine and Carly.

"Today's questions were straight up my nerd-alley," Joe said. "The final question? Who was the longest-running companion on *Doctor Who*. Can you believe it? Fate!" He took a long sip of soda.

"That's awesome," Marilyn said. "What did you win?"

"*We* won. *We* won. And you know *what* we won? Get this: an all-expenses-paid, week-long trip to …" He drummed his fingers on the table, "…*Hawaii*! To a brand new resort on the southwestern coast of Kauai. In a place called Pyramid Bay. How amazing is *that*?" He turned to the sisters. "I had a friend who went to BYU Hawaii. Visited him once. Oh man, incredible. I wanted to go there on a mission. Or even our honeymoon. But I've wanted to do it in style, you know? I don't want to compromise."

"Compromise?" Carly asked.

"Sure! Gimme five-star beaches, world-class snorkeling, the most succulent seafood. Nothing less. Do it," he slammed his palm lightly on the table, "in *style*!"

Marilyn was embarrassed. How vain did the Sisters think they were, now?

"Why didn't you tell me about this when you got home?"

"Well, I got off late," Joe said, "and you were busy getting dinner ready and all. I wanted to save it for when things simmered down and we were all together."

"Well, congratulations!" Josephine said.

"My cousin went to BYU Hawaii, too," Carly said. "He stayed there for two more years till he really couldn't afford it."

"Wait, so do we all get to go?" Tommy asked, mid-chew. Of all her children, Tommy had inherited the brunt of Marilyn's own homebody tendency.

Joe shook his head. "I'm sorry to say, Tom Bombadil. It's just Mom and I."

"Aren't you excited?" Josephine asked Marilyn.

"Oh, I am," she said. "It's just…"

"Just what, Mare?" Joe said.

"It's … water."

"Huh?" He furrowed his brow at the young women, as if to show solidarity with their own non-understanding. "Yes, Hawaii *is* surrounded by water…"

"*And*, you know I don't *do* the water thing."

Josephine and Carly's gazes now followed a ping-pong match in this odd, stupid standoff with her husband. He did have tendency to deny things that were inconvenient to his plans. Sometimes, it made him a fun go-getter. Other times—most times—an inconsiderate nuisance.

"What's the water thing?" asked Josephine.

Carly frowned. "And you're into octopi?"

"I almost drowned when I was four," Marilyn said. "At a lake up in Oregon."

"Whoa." Josephine set down her glass. "Yeah, that's enough to make water a 'thing,' for sure."

"Just how many angels *are* following you?" Carly said.

Marilyn didn't exactly remember what had pulled her out onto Gordon Lake, but it hadn't felt angelic. Nor had it been evil, really. Through the clouds of that early childhood hour lingered the silhouette of a thing large and alive, though not 'alive' in the way she was.

"Wait, so how did you almost drown?" Josephine asked.

"Uh…Mom?" Tommy interjected.

He was pointing at Troy, whose head was bent forward like he was about to collapse.

"Hey buddy!" Joe said. "Troy!"

"*Honey*?" Marilyn felt a pang in her chest. She hastily lifted his head up. His eyes were almost closed. "What's wrong?"

Consciousness returned to Troy's face. "I'm sleepy, Mommy."

She felt his forehead. No fever. He was actually a little cold, and pale.

"Are you not hungry?" Marilyn asked. That was a stupid question. He'd pretty much finished everything on his plate. "You ate well. Really well."

"It's probably just food coma," Joe said.

"Do you want to wait for dessert?" Marilyn asked Troy. "Or lie down and nap?"

He leaned in toward her. For the briefest of seconds, someone else stared out at her from her son's hazel eyes.

"Nap," he said.

He reached out and embraced her neck. She lifted him up and excused herself and carried him down the hall. Sounds of the dinner receded.

Troy's body heaved up, down, up, down under her palm. She had to hold him longer, like she'd done for Tamara when she had colic as a baby. She was not to lie him down and leave him, not just yet. She had to give him something.

As they passed the bathroom, Troy made a half-hearted gesture.

"Do you need to go?"

He nodded. He rubbed a fist over his left eye, making it red and puffy. Marilyn set him down and accompanied him into the bathroom. All at once, Troy's poise straightened. He snatched a rubber shark squeak-toy they called "Mr. Megs" from the rim of the bathtub, then adjourned to the toilet, lifted the lid himself and sat.

Given the contrast with how he'd been a moment ago, and her fresh, potty-training battle scars, she was struck by the sight.

"Do you want Mommy with you?"

Troy shook his head. He fiddled with Mr. Megs, whose mouth yawned with pointy, bendy teeth. He squeaked it.

"I'll be right outside the door, okay, sweetie?" Hand on the knob, Marilyn paused. "Didn't we put Mr. Megs away after your bath earlier?"

Troy bent the shark's tail back and forth, swimming it through some ocean in his mind. "Baldy likes to play with it."

"Oh he does, does he?" Marilyn knelt by the tub, unplugged the stopper from the drain. "Hey Baldy, we had a deal. Playtime's over when I say it is, remember?"

"He isn't there," Troy said distantly. "He's in the faucet."

"I see. Well, I'm sure he still heard me."

Troy began peeing and she left, clicking the door shut behind her. She leaned against the frame and listened to the murmur of dining room conversation, Tamara's one-word interjections by far the loudest.

Then—new murmuring, right on the other side of the wall. Troy was talking, it sounded like. Probably to Baldy, his "bathtub buddy" who had showed up sometimes over the last year or so, right around the time their cat Tardis had died.

Troy's murmuring stopped. In a burst of fear, Marilyn barged into the bathroom.

He was nowhere in sight.

"Troy?" The toilet lid was still up, the pee sitting there, unflushed. The Chewbacca shirt he'd been wearing lay pooled on the floor. She picked it up as she hurried about checking cabinets, the towel hamper and the shower.

All empty.

She bustled down the hall to the kids' bedroom, popped open the door covered with drawings and construction-paper cutouts blaring TOM, TAM and TROY. Soon it would be time for Tommy to get his own room, whenever they might afford the add-on.

"Troy?" she said. "Troyasaurus? Come on, honey."

Nothing.

"What in—?"

She turned and closed the bedroom door, just as Carly entered the hallway and smiled at her. "Sorry, the bathroom?"

Marilyn pointed, and the girl nodded. At the entryway, she stopped. "He okay? Troy?"

"Um." Marilyn tried to slow her pulse. "I'm actually trying to find the li'l stinker."

"Uh oh, he run away from you?" Carly frowned. "I thought he was tired."

"So did I."

Carly entered the bathroom and closed the door. Marilyn paced slowly back and forth. Paranoid thoughts gathered like hyenas on the fringe of her mind.

A yelp. From the bathroom.

Marilyn hurried over. "Carly? Everything alright?"

"Yeah," Carly said. She snickered. "There's a shark in the toilet."

Mr. Megs? She'd just been in there. She'd checked the toilet.

Against all desire, Marilyn walked back into the dining room and beckoned Joe with her finger, interrupting a discussion between him and Josephine.

They convened just inside the hallway.

"What's up?" Joe asked. "If this is about the Hawaii trip—"

"No. Troy got loose. I don't know where he is."

"Huh?"

"I was taking him to his room, and he needed to go to the bathroom. I asked if he wanted me to stay with him, he said no, which is already weird…then, when I opened the door, he was gone."

"He's squirrelly. Good hider. You sure he's not under the sink in there, or in the shower?"

"I'm sure. I checked."

Joe glanced down the hall, then toward the dining room. "Okay. Let's round up the soldiers for a little search party."

As he started back toward the table, Marilyn tugged on her shirt. "Can we not tell the Sisters?"

"How, exactly? They're here. They can help us look."

Resignedly, Marilyn nodded.

•   •   •

Tom and Tammy went about their search in a chorus of hinge-squealing and door-slamming. From another room, a bunch of plastic items crashed to the floor. Marilyn thought of her game and music CDs, all stacked on the desk in the den.

"Hey!" Joe called from the family room. "No pillaging! Pick it up!"

Marilyn formulated a mental list of all possible nooks and crannies, which she checked off: behind the La-Z-Boy recliners in the living room, under the kitchen sink (where her old cat Tardis had slunk one-too-many times), hers and Joe's shower stall, behind the bookshelf in the game room. On and on.

"Still nothing?" Carly asked at one point as they crossed paths in the kitchen. The dishes and utensils and food remaining on the dining table had become a melancholy sight, the ruins of a pleasant evening.

Marilyn sighed. "Still nothing."

"We'll sniff him out," Josephine said, reaching out to rub her arm. The gesture felt patronizing, like Marilyn was a mental patient on the verge of losing it. Then again, how much anxiety was she now broadcasting on her face? People could often read her surprisingly well, which she didn't like.

"Troy!" Joe called, his voice quavering a little. "Let's go! Not funny anymore! The Sword of Shame awaits!"

"He's gonna get *shamed*!" Tamara said. Just a plastic, retractable lightsaber they'd bought at Disneyland last year, the Sword of Shame had become the household's go-to method of either condemnation or honor, applying not just to the kids but to Marilyn and Joe, as well. One could be knighted ("Jedi-knighted", Tommy would say), or "stabbed" for some indiscretion.

Several times, Marilyn had to reorient Tommy and Tamara away from bickering back to searching. As she scoured the garage, she felt a waning connection to Troy, like he was a feather blown constantly beyond reach.

This makes absolutely no sense.

"Troy!" she called. "Please! Come *on*, man!"

She tried desperately to ward off certain thoughts: Troy as a bloody heap on Turner Road, or in the grip of a faceless cretin who'd lured him outside.

She hurried to the living room window and parted the curtains. Past the front yard and her own ghostly reflection in the glass, Turner Road lay quiet under the cold glare of streetlights.

She popped open the front door. "Troy?"

"Did he go outside?" Joe asked behind her.

"I don't think so."

Blame started creeping in. *Troy, you ruined the evening. Ruined it. Maybe the Sword of Shame should be in order. Or far worse.*

Returning to the house, she made her way to the kitchen, snatched a flashlight and slid open the door to the backyard. Plastic kid-cars and bikes sat next to cobwebbed patio furniture. The shadows taunted in cricketsong.

She shone her flashlight across the yard. "*TROY!*"

The entire house froze. A dog started barking not far away.

"Um, I think," Tommy said meekly from the kitchen, "I heard a noise in the ceiling."

Marilyn switched off the flashlight and rushed to him. "When?"

"Like two seconds ago?"

"Want me to check the attic?" Joe asked.

Marilyn didn't reply. She hurried down the hall to the attic door, placed her hand on the knob. Her family and the Sisters gathered nearby.

She popped open the door. The wooden staircase rising into gloom. Each rung creaked on her ascent. One made an ominous snapping sound, making her think she might plunge to the floor in a cloud of dust and debris.

Joe approached the staircase. "Watch for splinters. Nails, too."

"I know. I'm up here more than you."

She reached the attic. Boxes and bins radiated memory. Every step she placed more gingerly than the last. Roofbeams arched over her like whale ribs might have Jonah.

She switched on the light. The lone bulb sputtered on.

"Troy?" she said. "Are you up here? Somehow?"

Her eyes were compelled toward the table stacked with old board games. Under her feet, Tamara and Tommy thumped about, trading garbled statements she couldn't hear.

It was strange. Though she didn't think Troy was in the attic, she also had a feeling that every time she looked somewhere she would see him, that finding him was imminent if she could only "decide" where he was.

Movement on the far wall caught her eye. She turned. The lightbulb was …

What?

… quivering. By itself.

Chills flooded Marilyn. She stepped toward the bulb. It kept shaking, on and on.

"Mommy…"

She whirled around.

Troy was there, crouched near-naked under a table stacked with board games. Marilyn went numb.

Joe's footsteps climbed the stairs.

She hurried to Troy, knelt by him and embraced him. His eyes were wide and dewy, his legs bunched up so his chin rested on his knees.

"What on Earth are you doing up here?" she said.

"You *find* him?" Tommy cried from below.

"Hey," Joe said, halfway into the attic. His gaze fell on Troy. "Buddy, what's gotten into you? Why did you hide like this?"

"They said playtime's still going," Troy said.

"Who?" Joe asked.

"The people from the faucet."

"Oh," Joe muttered. "Is this more 'Baldy' talk?"

Still clutching his arm, Marilyn gently pulled him out of the crevice. They rose to their feet. His pale little potbelly jutted over the band of his underwear. His skin was pale, cold still.

Troy took her hand and they made their way to the ladder. The light no longer appeared to be shaking, and Marilyn flicked it off. Darkness closed on them like a giant phantom pincher and Joe descended the stairs.

She felt a thrum of vulnerability. Her son's existence seemed … flimsy, the space around him perforated for easy tearing and pulling away.

She lifted Troy into her arms and clutched his warming body against her own, feeling his roundedness, his there-ness, as they made their way down into the light of the house.

•   •   •

The Canyons below were a plentiful network, many smaller ones feeding into the enormous one. How far would they have to travel? She'd been to Gora Desert, but had never been to these badlands. Stories had been told of ancient warring tribes, of the exotic creatures in its rocky folds.

The wind howled. Gally, her Elvish companion of over four months now (thankfully Renee had renewed her subscription), unsheathed her sword and ran toward the trail sloping down the cliff face.

She, however, hesitated. She herself was a Myrulian Dwarf-Knight, genetically shaped over the eons to endure such a harsh native environment.

Jammies on, computer on her lap, and dishes piled up and totally *not* done, not yet, Marilyn explored the troll-infested Lhan'Ni Canyon, a mere stitch in the massive digital quilt that was the world of *Errowind Tales Online*. Troy lay sleeping in the crook of her arm. He was still pale, though not as cold. Periodically she checked his forehead.

Across the room, the TV underwent the restless schizophrenia of Joe's indecisive channel-changing.

"Hah, *Spooksters*," he said. "Nice."

Some of Marilyn's attention was drawn away from *Errowind*. It looked like an episode they hadn't seen. The crew was visiting a haunted plantation home not far outside New Orleans. The team's main guy stood interviewing a local medium named Lady Beaumont about what she perceived as the "abominable forces at work in this place."

"However," Beaumont added, "they can't touch you if you don't let them."

Just one look, and Marilyn knew: Beaumont was bogus. The woman seemed perfectly sincere. She was just a Little Leaguer convinced she could start for the Dodgers.

"She's not legit," Marilyn said.

Joe looked at her. "I never think *any* of them are. Why do you say that about her?"

"Just a feeling."

Joe chuckled. "Well, I will say, I definitely trust your 'feeling' over anyone else's. That's for sure."

The comment was genuine and unexpected. Marilyn brightened.

Returning more of her attention to *Errowind*, she typed a message to the three people she was now gaming with.

Random question: do you guys believe in ghosts?

She sat back, just now recognizing the tension in her shoulders.

Replies came back.

Sure why not?

Not really.

Depends…

Marilyn's fingers hovered above the keys, her eyes on the TV even though she wasn't watching right now. Troy squirmed, shifted his position such that she could feel his warm pure breath on her arm.

She wrote:

What about … anything else?

This time, the answers were universal.

What do you mean?

She dropped the subject and kept playing.

•   •   •

Toward midnight, she closed the laptop. She checked in on Tommy and Tamara, both calm lumps of bedsheet in the dark. Having requested a Mommy-Daddy night, which Marilyn herself would have insisted on, Troy now lay curled next to Joe.

She brushed her teeth, staring at herself in the mirror. Occasionally her gaze flicked down to the reflection of the bathtub faucet.

The whole, surreal evening had splattered itself across her attention, her every thought now chasing some different trickle down her mind.

Like Joe's out-of-the-blue Hawaii trip. Such random "luck"—what was that about? That was not something that happened.

He won it, chided a voice. *It's* Hawaii. *It's paradise.*

Stop whining. Never whine. You've got nothing to whine about.

She positively detested the *other* concern of hers—people were fit in Hawaii. All pictures boasted of chiseled surfer-abs and curvy bikini babes with colorful dresses thrown 'round their hips like bath-towels. Not to mention the "island girls", flower-clad and calendar-ready.

Pre-kids, Marilyn might've competed. She'd of course been fitter when she married Joe, a 26-waist, firm rear and legs. Now she had chunk; not a lot, but enough that the "would-be model" in her (so-called by her sister Pat, who was always flipping through *People* or *Us Weekly* even as she lamented moral rot in celebrity culture) had been buried under layers of unfashionable pudge.

Yet Marilyn's blue eyes still shone, and her hair remained long and silken and all-natural, much as the fortunate symmetry of her face. "You're so pretty, Marilyn," Aunt Sarah had said to her last Christmas. There was some green to her words, probably because the woman was only forty-seven and already on her fourth bout of plastic surgery.

Marilyn knew she tended to get drunk on petty resentment, letting it fog up experiences that should be savored. She told herself not to allow that to happen this time. This was an opportunity.

This was going to be a real adventure.

Yet she also assumed that, no matter what Joe might tell her now, he would be orchestrating a hard-fought campaign to get her in the water. She'd have to be firm.

Check that—*strong*.

•   •   •

She lay in bed, her brain whirring. Could they donate the Kauai trip to someone else? Surely there were folks far worse off who might have greater use for a gift like that.

It was the kids. The *kids*. Especially Troy. Neither she nor Joe wanted to leave them with Shane and Jeanie again. There was Joe's cousin Kevin and his wife Marge in Orange. They had their son Calvin, but she could ask. Have them over for a BBQ, or something.

Just then, a voice cut through her thoughts, shining on her mind a ray of absolute conviction:

You need to go.

Suddenly, the trip was without question. It was locked in. She felt this as clearly and immediately as she'd known that "Lady Beaumont" was self-deluded. It was deeper than an urging—it seemed to be a calling, weirdly, a wordless voice summoning her.

Eventually, her eyelids grew heavy, and her brain calmed.

She felt an odd sensation, like something was moving on her. Joe's hand, probably. It had been a while since he initiated in his sleep.

"Joe," she whispered. "Not now."

She turned toward him, opened her eyes halfway. Joe lay on his side, his back to her, body heaving slowly with each purring snore.

Marilyn blinked awake … and looked at the creature standing on her chest.

It was naked, its body fragile looking even as it emanated a mysterious strength. Its wide, round eyes hovered only inches from hers, glinting like its bald scalp in the glow of the security light outside.

Marilyn held her breath.

Baldy's expression was neutral. Pulse accelerating, she studied him. He was there, not a mere name, not a mere feeling, not a mere shadow out of the corner of her eye.

His eyes narrowed.

"You need to leave," Marilyn hissed, in as low a voice as she could muster. "You need to leave now."

For a second, the creature didn't react. Then it crossed its arms in a defiant *harrumph*, eerily similar to Troy's common reaction when rebuffed.

In fact, there was a quality about this creature that felt like her youngest son. As if it were a broken-off chunk of him.

"Give it back to him," Marilyn said. Her limbs trembled. "Give back whatever you *took* from him."

Their old cat Tardis flashed through her mind. Weeks of sleeping a lot, of waning energy. Weight loss. Vet calls. X-Rays. *No idea what's wrong.* Draining toward that moment Marilyn found him bony and lifeless by the side of the house.

No idea.

And Troy tonight, falling asleep at the dinner table.

"Did you," Marilyn squeaked, "did you take Tardis?"

Baldy's lips pushed up in a half-smile. Marilyn wrenched forward like one waking from a bad dream.

In a blink, the creature was gone. It felt gone, too, like it had taken all manner of its presence with it. Like it had actually listened to her.

Joe stirred, shifted onto his back.

"You okay, Mare?" he muttered, without opening his eyes.

Marilyn would have answered, but he was already snoring again.

2

"I wonder if they have any of those full facial masks," Joe said, as they made their way into the section labeled AQUA in big blue letters. "They're more expensive, but they leak less, and they give you more of a panoramic view."

The Kauai trip was now officially on the calendar. BlastFM had sent them their plane tickets and vouchers and "travel package," a garish pile of promo materials with their logo plastered everywhere in between photos of the Huna'ia Resort, which looked like a big slab of steel-and-glass barbecue ribs.

"Can I go play the golf balls?" Tommy asked, craning his head back toward the GOLF section where a putting matt sat, with putters and balls out for idle use.

"In a bit," Marilyn said. Golf—bah. She could only envision the golfers they knew at church, glinty-eyed salesman-types who carried their true god in their wallets. "Daddy wants to get swim stuff for our Hawaii trip."

Tammy frowned. "But you said you weren't going."

Joe turned back toward them, a pile-up of opinions at his eyes.

Marilyn stroked Tammy's hair. "I never said that, sweetie." She met Joe's gaze, already cooling with relief. "Daddy and I worked it out. Although he won't be getting me snorkel gear."

"Snorkel gear?" Joe said. "Oh *no*, I already registered you for a scuba license. You're going whole-hog, Mary-Lou."

"Har!" she said. "And *har* your face."

They stood before a section of fins and masks. Joe knelt and sifted through the options, scrupulously checking prices and, knowing him, where they were made.

"I really, really want to get you a set, Marilyn," Joe noted.

"Why?" They'd discussed this already. "I told you, if I go in the ocean, *if*, I can just rent one. Why buy one if I may not even use it?"

Joe looked up at her. In a voice quieter than expected, he said, "If you actually buy one, you might feel more compelled to go in. I know you. If we're there and I ask you about renting, you'll chicken out."

"How do you know?"

"You'll come up with something. You'll say you don't know how many mouths've been on that snorkel, or whatever."

This coming from the guy who was squirrelly about baths. About bathing his own kids, even.

"That sounds more *you*," Marilyn fired back.

Thankfully, Joe dropped it. Marilyn knew that look of his, though: slightly downcast, the slot-machine-spin of all histories and lives that might've been whirring behind his gray, distracted gaze. He loved her, for sure. He still celebrated without fail the day they met, for Pete's sake, which not even she remembered every year.

He picked out two sets of a mask and snorkel, and two pairs of fins in a netted bag.

"The Huna'ia Resort has fantastic snorkeling, apparently," Joe said. "And it's even better this time of year."

"Why?

Joe shrugged. "A fluke thing, I guess. Online there are lots of testimonials about people seeing all kinds of cool things now in Pyramid Bay. Way more than usual."

Well, what kinds *of 'cool' things?*

"Our suite's like a five-minute walk to the beach. You can't *not* go in." Joe held up his awkward bundle of purchases. "I'm getting you one. End of story."

"Fine."

"Is there a pyramid there?" Tommy asked, as they started heading back through the store.

"No, bud. It's named after a rock formation, I think." He handed one set of snorkel gear to Marilyn, who took it with a sardonic grin. Fishing out his phone, he said, "Siri, show me Pyramid Rock in Kauai."

The screen spat up a peppering of pictures. Joe clicked on the first one and showed it to Tommy as the others leaned in as well.

Marilyn recoiled a little. The "pyramid" looked more like the top of a witch's hat, a tower of dark lava rock stark against a fading sun. There was an ominous familiarity to it.

"Did someone make that pyramid?" Tommy asked.

Joe chuckled. "Kind of looks like it, doesn't it?"

"That's right by the Huna'ia Resort?" Marilyn asked.

"Uh-huh!" Joe seemed encouraged by her question.

She was going on this trip, sure, but had yet to work out for herself why. There was pleasing Joe, there was the dumb prospect of not taking advantage of sheer luck...

—you need to go—

...and then, there were the deeper, murkier reasons. The strange, anxious compulsion, the sense that part of her was already there, that nothing of this had been luck. That Pyramid Rock was like a needle-pointed broadcast tower, urgently dispatching to her some ancient, jumbled signal.

•　　•　　•

A new episode of *Spooksters* aired that night. Joe whipped up two bowls of popcorn and the kids huddled about the couch, Troy between him and Marilyn on the cushions. Tamara sat on Joe's other side and Tommy lay on the carpet, gazing at the primetime antics of poltergeists in a Hollywood Hills mansion.

"Is that close to us?" Tammy said.

"Sort of," Joe said, muffled by munching.

Toward the end of the episode, they interviewed a physicist about the science of ghost-hunting. He was an older gentleman with bold engineer glasses and a silvery ponytail.

Joe snickered. "Where'd they get this guy from? Spook Central U?"

Out of the corner of her eye, Marilyn saw him look at her. She just smiled and kept her gaze on the TV.

"The bottom line," said the physicist onscreen, "is that the phenomena we're talking about, that you've experienced, that I've experienced, that, I'm willing to bet, far more people've experienced than you might suspect, is just invariably part of the natural world, and it's a part science can't quite reach yet. But I think it'll catch up. Science is too curious. Too ravenous."

"Daddy," said Tamara, "can we watch something else?"

"There's only about ten minutes left," Joe said. "Okay, princess?"

What might science say of her experiences? Marilyn wondered. Not officially, of course, but what might be gleaned in the cracks between what they knew and what she knew?

Her phone buzzed with a text. It was from her younger brother, Shane.

Can you come over tomorrow sometime?

After some hesitation, she pecked out: I suppose. For a little while. Why? Everything okay?

A pause. Then:

It's not an emergency or anything. Not yet.

Not yet?

She wrote: Okay. What time?

•　　•　　•

Before going to bed that night, Marilyn fished out several books: *God & the New Physics* by Paul Davies, Neil deGrasse Tyson's *Astrophysics For People in a Hurry*, and *The Cosmic Detective* by Virgil Demian, whose kid-friendly show *Impossible Wonders* still reran on TV, much to Tommy's enjoyment.

She dipped in and out, flipped back and forth, tried to focus. All such wondrous things, sure. But at bottom, she wanted to know what energy *was*. Divine respiration? Matter was energy, energy matter. Light could be both a particle and a wave. There were different *kinds* of energies. There was kinetic energy and potential energy, and apparently other, more exotic kinds yet to be found. Like Dark Energy.

She'd sensed in Baldy a distinct consciousness. So, then, what was consciousness? Not just a quirk of neurochemistry. Rather, it spoke through neurochemistry, often distortedly.

Were minds refracted souls?

And, at the end, wasn't it all the same soup? More than anything, it seemed like whatever ultimate truth existed out there had far more kinship with the mystical than the mechanical.

These kinds of thoughts reminded her that she was seeing Shane in the morning, and a mild dread grew in her. She really didn't feel like getting dragged into another "faith versus reason" argument—not that she ever did.

She piled the books onto a shelf in the family room and made her way to the bedroom, where Joe lay sound asleep. She changed into her pajamas and, purposely foregoing any teeth-brushing or face-washing, she slipped under the sheets and cuddled against her husband, who uttered a low, unconscious "Hm."

"Love ya…" Joe muttered, barely coherent.

"Love you too," she whispered.

She laid there a while, eyes open. A church Elder had once told her: "Don't stray to seek out false truths." He had been talking specifically about internet surfing. Best not to callus one's hands with too heavy an intellectual spade or shovel.

Quite often, Marilyn felt she was poised on a teetering outpost, and that every thought she had about the world's overwhelming chaos was another stray gust of wind against her, further upsetting her balance toward the edge. And the closer that edge, the more belligerent those windy thoughts, whipping her with questions old and new, all lifted from every corner of her incomplete learning.

How could so much senseless *tragedy* exist? she might think. Was it all truly "tragic" as we thought? Trees or rocks didn't mourn. Way out in space, black holes might blithely swallow distant worlds. Volcanic supercalderas unleashed doomsday death to millions of innocent beings.

A 570-million-year-old creature, alien in appearance: what might the Prophet have made of such a creature?

Dumb! Dumb stupid thing to ask.

Or was Joseph Smith as small a man as any, one so stuffed with delusion that his flesh could not contain it, that his proclamations became little more than the supercaldera: a fiery eruption, ambitious in reach and preserving in its influence as many nearby souls as it might?

These and so many other thoughts would whip at Marilyn. It happened more often when she was a teenager. Some particularly strong gust would send her over, reeling so that, in the depths of her spirit, Marilyn would feel something like the freefall belly-tingle as she tumbled down toward a terrible dark chaos, one wild with the unjust, the unclaimed, the unknown, the *unknowable*. She would crash on the way into every blasphemous revelation until, then as now, she would seek the arms of a loved one and hold them in quivering silence, and receive her mother's, "Marilyn, is everything okay?", or Joe's silent embrace or Tommy's occasional, "I love you too, Mom—can I go now?", and so descend with blemished grace into the fine netting of her faith, positioned so as to catch her, to hold her, even as through the obscurity of the mesh she could still glimpse the darkness and the chaos living below.

3

Past the streets and strip malls lay the rocky hills of Chatsworth, outlined like a rugged vertebrate on the horizon. Shane had told her it was once an ancient seabed.

"In five hundred feet," chimed her phone, "turn left on Plummer Street."

She turned. The road drew away from commercial arteries into more secluded residences, winding through fields dotted with barren trees. The massive brown rocks loomed in powerful, purposeful disarray, Stonehenges laid by schizophrenic deities. Much as a child's discomfort with his combed hair and suit, the land seethed in scant tolerance of the neighborhoods tucked into its folds.

There was a shadow over this area. Marilyn tried to comfort herself by imagining old-movie cowboys roaming these hills, or William Shatner punching out a clumsy alien.

Something caught her eye. She glanced up toward one of the farther hills, squinting against the sun. What was there?

Whatever it was, it was massive.

Repelled by sunlight, Marilyn returned her gaze to the road. She shuddered. She thought to pull over, but this stretch of Plummer was sharp with blind curves and few shoulders. She kept driving, at a lowered speed.

What had she seen? She couldn't be sure. But the eye itself wasn't the only gauge. Many spoke of a "sixth sense", but Marilyn thought that shortchanged the phenomenon. There were "phantom senses"—counterparts of physical sight, touch, taste, smell and hearing that operated either in the mind, the soul, or somewhere in between.

The term "mind's eye" partially acknowledged this truth. But as far as she was concerned, the mind also had its own ears, its own nose, its own fingers.

And what her mind's fingertips now touched was something cold and enormous and still.

What rumbled through her mind's ears was a sound like breathing—great, raspy rips of air like those of a slumbering dragon.

The form in her vision lay draped across the Valley, a creature from the midnight abyss that had made its way to land. A giant poisonous thing, whose every quiver might incur a natural disaster.

There was chaos cooking in this thing's belly, and it seeped down these hills and through these rocks. Shadow-streams, flowing. And there were places where these streams appeared to pool: ponds and lakes of this spiritual venom.

One such place: the cul de sac up Wyndham Lane, where Shane sat waiting for her on his porch, hands tucked into his jeans, smile thin and wooden.

•   •   •

"I've already got the coffee brewing."

Marilyn gave a tepid chuckle.

"I'm going to let you do the sweetening, though," Shane called. "I ran out and got extra creamer for the occasion."

"Thanks." Marilyn ran her fingers through her hair. She resisted the urge to get out her phone.

Her brother's face leaned out from behind the kitchen archway. "No chance I can get you to go another mile?" He held up a bottle of

Kahlua, rocked it back and forth like a gameshow host showcasing a prize. "Maybe a teeny drop?"

"No way." Marilyn stood and walked over to the archway. Relax, she told herself. He's poking you as always. Except she was not in a poking mood. "It's bad enough you got me hooked on coffee."

Shane laughed. "Okay, *one*," he held up his thumb, "if you only have it when you're alone with me, you *aren't* hooked, and two," he flicked up his index finger, "with the category five blizzard of cream and sugar that you throw in there, it barely qualifies as coffee."

"I like to put syrup in it," Marilyn said. "Not sugar."

Shane picked up a nearby bottle of maple syrup and plunked it down next to a mug of steaming black coffee. Printed on it was a quote from Thoreau: *Go confidently in the direction of your dreams! Live the life you've imagined.*

"Thanks, Shane," she said. How many times in the last twenty minutes had she thanked him for some trivial little service, for leading her inside, for hanging up her coat, for telling her to use the master bathroom instead, for continuing in the tradition of forcing upon her a "strong" drink Mormons weren't supposed to have, a drink that with every sip came a sweet, buzzing guilt, yet which she nonetheless enjoyed, and enjoyed all the more because of the secrecy?

All this, and yet no thank you for driving all this way.

She fixed her coffee and returned to the living room, when Shane indicated the balcony and she followed. He set his cup on a table stacked with a couple books: a history of the Mediterranean and *The Unholy Ghost* by an Arthur Moore, who Marilyn knew dimly as one of those public God-bashers.

There was also an ashtray, a lighter and a glass pipe and a small pouch of marijuana which Shane began packing into the pipe.

He lit up and took a long drag. Marilyn sipped her coffee and turned her attention to the view before her: the hills of boulders dyed orange in the late sun, the Chatsworth Reservoir and the shrinking band of city beyond.

"So what's up?" she said. "Is Jeannie at work?"

Shane nodded. "Listen," he said, blowing out smoke. "It's Barb."

Marilyn's gut sank. "Huh?"

"I think…" Shane said with a sigh.

"What is it?" If her niece—well, technically step-niece—was already having trouble at college, she was prepared to heap all the blame on Shane, even as she recognized Jeannie's helicopter Mommying. "What's wrong with Barb?"

Other than the fact that she has the name of a 1950s country-club wife?

"Well," Shane sighed, "we think she might actually be, um, interested in…"

Sex? A cult? Communism? Lesbianism?

"…Islam."

Marilyn blinked. "That's unexpected."

"Tell me about it." He sucked up more smoke, blew it with defiance over the railing. "Jeannie, me and her dad all think it was her sociology professor, who's she's told us about before. He's from Tehran."

Marilyn narrowed her eyes. "Okay. So … what?"

About to sip his coffee, Shane snorted, spilling droplets on his denim. "Are you fucking kidding?" He set down his mug. "Google 9/11. Google ISIS. Honor killings. There's your 'what'?"

"Isn't college supposed to be about exploring ideas and, you know, finding yourself?"

"Of course it is. But as parents it's our job to give them a good flashlight in the dark."

"Maybe she was in the dark before, and now she's starting to see."

Shane stared at her. "See what, exactly?"

"See what's right for her." Marilyn gulped her coffee. "And I've told you before, please don't use that kind of language around me."

He waved her off. "You're drinking coffee."

Okay, so naturally that justified every more egregious transgression. With sadness, Marilyn realized her only connection to Shane lingered in micro-fibers of DNA. He was like a stranger that out of some baseless, sadomasochistic obligation she felt compelled to interact with.

For what purpose? It came from the Shane she liked to remember, the Shane of epic family game nights, when he would smack his cards down in assured victory, or the Shane so fatally certain he was going to die from his inaugural bee sting, or even, God, forbid, some of his sillier pious moments, like the time he'd caught her checking out the R-rated *Terminator 2* on TV and told on her. Though, in retrospect, maybe that was the seed of today's Shane.

"I've often thought religions, and religious people, are selfsame," Shane said. "Do you know what that means?"

She did, but she just sipped her coffee.

"It's a Shakespearean word," he continued. "It means persisting sameness through change. And I think that even though not all religions or religious people are the same, the impulses toward them come from similar places."

"Okay." Marilyn had a vague idea where he was heading with this.

"Barbara really likes you, Mary. She's always liked you. I think you have more in common with her than I do, or even Jeannie sometimes."

This startled Marilyn.

"And I was wondering," said Shane, his voice growing softer, "if you'd be willing to speak with her. I mean, we're no longer in agreement on Mr. Smith, you and I. But I imagine neither of us wants to see her bend knees to Allah."

"Honestly, Shane, I think Barb should follow her heart. If that means being Muslim, so be it."

Her brother's face fell. "You can't be serious. This from the woman who proudly held up signs for Yes on Prop 8. Speaking of gay pride."

"I was a *kid*, Shane. I didn't know any better."

"But you do now?" He took a drag. In puffs of smoke, he said, "What if Barb were gay? Hell, what if Troy or Tommy go all flame-o?"

"I wouldn't love them any less," she said. "I'd make do."

"'Make do.' As if *you'd* be personally crippled."

Marilyn ignored the comment. "Given how restless Barbara is, I don't see her sticking with anything. Not now. She's just finding herself."

The Islam thing did concern Marilyn, but not because it wasn't Mormonism. She had visions of Barbara covered in a black sheet, nodding her way through some rabid rhetoric or scrolling through websites with creepy symbols and pictures of masked, gun-toting men, their eyes as hard as those who'd bombed the parade.

Will you shut up? she told herself. After all, how many Muslims knew the same comforting light that she did, filtered only through a different prism?

"Listen," said Shane. "I'd be fine if you even converted her to Mormonism. That I can at least deal with."

"Would Jeannie want that?"

Shane shrugged. "I'd think so. It's not a death cult. No jihadis. You don't declare fatwahs on cartoonists who draw our favorite 19th century charlatan. Er, excuse me, *prophet*."

He shrunk in his seat a little. Fragments of notions and arguments pummeled her brain and Marilyn tried to make sense of them, to spit them out with arrowheads sharp enough to match those flung by Shane, who did read more "intellectually" than her fantasy books.

When she turned to look at him again, though, the world evaporated. He was no longer Shane. His pupils narrowed with a malice that seemed inhuman. The same features were there, of course, but lurking just beneath them was a distorted presence.

A symbol flashed through her mind, though she didn't know its significance:

If it was true, her notion that the mind had its own array of senses, she could "smell" a pungent, earthen scent. She could "taste" something sour and curdled.

And that mental finger, the one that could "touch" things unseen, drew across Shane's energy and found it rough and leathery.

Like scaled skin, in fact. Almost reptilian.

•　　•　　•

After spending barely two hours there, Marilyn left despondent and detached. Shane hadn't even asked about the kids, or Joe. She hadn't even told him they were going to Hawaii.

Lost in thought, she drove slowly down the hill. Utah was where she and her family should be. Max and Lillian and Uncle Dave and Aunt Sarah in Provo, vain as she was, and of course Mom and Dad in Salt Lake City. And they wouldn't live forever. What kept her close to Shane? Well, Joe, of course. Joe's work. And Marilyn herself had always hated snow.

She was approaching the intersection of Plummer and Wyndham Lane when she felt it: a strong sense that her attention was being pulled in a certain direction. The chime noise rang through her head, over and over. Like those musical chimes in *Errowind*, alerting her to something important.

It wanted her to turn right.

These stupid whims. This was why she shouldn't have coffee. It made her jumpy and anxious and impulsive. Just go *left*, she told herself.

The signal turned green. She waited. No one was behind her.

The chime continued. Turn right.

No. Turn left. Go home.

She squeezed the steering wheel. Other drivers zoomed by, some glancing at her. One honked.

The light turned yellow.

She went right.

She was going somewhere, but didn't know where. Only when she pulled into the empty lot of the Painted Cave Trailhead did something of her normal mind click back into place.

She had no idea what she was doing here. She closed her eyes and took three breaths.

Large oaks shaded a picnic area. The trail itself was one of two visible passages out of the surrounding stone. Marilyn glanced up through the windshield and driver's side window, working through something like stage fright. Like she was in the middle of a granite coliseum, its spectators never bored by human intrusion.

She climbed out of the car and shut the door and the noise echoed lonely over the land. Her gravel-crunch footsteps were loud, affirming her solitude.

Surprisingly, she was no longer nervous, or regretful. This was right. In the cellar of every human soul there was a small door, one leading to a shared cosmic crawlspace. In many, it was ignored, caked shut. Others, pried a little, maybe ajar.

These past few years, Marilyn realized, her own door had been creaking further and further open.

The oaks danced in their stillness. Approaching one, she placed a hand on its trunk, sensed an electric heat she'd never felt before. Was it all in her head? Or were her fingertips grazing the contours of some essential treasure stored in that crawlspace?

She pressed on down the trail, passing into the sliver of canyon. She was reminded of a childhood trip to the Narrows in Zion, the beautiful but unnervingly thin space between rock walls, lined with the wordless poetry of their age, the sky a blue ribbon above.

Though she was less than half a mile from the nearest main road, there was no traffic. No engines. No dogs. No planes. This wasn't a particularly isolated trail, either. There were picnic tables and dispensers of dog-waste bags and a kiosk discussing the history of the petroglyphs at the Painted Cave ahead, which was thought to be about a thousand years old.

But all of it felt … clear now. The tide of modern influence had receded, at least for a time. Marilyn felt a poignant connectedness. An ancestry awakening in her.

She knew refuge.

She knew home.

About half a mile in, the trail forked. A wooden sign indicated the glyphs were another .05 miles down the right path. Marilyn followed it, walking for another twenty or so minutes in what was mostly shade thanks to the lowered sun and massive, enveloping boulders.

She reached the cave. An iron gate blocked off much of the interior. Visitors were restricted to the recessed "foyer," where they could peer inside.

The cave breathed.

Marilyn approached cautiously, not only to avoid stumbling on the rocks, but to remain stable in the sudden suckerpunch of energy. She'd been to one or two Native American sites before, of other tribes, and they'd felt similar—the energy ancient yet whole.

Her entire body tingled. Her eyes watered.

Catching a moment to breathe, Marilyn looked past the grating. The cave air was cool on her skin. The rock paintings were on the cave's north wall. The designs varied in color and geometry. The more Marilyn drank them in, the clearer it became that they bore the brunt of the cave's energy. It fumed from those drawings, like steam off a cooked dish.

Many of the designs were sun-like. Crude people were also represented. Most of the artwork was quite symbolic, abstract.

However, Marilyn's attention did center on one drawing toward the back:

Suddenly, Marilyn understood several things.

It had come from deep water, that big dragon-thing across these hills. Or maybe it had stayed there over the eons, as the ocean slowly drained away.

She herself … somehow, she was connected to water.

And she was not alone.

III

620 A.D.

1

"Please!" she cried, in that unknown tongue. "Help!"

Though she was an unknown creature, her humanness was plain, at least to Kaimi. Not to mention the bewildered terror on her face.

Yet Kaimi's canoe glided past her, part of the collective push eastward. Per Chief Haunani's proclamation, they were to leave her behind. With his every glance back, he met direct eyes with the woman-creature. As though, out of dozens of eyes to select from, she could intuit something about Kaimi.

Her *mana* radiated.

Kaimi turned around, grimacing, grip tightening on the oar. Pain coursed down his back. He inhaled, straightened his shoulders and resigned himself to the movement of his remaining brothers and sisters heading onward.

Gray humps of other lands appeared in the distance. An unknown homeland stretched before them. Kaimi had not realized this rumored world constituted multiple islands, scattered perhaps like paint-dribbles from that last stroke of Creation.

"*Please!*" cried the woman-creature behind them. "Can you understand me?"

What tongue was she speaking? It sounded so alien, sharp points and edges on the ear. She might be cursing them.

She might even be the human form of the shadow-being that Kaimi had encountered underwater, when they were struck by that rogue wave.

"Kaimi," said his brother Makui. "Who is she?" He leaned in closer. "*What* is she?"

He didn't want to answer.

"Kaimi?"

"I do not *know*."

He rowed on against the sweet wet winds, the sea hissing under, the clouds grouping to tame the sun. He kept focused, though his mind burned with that singular thought of the woman-creature. That she was something of an omen, of malice and danger, unworthy of the guilt now breaking into his consciousness. Or his strange sense of connection with her.

•   •   •

As they had come in relatively small numbers, and had lost more on the Great Voyage, settling a land meant everyone shouldered multiple tasks. Chief Haunani had declared their new home on the shores of the largest, easternmost island in the chain. It was a place no less void of curious, questionable energy than the others, but also more open and desert-like, even as dense jungle loomed not far from the two basalt foundations that formed their bourgeoning hamlet.

In the homelands, which, to Kaimi's chagrin, Chief Haunani referred to more and more as the "Old Land", Kaimi's trade had been ink-art, or *tatu*. Yet his *Kupunakane*, or grandfather, perhaps hoping to undo some of the stain of Kaimi's father's fatal wartime cowardice, had ensured Kaimi was also practiced as a warrior and a survivor.

"Everywhere the world watches," said grandfather. "And every moment it waits to strike, with hands visible or invisible."

Then about ten years old, Kaimi refrained from asking if grandfather's words were a veiled reference to the shadow-beings he would sometimes glimpse in the forest, usually out of the corner of his eye.

Once, when Kaimi was working in a taro field, he thought he saw enormous eyes in a tree. Yet could not tell if the eyes belonged to the tree itself or to another presence, some being that had made itself partially known to him.

For much of his life, the visions had been manageable. When he was younger, he once thought they were dreams that had wandered away from their dreamer. Why no one else could see them as well Kaimi wasn't sure, but he'd quickly learned, more from his grandfather's apprehensive eyes than his words, that as a commoner in the village it was not his place to speak freely of those things which were the domain of priests or chiefs.

And yet, while Kaimi didn't remember grandfather's exact statement, he had remarked on the world as "dreamfruit," its every piece—people, creatures, wind and water, all land—uniquely shaped.

"All of us hold and perceive *mana*," said grandfather, referring to the Spirit operating in All Things. "But we must never presume beyond reason, or beyond our limits."

In his twenty-seven years, Kaimi had never spoken of the shadow-beings. He had convinced himself that no transcendent destiny would, or should, be availed to the son of a disgraced warrior who had been put to death for cowardice. Like those of his siblings, Kaimi's lot was to shed the suspicions and the dishonor of his father, to respect his place in the village.

Yet even without such heavier eyes upon him, he had always known humility and fear. Unlike his far brasher brother Makui, he did not seek any more attention than he already received.

"What did Chief Haunani say to you last night?" Makui asked him as he and Anakoni paddled their canoe down the coast. Kaimi busied about setting up the dragnet, one of the larger, sturdier ones that had made it through the Voyage.

"He wants *tatu* designs," Kaimi said, without turning. "To commemorate the new lands."

"For himself? Or—?"

"For everyone." Kaimi hoped his interjection seemed a fitting cutoff to Makui's words. It was the tone that most bothered Kaimi, the arrogant, almost resentful tone his brother carried especially toward Chief Haunani. Sometimes, Kaimi sensed in his brother's eyes many different Makuis, all competing for life. And in the untamed wilds of this new land, he worried that Makui's unpredictability would only worsen.

The ocean was calm, a rich dusky color. The sun seemed to shine that much brighter over these islands, like a parent beaming over a new child.

For only the second time since pushing out, Anakoni, the oarsman at the front, spoke up.

"How do you feel, Kaimi?" Anakoni asked. "About where we have settled?"

Kaimi glanced at Makui, who must have told Anakoni something about his suspicions. This sparked another concern: just how many had he told?

Kaimi said, "We are safe."

"What was the creature we saw? Do you know?"

Makui turned, ceasing to paddle as he awaited Kaimi's words. In that moment, Kaimi wanted to strike him, if only for risking a slowdown that would affect their catch.

But the question also pestered him, of course—every day, multiple times a day, he had been turning over in his mind the image of that yellow-haired woman-creature. The extreme *mana* emanating from her. The knowing. The desperation.

"It was a large seal," Kaimi said, gazing out to sea.

Makui laughed. "What kind of spell are you trying to cast over us, Kaimi?"

"It did not look like a seal," Anakoni muttered.

"That is because it wasn't." Makui resumed rowing.

The canoe hastened over the sea, saltwinds whirling about them. Perspiration beaded Kaimi's skin. Tiredness crept over his bones. He glanced off toward the center of the island, where a massive mountain bulged, crowned with clouds.

These lands … so sweet in their isolation, they seemed like artisans on a half-finished work. Had their arrival here disrupted its *mana*? Those who had begun exploring the islands for taro and breadfruit cultivation, and to begin irrigation projects, had not reported any large beasts. A man named Atoni had remarked on the difference in this new world's land and sea, how the earth had spent such time filling the reefs and coastlines with all rainbows of life that it had neglected the land.

The canoe slowed. Makui picked up his spear and rose, gaze fixed on something nearby in the water. He pointed. "Look."

A slick hump broke the surface. Dark gray-brown. Black flippers glistening as the little beast slunk under.

Makui told Anakoni to turn the canoe, as he stiffened into throwing position. "That," he said, "is a seal."

•   •   •

Steadily and efficiently, the hamlet came together. Candlenut torches marked the corners of open-air huts made of timber and banyan bark, furnished with coconut logs and mats and baskets of vegetable fiber. Remaining livestock stirred in crudely constructed pens.

The first shelter built had, of course, been that of Chief Haunani's, raised slightly higher. He had taken in two of the pregnant women, working to rebalance and restore their *mana* which the Great Voyage had expectedly drained. Other women would follow.

As the frenzy of the last several weeks began to simmer, it was understood that normal relations were to resume, that women were to once more start taking husbands, and breeding this tiny, fragile hamlet into something resembling the dignity of the old village.

Meanwhile, something strange was happening in Kaimi. With each passing day and hour, he felt more alien to the hamlet, even to those directly his kin, like Makui. His heart still ached for Akamu and Kaha'i, of course, as well as Haumea, Eloni and Ewelani, whose fates he did not even know and, in gloomy meditation, considered he never would.

Yet so many of his thoughts also circled the woman-creature in the waves. The rest of the hamlet, buried in duty, seemed to have banished the encounter from their minds. When Chief Haunani had pulled Kaimi in to discuss the commemorative *tatu* designs, Kaimi, fighting instinct, had asked if they might include the woman-creature. After all, it—she—had been the first life to greet them here.

Or to warn us.

Chief Haunani, however, had rebuffed him.

•   •   •

Late one night, Kaimi was pulled awake by an oppressive heat. There was the sting of smoke and ripe ancestral musk and squealing pigs and commotion and voices and the darkness aflutter. Alongside Makui and others, he hurried from his hut and saw flames lashing the night.

Chief Haunani's hut was ablaze.

Some villager had already taken to dousing the flames with water containers, to little effect. The trees beyond pulsed red, the smoke and ashy dust spiraling high as though desperate to join the clouds above, the clouds that had curiously withheld their rain now for a day and a half.

Once the shock of the sight settled, Kaimi saw the problem: the pigs were loose, bolting across the hamlet down toward the beach or to the tree line, grunting and squealing their liberation. One of them had knocked over a torch and set the chief's home on fire.

"They broke out!" someone cried.

He rushed over to the pen. The wood had been unbound and simply removed, left lying on the ground. No evidence of anything broken, or broken out of.

Then Kaimi noticed them—arrayed like birds on the far side of the pen, little eyes watching, attached to bodies he could only sense. They were human-shaped outlines, though far smaller than humans. They sat utterly still, so much so he thought perhaps he was just seeing things.

When he stepped forward, though, they hopped down from the pen and scampered off toward the trees.

Kaimi pursued the small creatures, taking one of several crude trails carved into the jungle. Soon he found himself in darkness. The wind moved through the trees and bushes. Kaimi thought it sounded like mischievous laughter.

*   *   *

Overseer. Grandfather. Protector. Mother.

Such were the words that rushed through Kaimi's mind at the sight of the enormous banyan tree in this forest. It seemed to have grown sideways out of the sloping ground, a great burst of earthen wisdom. It was old, dripping with roots and vines.

Kaimi could taste the breath of its centuries.

His companions, Chief Haunani, Makui and Akamu, also appeared stricken with awe as they approached the tree. They had been working for several days now to rebuild the chief's hut, and this tree would offer much material.

"We are meant for this place," Chief Haunani said, placing a reverential hand on one of the limbs.

Kaimi's gaze was lost in the upper reaches of the canopy, where a barely-visible being shimmered down the branches.

This time, Kaimi could not see the creature; he could never see them very well. But he *felt* it, its presence heightened in other senses: coarseness by some ineffable touch, foulness by some ineffable smell.

He could feel, he discovered, with "spirit fingers."

The being had claimed the banyan tree as its own. By the buzz of its paranoia, Kaimi was certain it would defend its domain however it could. This one was stronger than others he'd encountered, as well, less a brief shadow and more bodily. More apt to affect other bodies like him.

And it waited and watched now, as Chief Haunani strode toward the banyan, his grip tight on the stone adze. With the chief's every step, the being leaned down closer. Kaimi sensed intelligence in it.

Chief Haunani raised the adze. Acting on impulse, Kaimi sprang forward.

"Stop," he said.

The chief did so. The entire party did so. They halted, turned to him.

"What is it?" the chief asked.

"Yes, Kaimi," said Makui, stepping forward. "What is the matter?"

Kaimi's mind raced. The spirit-being in the tree slid down the main trunk, watching.

"Might we disturb the *mana* of this great tree?" Kaimi said. "By reaping it?"

The tree itself felt calm, like most trees. When he was a child, Kaimi had periodically wondered if every animal and every person wasn't just a dream of all the trees, visions for their amusement.

Chief Haunani was about to reply when he and everyone noticed suddenly: the adze was no longer in his hand. Nor was it on the ground.

"What—?" Chief Haunani cried, eyes widening.

Bewildered glances. Until Kaimi spotted the chief's stone adze lying an inexplicable thirty yards away.

Kaimi hurried over and retrieved the adze. Tingles burst across his forearms.

Wind blew through the woods. Gray clouds had been encroaching all day and had now overtaken the sun. Kaimi thought he could feel the wet tickle of rain.

Such wasn't all he felt, though. The texture of everything darkened, but it wasn't storm-darkening.

In a shot of fear, the being in the tree disappeared.

Like a prey fleeing a predator.

An enormous Something moved just beyond the trees.

It wears the wind and the stone, Kaimi thought. Like a mask. Like a costume. He trembled, breathed in a scent fertile and ancestral. His impression was that of a great lizard, one dwarfing any earthly lizard he had ever seen. And it lumbered not far away.

In his mind's eye, he saw a spiral shape. Much like the one he had seen underwater, right before the woman-creature.

"Kaimi," said Makui.

The wind died down.

"Kaimi."

Makui stared at him with a dark smile. The others watched him, too, as Chief Haunani approached him to receive his adze.

"What did you see, Kaimi?" Makui pressed.

He regarded his brother. Makui was not long into manhood, and eager for something to grasp. He had in him the soul of a hungry predator lying in wait.

The rest of them all stared at Kaimi now. Everything stared at him. This island had a million eyes.

"I see," Kaimi said, "nothing more remarkable than the normal person."

•   •   •

Kaimi woke with a start. Commotion again.

The others in his dwelling were awake, too. Voices rose nearby. The air was damp, suffocating.

Kaimi went numb with worry. Had the warring tribe from the homelands managed to find them here, across so many thousands of miles?

The entire village was roused, gathering around two figures in the dim pulsing light. A half-moon kept casual watch above. Many held spears and adzes. The sight of what was truly taking place made Kaimi wish it had, in fact, been another invading tribe.

Makui stood over Chief Haunani, now kneeling on red-stained sand as Makui, wild-eyed, held him down, a sharktooth blade raised in one hand. Blood ran over his knuckles.

"Haunani is no longer fit for us!" cried Makui.

"He guided us here," a woman named Ahu protested. "If not for him—"

"He is deaf and dumb," Makui said. "These new lands require new eyes and ears to guide us now." He scanned the crowd, his gaze centering on Kaimi.

For the briefest of moments, Kaimi detached from himself. He floated there, not believing the vicious scene playing out before him, half-certain this was a nightmare.

But then, the winds rushed him back into his skin, and he joined the others in advancing upon Makui, wrenching him from the bloody affair yet even with multiple bodies assisting it took considerable effort.

The sands reddened. In the frenzy, Kaimi once again felt detached. He wanted no more of this, this violent swaying from pole to pole that defined the affairs of man, regardless of whatever lands they occupied.

Because, he thought, maybe none of us were supposed to be here, or anywhere. Maybe humans had received an undue surplus of *mana* they could not sustain, and so maybe … maybe those like Kaimi were chosen.

Yes, perhaps, to some degree, Makui was right that he was special. But maybe he was not meant to operate in the confines of any hamlet or village. Maybe his destiny lay in the celestial planes of *Rangi* or *Papa*. In the shadows of the world. In the mysterious realms of those like the woman-creature.

Kaimi did not remember the next several moments. Some alien consciousness splashed over him, drew him away.

When he awoke, he found himself in the middle of the jungle, all chirping and buzzing around him.

He could hear the voices of his village behind him, but he did not want to go back. Indeed, he could *not* go back, not anymore, not when caught in this undertow of revelation which offered no clear direction. Even as, mysteriously, he knew a direction would come.

Through the darkness, Kaimi noticed a red glow. Pushing forward, his eyes adjusting, he saw that it came from the center of the island—from the summit of the large mountain there. Like the maw of some vengeful deity, warming its flame-breath.

Ready to erupt.

2

Present Day

The massive B'ylon Beast thrashed, struggling to buck her off as her Myrulian Dwarf-Knight's grubby warrior's grip held fast to its vertebrate. It was all timing, of course, knowing when and where to place that next, precise leap.

At last, she made it to the nape of its long, dinosaurian neck. She equipped the double-bladed axe and hacked away unsparingly at its throat. The Beast stumbled and writhed, roaring out its defeat. She just had to hold on and keep slashing. Over and over.

The Dwarf-Knight's double-bladed axe was far more powerful now. She'd upgraded it just before leaving for Hawaii, and for much of the duration of the flight had mercilessly availed herself of feral pigs, low-level orcs and even a poor Zoran sorcerer's apprentice, all of which had met the business end of her blades between the spottier moments of airplane WiFi.

A nudge—Joe.

Marilyn popped out her earbuds. "Yeah?"

"Promise me you won't be playing that game all this trip," he said.

"I promise," she said, staring again at the laptop screen. "Why do you think I'm getting it outta my system now?"

Joe smirked. He gestured past her toward the window. "Also, check it out."

She lifted the window shade up further, blinking against the sun. A green valley lay below, its lower reaches shaded by clouds orphaned from higher thunderheads. Reef-blotched seawater caressed golden beaches where tiny people walked and swam and where postcard palms clustered between sand and jungle. A small awe filled Marilyn. She closed the game and shut the laptop.

The captain's voice crackled on. They would be on the ground shortly.

•   •   •

Disembarking the plane and filing through the airport, Marilyn resolved that she was not *yet* in Kauai, not quite, even as she glimpsed the gold-laced palms outside, or heard the ukulele dripping from airport speakers, or passed the sharktooth tools, baskets and drums in a display case labeled *Hawaii's First Inhabitants*.

It was the moment the final sign for Baggage Claim led them out to a series of open-air huts, where bags and traffic circled and where people waited, their frazzled traveler's energy subdued by silken winds. The air was breathable candy.

Marilyn blinked. Grinned a little. She was *here*.

They approached the open-air luggage carousel. Warm wind whistled through.

God has blessed you.

"Oh man," Joe uttered next to her. His arms were folded, his gaze fixed on a TV hung near one of the rental car stations.

"What is it?" Marilyn asked.

He pointed. On the screen, a weatherman gestured to a swirl of pixelated clouds moving toward the southeastern United States.

Bolted in silver letters across the bottom of the screen: *Hurricane Warning*.

It looked like the storm was expected to make landfall in about a week, to sweep up through Florida and maybe across the Gulf of

Mexico. Though a tropical storm right now, there were fears it might become a Category 4 or 5.

"Gonna be more where that came from," said a man nearby.

Joe turned to her with a smile. "Good thing we didn't win a trip to the Caribbean."

•   •   •

She stood on the curb, taxis and other vehicles purring past her. They'd moved out from baggage claim. For the first time ever, tropical sun found Marilyn's skin, igniting in her a strange urge to rip off all her clothes.

And the *view*—the lush, ridged mountains so dynamic and luminous they seemed like Northern Lights resolved into physical form. The thunderheads sat over one end, their edges frayed in a kind of Lost World fog, a fog incomplete without the distant cry of a dinosaur.

"Pretty, huh?" Joe said, with a hint of, *I told you so.*

They continued toward the Hertz kiosk, an indoor facility where a rat-maze of people stood waiting. Marilyn reluctantly joined the line.

She leaned in toward Joe, brushing her cheek against his shoulder. "Thank you for this."

Joe's eyes shone with validation. "I did nothing but be the first to answer an obvious question. Well, obvious to me, at least."

"And to me. Not to mention half of England. Probably."

"Indeed." He embraced her with one arm and kissed her temple. "I'm glad to see island magic is already working its, um, well, magic on you."

As they slowly made their way through the line, Marilyn watched out the nearest window: the azure waters framed by coconut palms. Next to the garish monolith of a Coke machine, the sight floated there like a painting. In her mind, she added new brushstrokes: an 18th-century explorer's ship, creaking to shore; a pterodactyl slicing across the sky; a huge Leviathan body, pitching forth from the waves.

Then, about halfway toward the horizon, she saw it.

A white spray.

Marilyn gasped and pointed. "Whale!"

People righted, turned, their eyes brightening.

Joe frowned. "Wait, what?"

"*Look!*"

The spray had evaporated.

"There shouldn't be any whales here," Joe said.

"Why?"

Joe snorted. "Whale season's in the winter."

Marilyn barely heard him. *Come on.* Another spray. Prove Joe wrong. Don't embarrass me. It hadn't just been her imagination, no…

There it was! A second one!

Then another!

Excited murmuring shot through the crowd. Right behind them, an elderly couple gestured. "That's neat," said the wife, "there's a bunch of 'em out there."

"Wow," Joe said. "That's unexpected."

He turned to Marilyn with a giddy expression and that made her happy, especially as she felt responsible for it. Animals, she thought, were reminders of truth.

3

It wasn't just the sweeping newness of where she was. It was also the little newnesses, the road signs bearing musical names unlike anything you might find on the mainland, or the roving gangs (flocks?) of roosters and chickens, or the mere fact that Marilyn could keep her passenger's window down and not feel chilled by the air.

"You'll be my proud navigator," Joe said, handing her a folded-up map. They'd rented a red Prius.

"What is this? 1980?" she said. "Why aren't we just putting in GPS?"

They came to a stop sign. The town of Lihue differed little from the franchise-flowerbed of any modern plot of civilization. What distinguished it were the castles of mountainous jungle backdropping it all.

Joe sighed. "Screens, screens and *more* screens. I deal with screens all day. The movie I watched on the plane I swore would be the last screen I look at for a while, at *least* for today. I was hoping to add a little old-school adventuring to this trip."

"I want to take in the sights, too," Marilyn said, slouching in her seat.

"Mare, come on, you wouldn't be staring at it the *whole* time. And it's pretty straightforward. I checked ahead a little. We'll mostly be using just one highway."

The highway wound through a jungle-dappled valley. They passed a tunnel of foliage where leaves larger than Marilyn's head spiraled up towering trunks, where vines hung like telephone wires, transmitting secrets tree-to-tree, the sun flickering through the canopy.

"What animals live in Hawaii?" Marilyn said. "I mean, on the islands themselves?"

"Besides the poultry?"

"Yes, besides the chickens."

Joe shrugged. "Um, well, you got a lot of tropical birds." He cleared his throat. "Which *are* technically dinosaurs."

"True."

"And I could be wrong, but I think they have wild boars and goats. At least in Kauai."

"That's it?"

"I'd assume so. I mean, think about it. Think about how isolated these islands are. What would get here, except by wings or by boat?" He tugged on his seatbelt's shoulder strap. "Most of the critters were hauled over by the natives, when they first came."

"And they were, what, southeast Asian, right?"

"Polynesian. If we're ever on Oahu, we should go to the Polynesian Cultural Center. It was sponsored by the church, you know."

What was it like, she wondered, for those faceless explorers who first spotted those green humps on the horizon, those who arrived when this soil had never known human feet? When it was pristine and when it was virgin.

They passed through another glorious corridor of trees, then dipped down and the country spread wide open. For what appeared to be a quarter of a mile there was nothing but grasslands and the road's asphalt snake resting in it, no other cars and nothing but the sweet island breath and…

The man, walking with his head down along the side of the road. His gait was odd. Rickety, even. The picture of this figure, against all the empty acres, inspired in Marilyn a certain sadness.

"Slow down a second," she said, rummaging about.

"What're you looking for?" Joe asked.

She fished out her phone. In those few seconds, however, the view had lost its dynamism.

"No screens!" Joe said, mostly playfully. "Remember?"

"But I can't *control* it, Joe!" With the camera still on, she pushed the phone toward his face. "I'm no longer Marilyn with an iPhone. I am an iPhone, with a Marilyn expansion pack! Your wife is now a full-on app."

He shook his head, smirking. "Any chance for updates?"

"Hey, my code is *solid*, buster."

Road Walker Man was now only a few seconds away. He didn't seem to acknowledge the car rushing up behind him. His hair was dirty-blonde, his skin bronzed and his gait long and loping. The only thing he appeared to be carrying was a walking stick and a long cylindrical bag strapped to his back.

Pull over for him.

She clammed up on saying anything. They passed the Road Walker and she glanced at him and at last he looked up. In their fleeting eye contact, he smiled. Marilyn grew lightheaded with compassion. She watched him in the sideview mirror.

The Road Walker looked older than she, though not by much. Early thirties, maybe. Even at their receding distance, Marilyn could sense the sheer energy from those eyes.

"Dedicated hiker," Joe said. "Back there."

"I hope he's alright." Marilyn suddenly felt strange that Joe had spoken of the man, as if he'd been her little secret.

"He looks fine to me."

The sun slid behind clouds, dimming everything. Marilyn yawned.

"I'm hoping to get to the resort by five," Joe said, with a glance at the clock. It was 3:32.

"Seems doable." Marilyn closed her eyes.

The car and all their surroundings melted together, grew slow and bloated and bleary. The last thing she noticed was a sign:

Kekepania Falls … 3 mi.

Then she was out.

She felt water. Near.

A waterfall, specifically—first, only a rushing noise through the trees, drawing her toward it, until…

She passed through an opening in the trees, where she could see it. Where every step fed on its magnificence.

The cliff face rose at least a hundred feet high, all mossy-slick and sprouted with ferns, its surface like the rugged cheek of a dark wise giant, long hushed by the water's caress. The bottom pool was inky, deep. The jungle huddled close, as if straining to hear the fall's every babble.

Marilyn walked to the water's edge, head craned up. She took in the totality of the waterfall, as well as the individual drops plummeting down, down, down. In that image, certainly, as He had in virtually all corners of Creation, God had left a metaphor.

As her gaze passed over the waterfalls, however, she thought she saw something—a human-like figure behind the rushing worble, *head and shoulders drawn by crystal drops. As improbable as a flock of birds forming a face in the sky, and yet it was there.*

She's watching me.

Marilyn waded in farther, up to her knees. Looked closer.

The human-like apparition faded, like an optical illusion.

Or, she thought, an essence gone back into its thing.

•   •   •

She started awake.

"Are we lost?" Marilyn asked.

"Huh? No." Joe chuckled. "Despite our navigator skipping off to dreamland."

She sighed. For a second she thought dusk had fallen, but it was only the thunderhead above, throwing doomgray over the land. Rain dotted the windshield.

"Looks like the weather's turned," she muttered.

Joe leaned over the steering wheel, squinted up at the clouds. "It'll pass."

She looked at the time, which now read 2:19.

Marilyn frowned. "Wait…"

"What's the matter?"

"Did you fiddle with the clock?"

"Why would I do that?"

"I could've sworn that when I fell asleep it was already past three-thirty."

Joe smiled, tongue bulging his cheek. "On vacation ten minutes and you're already keeping track of time. For shame!"

Marilyn checked her phone. Indeed, 2:19. Her arms tingled. She'd must've just misread the clock.

They rounded a bend, and he was there again.

The Road Walker. Striding along the side of the highway just as before, head down. Marilyn frowned.

"Whoa, how did he get ahead of us?" she asked.

"Who?"

"The guy walking up ahead," she said. "You see him, right?"

"Um, yeah, I see him." Joe leaned back in his seat, arms straight and hands fixed firm on the wheel. He looked ready to floor it. "Dedicated hiker."

She sat forward. "Okay, *some* glitch in the Matrix is going on."

"What're you talking about?"

"Let's pull over."

"What?" They were fast approaching the man, who, as before, hadn't yet acknowledged them. "Mare, are you nuts? He's not even hitchhiking."

"Please, Joe."

The man was zooming up and up. It would only be seconds before he'd be gone again.

"Joe!" Marilyn cried. "Please stop *now*!"

"Jesus!"

They screeched to a stop a few yards in front of the hiker. Joe took a long inhale, murmured an apology for taking the Lord's name in vain. The agitation on his face had hardened into anger. There was desperate unknowing in his eyes.

Marilyn turned to her passenger's side window, as the man stopped before her. She was taken aback by how different he looked. It was nothing easily identifiable. The clothes and features were the same, yet someone … *new* shone through the man's expression.

"Marilyn," Joe hissed beside her.

"Hi," she said to the man. "We wanted to make sure you were okay."

The man smiled, watched them with what something like humored skepticism.

Joe gripped her forearm. "What on Earth has gotten into you?"

"Aren't we here for a new adventure?" Marilyn said. "It looks like this guy's in the middle of one."

Though she'd no real grasp of her own motives, there was clearly something deeper at work here than a thirst for random bohemian adventure.

"Here's what's going to happen," said Joe. "We're going to be heading off to our own adventure, and leave this gentleman to his own."

Marilyn looked back at the man, who was still standing and smiling. He looked different again.

His eyes. His eyes are different, like another person's.

"Just hold on," Marilyn said. "If nothing else, do it to be kind. Maybe he needs help."

Joe leaned over her to address the man. "*Do* you? Do you need a lift? You hurt, lost, anything?"

"You apologize for cursing," Marilyn said, face flushing, "but not for asking someone so crassly if they need help?"

The man's mouth contorted, like a cow slowly taking its first chew of cud. "I d-d-don't," he said, struggling against the stutter. Then, in strangely calm, smooth speech: "Our f-feet are sore. But don't need help."

"There you go," Joe said, and hit the gas. He nearly turned right into a passing car, which unleashed a furious, trumpeting honk. "Yeah, yeah, jerk-off! I see you, I *see* you!"

"Be careful," Marilyn called out to the hiker.

She couldn't hear his reply, though he did appear to give one. By the movement of his lips, she thought he said, "You too."

Joe turned on the radio. Two words hung in Marilyn's mind. She was a little surprised when Joe himself brought them up.

"Did he say, '*our* feet are sore'?"

Marilyn ran her fingers through her hair. "I think so."

"Hm." Joe notched up the radio's volume. "He was hiking alone, right?"

4

And there it was, like the passing of one dream into another.

The Huna'ia Resort lay at the foothills of a crescent mountain range. Driving out over the valley, Marilyn was nervous, but not. She was excited, but not. It was like her skin now hosted multiple Marilyns from multiple realities, all trading sights and reactions.

No doubt about it: the resort was gorgeous, and the integrity of its perch, nestled among red earth and jungle, facing down the ocean, inspired in her morbidly comforting notions that it existed at some place unreachable by any apocalypse that, these days, only seemed more and more inevitable.

Marilyn felt charged. There was a self-enclosed completeness here. A protective energy.

The palms' hypnotic sway was a good distraction from the other thought: protective against what?

For now, yes, darn it, she would allow herself the stupid fantasy. She was royalty, arriving in a chariot to this lush estate.

Princess Toomey…Princess *Marilyn*…?

Duchess Toomey! There we go. *Duchess Toomey, would you kindly step this way?*

Joe pulled up the wide arching driveway and stopped. A toothy-smiling young man—Polynesian? Indigenous? Marilyn wasn't sure how to refer to him—hurried over with a luggage cart. Joe popped the trunk and he and Marilyn climbed out.

"Do you have all the info from the station?" Marilyn asked.

"Yep," Joe said. He nodded to the bellhop whose nametag read 'Carlo.' "Check-in should be smooth."

"Welcome," Carlo said, as they began Tetris-ing the luggage on the cart. "How are you two today?"

"Better for being here," Joe said. He stopped and drew a long breath, his contented, appreciative expression almost theatrical. "Love that tropical seaside air."

"Where're you visiting us from?"

"Los Angeles."

"Ah, neighbors!" Carlo said with a chuckle. "In a manner of speaking, y'know."

Marilyn thanked him for his efforts as he trundled their cart up the walkway into an extensive courtyard. Vivid green ferns reposed over a rocky grotto, babbling with a waterfall. Koi fish darted about a small, inky pond.

She held up her phone to the scene. Just as her thumb twitched to snap the picture, Joe elbowed her.

"Hey, not bad, huh?" he said, before turning to the concierge's desk.

Marilyn took another picture and uploaded to Instagram, with the caption *Arrived!*, #hawaii #grateful #highlife #adventure. She wondered if these first couple days, if not the entire trip, would see from Joe a series of unsubtle *I-told-you-sos*.

"You picked a very good time to come," Carlo remarked. "The bay's been very active."

"Oh yeah?" Marilyn said. "How do you mean?"

Big sharks, is what he means. Big marauding marine life with huge maws or stickers or stingers or venom-tipped teeth or poison whatevers gathering all for you, all for you.

"Just a lot of extraordinary diving and snorkeling opportunities," Carlo said. "We've had turtles, rays, all kinds of fish. Even whale sharks. I ran into a monk seal out here yesterday."

"We saw a regular whale, actually," Marilyn said. "From the shore in Lihue."

Carlo nodded. "Yep. Not sure why they're here."

"What about octopuses?" Marilyn said.

"They're out there, for sure. You'll probably pass over a ton of them without knowing. My brother's dived for ten years now and has only seen two."

"Okay!" Joe said, returning. "We're good to go. Room 812."

He handed her a keycard as they headed toward the elevator. They passed a glass display case and a little accompanying kiosk. Marilyn let out a little gasp when she saw what was inside.

"Are those bones?" she asked.

Unknown Ancestor, read the kiosk. *These fragments of an unknown native man were discovered during construction of the Huna'ia Resort and date back nearly 1,500 years old. They are thought to be from one of the first waves of people to the Hawaiian islands. As no other remains have been found in the area, it remains unclear why this man was alone.*

She shivered. The account left her feeling empty, and unexpectedly sad.

"It is amazing," said Carlo, "the amount of secrets these islands still have yet to tell."

They continued to the elevator. Just as Joe leaned in to push the button, one opened. Out spilled several well-tanned residents, smiles on their faces, towels over their shoulders and flip-flops suck-smacking the pavement.

"Ahh," Joe said. "Suntan lotion, chlorine and sea-salt. The scented symphony of vacation."

"An olfactory orchestra?" Marilyn said. Carlo grinned at them as they filed into the elevator, but was clearly a little bemused. "Sorry," she said, "our sense of humor doesn't always go down smooth."

"Oh, no, it's fine. We want you to have fun, y'know."

"How long has the Huna'ia Resort been here?" Joe asked. "It's fairly new, right?"

"Two years only." Carlo's gaze was on the elevator's ascending numbers as he spoke. "Give or take, y'know."

"It's such a cool, cozy area of the island," Joe said. "Neat bay, beautiful mountains. Was there anything here before?"

Carlo shook his head.

"Kind of surprising."

"Well, it *is* pretty isolated," Marilyn said, partially under her breath.

"It wasn't even just that," Carlo said. "They wanted to build here for years, I think, but kept running into problems."

"Legal?"

"Some of it, yeah. There was a lot of tussle with the owner of the land, who was hesitant to sell it. I think they passed away, though, and that's when things became easier, y'know."

"I *don't* know," Joe said, smiling. "That's why I'm askin'!"

Marilyn backhanded her husband across the arm. "*Joe.*" She addressed Carlo. "Sorry again. What did I say about our sense of humor?"

The bellhop waved her off. "Don't worry about it."

"Speaking of going down smooth…" Joe's attention had shifted to a framed advertisement. *Tsunami Sushi*, it read, *Beachside—Just north of the main pool!*, complete with a little map and colorful pictures of raw fish and rolls. "How's this place?"

Carlo shrugged. "I haven't tried it. But I hear great things."

"Sushi?" Marilyn said. "Really?"

"Come on. It'll be a good way to kick off the trip. Something new."

Marilyn snorted. "*All* of this is something new."

•   •   •

Joe slid the keycard into the lock. With a chime, the door opened to— a mistake.

That's what this had to be, right? Even though she'd seen something like it in the brochure, had known not to expect the typical Spartan arrangement of all other hotels and motels she'd been to, she instinctively rejected the unbelievable spaciousness, the whole kitchen area—with an island!—and the airy living room with a big, marshmallowy sofa and the sliding glass door to the sun-traced balcony.

"This is incredible," Marilyn said. She snapped a few photos with her phone. "Chilly in here, though."

"Yeah, what's the AC doin' on?" Joe asked Carlo, as they schlepped in their luggage. "AC in Hawaii should be outlawed three times over … y'know."

Marilyn walked over to the air conditioning unit and turned it off with a decisive *thunk*. "First World Problem solved, Sir Toomey."

Joe led Carlo out and shuffled off several dollars into the bellhop's palm. "Thanks a lot, man. Appreciate it."

Carlo grinned and waved back at them both. "Have a wonderful stay."

"Thank you!" Marilyn wanted to stop him, to ask more what he might know about the history of the area, its previous owner, but the questions stalled in her throat.

The door closed, and Joe turned to her. "Well!"

"Well!"

They made their way to the balcony, where they slid open the glass door and looked out upon the bay. Everywhere rose the susurrus of waves and wind and voices and light whirring traffic.

Joe leaned on the railing. Marilyn held up her phone and, rotating, took several successive pictures.

"Doing a panorama?" Joe asked.

"You know it." She finished and uploaded the photo to her socials: #nofilter #highlife #hawaii #fantasyadventure.

"Drink it in, Mare." Joe's voice was ambiguous, vaguely sarcastic.

She slipped her phone in her pocket and began caressing Joe's arm. Without meeting her gaze, he reached up and took her hand in his, and the two gazed over the palm-lined streets of the resort villager and the tiny ant-sized people lying on the shore or frolicking in the surf, and the contrived greenery of the golf course and the two indigo pools decorated with rocks and waterfalls and one large, serpentine slide and the outdoor Tiki bars where folks sat shirtless and sipping.

On the right side of the bay, rising at the very end of the short peninsula, was Pyramid Rock. Marilyn noted it.

"It looks like the island is raising a lance," she said.

Joe sniggered. "Against the sea?"

"No. Just against bigger islands. It's *Don Kauai*."

Joe smiled and shook his head. "See anything out there?"

"Nope," Marilyn said.

"I meant the ocean."

"I know. Nothing out there I can see."

Joe drummed his palms on the railing. "I'm sure we'll see plenty once we get out there." He started back toward the room. "I'm gonna start unpacking."

She was alone on the balcony. Marilyn inhaled long, deep, and watched the sea. Way down toward the southside of the bay, people jumped from a higher perch on the peninsula, shouting and splashing down not far from those snorkeling.

A cold anxiousness rose in her, but she tried to beat it back.

—you need to go—

She looked again, seeing nothing of the large dark form that had just been gliding about near Pyramid Rock. After all, it was nothing more than cloud shadows cast on the surface.

Probably.

5

Their oceanfront seat at *Tsunami Sushi* offered a beautiful view, promising even more delights as the cloud-dotted evening suggested a glorious first tropical sunset.

"This," Joe said, nodding. "*This.*"

The waiter arrived out of nowhere, wearing a loud Hawaiian shirt and a wide, attractive smile. His nametag: *Will.*

"Can I get any drinks started for you?" He unveiled a long menu. "We've got plenty of signature cocktails, premium sake, craft beer…"

"No, thank you," Joe said. "Just a Diet Coke for me."

Marilyn cast an eye toward the menu. "Any virgin on there?" Her face flushed. "I mean any*thing* virgin on there?"

Will's boyish grin grew. "We have the virgin pina colada, lava flow and margarita."

"Oh! Pina colada, please."

"You got it."

With a wink, he hurried away. Joe was already poised over the sushi menu, brow crinkled. He cleared his throat with tutorial authority. "Do we want to walk on the wild side and get sashimi? That's the raw fish."

"I can read, Joe."

After some back and forth, they settled on rolls and nigiri of the shrimp, eel, and salmon variety. Joe argued for the tuna but Marilyn, her conscience prodded by a recent article about overfishing, vetoed the choice.

"Don't get all activist on me, Mare," Joe said, half-grinning.

Caring about the planet. That's activist now.

"No octopus, though," she said. "Got it?"

Joe shrugged. "Fine. They're too chewy, I hear."

"They're smart."

He smirked and shook his head. "You and your octopi."

"Octopu*ses*."

"Well," Joe said. "We might just *see* one snorkeling."

"Really? Does an octopus need a snorkel mask?"

Joe gave her a quizzical look, just as Will the waiter returned. He took their order and asked, "This round one, I take it?"

"We'll see," Joe said.

She wanted to engage the waiter more, to keep him there because now she and Joe were alone and facing one another, with no kids and no distractions.

Reflex prompted Marilyn toward her phone. She homed in on Instagram, where the likes and the loves and comments on her pictures so far were well underway.

Kevknight609: Freaking beautiful!

Moonstargoddess88: Tots jelly! Ur hitting the beach now right???!!

FlameChick_309: Well-deserved vacay!

NightFairyMeg: Magical place fit for a magical lady…

Breathtaking, wrote Aurora_Pixie, or, Jen, one of her best *Errowind* friends, almost as sunny and beautiful as you! When u comin to Seattle?

Joe sighed. "The phone that quickly? Really?"

She put it down. "Sorry. Just want to share the goodness."

"I know." Joe poured soy sauce into two trays. "I'm sorry to be an ogre about it. I'll try and scale that back."

"I get it." She really did resent the bewitching power of this thin slab of plastic and silicon. She'd read somewhere, probably in one of their quantum science books, that the very base of the world might well be pure potential. That beyond anatomy or biochemistry, people were made of the stuff of ideas, of concepts—of anything-ness. They reveled in What *Could* Be. Now, tech wizards had put us in touch with our deepest cosmic inheritance, having slipped into our pockets a whole universe of potential far more enticing than any defined, present moment around us.

The sun inched down toward the horizon, now a glowing amphitheater of clouds and colors.

"You know about the green flash at sunset?" Joe asked. "It's rare, and you have to really keep your eyes trained. My friend Rob saw it happen when he was at BYU here. Only once, though. In four years!"

"He was probably too busy chasing all the surfer girls."

"Hah. Right." Joe glanced distractedly toward the kitchen area. "The waiter hasn't brought my Diet Coke."

"Just remind him."

He tore open his chopsticks packet and began folding it into crude origami. "I hate waiters who don't actually write down orders."

"Don't bash our waiter," Marilyn said, in a lowered voice. "I like him. He's cool."

"That's because he's flirty with you." Joe chuckled. "Which is understandable. You *are* quite the looker."

"No, I'm not. I wish I had more time to get in shape before coming here."

"Mare, stop it. You look great."

Marilyn considered driving home the point by acknowledging the stunning set of curves and legs striding from the ocean nearby, but she dropped it. She hated how some women looked like that in real life.

Joe slid his hand across the table and took hers, and she returned a brief squeeze. "So I was thinking," he said, "that tomorrow morning we officially christen our new snorkel gear. We can pop outta bed, stuff our faces with the breakfast buffet, maybe practice in the pool and *then*—whip on down here and see what's cookin' in the water."

"Maybe," she said.

"Unless you'd rather go parasailing."

Will appeared with two plates lined with rolls and nigiri. "Alrighty, we got round one here."

"Wow, that was fast," Marilyn said. "I haven't even opened my chopsticks yet."

The waiter beamed. "What can I say? I'm a fast fisherman."

"You caught 'em right out here, right?" She pointed toward the water. "That's what we're paying the *big* bucks for, after all?"

"I caught 'em with my bare hands." Will quickly mimed a choking gesture.

Joe mixed some wasabi into the soy sauce. "Weird that sushi would be easier to wrangle than a Diet Coke." Though clearly meant as playful, there was a chilliness in his voice. "Or her … what was it you got, Mare? A virgin pina colada?"

"It's not a huge deal," Marilyn said. She held up a palm over her mouth and fake-whispered to Will, "Soy sauce just fatally dehydrates him."

Will clapped his hands together. "I'm sorry about the drinks. I'll get those right now."

"Thank you," Joe said.

A seasoned ramen-eater, Marilyn was at least partial to chopsticks, though she'd now edged past that initial comfort into hovering ambivalently over which sushi to try first. The rubbery veneer wasn't too appetizing, but she appreciated the presentation.

"I almost don't want to mess any of it up," she said.

"Oh stop," Joe said, chewing. "Mess it up good. It's an insult you don't."

The plan she'd formulated was to start with the more familiar (and cooked) shrimp nigiri and graduate from there. But then she snatched up the salmon and popped it into her mouth.

"Ack!" Joe pointed to the tray of soy sauce and wasabi. "You gotta dip!"

"Too late." She chewed slowly. Not bad. Fresh. Succulent in its own way—

—*writhing*—

Marilyn recoiled a little.

—a flurry of light and shadow and streams of bubbles and muffled sounds and a chaotic smear of movement and panic and all blue and pressure all round and the massive purging sweep ongoing, *ongoing* and—

—more light blazing and hopeless squirming and the futile grasp for breath and wet wrenching *spasms*—

"Mare?"

She inhaled quick and sharp, sucking stray rice down her throat and forcing out a series of coughs.

"Sorry." She cleared her throat. "Must've gone down the wrong tube."

"You okay?"

She swallowed. "Yeah, I'm fine."

"It's good, right?"

"Yeah, not bad."

She closed her eyes, swallowed and gently set her chopsticks down.

"You're not done, are you?" Joe said.

"No, I'm just going slow. I'm not stopping you, though."

She looked down, lost in thought. After a few breaths, the final waves of that primitive, unknowing panic faded from her. If she had to describe it out loud, it was almost as if—briefly, brutally—she'd been drowning. But not as herself. More … as a fish.

"There it was!"

Marilyn snapped back to attention. Joe's gaze was on the horizon.

"Green flash! I saw it!" He looked at her. "You missed it, didn't you?"

6

"Heyooo!" Kevin said, his face distorted by pixels.

"Hi-ho yourself," Joe said. They had set up his laptop on the desk in their bedroom. "Hey, Margie."

They waved, as Kevin and Margie's own hands blurred across the screen.

"I saw your panorama from earlier, Marilyn," Margie said. "Looks absolutely beautiful."

"You have any Kalua pork yet?" Kevin said, randomly. Never had Marilyn interacted with him and Margie in this context, and she was struck by how insincere and…well, dopey they seemed. Maybe the stage fright of Skyping.

"Not yet," Joe said. "But we did have some top-notch sushi. And BlastFM signed us up for a luau in a couple days."

Marilyn looked at her husband—this was the first she'd heard of the luau.

"So where are the little goblins?" Marilyn asked, trying to keep from her voice the sting that they weren't there when the session had started.

"Oh, they're right here." Kevin tilted the screen to reveal the pixelated blotches of Tom, Tammy, Troy and Calvin kneeling across the room on the living room carpet, busying themselves with what looked like a board game. "Guys! We got it up. Come over and say hi to Mom and Dad!"

The threesome sprang from their position and bounced over. With divine timing, they filled the screen just as it de-pixelated. Marilyn's heart unclenched. An absolute love swept over her.

"What're you guys so absorbed in over there?" she asked.

"Kevin's game!" Tammy said. Next to her, Amy tried to quietly correct her by saying "*Uncle* Kevin," but Tammy remained steadfast in always just saying 'Kevin'. "He invented it."

"Really?" Joe said. "I didn't realize you were a game designer, bro."

"It's just something I've been tinkering with," Kevin said.

"Do you guys want to see our suite?" Marilyn said.

"Huh?" Tommy said.

"Our hotel room!"

"Oh, yeah." Tommy pointed at them, shoved his face forward so it blotted out half the screen. "I can see some of it. There's a lamp and a painting and stuff behind you."

"*Psssh*. This is just our bedroom. Lemme take you all on the grand tour." Not without some gratuitous, *careful-with-my-gear* help from Joe, Marilyn lifted the laptop and turned it toward the rest of their room.

"Nice," Margie said. "Is that a whirlpool tub in the bathroom?"

"It is."

"Please tell me you've inked some time for a bubble bath."

"It won't go wasted."

Tommy started to say, "It looks kinda sm—whoa!"

Marilyn had taken them out through the bedroom door into the living room, where like an awkward spokesmodel she showed off the kitchen, the giant TV, the leather couch, even the other bathroom by the entrance.

"That's like the biggest hotel room I've ever *seen*!" Tommy said. "How come we've never had one like that before?"

"Because it ain't comin' out of our wallet," Joe said, stepping alongside her.

"But this is just the boring old inside," Marilyn said, striding toward the balcony door and reaching for the handle.

Joe brushed her elbow. "Wait, you're taking it out there?"

"Yeah." She slid open the door, the sweet warm night billowing in. "I'll be careful. I won't drop your computer eight stories."

Marilyn edged out onto the balcony. She rotated the laptop all around, trying to encompass everything of the pool area lined with Tiki torches and the palms dark against the bay's moon-drizzled waters. "I wish you could feel the air. Every breeze is warm."

"Looks pretty dang gorgeous, that's for sure," Kevin said. "We're green over here."

Marilyn looked back at the screen. One face was missing.

"Where's Troy?" she asked. "You're not crowding him out, are you?"

"Troy went back to the game," Tammy said, pointing.

"Huh?"

One of them shifted the monitor enough so that she could see Troy back at Calvin's side, hunched over the scattered pieces of Kevin's game.

"Hey Troyasaur!" Marilyn said, voice raised. "What're you doing back over there already?"

Troy turned around and said something, but she couldn't understand what it was.

"What did you say, bud?" Joe asked, leaning in.

Tammy played translator. "He said the water's alive—"

Troy's garbled voice rose in the background. This time, both Tammy and Tommy relayed what he said.

"And that it's bad—"

"—and it's bad." Tammy rolled her eyes. "Whatever. He's being dumb—I mean, weird."

Marilyn's chest clenched.

"Can't be any worse than how bad the water is here," Margie said. "I read this morning our local beach got an F for the pollution. Can you imagine? How long will it take for us to clean up our act? Literally."

•　　•　　•

After brushing her teeth, Marilyn closed the bathroom door and sat on the lid of the toilet, trying to collect herself. Random shivers broke out over her.

At some level, Marilyn welcomed a juicy airplane cold. It would be an excuse to rest, to remain unbothered by Peppy Joe's activity list.

Besides, she was here for a reason. What that reason was, though, she wasn't sure.

Phone in hand, Marilyn opened Facebook. Her notifications were in double digits, but it was the first thing on her feed that drew her attention the most:

Facebook Memories
We thought you'd like to look back at this post of yours from 1 year ago.

God doesn't text! He CALLS you!
Though it's always a nonlocal number.

She'd forgotten about writing that post. Encountering it again, Marilyn was impressed with her own wit and wisdom. She'd mixed "spirit" with friendly advice and added a smidgeon of quantum-science humor. It had garnered almost seventy-five reactions, most of which were "Loves." Then there were the comments:

So true and so beautiful. Like you!

Wisely, you speak, Master Marilyn.

…and He won't leave a voicemail, either! So you better Answer when He calls!!!

God's Light shines so radiant thru u and your family thank u God bless Mary!

Toward the bottom, her brother Shane had also left a comment: a link to a clip titled "George Carlin Dismembers Religion." Marilyn was certain she'd never watched the video.

Indeed: purpose had fortified her. Purpose was taking shape on a blurry horizon. And now—

—God doesn't text—

—it was close, calling out to her, even if much of this purpose remained stubbornly unclear.

The water's alive.

And it's bad.

—He CALLS you—

Marilyn set her phone by the sink, clasped her hands and lowered her head.

"Lord, I don't know if this Facebook thing is at all a sign," she muttered. "But seems as good as any, am I right? Kind of ironic, too. Since it's, y'know… text."

She rambled, stuttered, chastising herself for such flippant prayer.

"If I do have something to do here, if you called me here for a reason," She hesitated to utter the next word. "For a mission…"

Yes.

The word bolted into her consciousness. Marilyn was reminded of that evening when Troy had vanished into the attic, when the whole notion of this trip had been thrown at her and how later that night she'd been struck by the conviction that she was going, that she had to go.

That Joe's radio-contest win was hardly a fluke.

God had placed her here, at this moment.

Stop this.

"…whatever your plan for me, for my family, you know I trust in you, and your Love."

Marilyn sat back, unclasped her hands and stared at the watercolor of Pyramid Bay hung on the wall across from her.

False prophet.

Yet how could she be sure?

A knock. "Mare? You alright?"

These were dangerous thoughts. Of the many divine rays that had shone through Joseph Smith, surely the doctrine of personal revelation ranked among the brightest.

But as today's church was quick to point out, said doctrine had also blinded many to their own corrupting misuses and misinterpretations.

God, after all, wished spiritual intimacy and unity, not hopeless fragmentation.

"Yeah." She turned and flushed the empty toilet. "Coming out."

•   •   •

Not ten seconds after lights-out, Joe began stroking her arm. What she hoped was only a touch of grateful tenderness soon became a series of light pecks on her arm which traveled up her shoulders to her neck.

Marilyn caressed the back of his shoulders. "I see where you're goin' with this."

He made his way to her ear and rubbed it a little. Marilyn moaned, her usual moan that concealed the fact that he always bit too hard.

"It'd be an incomplete first night otherwise," Joe whispered in her ear.

"At least you're not asleep for this one," Marilyn said.

The kissing stopped. Joe leaned up and looked at her with mild bemusement. "Why do you say that?"

Marilyn snorted. "Why do I *say* that? You know you're infamous for that."

Joe sighed. "Okay, but you know I don't like hearing about it. It makes me feel like a rapist."

Marilyn *tsked*. "Honey-bear-sweetie-pie-loverpants, if you were raping me, I'd knock you awake and stomp all over you, and maybe cut you with the Sword of Shame."

Joe sniggered. "The Sword of Shame is plastic."

"So you *know* how hard I'd swing it."

This time Joe full-on laughed. "I love you, Marilyn Toomey."

She wasn't sure why she hesitated. "I love you too, Joe."

Though his brow furrowed, he seemed uninterested in following up on that two-second pause. Likely because of the erection prodding her thigh.

She pulled him in. Not without some awkward maneuvering, he mounted her and they kissed, feeling the shape of one another's smile.

• • •

Pain throbbed across the back of her skull. In semi-waking delirium, Marilyn imagined her head in crocodile jaws.

She was lying on hard carpet.

Fell out of bed?

But everything was pitch black and she felt enclosed, like the dark had grown tissue and was pressing on her.

She felt around. Wall in front of her. Scratchy. Also carpeted. Wall to her side.

I'm in the—

A loud chime startled her. A lighted line split the dark in front of her, and the whole room lurched as the line widened and the—*elevator, the elevator doors*—parted. A liquid coldness rushed in about Marilyn's feet, rising to her knees.

The hallway was flooded, the air bloated with primordial odors of salt and dead fish. Lamps buzz-flickering down its stretch.

She tried to remember what had happened, but could recall nothing through her hammering heartbeat and mounting breath.

Had a storm hit? A typhoon?

Marilyn hesitated to move forward, until the elevator lurched again and the doors threatened to close once more, forcing her in clumsy splashes out into the hall where she looked up and down and saw only doors and dimming lights hovering over the disturbed surface of this eighth-floor lagoon. One of the nearby lamps died in a final gasp of sparks.

"Joe?" Marilyn cried, dragging ripples toward their room. "Hello?"

She rapped on the nearest door—843—even as she kept on trudging, running trembling fingers over the wall. *Something touched me, touched my LEG.* She glanced around and thought she caught the impression of a snaky thing swimming away but as there was movement everywhere—*Water's Alive*—it was difficult to tell anything.

"Is anyone here?"

She pounded on the nearest door. It shuddered open, enough to unleash a tide of seawater, now to her thighs.

"Joe!" Marilyn hugged the opposite wall, splash-dragging herself closer and closer to their room.

"Marilyn," said a voice.

Joe was there, in the newly opened room, naked but for his boxers and striding toward her. Something about his loping, almost frog-legged gait was wrong. She stepped back.

"Joe…what are you doing in there?"

He halted, staring at her with a blank expression.

"We're in every room, Marilyn," he said. "Until we're not."

Joe's mouth quivered, hung open and hung low. Marilyn thought she could see an eye blink open at the back of his throat. Then his lower jaw dislocated and fell into the water, and it was not a jaw but a little humanoid creature—one of many, in fact, for his whole body trembled with hundreds of much tinier bodies composing it.

Pair by pair, tiny eyes blinkered open. A watching constellation. Their heads snapped to alert. The Joe-composite began dismembering itself right before her eyes, flesh-colored creatures pulling apart and plopping into the water below.

Marilyn gasped and stumbled backwards, collapsing with a large splash. The water drowned her scream and she coughed and gagged as she flailed to her feet.

"Mommy!"

She stopped breathing, willed her heart to stop ramming, just for a *second*—

"Mommy!"

"*Troy*?" Soaked and shivering, Marilyn pushed forward toward the voice, which she thought might be coming from her room. "Troy where *are* you sweetie are you okay?"

812. Their room.

The door was open, looser furniture like chairs and tables and lamps stirring in the chop. Through the thunderous sound of rushing water, the crying of a child reached Marilyn's ears.

Troy stood bare-chested on the living room balcony, waist-high in the currents flowing past him through the railing and over the edge. The source of the waterfall noise.

"Troy," she called. "Get *away* from there!"

He didn't budge. How was he managing to stand so still in the pull of all that water? Marilyn strode through the room toward her son, trying to avoid some of the hard-cornered debris.

"Come here and look, Mommy," Troy cut in. His voice was deeper, his tone demanding.

Marilyn made her way to the balcony, where she lifted Troy dripping into her arms and hugged him tight. Any of what they said was subsumed by the noise of the nightwinds and the waterfall over the balcony, which, as Marilyn quickly saw, wasn't unique: every visible balcony across the Huna'ia Resort spouted water, water that rushed and roared toward the darkness now covering the bay.

The darkness was total, too. As if the sea had fastened shadow jaws upon the village.

·   ·   ·

Marilyn awoke, Joe snoring beside her.

Her pulse ran, her stomach was knotted and there was a dull throb in her temples. Across her body, a tense conference seemed to be taking place about whatever dream had visited her.

She turned on her side and checked her phone. Only 10:45. She was surprised. It felt like hours had passed since they'd finished their lovemaking and turned in.

She was wide awake.

Moving carefully so as not to disturb Joe, Marilyn peeled back the sheets and sat on the edge of the bed. She used her phone's flashlight to walk quietly out into the living room, scrounge for the laptop then set up shop on the kitchen counter.

The world of *Errowind* threw a dull blue glow on the darkness. Jen from Seattle was online, as were Renee and Frank, from the UK.

Hey! Jen messaged. *Look who's back. The Hawaiian princess!*

Heh, hardly, Marilyn replied.

Not long ago, and for the third time, she had re-customized her Myrulian Dwarf-Knight, who was technically a female though she'd still given her a big red beard, some of which was braided along with two braided ponytails down her armored back. She sported a new, gilded jerkin of chainmail, and Marilyn had even fashioned a silver dragon's mouth to the handle of her double-bladed axe.

Errowind's character-creation system was amazingly detailed, to the point where she felt ownership over her dwarf, having sketched out ideas before implementing them. Some of the drawings of her Dwarf-Knight, like her old D&D necromancer Gabriya, had been "Favorited" by fair numbers of DeviantArt folks and Instagrammers. All very cool, but the honor she was most proud of? The game's lead designer had "Liked" the one of her Dwarf-Knight riding a wind-demon, which had made her squeal.

She played for forty minutes before the blue light started giving her a headache. She paused, rubbed her eyes and for a moment sank her face into her palms.

In returning to the screen, she saw her Dwarf-Knight frowning at her, tapping her booted foot. Just a clever "idle animation", though sometimes it did seem like the character suspected her presence.

Increasingly, Marilyn felt restless. Here she was, exploring a phony world when outside sprawled a whole new *real* world to explore.

She said goodbye to her gaming friends, closed the laptop then went about quietly dressing. She headed for the door before turning and snatching the keycard from the counter.

Pulling the handle slowly, she popped open the door and tiptoed out.

The door clicked shut behind her. She grimaced. Waited.

Then headed off.

She took the stairs down. It was by the sixth floor when Marilyn realized she'd forgotten her phone. She stalled on the step, feeling naked, surprised with herself. She decided not to go back, telling herself she wouldn't—shouldn't—be long.

7

Making her way to the beach, Marilyn removed her sandals and sunk her toes in the sand. The bay was almost like a Hollywood backdrop, the full moon bejeweling the dark sea. The stars winked down.

She dared herself to walk closer to the water. Yellow signs came into view warning of possible riptides. How on Earth could Joe want to go snorkeling tomorrow? She had to get out of it. Maybe say the sushi had made a vengeful return. Or, better yet, just plant herself firm and *not give in*. Yes, there'd been times she was glad Joe had pushed her past her innate reluctance (snagging a slot at *Realms of Magic*'s art exhibit came to mind), but too often she was simply afraid of triggering an argument.

She continued south, or at least what she thought was south. The Tiki torches flirted with the shadows of the empty pathway and shoreline. All was quiet, no traffic or voices.

Outrigger Rides—$20 per person, said the sign.

There were several of them, massive canoes lined up across the sand next to a kiosk and collapsed umbrella. In the dull throb of the nearest torch, she read the rest.

Outrigger canoes were staples of early Polynesian and native Hawaiian life and maritime navigation, often carrying whole tribes, even societies, across thousands of miles of open ocean.

Maybe she could convince Joe to take a canoe ride, instead of snorkeling?

"If you push one end," said a voice behind her. "I'll push the other."

She whirled around. She knew the face, though it took her a moment. It was the smile that did it. Released from *Tsunami's* contractual shackles, it seemed to stretch that extra, authentic inch.

"Mary, right?" said her waiter from earlier. He was still dressed in his Hawaiian work shirt, but it was untucked and he now wore shorts and flipflops. In one hand he held a small cooler.

"Wow, you remember my name?" Marilyn said. "Shouldn't it be the other way around? You were the one with the nametag." She pointed. "But you took it off!"

"No worries. I just overheard your husband say your name and it stuck."

"Because 'Mary' is so memorable? Though that's not *quite* my name."

"Oh no!"

"It's Marilyn."

"Bah, sorry about that." He stuck out his free hand. "I'm Will."

They shook. "Right! Nice to officially meet you. And I won't forget your name this time … Bill."

"Uh…"

Marilyn gave him a light punch on the shoulder. "I'm kidding, good sir. Although if you were Bill, it might've stuck. It's almost as memorable as Mary."

"Is your husband with you?" Will asked.

"He's zonked out."

"So you're out and prowling." He hesitated. "Not like *that*, I mean."

"You could say that. I get curious. I stray." With a soft snort, Marilyn added, "Not like *that*, though."

Will gestured beyond her. "I'm meeting a few friends just up the beach here, if you want to join us. It'll be chill. Bonfire, some grub, some drinks."

Marilyn smiled. "How far down the beach?"

"Literally like a twenty-minute walk from here."

The anti-social part of her, the part that just wanted alone-time to drift, to reflect, to turn off obligations and expectations, thrust a futile blow at her desire to be pulled into some adventure.

"Hm," she muttered. "Sure, why not?"

"Great." As they started off, Will held up the cooler and patted it. "And don't worry. We got virgin options, too."

• • •

They'd set up a little makeshift bonfire on a smaller beach just south of the resort. The thought occurred to ask whether a fire was even legal, but Marilyn kept quiet.

"Hey folks," Will said.

The small group turned and offered their greetings, the two women smiling wide and the other guy raising his can—what Marilyn assumed a beer—in a singular toast of, "Yo, yo! Billiam has arrived!"

"I brought an impromptu guest," Will said, gesturing to Marilyn. "This is Marilyn. *Not* Mary."

He smiled at her. Marilyn hoped her return smile wasn't as sheepish as it felt.

"Marilyn, this is Colin, Vanessa, or Ness, and Tatiana."

Such *young* names, she thought, waving. "Nice to meet y'all. Sorry, I swear I'm not Southern."

"Grab a drink!" Colin said, pointing out the two coolers already there at the edge of the firelight. Immediately she sensed far more welcoming energy from him than the women, who seemed to bristle at her arrival.

"Thank you. Do you guys have any sodas, by chance?"

"I brought sodas," Will said. "These people never bring mixers or anything."

Colin snorted, slipped his arm around Tatiana. Vanessa held a skewered hot dog over the flames, gazing into the fire in a way that intrigued Marilyn. Though she was already quite pretty, the fire-shadows and flowers in her hair conspired to make her look elemental.

She fished a 7-Up from Will's cooler.

"This is a special privilege, I hope you know," Tatiana said to her, with a playful grin. "Firepit Fridays are secret. Kind of."

Will winked at Marilyn. "She tipped well."

"Marilyn," Vanessa said, gesturing. "If you want a hot dog, please help yourself."

"Thank you, Vanessa. Er, Ness, right?"

The girl smiled, which sent an unexpected bout of butterflies through Marilyn's stomach. She wanted Will's approval, sure, and everyone else's, but she inexplicably wanted Vanessa's most of all. Maybe it was the way the woman seemed so detached and, well, bohemian.

Marilyn felt stiff and awkward but tried her best in answering and asking questions with a high and excited voice, forcing her arms into big theatrical gestures. At one point, she even flung a small geyser of soda toward Tatiana, who recoiled with an uneasy laugh.

"Sorry," Marilyn said. "I guess I have a splash zone."

Unsurprisingly, all four of them worked in the resort village. None of them had known one another before moving from the mainland to Kauai. Colin and Tatiana had met in a surfing class, and Colin had met Will working at a nearby coffee shop, "Lava Java," where Vanessa would come regularly to strum her guitar.

"Wait," Marilyn said, looking at Vanessa. "So what do you do?"

"I give jet-ski lessons," said Vanessa. "And bartend in the evenings."

"Jet-ski! That's cool. Like the motorcycle of the ocean."

Vanessa smirked.

Between plans for a surfing TV show, record labels, art galleries and food trucks, all four vibrated with ambitions beyond Marilyn's reach. Hearing their chatter simultaneously exhausted, depressed and inspired her. She envied their certainty of the future. Life was wide open, accommodating of big dreams.

"By the way, Tats," Vanessa said at one point. "I'm pretty sure that guy today was from the Lofts."

Tatiana frowned. "What guy?"

"When we were surfing this morning, off Ohana Point. The bearded dude who strolled out of the jungle and just sat and watched us for a while."

"That's not a little creepy," Will said.

Vanessa shrugged. "Tatiana found it creepier than I did."

"It would've been okay if we hadn't been the only ones out there."

"*You* wanted to go at seven AM!"

Marilyn leaned in. "What are the 'Lofts'?"

Colin turned and pointed off into the darkness, as though it were across the street. "It's a community out in the jungle, farther inland."

"Bloodthirsty cult?" Marilyn said. "Or hippies? Or bloodthirsty cult of hippies?"

"No. Hope not, anyway. I barely know anything about them, honestly."

Vanessa pulled out her smartphone and opened what looked like ten Louvre's worth of pictures, impressing even Marilyn.

"I hiked by there maybe three weeks ago," Vanessa said, "and got some pics. I think I could've gone up to it—they're supposedly pretty friendly, though weird—but it was outta my way."

"May I?" Marilyn said, already in the act of taking her phone.

Vanessa nodded. Marilyn peered at the photo, zoomed in a little on the elaborate banyan tree centered in the frame, rising and spiraling its massive tendrils out like some alien long landed there and petrified over.

Yet it was the opposite of deadness. It exuded life, the tree-sun of its solar system, and wrapped around its trunk and scattered across its bulging branches were treehouses complete with wooden walkways and bridges, an above-ground village straight out of any fantasy art or cinema.

I know that place. Though Marilyn had no idea how, or why.

I know those trees.

"That's the Lofts?" she asked.

"Uh-huh."

Marilyn was about to hand the phone back when she noticed something in the photo gallery.

"Wait." She pointed with her thumb. "What is this?"

Manners prevented her from clicking on it—she felt rude clicking on photos she wasn't "invited" to see—but in pointing she accidentally brought it up, and there was no mistaking it: by astonishing coincidence, Vanessa had downloaded one of her drawings, a charcoal rendering of a half-dragon, half-octopus that Marilyn called "Dractopus." She'd sold the original at *Realms of Magic* a year ago.

"That's my tattoo," Vanessa said. She turned to illuminate her left leg in the firelight. Indeed, that same tentacled, winged creature was coiled up her calf, sliding over her knee and across her firm rounded thigh. On her skin, the creature had assumed a three-dimensional quality.

Marilyn felt a giddy rush, but told herself not to make a big deal about it. In fact, why push it at all? She'd just met these people. She didn't want to come across as vain. At the same time, how the heck had Vanessa stumbled on it? It did live a certain life online, on DeviantArt, on Instagram, on Pinterest and other places. Maybe it had just found her, like a stray snowflake.

"That Lofts place looks like something out of *Errowind Tales*," Marilyn said. Ignorant glances went around. "I guess no one here's a gamer?"

"Does *Minecraft* count?" Will asked.

"The funny thing about the bearded guy this morning," Vanessa said. "Every time I looked at him, he looked, like, different. You know how certain things look new or unfamiliar from certain angles? It was like that, only I wasn't looking at him from any other angle. He just seemed like a new person every time I looked at him, even though he didn't change or move much."

"That's weird," Tatiana said.

The Road Walker, Marilyn remembered.

"I had the same thing happen to me, actually," Marilyn said. "On the way here. There was a hitchhiker. Like you said, he just looked…different every time I looked at him."

"It's the tropics," Colin said, after a long gulp. "It constantly refreshes you."

Glancing toward the sea, Marilyn caught sight of a dark hump breaking through the band of moonlight. A cloudspray puffed up, hurried off like a bashful specter.

Marilyn pointed. "Hey! Whale!"

Conversation ceased. The creature couldn't have been more than a hundred yards out, having breached just beyond the farthest breaker.

The small crowd gathered behind her. Will stopped next to her.

"Where?" he asked.

"They've been around lately," said Tatiana. "Though it's not their season."

"Might be climate change or something," Vanessa said.

Colin laughed. "Not every hiccup is climate change."

Will piped in. "Who says nature has hiccups?"

"We're poison," Vanessa continued. "I mean, what does the body do to poison? It tries to get rid of it."

Marilyn frowned. The words cut deeper than expected. Marilyn saw humanity as a sad, vulnerable thing that simply tried best it could. Funny, since in conversations with right-wing church members, usually online, or even in her terser spats with Joe, she often took a stance more like Vanessa's: that humans had undermined God's trust as stewards of the Earth.

"There it goes! Holy shit! Look!" cried Vanessa. "I think it's got a baby with her."

"A calf," said Will.

"Whatever!"

Two dark humps rose now, one bigger and one smaller. Dual sprays shot into the night air. The mother wheeled through the water.

"They're so close!" cried Vanessa.

"Uh, what're you doing?" said Will.

It took a second for Marilyn to realize his attention had centered past her on Vanessa, now topless with her shirt and hair-flowers lying on the sand as she hopped about removing the rest of her shorts. Marilyn gasped.

"Please tell me you're *not* going swimming," Marilyn said.

"They're whales!" Vanessa said. She scrambled on toward the tideline, sand and suds warping whatever grace she might've otherwise displayed. By the way her feet haphazardly slapped the wet sand, Marilyn was afraid she might twist her ankle.

"Well shit." Will set down his drink. "She can't go alone."

"You've gotta be kidding me."

"I've been in this water a billion times. Even at night."

By now Vanessa was hip-high in surf, not looking back as she dove forward with a merry "*Whoo!*", a rebuke to the more pensive Vanessa Marilyn had met moments ago. She began breast-stroking out beyond the waves.

Watching her, Marilyn shuddered.

Tatiana landed a playful backhand to Colin's chest. "You aren't goin' in?"

"Hell-fucking-no," he said. "Andrew said he thought he saw a shark here the other day, while surfing."

"Probably a dolphin," Tatiana said. "But there has been a lotta stuff lately."

"Animals, you mean?" Marilyn asked, remembering Carlo's remark.

"Yeah. There were like manta rays here the other day. One dude even said he saw a whale shark out by Diamond Rock."

"Really?" Colin said. "Damn. Crazy."

Will seemed to hear none of this as he now raced bare-chested toward the water, becoming a little silhouette before the sea. Marilyn gripped her 7-Up tighter, partially crumpling it.

On reaching the tideline, Will stumbled. And cried out.

Marilyn was the first to mobilize. She dropped her soda and hurried over to him, Colin and Tatiana closing in behind her.

"You okay, dude?" Colin asked. "Oh fuck! *Fuck*!"

Marilyn looked. Grimacing, Colin hopped backwards on one foot like he'd just stepped on a nail. Tatiana tried steadying him but in Colin's tipsiness both collapsed backwards. Colin screamed as Will screamed and as Marilyn knelt there, the tide sweeping chilly waterskirts about her waist and knees, she saw the many strange bulbs glistening in the sand, with more washing ashore, rolling and blinking in the wan light.

They were eyeballs—hundreds of them all scattered, long thin optic nerve tendrils snaking back toward the sea.

"Fucking *man*-o-wars!" Will howled. "They're everywhere! God*dammit*!"

Just like that, whatever loopy reality she'd just inhabited went away, and what had been eyeballs were now gelatinous, tentacled blobs dotting the beach.

Another wave was coming in. Marilyn urged Will up, hooking her hands under his armpits. He batted her away but apologized immediately. Paranoia flooded Marilyn as she tip-toed on the balls of her feet over the darker stretches of sand, back toward the bonfire.

"Ow, ow, ow," Will muttered, staggering. "They got my hands and feet and one knee." Touching dry sand, he turned and whistled out toward the water. "Ness! Get *out* of there! Portugese man-o-war!"

Vanessa looked about halfway to the whales. She'd turned and was backstroking, her head a tiny punctuation mark in the water.

"What?" she called back.

Will cupped his hands over his mouth. "Man. O. *War*!"

"I don't see any!" There was petulance in her voice.

"Well we *feel* them!" Much of Will's reply was drowned in the hissing crash of a wave. There was an itchy sting on Marilyn's right leg, which she hoped was just sympathy pain. Nothing looked out of the ordinary.

With an irritatingly relaxed pace, Vanessa began circling back toward the shore. Marilyn almost hoped that the free-spirited swimmer would cry out in pain, be shocked into some kind of urgency.

"She's coming back," Tatiana noted. She still tended to Colin, who lay stretched out on the sand. "Do you think you guys need to go to the ER? Marilyn, are you okay?"

She nodded, as Will waved his off the prospect of a hospital visit. Marilyn said nothing. She would've felt obligated to join any trip to the ER, but she was eager to get back to the room. The longer she was out here, the more she felt like she was betraying Joe.

Vanessa was still swimming toward the shore, turned away as she backstroked. Another wave rose and briefly eclipsed her. A breeze rolled in.

The wave leveled off and Vanessa again came into view, as did another shape breaking the surface no more than thirty yards behind her: a rugged, lumpy thing somehow darker than any other silhouette. The water around the shape didn't appear to move naturally, not the way it had for the whales—especially odd given its far larger size.

"What is that?" Marilyn said.

Tatiana looked out to sea. "What is what?"

Vanessa stopped for a moment, then continued swimming at the same pace until she strode cautiously ashore.

Though it might've been the dim light, Vanessa looked paler, distracted, her gaze hastily surveying the beach.

"Are you okay?" Marilyn asked.

"Um, yeah." Vanessa checked her arms and legs. "Nothing got me, thankfully."

"What's wrong? You look frightened."

"What's *wrong*? Are you serious?"

Marilyn dropped it. They discussed Vanessa's dumb luck, whether to finish off the booze that night, whether Colin or Will should call in sick tomorrow. As they did, Marilyn noticed Vanessa glancing around furtively, looking confused, as if uncertain of her surroundings. She had the sense that Vanessa's frightened expression had not been because of the man-o-wars, but she would say nothing more.

Between the warm breeze and persisting bonfire, Marilyn stood cold, and began to shiver.

•   •   •

Joe popped open the door just as she went to slide her keycard into the lock.

"Holy *Moses*, Mare," he said. "Where *were* you? Why didn't you take your phone?"

"I needed to stretch my legs." Walking in, Marilyn moved to lightly elbow Joe in the side, but he tensed and backed up a step. "I'm so sorry I didn't leave a note."

Joe gave an incredulous chuckle. "Think for a second if roles were reversed. You wake up in the middle of the night—"

"It's only midnight."

"—to find me gone, with no note or text. Spare me the denial that you'd be freaking out. Especially given, well…"

"Well what?"

Joe sighed. "With what happened in San Fran."

"Because every time I take a walk by myself I'm gonna run into a terrorist attack?"

They went into the bedroom. Joe's hands were clasped behind his skull. Marilyn felt a twinge in her chest. With his own affected melodrama, her husband had an unwitting knack for making others feel crazy.

"That's not what I mean," he said. He sat on the edge of the bed and stared up at her. She resented his sad, gray eyes. "Weird stuff follows you. Weird situations follow you. Look at Gordon Lake."

"I was *four*."

"But you're still afraid of swimming, right? I mean, look where we are. If you'd had your way we wouldn't even be here, cuz of what happened when you were four."

"So I'm not allowed to do anything on my own now? You want to throw a dog leash around me when we go out? You want to follow me into bathrooms, make sure I don't fall in and get eaten by a terrorist alligator up from the sewer?"

"Where *did* you go?" Joe asked.

"Down along the beach. There's an invasion of Portuguese man-o-war going on, actually. Couple folks just got stung."

"Just tonight?"

Marilyn nodded. "Yup. So the beach'll probably be closed tomorrow."

"Hmm."

"They have outrigger canoe rides, I saw."

Joe gave a suspicious glance. "If the beach is closed, they wouldn't be doing the canoe rides."

She said nothing.

"We can mosey up or down the coast," Joe said. "Find another snorkel spot for now. Though that's too bad since right now the snorkeling here is supposed to be great."

"It probably won't be closed for long."

"You'll love it, Mare. I promise." He cleared his throat. "I'm glad you're alright."

Joe stretched out in bed and Marilyn began to disrobe.

She looked out the bedroom's balcony door, left partially open for the breeze. The bay was calm, breathing the tide in, the tide out. It sounded normal, but there was unknown menace in it.

Water's alive, Troy had said.

8

Large gray clouds had moved in, dimming the sun. The air had rain on its breath, even as it held to its honeyed warmth.

"Press your tongue to the roof of your mouth," Joe said, chest-high in the pool, "then hold your nose and blow. That'll equalize the pressure."

"Okay." Marilyn hated how nasally the snorkel masks made her voice, which she already imagined too high. "But I don't plan on diving down or anything."

"Never say never—"

"I never *said* 'never.'"

Joe finger-gunned her. "Yeah, y'did."

A quick roll of her eyes, and Marilyn slipped back beneath the surface. She regretted that they'd chosen the larger, "main" pool in which to practice her snorkeling.

"Marilyn!" Joe had said moments ago, when they'd gotten in. "I didn't realize you could swim."

"What're you talking about?" She adjusted her snorkel after a brief warm-up around the shallow-end. "I can swim. I don't mind pools."

"I knew you could *swim*," Joe said defensively. "You just seem more comfortable in the water than I anticipated."

Well, truth be told she was surprised at her, too, not only with the swimming strokes that had so readily returned from the mists of fifth grade, when Mom had forced her into Instructor Keith's burly arms at the Y, but the naturalness of being in water. Maybe she could delude herself that Pyramid Bay was simply a much bigger swimming pool.

"I know you don't plan on diving," Joe said, "but with the waves and everything, trust me, you're gonna get water in your snorkel. You can just blow it out. Try it."

Marilyn nestled the mouthpiece between her lips and dipped down. The shouts and murmurs of the area grew garbled and distant. She sank low enough to fill the snorkel with water, rotating as she did, observing two kids chasing one another across the pool's bottom.

Wish Tommy, Tammy and Troy could be here.

Sucking in breath, she drifted up and blew the water harshly out her snorkel— "*Pffffffffftthpppfff!*"

"Wow," Joe said. "Going for the whale spray, I take it?"

Marilyn spit out her mouthpiece. "Pretty much."

"Just imagine when we do it for real," Joe said. "There's so much to see."

•   •   •

Awaking not long after sunrise, Marilyn lay in bed listening to Joe breathing, to the distant waves rushing and receding with maddening calm, to the excitable voices filtering in downstairs from all corners of the resort, all so light with play. Empty of burden.

Go back, all of you. Go back to bed and stop being so happy and stop thinking life was left back at the airport, that it was obligated to leave itself there...

Indeed, that's what maddened her: the people that were up and pulling the day with it, forcing it on her. That, and the beach had clearly reopened.

She lay still, trying to calm her heartbeat.

"Oh, you're awake."

Joe's half-open eyes peered at her. His expression glowed with anticipation, only heightening Marilyn's nervous irritability.

"I'm awake," she said.

•   •   •

A large sea turtle lay farther down the shoreline, so inert that Marilyn had trouble distinguishing it from the backdropping rocks.

"Look at that big guy," Joe said. "I'm glad no one's hasslin' him."

"It's still early," Marilyn muttered, planted on the sand as she strapped on her fins.

"Who knows," Joe said. He lowered his mask over his eyes. The snorkel hung like some floppy vestigial appendage at the side of his face.

Marilyn stood and looked at the turtle. Its crusty eyes slowly opened and closed, its reptilian hide a temporal atlas of all the tens of millions of years collected under its shell.

"We'll probably run into some of his friends out there," Joe said, extending his hand. "Ready?"

With a breath, Marilyn took his hand. In his eagerness, he nearly pulled her off her feet. She stumbled, narrowly avoiding a faceplant in the sand.

"Hold *on*." She released his hand and began fiddling with the strap of her mask. She glanced around for anyone watching.

"What's the matter?" he asked. He waded knee-high into the surf.

"It's a little tight," she said. "It feels like it's going to suck out my eyeballs when I take it off."

With a sigh, he started toward her. "Here…"

"No, just, hold on. Like I said. I *got* it."

Truthfully, she wasn't exactly sure if she did. But after some tugging—and painfully tugging several locks of hair—the mask loosened. She adjusted it, then stepped forward with an arching, fin-plopping stride until the little waves scuttled in about her ankles.

"Chilly," she said.

He laughed. "It's Hawaii water. Not Vancouver Island."

"Doesn't matter. It's always a shock at first."

Joe tugged at her again.

"No, please, don't *pull* me," Marilyn said. She again let go of his hand. With a surrendering gesture, he backed off.

It was up to her now. There was nothing left to adjust or put on. No delay between her and the ocean that playfully cajoled her.

In a huff of protest, Joe turned, dove in and pushed off, snorkel cutting across the surface.

Goddammit, Joe. The thought was so strong it nearly leapt through her lips.

Marilyn took a deep breath through her mouth and closed her eyes. Then, before she fully gave herself permission, she was tipping forward, waves closer and closer and so clear she could see a school of small yellow fish at her feet.

She slipped in. Hazy cold chaos engulfed her. So many fish so close to shore. She fitted the water-filled snorkel and inhaled a mouthful. Her throat and lungs convulsed, forcing her to surface in a fit of coughing and spitting.

Marilyn poured out the remaining water and blew into the snorkel. She snuggled it between her lips and, before any more thoughts could catch up to her, speared herself into the breakers.

Something clasped her elbow. She whirled around to face Joe, now mostly submerged and floating just below her. He grunted like a caveman and pointed ahead toward the mounds of coral blizzarded by fish, beyond which loomed the great blue wall of the open ocean.

He took her hand. Marilyn hesitated. There was no one else in the general northwest part of the bay, the direction he apparently wanted to go. By contrast, the southern section brimmed with other snorkelers, reef-jumpers and swimmers.

Joe swam them farther out. They passed over urchins and starfish and drab, brown-white splotches of coral, porous with innumerable passageways and cozy havens for foraging fish.

Maybe it'll be okay. Maybe we'll have an adventure and see something no one else has seen or will see. Maybe it'll be a memory shared by only the two of us…

But the farther out they swam the colder Marilyn became, and it wasn't from the water but from something within. She dreaded that unpopulated stretch of reef, that merciless blue nothingness.

There's a reason no one else is over there. They feel it. Subconsciously they feel it.

Marilyn tugged Joe's hand. He turned, eyebrows raised. She pointed toward the southern peninsula that buzzed with the frolicking noises of any community pool. She indicated she wanted to surface. He followed.

Spitting out snorkel and seawater, Joe asked, "What is it?"

Marilyn put extra effort into pumping her legs to keep afloat. Between that and her general anxiety, not to mention being out of shape, her breaths were already coming harder.

"I want to go that way," she said, nodding.

Joe frowned. "That's where everyone else is."

"Exactly."

They lingered in silence for a second.

"Joe," she said. "Please just be reasonable."

He guffawed. "Did you really just say that?"

"Okay, I'm going," Marilyn said. "I'll meet up with you later, if you don't get eaten by something."

Without waiting for a response, she wedged the snorkel back in her mouth and pumped off, kicking and stroking with what was assuredly all the grace of an arthritic dog, but moving as fast as she could. And, most importantly, not looking back.

The blurry swimmers took on further definition, and she passed into the welcoming aura of fellow humans out of their element.

The rock wall rose nearby. Silvery fish darted past her in a dizzying school, so supernaturally coordinated.

Massive movement by the rock. Heart palpitating, she stopped and watched the cyclone of thousands of those same fish feasting and flitting across the great bulges of coral. They looked as one enormous entity, scaled by so many bodies glinting in the morning sun.

Other fish moved below, hued like broken-off bits of rainbow. Among them were the big-lipped types she'd seen in pictures (those with the *looooong* Hawaiian name), the long trumpet yellow-fish and the needlefish bobbing like syringes near the surface.

Marilyn floated, watching, every breath a whooshing typhoon in her ears. There was a primordial vibrancy here, faint echoes of the time when life itself was a new concept.

Poking her head up, she scanned for Joe but couldn't see him.

Keeping near the wall, Marilyn hesitantly pushed farther out, watchful of the reef-jumpers. A tickle in her gut. The rolling meadows of browned coral spread out beneath her, and she imagined herself some great flying deity, cruising over an alien landscape. She watched closely for octopuses.

More fish appeared. Brilliant yellow. Green. Striped. Spotted. A whole matrix, at once mindless and mindful.

One rule of snorkeling became self-evident: follow the people-clusters.

There was a cluster farther west, just past the peninsula's end. While beyond the main crowd, and thus farther than Marilyn was comfortable going, she made her way toward them, keeping near the rock wall. Small waves washed over her, sometimes dumping water down her snorkel. One gulp of seawater almost made her gag.

She willed herself on. The water grew colder, goosebumps breaking out on her arms. To her left, there was a rugged, rounded spire, fuzzy with growth and aflutter with fish, then—

—it dropped off, precipitously. Sunbeams danced like silent wind chimes through the surface. She slowed, muscles tightening. Murkier out here, too. Or was her mask acting up?

Surfacing, she rinsed her mask, reset it and looked around. Across the bay, the namesake "pyramid" rose like a steady odometer needle against the horizon.

She removed her snorkel. "Joe!"

A wave rose, briefly blocking the other end of the bay.

Leave now, said a wordless voice.

Coming to the surface had also sparked paranoia about whatever lurked beneath her, and she slipped back under again.

Something flashed in the corner of her eye.

Nothing there.

Tingles danced in her chest, up her throat. On higher and higher alert, Marilyn glanced around. A wave pushed against her. Another wave came, stronger. The feeling was that of a mysterious child testing her patience. Was this a riptide?

At this point, Marilyn imagined she could be making a break for shore, but the compulsion wasn't there. It was as if two large urges in her, that of the adult and that of the child, of the hungry explorer and Mom-Marilyn, were canceling each other out.

She hurried to the cluster of people, all of whom monitored something far below.

Marilyn saw two black kite shapes gliding along the bottom, less clear given the depth until three more appeared out of nowhere, much closer and flapping their wings (*fins*?) in elegant unison.

"What's over there?" someone called behind her.

A close, clear reply: "Eagle rays!"

Enchantment swept over her. She felt it also from the strangers floating close by, the two older kids with their dad and a young guy, maybe late-teens, and three other women all older than she. The energy was palpable with discovery and revelry.

Teetering between wonder and terror, she thought, I'm really here. *I'm really* doing this.

She began following the nearest eagle rays, as they swam onward. Breathing hard, Marilyn forced herself onward. Wait till *Joe* heard about this. The regret on his face. The envy.

She trailed the rays at a respectful distance. She glanced behind her to keep her eye on the people, some of whom, she was relieved to see, were following her.

Marilyn swung back toward the rays, but they were no longer there. Just unblemished blue.

She frowned. They hadn't been moving *that* fast. She turned back to the fellow snorkelers behind her, but they weren't there. Her eyes met the same resounding blueness, all around.

No sign of anyone. No sign of the reef.

One breath … and Marilyn sucked in a lungful of seawater.

Panic detonated across her body. She looked up—the surface glistened a good ten yards above her. Somehow, she'd been submerged, though she'd never dived down herself.

With motions less of a swimmer than a prison escapee tunneling to light, Marilyn ascended.

An enormous shape interrupted her path. She screamed into her snorkel, blowing out a spray of bubbles.

It was something like the eagle rays, only far larger. A *manta* ray, gliding over her with all the grandeur of a solar eclipse, its underbelly a ghostly white.

My God.

Chest wrung tighter and tighter, she kicked her way past the ray toward the surface, where she exploded, gasping. Summoning what she could of her strength and presence of mind, she screamed, "Help! *Help!*" in every direction of every splash she made…before realizing how far her voice would have to travel for the nearest ear.

She was the frightened child floating impossibly out on Gordon Lake, the child whose ignorant heart still beat in her, whose spirit had been caught in the unbreakable cycle of that moment, watching her family faraway as they cried out to her from the shoreline.

Except now it was only the cold, passive face of the Huna'ia Resort staring at her from the beach, the people mere bugs drifting over sand and surf.

She had to be well over a mile out.

"Hey!" She closed her eyes and bit her lip so hard it bled immediately. "*Heeelp!*"

Something was happening and it was happening to *her*. Something wanted her, had lured her all the way out here—

"*Heeeelp!*"

Head tilted down, she saw no bottom, just her fins and legs hovering over abyss. Aching and exhausted, Marilyn made determined strokes toward the bay.

She was also no longer alone. Though the manta ray was now barely visible, Marilyn could feel the thunderous specter of other life nearby.

Glancing around brought back only vague apparitions, undecided between whales or giant sharks or *krakens*, for all she knew. Yet Marilyn picked up the squeal-clicking of what she thought were whales, and then, not far away, she made out dolphins—a whole pod slicing through the sea toward Pyramid Bay.

They're all going in the same direction.

Far to her right, two turtles swam with lethargic grace. Well beyond them, like discolorations on the deep, were the outlines of what had to be whales. Any thrill Marilyn might normally have experienced, though, was but a dull pinch on a colossal body of nightmare.

In that second, nothing existed in Marilyn except the command to flee. She darted away, clawing and kicking and heaving and hoping to rip a wound in these waters.

She slowed. Several dozen white splotches began appearing in the water.

For a second all Marilyn saw was white. She stopped, fearful to the point of nausea. Had she seen it on TV, some nature documentary, she might've found surreal beauty in the sight around her. Yet, while exploding stars might dazzle from the telescope, you shuddered to think of the poor worlds in their path. Beauty often required buffers.

And there were no buffers now between her and hundreds of jellyfish.

They, too, appeared to be shifting toward the bay. There was a spectral quality not only in their movement but in the suddenness of their existence. She started to swim away but more and more appeared. Under, behind her and to her side. Ballooning, pulsing. Paint-dabs out of nowhere. Her heart rammed. There weren't hundreds. No.

Thousands.

By now she was hyperventilating, taking in mouthfuls of seawater, feeling like she was drowning even when she surfaced.

"Help!" she cried in a gulp of air. Her muscles ached. Water tore at the sky, sloshed over her.

Bolts of tremendous pain shot up her leg. She screamed. The ocean rushed in to silence her. Coughing, sputtering, Marilyn dipped below and saw the squiggly tendrils draped over her calf. Spots across her vision.

Hopeless.

Then—a slim passage opened before her, maybe ten feet under the surface. Ringing with pain, Marilyn moved down toward it. Lightning thrashed her arm—more groping tendrils. She jerked away, shrieking bubbles, snorkel thwacking her jaw.

Oh God please help me save me Lord please PLEASE—!

In her haste, her limbs seemed to disappear. She shot to the surface, sucked in air and gasped breath after breath. The sun flashed across her vision, blinding. The burn of saltwater in her nose, her eyes. Her mask leaking.

Her vision cleared. She looked toward the bay.

The people were gone. The umbrellas, the Tiki huts, the torches, the towel stands, the surf shops—gone.

Gone, too, was the Huna'ia Resort.

•   •   •

There were two ways this could resolve itself, Joe Toomey mused as he watched Marilyn flap her way toward the southern peninsula. Either she was going to come back all drunk with excitement, insisting how grateful she was for his gentle urging into the water, speaking of how many things she saw and how she couldn't wait to do it again, or, *or*, in several minutes she would make a frantic return to his side and grip his hand tighter than ever before, realizing this kind of adventure, like almost all adventures, was best with company.

He floated about ten or so feet above the bottom coral, the sound of his every breath Darth Vader-ing in his ears.

Come on, Marilyn, you know you want to turn around. Come on. What's the point if we're not doing this together, especially for the first time?

No dice. She became slightly transparent, little more than a pair of stroking fins against the distant rock and sun-washed blue.

How far had he gone in upsetting her *this* time?

This was not the time to dwell on such pettiness. There was a whole ocean to explore. Not only that, but an ocean (alright, a bay) positively brimming with life, just as the concierge and bellhop had suggested.

Fish zipped all round. Plenty of clownfish ("Nemos!" he could hear Tammy cry), and yellow tubular pipefish and tiny pufferfish and those beautiful rainbow-hued ones and so many others he wished he knew the names of.

Now *that* was a good idea: a high-tech snorkel mask that could identify the creatures in front of you. The whole waterproofing thing might be tricky, though. And would it have WiFi? He'd have to file that one away for R&D, like so many other ideas that Marilyn would probably just chuckle at if he told her about them.

He swam down, releasing pressure with the Valsalva and cruising northwesterly over that coral society, taking in its beautiful denizens and the—*eel*! The moray hovering with its evil toothy grin in its lair, and the, wait, was that …?

The rock was moving, opening a pair of bulbous eyes and … holy cow! It *was*! An octopus! Spreading camouflaged tentacles across a rock.

Marilyn, you're missing out!

Swimming near the bottom of the bay, he began hearing a clicking, whistling noise. He adjusted his mask, figuring it was air escaping, but no…

Whale-song!

He looked toward that wall of ocean, now maybe a hundred yards away. No shapes he could make out, sadly. Sound carried quite a distance underwater, of course.

Marilyn—where are *you?*

Lungs burning, Joe ascended to the surface. With every foot he climbed, the whale-song grew fainter, and then the outer world rushed in on him.

"Mare!" he shouted, spitting out saltwater. "Yo, Mare! *Marilyn*!"

He couldn't distinguish her from the dozen or so others bobbing in the chop near the southern peninsula, where teenagers cannonballed from higher perches on the lava rock.

"Marilyn!"

All sun-glitter and swells and dark heads and distant boats, and no obvious sign of his wife. Joe felt a sting of isolation.

After de-fogging his mask and sucking in a breath, Joe replaced his snorkel and was off again, cutting along the surface. Weeks ago, he might have grown tired by now, but the impending Hawaii trip had compelled him to finally man-up and, for the first time in his nine years at WaveSystems, take advantage of their gym's indoor pool. He'd bulked out a little in the right places, too, especially in his arms. Marilyn had not made any comment on it, if she'd even noticed. Par for the course.

The bay stretched deeper, the water bluer and chillier. Coral grew scarcer; what was once a busy continent had become a patchwork of islands in the rippled desert floor, tended to by only the occasional small fish.

To his right, at the bay's northern end, the peninsula sloped away like a rugged black mountainside. The area was strangely empty.

He had to take advantage of his current independence. Had he still been holding Marilyn's hand, there was no way on Earth he would have made it out this far.

Sunbeams flickered just below the surface. Everywhere the ocean hummed. He peered north, south, hoping to catch sight of some impressive form.

As though by divine tease, his mask began to fog up again. Joe cursed, then popped his head above the surface, removed his mask and snorkel and rinsed them out.

He faced the southern peninsula, now farther away than he'd anticipated. By rough measures, he was about eighty yards beyond the official edge of Pyramid Bay's reef.

After strapping on his mask and snorkel, he looked underwater again—

—and froze at the sight.

It had come out of nowhere. His body seemed to react before his brain, which refused to accept the scene even as all heat drained from him. Joe grew colder than the sea. His heart pounded.

Not fifty feet ahead, between him and the reef, was a huge shark. Its dark stripes thwarted any attempt to identify it as one of the more harmless species: it was a tiger.

At least a dozen feet long.

Joe kept movement to a minimum, though he was positive the thing could smell his fear, maybe even feel his tiniest vibrations. Its yellow demon-eye regarded him, its barbed teeth revealed in the jaws hung partially open.

Stories he'd heard flashed through him: the young surfer who'd lost an arm, the woman who'd been dragged down on her honeymoon…

Joe muttered a string of prayers, half-conscious of what he was even saying. God had to protect him. He had to be there for Tom, Tammy, for Troy. Had to care and provide for them and for Marilyn. Had to be a brother. A son to his ailing mother. And he had projects that needed realizing…

They floated there. The shark moved so slowly. Why wasn't it swimming away?

—because it's going to spring any second—

While possible that his brain was just trying to calm itself, he began sensing the creature had no interest in him. That it was dispirited somehow. No obvious injury. Maybe sick? Did sharks *get* sick?

The shark jerked—but not toward him. Its head and tail thrashed about violently, a spasm of combative panic against some unseen combatant.

Just above them, a wave formed, except it was pushing *away* from the shore. Joe scrambled to avoid the rogue current but it swept across him, shoving him another twenty or so feet out toward the open ocean.

Remembering advice he'd heard as a kid, he swam perpendicular to the current, throwing up huge flowering splashes. He swam at full speed toward the southern peninsula, toward people.

Passing into the forest of pale kicking limbs, he searched for Marilyn but couldn't see her. He surfaced and spit out his snorkel and slid his mask onto his forehead.

"*Marilyn*!"

Some glanced his way. Joe welled up his breath and cried: "*Shark*! Everyone! Tiger shark right here!"

More eyes on him. Heads popped up. Teenaged jumpers stopped cold on the perch.

"What?" someone called.

Another: "He said there's a *shark*!"

The news spread fast. Some of those snorkeling scrambled out onto the peninsula right then and there, despite the crashing surf and sharp rocks. Others cut a harsh beeline for the beach amid random bursts of curse words and, on the part of a couple men, hollers of transparent machismo. Still others refused the exodus, seemingly unbothered by it.

Soon he was in the shallows, grateful for the feeling of sand and stray coral under his soles. He removed his snorkel and mask and staggered ashore. The word "shark" spread across those luxuriating on towels, chairs or umbrellas.

Two lifeguards appeared and began blowing their whistles, waving all remaining folks from the water.

Joe sat watching, waiting.

Finally, two breakers out, she emerged.

She was on all fours, and seemed to be struggling. Joe stood and hurried toward the surf. Much as that first, shocking moment he'd seen the shark, however, his brain revolted at the sight his eyes were feeding him. It had to be wrong. Had to be an optical illusion.

"Marilyn?" he almost screamed.

"Ma'am, are you okay?" a lifeguard called, as he trotted into the surf.

She raised a hand and stood up. She didn't seem to be hurt, thank God.

But she had no mask or snorkel. Her hair was longer. Matted. Dirty. There was a long scar across her stomach he'd never seen before. She was at least twenty pounds thinner.

And, she was utterly nude. Her body was lean, taut, firm-looking with wiry muscle, and her skin bore a tan she'd not had just this morning. Somewhere in this flurry of insane visual processing Joe also noticed that her pubic hair, normally well-maintained, looked like it hadn't been trimmed in weeks.

"Oh … my God. Marilyn, what's going on?"

She stood in the waves, dazed. The term *recalibrating* whipped through Joe's head. She looked like someone who'd spent months out in nature.

This was not real. Simply not. This was the capper of a crazy dream he was having. He would be up any moment, tap the Marilyn he knew awake and they would head down to the breakfast buffet, and he would tell her about this dream and she would half-listen, and chuckle.

Attention on her grew. She seemed to become aware of it only belatedly. And, in so doing, rose measured hands to cover her breasts and crotch, like some Venusian nymph ambivalent about joining—rejoining—earthbound affairs.

IV

1

620 A.D.

Hacking and spitting, Marilyn removed her mask and snorkel. For several pulsing seconds she floated arms out and eyes closed, catching her breath and her sanity, feeling the weight of mucus on her face.

The sun glared down. A sense of emptiness yawned beneath her. She shook her mask, then, blinking, she laid the goggles over her eyes without strapping them on. She looked down and around.

No jellyfish. No turtles. No fish. No floor. Just a vacuum of sea, her feet kicking at blue fathoms below. How deep was it? Even sunbeams couldn't make it too far down—the dark exhausted the light.

It had not been a freak riptide that had put her where she was. No. Riptides were one of many dumb, blind movements of a dumb, blind element. What had happened to her was somehow intentional. It had not been a natural movement, but a warping of nature.

She closed her eyes, taking deep long breaths. Her head lulled to one side. Everything was blurry. She felt light and tired and unreal. Especially loud, the *slop-drip* of her every motion against the surface.

Where was the resort?

An urge to swim forward met only cold paralysis. If she stayed, she reasoned, it wouldn't be long before Joe and everyone would find her.

Yet … shaking uncontrollably, she began to swim. And as she did, Marilyn entered an internal realm stripped of thought, a total, uncomprehending blankness.

"Help," she sputtered, almost involuntarily. Saltwater filled her mouth and she spit it out. "Help."

Who're you talking to?

She swam at a measured pace, pushing past the swells. Her muscles clenched, her breath broken by wet coughs and snorts. The coast dwelling an unreachable distance.

Where was the *fucking resort?*

With every stroke, the resilience of her logic grew weaker before the sight of what was certainly still Pyramid Bay, just utterly overgrown, unshaven by any hand of civilization. Where the big towering resort once stood, where the village and the golf course once sprawled, where Will and his friends might have lit up another Firepit Friday, there existed nothing but verdant jungle pushing toward the sea, leaving only a thin margin of sand.

A harsh warm wind blew.

A soft hissing spray to her right. She looked. A thin gray shape sped past her.

Then another.

Sharks?

Dolphins.

Adjusting her mask and snorkel, Marilyn dipped her head under and saw the sleek gray forms of her sudden companions streaking about, squeal-clicking. Their heads nodded, bodies ribboning through the sea.

Marilyn had ceased to recognize the state she was in: a mixture of relief, exhilaration, curiosity and terror. She wanted these dolphins near her as much as she wanted them anywhere else. They were creatures in their element, and she was anything but.

Several grazed her. Another's tail bopped her thigh. Initially swimming in random patterns, they began circling her, taking turns brushing the surface. Marilyn sensed their energy. There was an air of bemusement, of inquisitiveness. Like they were debating what they might do with her.

Please leave me alone.

The squeal-clicking grew louder, and with it her anxiety and even anger.

A large form crept into the corner of her eye. She glanced. Nothing there, and yet there was.

There was a Bigness, an Oldness, haunting these waters. A Presence.

She picked up fragments of an image: a large, blurry silhouette, multiple long limbs some of which snaked like tentacles, a massive body...

Another thing came to her, too, stronger than anything else. A symbol, one she'd seen before:

She had no idea what it meant, but she recognized it. She had seen it after leaving Shane's that one afternoon, before visiting the petroglyphs.

Was there some connection?

Something prodded her back. She turned—a dolphin, right *there*, so close she could see the nicks and bumps on its flesh. Wide, grinless grin. Its blowhole contracted. The eyes heavy with knowledge it tried to convey.

Another approached her leg. Marilyn moved to evade but the creature nudged her knee. Desperate squeal-chatter, urgent. Maybe urging her onward. To get out.

Several dolphins broke away toward the Presence. Marilyn's chest seized.

Stay away.

The dolphins slowed, orbited the Presence. Confident but cautious. The Presence itself lost definition, sinking between the sunbeams and ocean shadows. For all intents and purposes, it became water again.

A calm fell. Dolphin-chatter ebbed to a few clicks.

Everywhere, blue hummed.

Suddenly, the dolphins erupted in chatter. The ocean stirred and then surged. The dolphins nearest the Presence reeled back as they struggled to right themselves.

A distortion grew in the water, something like a shockwave that expanded quickly and swept Marilyn and the rest of the pod into its path, thrusting her away and knocking her against several dolphins' frightened tail-thwapping.

She kicked and gasped and cried. The snorkel came off and seawater once more rushed down her throat and she gagged, knew again that she would choke and that she would drown.

With water swelling her ears and bloating her sinuses and burning her throat, Marilyn homed her remaining strength on one thing: swimming to shore.

She looked back at the dolphins, scattered enough from her they hung like shards of a shattered thing. They were frightened and disoriented themselves. Marilyn's heart sank. She wanted to help them but had no idea how.

Go go GO.

She swam, daring the ocean to push her back. Only briefly did she turn to look again. Though hard to see through the fizz of her own wake, the pod was still there but distant. None seemed to have followed her this far.

The Presence became visible again: a ghostly blot on the blue, its arms spread so that it was hard to see where they ended, and the ocean gloom began.

Marilyn wasn't sure why she didn't see them sooner than she did. In all the choppy pandemonium, though, her attention reserved focus strictly for the big, broad things.

But there was that one rolling swell, rising before her and obliterating the horizon and even much of the island. She rose with it, and when she reached its peak, she could see a collection of logs not far away…

No, not logs.

Canoes.

Like those outrigger canoes, except these seemed larger than any of the ones available for $20 rides by the resort. But maybe that was also due to the bulging sails and masts, or the spaces in them crowded with what looked like crops and open wood crates and even living things.

Marilyn formed no immediate impression of the people rowing these vessels. They were simply *people*, at least people-shaped, and the sight of any person against this sudden, bewildering wildness, against the horrific loneliness, gave her delirious relief.

"Hey!" she cried. "Hey! Help! Help me *please!*"

Maybe she'd come across a tourist group, an "authentic outrigger experience" or something. They would see her and pick her up and remark on how absurdly far the current had taken her, how lucky she was they'd come by…

"Please!" she yelled, splashing closer. "Hey!"

Her gaze bounced from face to face, all of which were stern, largely expressionless. She sensed fear, caution and great weariness.

"Can you understand me?"

No, of course they can't.

But she refused to believe that. They had to. *Had* to. They were all thin and dark-skinned and many bore what appeared to be elaborate tattoos and there was one standing man, not rowing, who issued commands in a wholly unknown language.

One by one, their faces turned away from her, like she was some curiosity no longer worth curiosity, or maybe the standing man had commanded they ignore her. She grew angry, because no, it couldn't *be—*

Yet one man continued looking at her. There was a softness about him. Like many of the other rowing men, he sported a lean, wiry body, dark bronzed skin and a broad face, his inky black hair pulled back in a tight bun.

If all these people constituted a wall, this man was a thin passage in that wall: a place where something might get through. He looked frightened, shy. Marilyn felt an exchange…like a quick gust of wind through that passage, offering little clarity beyond some assurance of an understanding. Whatever that understanding might be.

Then, even that man turned back, and the canoes continued onward. Marilyn bobbed dumbfounded and numb in the chop.

The numbness gave way to rage. Her fingertips quivered with a desire to kill something. To tear flesh. To rip piece by piece. How callous they were toward another human being—

You aren't a human being to them.

Her thoughts now mimicked the sea in which she struggled, sloshing between the coherent and the crazy.

They were frightened of you.

The realization pressed harder, but still she refused to acknowledge it. Those in the outrigger weren't natives or putting on a show. They were—

No.

She had not drifted off-course toward another part of the island. She had drifted—

—stop—

—to another—

—say it—

—time.

2

Present Day

Once, when she was a kid, she'd wanted nothing more than to have a flying dream.

It's always so neat, Mom would say. She had them regularly. Dad had them, too, but not as often, and they didn't appear to make much of an impression on him. Even other kids had them—her friends at school, her older siblings. Marilyn felt unfairly excluded from an enchanted place.

Then—one night, in her dreams, she was back in the middle of Gordon Lake, reliving the bewildering, surreal trauma. Watching her family faraway on the shore. The Big Stranger stirring under her.

She wanted to swim, but it turned out there was no point: she could just fly!

And she took off, up and up and up. The wind buoyed her. She could soar, and she thought deep down, *Finally!*

Finally.

Marilyn had started to fly. Like a cruel prank, though, the wind died, her body became granite and she plummeted down screaming and flailing, the dark lake swift and brutal upon her.

When she awoke, her legs were drenched with sweat, and her stomach persisted in releasing her dinner across the sheets. Never had a dream pursued her so viscerally into the waking world. Never again did she feel so strongly the queasy roil of some World Between.

That is, until she collapsed, nauseated, trembling and naked, in the surf before Joe and the lifeguards and dozens of onlookers.

•   •   •

Her first thought: *Hawaii has hospitals?*

And they looked the same as any other hospital? Though, as she quickly found out, this wasn't a hospital so much as the resort village's local clinic.

Joe hovered over her, his expression tugged by any number of smiles and frowns. "Marilyn, I don't even know what to say." He took her hand and squeezed. "What happened to you?"

She did her best to restrain the tears, but they came anyway, and when the first one fell they all rushed down her cheeks and everything became a liquid blur.

She cleared her throat. "I don't really know."

Joe cocked his eyebrow. She looked at her arm. Definitely thinner. She'd known she was thinner, of course, when walking naked up the beach. Physically, she felt lighter, leaner, fitter.

But it certainly hadn't been *her* that had done it. Right? She'd gone snorkeling, had broken from Joe in a huff and, pushing against fear, joined those others at the site of the eagle rays…

That was where things started breaking down. And while she couldn't penetrate that memory fog, she found she could, in fact, graze those touchable moments, hours, whole days hidden there. It was a kaleidoscope of imagery and vague sensation.

It was like standing too close to an impressionistic painting. If she could give herself time and room for perspective, something might come into focus.

"Clearly," Joe said. "*Something* happened. What do you remember?"

"It's really hard right now," she said. "But I think I will. Remember, I mean."

"Well, I mean, there's … no logical explanation. At all."

"There has to be."

"Yeah. You know what I mean, though…"

She watched her husband. Even as awed terror filled him, a manic curiosity wasn't too far behind.

"And," he pressed, "you're sure you don't remember a *thing*?" He gestured to her abdomen. "Where did you get that scar?"

"I d-don't remember."

She would have to, though. Otherwise, there was no way to reconcile that, while Marilyn may have been physically lighter, some burdensome cargo had been put on her spirit, portioned out over a period of time that had, somehow, been removed from the normal continuum.

How else to explain the fact that she had lost twenty pounds in, what, forty *minutes*? How else to explain this feeling of "long lost reunion" with Joe, her excitement for it but also the somber notion that something once binding her to him had come undone in her heart, withered by absence?

"I do," she said. "Not really, but I know it's there. I feel like…"

"Yeah?"

"I feel like the files are in the cloud. And I need to crack the password."

"Well, um, I'm often the man for that." He placed his other hand atop the one already holding hers. "Though actual memory 'software' takes me longer."

"I'm sorry," Marilyn said. "I'm sorry for humiliating you. For ruining our vacation."

"It's not ruined—"

"I'm gonna be the notorious, confused naked woman around this place."

"I doubt this has made you famous. At most, a good dinner anecdote. I told people you'd just lost your suit, which is true. *How,* um…"

"Please stop."

"Sorry."

She would have to be patient. And she couldn't leave here. Not anytime soon. There was something here, something happening. That was maybe why she had to stay as long as she had to: if the memories were going to drip back into her, she couldn't disconnect the IV tube.

Resentment surged in her. Frustration.

"Marilyn," Joe said with a sigh. "I know you might feel, um…hesitant telling me certain things. I know you tend to believe the *Spooksters* stuff more than me—"

"Joe…"

"It's just, I do recognize that unbelievable things happen. I know miracles exist. I know that the amount we know about Creation can be pinched in God's thumb and forefinger. I know all this."

Joe hesitated. Marilyn studied him.

"And whatever's happened…I mean, come on." He gestured at her with both hands, as if her very existence made his point. "I can't deny it. Something unbelievable happened to you."

Yes, it did. Marilyn found she could think it a million times over, but still couldn't *grok* it. Was it because she couldn't remember? Maybe. She had long known unbelievable things hid in the corners of her life. But something like this felt like an upheaval. An exile from her life.

Somewhere within, she tried desperately to electrify back to life the connection she had (or thought she had) with Joe.

"I understand," Marilyn said, feeling robotic and lame.

•   •   •

Marilyn was discharged later that day. Beyond a few overshot mumblings about infection, diabetes or cancer, the doctor could offer no decent explanation for the unheard-of weight loss. The results of two blood tests would be forthcoming within the week.

By all other metrics, though (reflexes, heartrate, blood pressure, sinuses and a standard but nonetheless embarrassing probe into Marilyn's medical history, as well as the health of more private regions) little seemed awry. Her gums were inflamed, though, and her teeth appeared unbrushed for weeks.

"Do you want to just go back to the room and rest?" Joe asked as they stepped from the clinic into the sun.

No.

Yes.

A steady breeze blew, rain-scented—a harbinger of the gray mass of clouds rising in the east.

"That's probably for the best," Marilyn said.

Joe smiled. He slipped his hand in hers and they started walking through the small labyrinth of clothes shops and cafes. The honeyed voice of IZ drifted from the mall's speakers.

Approaching the palm-lined path toward the actual resort, Marilyn noticed a sign hung from the very end of the mall area: *Lava Java.* IZ's island tones faded before a live acoustic guitar, and a female voice singing a throaty rendition of *Walking on the Moon.*

Peering through Lava Java's large windows, Marilyn spotted Vanessa's profile in the corner, seated on a stool before a mic and crouched over a guitar. Though she wore a porkpie hat and was harder to make out, Marilyn recognized her right away.

"Hey," she said to Joe. "Can we stop in here real quick?"

"Why?"

"I met that singer the other night." Saying *the other night* felt strange and wrong. "I want to ask her something."

"When did you meet her?" His features stiffened. "Oh. Was that on your late-night solo trek?"

"Yes. We met at a little beach bonfire."

Questions gusted across Joe's eyes, but all he did was shrug resignedly. Hands in pockets (this felt significant to Marilyn, like he meant to deny her the pleasure of holding his hand) he followed her inside.

A thick, inviting coffee aroma. Marilyn's gaze centered on Vanessa, who threw her a furtive look as she continued with the song. The woman wore ripped-knee jeans, covering all but a few tentacles of the Dractopus tattoo.

There were only a few others in the café, including a hipster barista.

When the song ended, she offered a little golf-clap and waved at Vanessa, who now gave her a genuine smile as she removed her guitar and set it down carefully.

"Hey there," Vanessa said. "Mary, right?"

"Marilyn."

"Oh yeah, sorry."

"This is Joe," she said, gesturing.

They greeted one another and shook. Vanessa shifted her weight. Before any small talk came up, Marilyn leaned in and placed a light hand on Vanessa's elbow.

"Can I ask you something?"

"Uh, yeah. What's up?"

"What did you see the…other night?"

Vanessa frowned. "You mean the night of the man-o-wars?"

"Yes. When you were coming back from swimming. I saw, well, I was watching you."

Though Marilyn was unsure about her phrasing, the change in Vanessa's expression indicated she'd hit upon her subject.

In a lowered voice, Vanessa said, "You saw it, too?"

"What's going on?" Joe said, leaning forward. "What did you see?"

"I…didn't see it, no," Marilyn said. "Or at least, I didn't see anything strange *then*." She hesitated. Against her own impulse, she pressed, "Tell me what you saw."

Vanessa put a hand over her face. "You mind if I get a coffee first?"

"Sure."

Vanessa went over and ordered from the barista. She turned and, in her polite-yet-disconnected manner, asked, "You want anything? I get a thirty-percent discount."

"I'll have a regular coffee, thanks," Marilyn said. She felt tired, and the jolt would do her well.

"Mare…what?"

She faced Joe.

"You're a *coffee* drinker now?" he said.

Oh, get a grip. For a half-second Marilyn considered what to say, before abandoning the effort and turning to Vanessa.

A hand clamped her elbow and wrenched her back around, harshly enough that in a spasm of aggression she pushed Joe back. He froze, looking shocked and sad, which wrung Marilyn with guilt.

Vanessa approached with two coffees, one of which she held out for Marilyn. Joe stood between them and to the side, watching. All she was doing was taking a damn cup in hand. But Marilyn's self-consciousness might well have been that of a kid shoplifting for the first time.

"Shane's made me coffee before," she said to Joe. "It's alright."

Joe snorted. "Shane? Really?"

She hesitated to sip. The cup in her hand seemed to magnify its temperature by several degrees, stinging her palms.

Joe shook his head. "People and their secrets." He started walking toward the exit. "I'm going to wait for you outside."

"Okay."

At the door, he stopped and turned. "Or do you want to just meet back at the room?"

"Whichever. I won't be long, I promise."

She tried to throw him as full a smile as her mood might allow, but he just nodded and ambled out into the sunlight.

"Is everything okay?" Vanessa asked. "I hope I didn't step on any toes—"

"No, you didn't." They started moving to an open table. "It's a long story. Thank you for the coffee."

Confusion flashed across Vanessa's face.

"Did you want me to comp you?" Marilyn asked. "Sorry ab—"

"Hey, no prob." Vanessa scrutinized her. "I was more trying to place what looks different about you. It took me a second to recognize you when you came in."

"How could that be?" Marilyn said with a dry grin. "We've known each other for so many seconds."

Vanessa chuckled. "Yeah. And it was night. And I was kinda drunk."

"Which is why I thought you were insane for diving into the ocean after that whale."

Vanessa shrugged. "Will brings the beer. I bring the batshit."

Marilyn took a tiny, cautious sip. It was so hot it burned the tip of her tongue and she could barely taste it.

"Oh, that's black, by the way," Vanessa said. "In case you wanted to sweeten it."

Marilyn smiled and took her coffee to the condiments counter. In popping the top, she spilled some over the rim. She winced at the burn on her finger.

Sighing, she poured in her liberal dosage of cream and sugar, resisting the temptation to glance outside to check on Joe. Then she returned to the table.

"You're a good musician, by the way," Marilyn said, gingerly balancing her coffee.

"Thanks." There was a mix of fear, wonder and impatience about Vanessa. "So … I mean, what did you…?"

"Yeah, so, the other night. When you were coming back out of the water—"

"You weren't there," Vanessa said. "None of you were there."

"What do you mean?"

"As I was swimming in…" She fidgeted in her seat. "And, believe me, this could be nothing—"

"Or not."

"Well, I don't know *what* it was," Vanessa said. "I'm coming in and a wave crashes over me. Not too strong, just big enough to put me under for a couple seconds. When I came up, the beach was dark. Again, no one was there. It didn't even look like the beach itself was still there, like there were trees all crowded around it.

"I just remember: darkness. I don't even think I could make out the village lights. Like, *nothing* was there, and then, like, the surf splashed over me again and the fire was there and you were all there standing there again yelling about the jellyfish, or whatever."

Marilyn sipped her sweetened coffee. Almost immediately she thought she could feel a buzz, but figured that was in her head—and, maybe, due to the heartening sense that she wasn't the sole guest to Pyramid Bay's strange gala.

Vanessa hunched her shoulders. "I think I got turned around somehow. Like, I happened to see a different part of the island."

"Do you think," Marilyn began, laying a hand on the table, "you saw something more?"

"More?"

"Uh-huh. You know, like a parallel reality. Or time-slip."

"Time-slip?"

"Yeah. Have you seen that show *Spooksters*? About ghost-hunting and paranormal things?"

Snickering, Vanessa shook her head.

"They've talked about it," Marilyn went on. "It's like a moment from the past, bubbling up to the present. No rhyme or reason. Then it just *pops*."

"I have no idea, to be honest. That's weird to think about, though."

Marilyn frowned. How could someone so young, so ostensibly bohemian, be so disconnected when it came to the possibility of life's weirder excesses?

"You also said something about the man who watched you and…?" Marilyn said.

"Tatiana?"

"Yes. While you were surfing?"

"Yeah…"

"How he'd change every time you looked at him."

"He didn't, though," Vanessa said. "That was just—"

"But it *felt* like it, right?"

Vanessa paused. Multiple expressions tugged at her face. She gulped her coffee. To Marilyn, all this was just an elaborate 'yes' to her question-statement.

"You said he was from that treehouse village."

"The Lofts. I kinda just assumed he was."

I know that place. Marilyn had thought, when seeing the pictures of the Lofts. *I know those trees.*

"I met someone like that," Marilyn said. "Driving here. Every time I looked at him there was a different-ness to his eyes. Like a new soul coming to surface. What was weird too is that, through it all, he looked familiar." Marilyn crossed her arms, watched the steam from her cup rise like a vacating spirit. "Do you think he could be from that village, too?"

Vanessa gave a sustained shrug. "Honestly, I probably know less about any of this than you. I mean, what about you? What shit have *you* seen?"

At this, Marilyn froze.

•　•　•

The whole time with Vanessa, Marilyn avoided looking outside to check on Joe, preferring instead a kind of Schrodinger's cat approach to whether he'd stayed or left. In truth, she dreaded either possibility.

Vanessa had scrawled her phone number across the coffee receipt. "If you want to hike out to the Lofts sometime, here," she'd said, "hit me up. I'd be happy to get closer, if I've got a companion."

Marilyn took the receipt. "Thank you. I thought they were supposed to be friendly?"

With a shrug, Vanessa said, "Never know."

By the time they parted, Marilyn's coffee was still half-full, the caffeine in her veins demanding that she move.

When she walked outside, there was an elderly couple sitting on Joe's bench.

Marilyn scanned the courtyard. No sign.

"Joe?" she called out tentatively.

Crowds. Couples. Nothing.

He must've gone back to the room.

She began making her way toward the Huna'ia Resort, passing palms and flat lawns where lotion-glistened bodies lay on towels and lounge chairs.

Marilyn idly glanced up at the resort. She stopped. A cheery couple—maybe hers and Joe's age, maybe even younger—passed by and caught her expression and tried to follow her gaze. She heard, "What's she looking at?" muttered at a careful decibel.

How to answer them, if she did? Look at the very top of the resort there, she might say, toward the northeastern corner. Look hard. Focus. Like those old Magic Eye 3D pictures. See that shimmer, the hint of *there*-ness, like a shadow moving in the dark. And like the dark, wait for your eyes to adjust further, to carve out the thing there, crawling up the building in big, arching strides.

Keep watching and maybe you'll feel it, too, with those fingertips of a long-dulled Other hand: that which grazed dreamskin, or brushed spirits. Or tingled once with the real world's only answer to magic.

By the time she made it to the lobby, the coffee was running rampant in her veins. With still a quarter left, she threw it out before bypassing the elevators and moving toward the stairs, which she had all to herself.

She climbed them swiftly, sometimes leaping up two or three at a time like she would as a teenager. No side-ache. No cramps.

She thought: I'm fit.

Reaching the eighth floor, Marilyn paused, then entered the hallway. Goosepimples formed on her arms.

•　•　•

"Just tell me…"

Joe trailed off a moment. Fanning his fingers, he added, "Just *tell* me."

Marilyn sat on the edge of the couch, hands on her knees as Joe stood by the TV. It didn't feel right or real that this conversation, imagined multiple ways, was in fact taking place. Her whole body was prickly.

"Please, Mare."

She said, "I'm sensitive."

"Well, I got *that*—"

"No. Psychically, I mean. *A* sensitive. As in, spirits."

Joe's features tightened. "Alright." He bobbed his head. Marilyn couldn't tell if the action was satirical or not. "That does actually explain some things."

She blinked twice. "You believe me?"

"Sure. I mean, okay, no, not 'officially.' But, like everything today, it'll take a while to download."

Marilyn nodded. "I get it."

"So how long have you been 'sensitive'?"

"I want to say all my life."

"But?"

"I don't know how, or why," Marilyn said, "but I think I shut it down sometime when I was a kid. Maybe moving from rural Oregon to Los Angeles, with its crazy energy, helped me ignore them even though I knew they were there. It was like I developed a cataract. Then, that cataract was ripped away four years ago."

"What happened four years ago?" Joe almost cut himself off: "Oh."

"Yeah. After San Francisco, after Troy was born, I felt them more. Then I saw them more. Not well, but still."

"You've never mentioned this."

"I found I could adapt," she said. "Carry on. These things were just elements of the earth, I told myself. Which I still believe. Just frequencies we can't hear, or wavelengths we can't see. Most of us, anyway."

She liked to say she kept her perspective Big. While relishing factoids as much as anyone else, Marilyn often pitied those dedicating their lives to small things, to dissecting categories and subcategories, to parsing out, not unifying.

Yet somehow, the existence of these beings had been an aspect of the world segregated from all that Marilyn ultimately knew to be important. God, Fellow Man and Family—those formed the sides of her life's pyramid ("Well, and *Errowind Tales Online*, too," she'd always quip). Everything else was just noisy runoff meant for the science lab, the politician or the crazy man on the street corner—so she had long told herself.

Joe said, "And you just have more of the right … bandwidth?"

Marilyn hesitated. "So does Troy, I think."

Joe blinked. "Troy?"

"Yes."

"What do you mean?"

"You know Baldy? His imaginary 'bath-time buddy'?"

"Uh. Sure."

Marilyn inhaled. "I've seen him."

"*You've* seen him."

"Uh huh." In a lower voice, she added, "I've spoken to him."

"Um." Joe backed up a step. "Okay. So you're saying he's *not* imaginary."

"I don't pretend to understand the ins and outs of all this, by the way."

"I know you don't. But, wow. So, wait. Troy told me once that Baldy was a tiny dwarf or something. Only like a foot tall."

And here we go, Marilyn thought. Say the word "spirits" and people think dead aunts and uncles, childhood pets or Lincoln brooding in his White House bedroom. Well within the scope of ordinary comprehension.

"I'd say," Marilyn looked at the floor, "he's more like a foot and a half."

"What?"

"He's not a regular human spirit. None of them are."

"Okay, so what the hell does *that* mean?"

"I don't see conventional spirits," Marilyn said. "I don't see people-ghosts. I see…non-human things."

The word squeaked out between Joe's lips, "Demons?"

"No." *Maybe*, she thought. Some, like the huge reptilian entity by Shane's house, did feel malevolent. "I think they're more like animals. Animals in an invisible wilderness around us."

"So, animal spirits?"

Marilyn sighed. "No. I mean I can see spirits that've *always been spirits*. They're not like anything we know. They're big, tiny, medium. Sometimes colossal. And they're usually connected to water. Or at least, the ones *I* see are connected to water."

Joe crossed his arms, gazed at the floor. "I'm guessing that's where your mage character came from?"

"Huh?"

"Your mage character. Gabriya, was her name? In our D&D campaign, ages ago."

"Gabriya." She almost whispered the name. It had been years-going-on-decades since their last bout of *Dungeons & Dragons*. Heck, she'd been pregnant with Tommy.

"She could see ghosts, or something," Joe said. "She was a medium, and necromancer. Wasn't she?"

Marilyn smiled wanly. "I'm not a necromancer."

"And, Gordon Lake. Your near-drowning. Was that anything—?"

"I think that was the start of it, yes," she said. "That's why I shut it down after."

"You always told me you don't remember swimming to the middle of the lake."

"That's because I don't think I did. Swim, I mean. I think it pulled me out there."

"It?"

"I called it the Big Stranger, in my head. I don't remember much about it, at all, because it was dark and blurry and I was four years old and terrified, but I remember huge eyes, and the feeling of being watched and wanted, somehow."

A thick cloudbank of possible follow-up statements settled on her tongue, but she swallowed them back.

"Are these things, like, interdimensional?" Joe asked.

"I don't know. They feel both natural, but not."

His eyes narrowed. Marilyn collected herself before continuing.

"What I do think," she said, "is that they're the source of what people call faeries, or cryptids, or myths. Mermaids, elves, nymphs, dragons. Maybe Bigfoot. But none of them are exactly *any* of those things. Again, not that I've seen, anyway."

Joe just stared at her. *There's an invisible world, with (largely) invisible beings.* Was that such a blasphemous revelation? Reality tended to bulge where you thought it didn't. Or wouldn't.

Yet what *did* it say about the world's major faiths, including her own, that they basically neglected the existence of these "creatures"? Islam still had *djinns*, so she thought. For the most part, though, any such being nowadays would be forced to hole up in the dark, rusted chests of heathen history and pagan mythology.

What of her other truths, then?

About God?

Christ?

The prophets and those to come?

Maybe I'm a prophet.

"I don't know what they are, or what their existence means," Marilyn said. "Are they born? Do they die? Do they reproduce? I don't know. I don't even think I can see all of them."

"What do you mean?"

"What's it called when a color goes from dark to light, or vice versa?"

"A gradient?"

"Yes. I think there's a gradient to them. Not with color, but density. I mean, because we have bodies, we're heavy. We're flesh and blood, right?"

"I hope so—"

"So, imagine us on the 'dark', heavy side of the gradient. Most people can't see beyond the dark. But there are lighter and lighter things. Again, I can't see them *all*. I can probably only see up to the 'gray' section." For the first time in several long seconds, Marilyn made eye contact with her husband. "Does that make any kind of sense?"

"It's a brainful, is what it is."

"I know."

Joe caressed his scalp. "How does this line up with what happened this morning? With you being skinny, having longer hair?"

"I don't know, exactly," she said. "But I am sure there's something bad out here. In the bay."

"Something bad as in, one of these spirit-animal things?"

"Yes. Or several. I mean, again, I don't really know. And there's something that's going to happen that I'm connected to. Or, that I need to stop."

"Are we Captain Marvel here now?"

"I'm serious. I think that—" Marilyn cut herself off, but knew she was doomed.

"You think that…?"

Just say it.

"I think that God called me here." She almost added, *It's my mission,* but refrained.

Joe's eyes widened. "I'm not sure what to say to that."

"It's not something you can deny, easily."

Joe studied her with a defensive *Yeah, I know* expression.

"Just, please: trust me."

"I still don't understand how this has anything to do with you being naked and losing twenty pounds in an hour."

Marilyn closed her eyes in a long, processing blink. "We have that book, *The Cosmic Detective,* by Virgil Demian. Did you ever read it?"

"Awhile back." Joe looked skeptical. "Why?"

"I looked at it again, recently. There's a section on baby universes. Little bubble-offs from the main one. I'm wondering if I took a kind of side-trip into something like that. I was gone for a long time, for *me.* For you, though, and everyone here, it was minutes. Maybe even seconds."

"I suppose that makes sense in a loony, theory-of-relativity way. But still—why did that happen? What's going on?"

"I'm trying to find that out."

They stood quiet for a moment, struggling to digest all that had been spoken, and, perhaps, all yet unspoken.

Both heard it at the same time.

"Is that—screaming?" Joe said.

They went to the balcony and gazed out over the railing. The screams had been varied and somewhat distant, coming from the beach where people had gathered. Another people-cluster, Marilyn, thought, like when she was snorkeling, this time clustering around…

"Oh wow," Joe said, hand raised to shade his face. "I think that's a shark. It might even been the one I saw."

Through the ring of people, Marilyn could make out fragments of the creature stretched out on the beach. Definitely a shark, by the tail and the stripes. Big.

Dead.

She saw something, too: perched on the southern peninsula, as if consciously isolated from the crowds, was a tall man with blonde hair. Even at this distance, she could tell immediately who it was—the Road Walker.

Marilyn hurried away from the balcony, toward the front door. She didn't bother to field Joe's frantic questions. He'd catch up.

3

620 A.D.

That silly disastrous afternoon Dad had tried to teach her golf, when she'd stood on the green mat in their backyard facing the "driving net," a perplexing name because it had nothing to do with, well, driving.

But to any of her questions Dad would reply with the same huffy insistence on the task at hand, and repeat what had become that afternoon's ritual chant:

"Just keep your head down."

His voice now looped through her head as she swam. No looking back. No tilt to the side, not even a glance forward. Swallow the seawater. Breathe past the lack of breath, the pounding chorus of her pulse, peer through the spots across her vision.

Keep your head down.

Blotches appeared far below. Though she ignored them at first, Marilyn soon identified them as rocks. They grew clearer, more plentiful, as did the yellow sand and the fish blurring about.

As the reef itself loomed, it was like Creation re-emerging from a void into which it had carelessly stumbled. Brilliant hues of red and green and blue and yellow burst across her vision, a radiant, healthy coral reef that was unlike anything she'd seen just before, with Joe.

Toward shore and the world was an oppression of seawater. Not fifty feet from the beach, a wave curled up around Marilyn. She relinquished herself to it, thinking all the while that she could see faces in the foam.

As the surf thinned, she tried awkwardly to plant her finned feet on the sand, but her shin and her knee grazed sharp coral. She winced.

Crawling up the beach, Marilyn spat and heaved and hacked. She ripped off her fins, mask and snorkel and threw them to the side.

She wanted to sleep for a hundred years.

For what felt like hours, she lay face-down on the sand, ocean salt mixing with that of her sobs. She crunched sand in her teeth. A breeze blew over her.

Opening her eyes, Marilyn noticed a nearby line of palm trees caught in the wind. One after another they bent toward her, whispering to their neighbor like children playing Telephone, until the tree closest her swayed down, fracturing the sun in a spidery dance of fronds.

What do you have to tell me? Marilyn thought, before darkness overcame her.

• • •

She awoke. Some of her energy had returned. The wind and the waves and the trees carried on with their gossip.

And she was ravenous. And thirsty—her throat was parched, and the more she dwelled on it, the more dehydrated she felt.

Slowly, Marilyn wandered down the beach. Spotting a big enough passage in the tree line, she edged toward the jungle.

Part of her insisted none of this was real. And it wasn't just the time-slip (or whatever it was), but the messy, unrestrained purity of a nature uninhibited. Everywhere she'd ever gone held some markers of civilization. This place, however, was utterly clear of even the inkling of people.

The jungle was a green, slow-motion explosion. The broken cosmos of shadow seemed to move all around her, too, as if representing a twin-jungle struggling to impose itself.

Hunger grew, its nails sharp. Fatigue returned in pulses, but Marilyn sprinted forward, listening for any sounds of running water, hoping to spot any fruit—or anything—that looked edible.

Where were the Keke-something Falls they'd passed on the highway? Did it even exist here? Maybe, but it had been at least twenty or so minutes by car alone. And certainly no highways existed here. She had no map. No compass.

No direction.

An awareness hummed louder in her, like an appliance switched on. Marilyn felt vertigo. She could feel by her Other "fingertips" certain textures—unseen beings quivering with unknown life. In a bed of waist-high grass stood a tall, twisting tree, dark in color and festooned with foliage where shapes moved, half-living things that called the tree home.

She turned around. The jungle had swallowed her. She couldn't even hear the ocean waves.

•　　•　　•

The few forests she'd hiked had all felt accommodating, the trees staidly supervising the pleasure of travelers in their midst. Paths had been laid down, and, like a story, all she had to do was follow it.

This jungle, however, mocked her. Chuckled at this new creature's clumsy strides, this creature greener than it.

The *everywhere*-ness. Marilyn tried to convince herself that, on the other side of every other blink, her time, her world, had to be waiting for her. If these unknown forces could sweep her here so quickly, they could just as easily return her.

That was not to be, though. This situation, whatever its nature, was probably like breaking something: quick to make, complicated to repair.

Wormholes, Marilyn thought randomly, recalling her superficial bouts of science-reading. Were there wormholes in Pyramid Bay?

Thoughts of Tommy, Tamara and Troy struck her, like sniper-shots. She was simultaneously hollowed-out and very heavy. Marilyn cried, feeling more useless than ever. But she was *going to see her babies again*. She had to have faith. God would not abandon her. Even if this was a test. Even if she was failing it.

Sprawling mosaics of fern and ivy covered the jungle floor, woven that much denser by the banyan and koa roots that rose from the soil. Daylight could make few suggestions to the green dusk. The trees were large and bearded and twisted with untold time, their limbs outstretched like carnival showmen offering turn after turn in the gloomy, selfsame labyrinth.

Her Other senses felt cleaner here, too. More direct. More reachable. So many shapes of various life and things not quite life, that perhaps were or could be life. They were there, gliding about the world's edges. Drawn to her, God knows why.

Could she just…ignore them now?

No. Her flame burned too bright, the moths in riotous attraction. Was she a beacon? Why?

Because I can see them.

And by seeing them, she could confirm them. Kind of like some of the quantum stuff Marilyn had read about. Maybe all they could see were the lights of those who could feel them, burning as illuminated havens in a sea of darkness.

A random voice rose into her mind, a quote from someone that Marilyn had dismissed as a fraud—Lady Beaumont, the overly made-up medium on that one *Spooksters* episode.

She had said: *They can't touch you if you don't let them.*

For whatever reason, right now, this felt true. Even if Marilyn wasn't quite sure how to take it.

Many of the spirit-beings she had felt over the years had been connected to water. Could she, then, use that somehow to find water now? Use these Other senses like a…what were those things called? *Dowsing* rods, that was it.

A memory came back to her, but it wasn't real. It was a memory of a dream—the feeling of water near, the beautiful falls painted on her mind's eye as she dozed in the passenger's seat, while Joe drove them to the resort. The sense of some maternal essence behind the curtain of water.

The Kekepania Falls. That was it.

Her experience with the Other senses had been largely passive, like wind blowing upon her. She had never activated them herself, never put them to "work" the way she might her physical limbs, or eyes, or nose, or—

Marilyn closed her eyes, tight. She reached out what she thought might be her phantom "hands", the one Other sense that, besides the eye (her "mind's eye, after all), she was most familiar with.

For a second, it was like she was floating in a lava lamp, having entered a realm of zero-gravity, of very few rules beyond pure chronic existence.

Gradually, the ache of her physical body receded. A vision came to Marilyn, that of lacy white waters cascading down green mountainsides. Deep hidden pools. Smaller rivulets tucked in shadow. There were spirit-beings hovering. Watching. Feeling her as she felt them. Some were faint, others more distinct.

Some beings, Marilyn noticed, were more frightened than others, too. They seemed to be the "lighter" ones. Softer to the touch.

There was a range of there-ness, reminding her of *Errowind Tales* with its two "species" of phantoms: shades and shells. *Shades* were the lightest, their influence no greater than a shadow on the wall. *Shells* were heavier, able to frighten or curse you.

Marilyn opened her eyes, and, cautiously, stepped forward. That step became two.

Almost on a lark, she called, "Hello?"

The trees drank her voice in two echoes.

Third step. Fourth.

Then, she stopped. A sob ripped up her breast, bursting out in a spray of spittle and tears. She placed ginger fingertips to her temples, like flimsy levees to stand against some flashflood of emotion.

"Lord," Marilyn muttered, "what am I doing here?"

You're praying *now*? cried an inner voice. What good is that going to do?

What good has it ever *done?*

God brought you here, countered another. God brought you here to see, to heal, to understand.

Then again, maybe nothing was actually expected of her. Maybe she was simply one of many "special" people forever caught in the ebb and flow between her world and another. Limited by her own will and capacity.

If she were honest with herself, increasingly her faith felt like a container that had sat in the refrigerator for a long time. There to greet her, sure, but not really indulged, not *really*, even as she would never be so wasteful as to throw it away. Then, of course, there was that day when one finally popped the lid, only to discover a crust of mold over what were once-nourishing contents, too long neglected.

Fear, of course. All along, it had been fear. Fear that had kept her suspended above the chaos of a deeper nature. That had kept her from plunging down.

But she had plunged now. Far beyond imagining.

4

Present Day

She and Joe could only get within twenty yards of the dead tiger shark. The waves tugged and batted the carcass, as if trying to wrest it awake. An aura of terror and violence clouded the animal, fading now with the peace of its death.

Farther down the beach, half-naked onlookers clustered by the tideline. Some stood watching while others waded into shallow breakers, where a glistening mound of gray flesh came into view.

Shrill whistles rang out, hailing the arrival of more lifeguards who shouted for the gathering sea of people to part, to maintain their distance.

"Is that a dolphin down there?" Joe said, through heavy breaths.

"I think so," Marilyn muttered.

A lifeguard passed by and Joe called to him. "What do you think happened?"

The lifeguard shrugged. "Could be they fought one another to the death."

It took Marilyn a moment to realize he was talking about possible combat between the shark and the dolphin. He was right about there being a fight, but wrong about the opponents. Of course, having no real answers herself, she kept her mouth shut.

"What's going on, Mare?" Joe said. "Why are there suddenly dead animals in the bay?"

That Joe would address that question to her was both scary and encouraging. Less than half a day ago, he would have assumed there were toxins or some wildlife disease, that it was clearly an issue for faceless bureaucrats and marine scientists.

Marilyn glanced across the bay for the blonde Road Walker. No sign of him.

"We'll find out," she said, almost adding, in a pang of remorse, *And I'll remember.*

•   •   •

She'd left her phone in the room, and kicked herself for it. How many times did she have to go back to her damn room, that quaint little port in the storm, when she was supposed to be confronting the storm? Whatever that storm was.

Two minutes past the beach, Joe tugged at her arm.

"Marilyn, do you want to eat something?" he asked. "Or rest at all?"

"I can't. I *can't.*" She half-gestured to the current of foot traffic heading against them, onlookers drawn by onlookers, as if to warrant her urgency. *Get away,* she wanted to tell them. *Get away from this shore and this sea.* "I need to follow a lead."

"Follow a lead? Like a detective?"

"Did you not register what I told you?"

"I know. Something bad is going on. Something weird. *Clearly* there is. I can see it. But…"

Marilyn remained silent against a rush of sympathy for her husband.

"Wherever you're needing to go, can I come with you?"

"I want to see about a place in the jungle," she said. "You can hike to it, apparently. So I don't see why you can't come."

"What place? Why?"

Telling him it was a village or community, about which she knew next to nothing, would likely invite prejudices of drug-farms, sex-cults or other stupid things. Nor did she want to tell him that the blonde

Road Walker (might) be connected to all this. Or that she'd somehow been to the part of the jungle where the community was, though right now she didn't remember how—or exactly when.

I know that place.

I know those trees.

"It's called the Lofts," Marilyn said. "Vanessa, the musician from the coffee shop, can take us there. That's why I wanted to talk to her."

Joe ran his fingers over his scalp. His eyes widened a little. "Can we at least get some food before we go hiking into the middle of some jungle nowhere-land?"

Marilyn sighed. "Fine. Get a couple stools at the poolside Tiki hut. I'll be down and meet you in a minute." She reached over and took his hand, a motion which felt awkwardly middle school. "Okay?"

•　　•　　•

Reaching the suite, Marilyn snatched her phone from the coffee table and, after minor digging, unearthed the paper on which Vanessa had scribbled her number.

She dialed.

As the phone rang on the other end, she walked to the balcony and stared out at the bay, at all the people and vehicles now gathered at the beach, the water empty of all tiny human heads or splashing limbs. The stormclouds had drifted closer, eager to swallow the sun.

To Marilyn's dismay, she got a default outgoing message.

Beep.

"Hey Vanessa, it's Marilyn, from an hour ago. Heh. If you can swing it, I was w—"

Click. "Hello?"

"Oh, hey, it's Marilyn."

"Hey!" Surprisingly, the woman sounded pleased to hear from her. "I'm about to head off, actually."

"Where're you going?"

"Just…somewhere. I'll decide on the way. I was gonna go to the beach, but I just heard they're finding dead animals down there, or something."

After a moment's hesitation, Marilyn said, "Do you mind waiting a bit?"

•   •   •

It was set. In an hour, Marilyn and Joe would meet Vanessa in the main lobby of the Huna'ia Resort. To Joe's likely chagrin, they would have to eat quickly, though in all honesty she herself was too keyed up to want to eat much.

She also regretted agreeing to Joe coming along. Yet the reasons for not wanting him along remained unclear. As with many previous situations nowhere near this strange, she was wary of petty tensions that might arise.

Making her way toward the agreed-upon Tiki hut, Marilyn saw Joe at the southwestern corner, finishing the last gulp of a drink.

She brushed his shoulder as she slid into the adjacent stool.

"Everything okay?" Joe asked her, without making eye contact.

"We're meeting her in an hour. In the lobby."

"An hour."

"Yeah. That should give us enough time to wolf something down."

"Should, I guess," he said. "I ordered for us. Got you tacos."

"Okay. Thank you." She studied Joe. Something was off. His posture was slouched more than usual, and words came out his mouth in a kind of lazy roll. His energy felt calmer, but…diminished.

"Joe," she said. "What's up?'

He looked at her. His eyes were distant. Before Marilyn could form any precise thought, the male bartender came by and set down a glass full of beer. Joe's expression turned to one of absolute shock and horror—the horror of an unexpected spotlight.

"This one's on the house," said the bartender, who acknowledged Marilyn without any understanding of her growing shock. "You hear this guy had a run-in with a *tiger* shark today? That's worth a free beer."

The bartender shuffled off. What Marilyn thought might be bile scorched the center of her breast, rose sour to the back of her throat.

"You give me crap for the coffee," she said, "and you're sitting here having *beer*?"

Joe said nothing.

"What did you say back at Lava Java?" she went on. "People and their secrets?"

Joe's hand squeezed the plastic glass, denting it.

"How long have you been secretly drinking, Joe?"

"Not long," he muttered. "Off and on."

"Well, I gotta hand it to you. I never smelled it on you."

"Oh come on. I don't do it that much. I've never, ever even drunk a drop anywhere *near* the house. I'm just…"

Just what? she wanted to blurt. But Marilyn considered she could have filled in any number of accurate possibilities: Just lonely. Just neglected. Just overwhelmed at work. Just tired. Just gassing up my ego. Just wanting to float. To wrench away.

To escape.

"Joe," she said, turning away. "I'll see you later."

Marilyn hurried off. As she passed the pool, she glanced back at him. He remained on his stool, frozen, still clutching the full waiting glass.

•　　•　　•

The moment Marilyn climbed into Vanessa's rundown hatchback, she was powerfully and unexpectedly transported by scent to the only farm she'd ever visited—Uncle Jeffrey's, just south of Salt Lake City. The backseat was littered with hay, clipped bags and a black cage encrusted with stains.

"I got chickens," Vanessa said matter-of-factly as they settled in. "They're my ladies. And my main source of protein."

"You eat them?"

Vanessa snorted. "No. The eggs. Supermarket eggs got nothin' on the fresh feathered-butt stuff."

Marilyn smirked. "Is that your next album? 'Feathered Butt-Stuff'?"

"Hah. Could be."

"There're chickens and roosters all over the place here, I've noticed."

"Yeah. They got released by a hurricane in the nineties. Little raptors. It's our own miniature Jurassic Park."

Vanessa turned the ignition. The dashboard lit up and the hatchback growled, chugged, then whimpered down.

"Oh, come on."

She tried again—same thing.

"Okay, that's it." Vanessa popped the hood. "This puppy don't know what she's up against. I got the Frankenstein touch."

Marilyn frowned. "Frankenstein touch?"

"Yeah. With cars. Or any vehicles, really. I can zap 'em back to life."

Marilyn waited as Vanessa went to work behind the raised hood. There was rummaging and soft metallic sounds. Why did she herself not know more mechanical stuff? Joe had never been particularly handy in that department, either. At least someone in the household should be.

Moments later, Vanessa returned to the driver's seat, hit the ignition and—success!

"What'd I tell ya?" she said, going to shut the hood. "Frankenstein."

•   •   •

The highway and the Huna'ia Resort village became a shrinking panorama in the side-view mirrors. Vanessa hadn't asked about Joe's absence, which caused Marilyn to wonder if during their phone chat she'd even mentioned his wanting to tag along.

He wanted *me to see him. He wanted to get caught. It was a protest. He didn't want to go.*

For a short while they took the same highway she and Joe had driven to the resort. Soon they were in the hills and navigating roads that narrowed with every acre, as if this lonely strip of asphalt, the only visibly manmade object out here, grew further intimidated at the lording jungle.

"Do you remember where the Lofts are?" Marilyn asked, suddenly recognizing the lack of any GPS or map.

"Uh huh. I was by there the other week, remember? Just gotta retrace my steps."

Marilyn studied her companion. Vanessa had foregone the ripped jeans for a pair of athletic shorts that deferred liberally to her long, toned legs. She tried to glimpse more of Vanessa's "Dractopus" tattoo, that beast that had begun in her own brain that now, magically, lived its own life beyond her. She could only make out the gaping-mouth and snatches of its tentacles.

Marilyn drew out her phone and pulled up an Instagram picture Joe had taken of her at the *Realms of Magic* convention, standing next to her charcoal original of the Dractopus.

"Hey," Marilyn said. "Wanna know something crazy?"

Vanessa lowered the volume on the music. "What's that?"

Marilyn showed her the picture. Vanessa slowed the car as she looked. Her eyes widened.

"Holy *shit*," she said. "Wait, what? That's *yours*?"

"Yep."

"That's fucking *insane*. I mean, how *insane* is that? I found that reshared on Twitter and fell in love with it."

"The world weaves weird threads," Marilyn said.

"I love that," Vanessa said. "'The world weaves weird threads.' Careful. I might get your words of wisdom inked on me, too."

Marilyn felt a cleansing swell of validation. "I wouldn't complain."

Vanessa chuckled. "You could start a religion on that."

"What? Weird threads?"

"Uh huh. And then you could actually wear *weird threads*. Get it?" She shook her head. "Man, that's fuckin' *psycho*. Wow. What a fucking insane coincidence."

Marilyn smiled. Somehow, the obscenities made it even more complimentary.

Several minutes beyond a cardboard sign for *Homemade Banana Bread*, they found a reddish dirt road pocked with puddles and several brain-rattling bumps.

When was the last time I ate? Marilyn wondered. She had eaten a small breakfast that morning, technically. But that was weeks ago.

•   •   •

Joe wasn't sure how long he sat at the Tiki bar, squeezing the plastic glass harder and harder, watching the beer rise like amber magma toward the rim. He imagined just clenching a fist, bursting it all over the bar.

Because he was sure of at least one thing: he wasn't going to drink this one. No way. Didn't matter if it was free. His marriage may have just drowned in it. *So dramatic.* Yeah, well, such thoughts forgivable with the way Marilyn had walked off, her gait so determined, so final.

Joe had watched her go for only a few seconds. His heart pounded. Sweat tickled his skin. He felt queasy.

I was in the clear, he thought. He only had one. *One.* And he'd finished it just in time and she was none the wiser and of course, of *course* he had to let slip to the bartender about his tiger shark encounter, and of course, of *course* the bartender had to be nice and, like some smiling, unwitting agent of divine retribution, bring him "another" and bust him wide open.

Watching other couples young and old congregate under the awning, Joe wondered why he'd even taken the risk. By now it had been three months since his last drink, a single glass of wine to calm his nerves amid business associates. It was wrong, of course, against his faith and as with any sin he had prayed for forgiveness every time.

It's her fault.

Several TVs flashed over the bar's central island of bottles. Of those Joe could see, one played a baseball game, the other a series of advertisements—until the show in question returned and Joe recognized it immediately: *Spooksters.*

Yes. It's her fault.

The volume was low, but the captions were on.

NARRATOR: *The team has hunkered down at the infamous Spahn Ranch, in Chatsworth, California—*

The investigators had gathered in a sunbeaten, outdoor area. Behind them, a horizon of large, primordial rocks. His brother-in-law, Shane, lived somewhere in that stretch of hills. Likely he'd never known of his older sister's…sensitivities.

If all this "spirit-being" stuff was true, Marilyn had to have kept her secrets bottled deep, wedging herself between her mom's ilk of the frightened faithful, and Shane's non-believing mockery.

In his mind, Joe tried to replay the discussion in the hotel room, if he had come across at all as mocking. He didn't think he had. He'd been frightened, of course.

And still was.

NARRATOR: *On initial survey, the team finds a strange symbol across the walls of several rooms—*

Joe watched as the camera zoomed in, focused. Spray-painted in black across the wall was the crude outline of what looked like a lizard with a coiled tail:

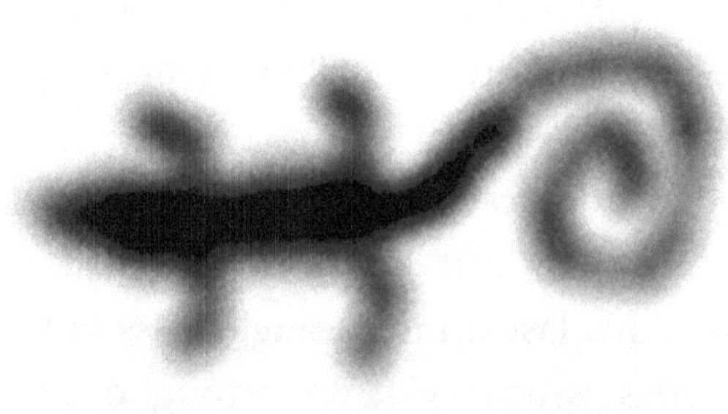

Looking at it, Joe knew a rush of futility, debilitating aloneness before uncaring Largeness. He felt weak. Small.

In one swift, uncontrollable motion, he downed half his beer, enjoying the burn of every gulp.

He set the drink down and pushed off the stool. The buzz came fast, rocking his mind between moods of carefree relinquish and helpless despair. Moving mostly on autopilot, he made his way back toward the beach, studying faces as he walked.

One of his scarier thoughts was that human beings had unwittingly crossed a point of no return. The slow, clarifying burn of society, and all the awareness "progress" had opened in us, was driving us to oblivion. *Knowledge is power*. And we knew more now than anyone before.

Yet maybe it was *not* knowing things that had sustained us, compelled us in our starry-eyed ignorance toward new unseen futures, unburdened of the cynical paralysis we now faced, where God's wonders became a splatter of Google Image thumbnails, ideas mere dental-floss strings of letters quickly discarded, as we understood that more information and more access than ever before had not freed us, but sent us into even greater, terrified submission.

Somewhere, maybe, we had failed to reconcile key revelations, at key times.

Signs were being erected around the shoreline, warning people away as lifeguards and plainclothes officials milled about the surf. From nearby pathways, people looked on, the colorful bloom of their swimsuits and towels and umbrellas a bright contrast to the somber atmosphere of unknown tragedy. Anger rose in Joe.

"Oh my God," said a nearby woman.

A charge went off through the surrounding crowd, everyone spotting it the second she spoke.

A massive body floated several breakers out. Dark. Round. Slick. For a moment, the white surf camouflaged the white barnacled fins, but soon they came into view, too.

The juvenile humpback was turned belly-up, exposing the striations on its underside.

"What is going *on*?" someone else cried.

Joe shivered. All of a sudden, the world was losing interest in keeping itself together. And if he was being pulled into this change, this chaos, what else could he do but persist as he'd always done in encountering strange new things: maintain his faith, sure, and use his mind, the greatest instrument God had gifted him, to try and understand.

Joe walked hurriedly away from the crowds. He found a secluded hammock hung between two palms and sat on the edge, depressing the cloth to the ground.

He pulled out his phone and dialed. After two rings, Kevin picked up.

"Hey Kev, it's Joe."

"Hey! What's the good word from paradise?"

"Could I speak to Troy?"

"Uh, yeah sure, of course."

A pause. He closed his eyes. Breathed.

A clatter, then: "Daddy?"

"Hey, Troyasaur."

"I just finished a puzzle!"

"That's awesome, bud." He glanced around. "Maybe you can help me with another one."

A pause. After a moment's hesitation, Joe continued.

"Tell me more about Baldy," he said. "And his friends."

1

620 A.D.

The mountain rose black against the red corona. Fire-tongue, tasting the heavens. Fire-fingers reaching over the rim.

Despite the air's growing warmth, Kaimi was racked with chills. The mountain was the only thing visible besides the stars. Right then, it was easy to believe that he and it were among the remainders of existence.

For a long moment, Kaimi's identity clung to the slippery driftwood of a few blurry impressions and half-memories. He had rushed upon Makui, who held Chief Haunani in the grip of some terrible, traitorous desperation, animated by faith in Kaimi's "specialness."

Then—his mind had gone blank, and Kaimi had found himself in the jungle, peering up at the glowing volcano.

Kaimi turned southeast. Sprinkles of firelight. The village. What had happened there? What *was* happening there? His throat closed.

The air grew warmer by the minute, the stars swallowed by rising black clouds. Kaimi thought he could feel and even see—faintly—the dim flashes of ash flurrying down the darkness.

He breathed, coughed.

He could not simply abandon his people, particularly not when it was his brother who'd so disrupted everything.

The village is in chaos.

But, there was the mountain. It beckoned him. It wanted to reveal something about itself, to boast of its sheer existence and the power cooking in its bowels. It called especially to those like Kaimi.

Because while any creature with working senses could feel its heat, could taste and smell the smoke of its breath and see the girth of its stormbody, it was a unique eye that could glimpse its *face*—and those yellow, reptilian eyes that burned back to some Age before ages.

Reptilian, he thought. Much as the giant being he'd sensed in the jungle, when they were collecting wood.

Kaimi kept his gaze on the mountain. Against the smoky bloodlight, a shape began to materialize. Perched on the side of the volcano, the entity was colossal. With its ridged contours, it appeared like a ghostly extension of the mountain itself. Same for the rising tail, coiled like some snakes.

Kaimi felt like they now stared at one another.

Then, it moved. The thing's great head swung away, the great limbs rose and the great body edged down the mountain. In no more than three strides, the Reptile lost distinction against the shadows and the smoke, its disappearance so swift that Kaimi wasn't sure it had been there at all.

Except he could still feel it, by the soft graze of "spirit-fingers". It was there and it was drawing away to some other place.

Toward the sea.

Lightheaded, Kaimi made his way back down toward the village. Acrid smoke-odor sharpened. The ground shook. He stumbled, struck a tree and crashed several yards through thick brush, reigniting recent wounds.

Covered in soot and mud, he rose cautiously and peered at what he could see of the village. The chief's house still burned, but the flames would likely be out soon. Some torches still burned. The ground scuffed with the movement of so many though he could see none of them.

Something like voices reached him on the oceanwind, as did what sounded like the faint bellow of a conch shell, but he didn't trust his ears.

The scent of terror and panic hung on the air. The spirit of the village, the collective hues of its *mana*, brooded on the sad, murderous haste of its desertion.

Kaimi stepped into the village grounds. He knelt to examine the impressions in the soil. Footprints indicated many had been running, in multiple directions. Chaos had seized the village. Probably they had retreated at the volcano.

And you abandoned them. Though he didn't remember doing so.

Kaimi caught sight of a body lying prostrate near the remnants of Chief Haunani's home. He made his way toward it. Even without looking, however, he knew the villager was dead.

As he knew it was Chief Haunani.

In the torchlight, he looked at his own hands: dried blood on both. His chest clenched. His stomach plummeted.

Haunani's skull had been crushed, slick pulp surrounding his head. Blood had congealed on his nose and mouth. The lone visible eyeball had been pushed partway from the socket, the reflected glint of fire granting it a dull impression of life.

Nearby lay the blood-slicked sharktooth blade that looked like Makui's, though he couldn't be certain. Kaimi was shocked. From what he could remember of the conflict, before the blackout and before awaking in the jungle, Makui had been outnumbered. If fortune had turned against Haunani, that meant Makui's rebellion had more sympathizers than Kaimi had ever suspected.

Shaking, Kaimi placed a palm on the chief's back, closed his eyes and uttered a prayer. He felt tears stirring, and a great, reverberating sadness. Yet the sadness centered less on Haunani than it did on the sheer scope of all his recent loss.

The night grew redder, an angry sunrise over the tree line. Everywhere the grumbling of the earth.

He hurried to the beach, where he was surprised to see several canoes remaining. Kaimi pushed one toward the surf and, as he ran, a burning pain tore up his leg. He cried out and collapsed. He had known this pain before as a child, and knew exactly what it was now: the long-limbed floaters had washed ashore, their tendrils fiery to the touch.

Adrenaline surging, Kaimi shoved the canoe past the harshest waves, settled in and began to row. The sting was a reminder. Even if he were being summoned by spirit-beings, he was still a body, subject to the many punishing hands of the elements.

•   •   •

His true family had long disappeared over the horizon—in the "Old Land", as Chief Haunani had so callously called it. Makui surely had felt this vacancy, too, which was probably why he'd acted as he had.

Kaimi slowed his rowing. The ocean whispered all about. He glanced back at the shoreline, those beads of remaining torchlight against the black jungle, and the rumbling, pulsing red growing up the sky.

Streams of fire shot from the mountain, certainly big enough to incinerate him in one stroke.

Shipping his oars, Kaimi reluctantly felt the blood encrusted on his hands. He shuddered violently. Tears flowed from his eyes, everything of every hour of every day for the last several months, the sludge of it all pressing at his every pore. He sobbed into the dried blood on his palms.

You have a mission before you.

Yes. He had to follow the Reptile being. It was time to glimpse meaning behind a world which had long treated him and his tribe with such brutal indifference.

Bobbing on the ocean, he wiped his eyes and his face, tried to banish all thought in order to reach his mind, to reach his spirit-fingers across the night, the ashwind and the seasalt, to graze the presence of the Reptile being. To pick up its scent.

He saw the coil of its tail, that immense spiral shape. He had seen that shape before.

His head snapped up. The northwesterly view before him was, save a few stars, featureless in the dark.

Except two of those lights weren't stars. They were the eyes of the Reptile, raised above the sea.

With renewed vigor, he took up the oars and rowed onward.

2

620 A.D.

The inner war was over: this *was* real. She'd slipped through some loophole in physical law. And if this crazy thing were real, was it so unreasonable to expect a clear answer for why it was happening?

Probably. That show *Spooksters* had interviewed people who'd claimed to have "time slips", and, as far as the witnesses could tell, there'd never been any rhyme or reason to their experience.

Everything hurt. What little of her the sun had managed to find through the thick jungle canopy had started to feel slightly burnt (sunscreen must've worn off, she thought with a fatalistic snicker) and Marilyn could feel the calluses and blisters forming on her feet.

Soon, however, hunger pangs distinguished themselves from the rest of her aches and sores.

How could she possibly forage for herself? What about clothes? Shoes?

Medicine?

Clouds passed overhead. Hard to tell, but she figured it was mid or late afternoon. Pressing forward, she felt new reverence for her own species, all the nameless survivors that had carried us from caves to civilization.

She began feeling feverish. Several times she spotted what looked like edible fruits, and she would pick them and examine them and, depending, lick them or merely nibble on them. One she spit out, for its sourness. Could she eat any of the bugs? Birds? The thought made her sicker than the hunger.

She knew nothing, and was terrified of what she didn't know.

At one point, something flickered into view between two koa trees. Had to be her dehydration, she guessed, her tiredness, her hunger. She'd seen TV documentaries where people stuck out in the wilderness went crazy.

Except with her, there *were* "other" things out here. She knew this. All nature was haunted. And, if things got really bad, how would she be able to distinguish between the Other visions, and the madness?

Don't worry about it, said a voice. *You've always been nuts.*

I have been, haven't I? she thought. It was just being forced out of her now.

But this notion did nothing to dissuade her of the sight flickering into view between the two koas. Because it had right angles. It was fake green. It had writing.

A road sign!

As fast as she could, Marilyn hurried toward it. She fell instantly. Pain erupted, but nothing like a sprain or break, thank God.

She looked up once more. The sign was gone.

Her heart sank. But she knew it hadn't been a hallucination. It had been too detailed, too real.

Hope crept into her soul. She was still entangled with her time. It was still "there." She just had to unearth it again, and make it stick.

Or, make *herself* stick.

She was positive of at least one thing the sign had said:

Kekepania Falls…3 mi.

●　●　●

Mostly she used the sounds of water to guide her. She tried engaging her Other senses again, but this time they felt less stable, like trying to grasp a dream you were meant to forget.

Of course, no evidence of any trail existed here when Marilyn, bleary and aching, drew closer and closer to that thunderous rush of water. It struck her, how something could sound so *right there* yet be utterly invisible, well-concealed behind the jungle's many surfaces as if the trees were playing their own version of hide-the-ball.

Eventually, she discovered an opening: a thin passage through overgrown rock wall. Vines hung across the passage, as if meant to sew together an irreconcilable wound. She brushed past them, even snapped them out of her way and emerged into the small coliseum of earth, the circle of craggy, redstone rises laden with growth.

The pond was there, rich and dark. The waterfall was wider, too, crashing fuller, stronger than she remembered from the dream she'd had while driving to the Huna'ia Resort.

On reaching the pond, Marilyn collapsed into it as one might a mattress at the end of a long day. She gouged her knees on gravel, stung her sunburnt face on the surface. Water filled her mouth, her nose. She coughed it up in bubbles and mucus, pushed forward and drank through every pore that cleansing coolness before rising and stumbling toward the waterfall, where she cupped her hands and slurped the pure elixir that had never known human lips.

Water, mom had once said, *is plain evidence of God: a basic thing, needed by all things.*

On filling her belly, she stepped into the waterfall's splattering thunder. The roar and the wet and the chill enveloped her. She imagined they were breaking her down, that, drop by crystalline drop, the water was taking her with it.

Behind the waterfall: a cove, yawning and dark. Inviting. She suddenly yearned for shelter. And not just a physical shelter, but a haven—a pocket in which to conceal herself from all the openness, all the unknown-ness.

Marilyn stepped farther into the cove, the waterfall just behind her now. Like a moving window curtain, she thought. Blurring out everything. Her mind felt splintered. Everything about her— emotionally, physically, intellectually—was upheld by toothpicks.

She hugged the cove's moss-slick wall, treading shin-deep water that became knee-deep.

Finding a decent platform, she lowered herself down and sat hugging her legs, knees bunched up to her chin. She trembled, pressed up against the rugged wall of the cove. Her muscles knotted. Blood-pulse in her ears.

The faster she breathed, the faster her heartbeat, the more Marilyn imagined they might punch holes in this cosmic fabric, this dream-layer enshrouding her.

•　　•　　•

Marilyn awoke—in bed.

No water.

No wind.

Only the soft, rhythmic nuisance of Joe's snoring.

She lifted her head from her pillow. Distant traffic whirred. The sideyard light threw its funereal glow through the curtained bedroom window.

She was home. *In Los Angeles.*

Marilyn lay there for what felt like a long while, waiting for the whole scene to crumble. The entire harrowing sequence—the flight, the snorkeling, the terror in the water—was now a hazy, anxious hyphen between her going to sleep that night and this glorious moment of realizing it was all a paranoid dream.

"Mommy?"

The dull outline of her youngest son appeared in the doorway.

"Troy?" she said, in a croaky voice. "What's up, sweetie?"

"I wanna show you something."

He didn't wait for her, his footfalls pattering halfway down the hall by the time Marilyn rose from the sheets and followed.

Troy stood at the living room window, little fingers splayed on the glass. Surely to leave marks.

"There are dogs outside," he said.

"What do you mean, buddy?"

He didn't look back, nor did he reply. She walked over to join Troy at the window, where she met with the sight of numerous, canine eyes glinting across her yard, across the street and beyond. Dozens and dozens. Maybe hundreds. Heads cocked and watching.

There were no other houses nearby, either, not that she could see. The Campbells, the Williamsons, the Rowans…no neighbor seemed to exist. Their home sat alone in dark sprawling space, empty but for these gathering dogs.

"Honey," Marilyn said, "what's going on?"

"Let's go out to see!"

Troy ran from the window, toward the front door. Marilyn panicked.

"Troy! Get back here!"

Next thing she knew, she was outside, Troy pressed tight in the crook of her arm as they stood among the field of watching dogs. Glowing stars above. Their house seemed to exist on a chunk of ragged terrain, an island floating through the universe.

It's cold out here.

Troy said, "The dogs are sad, Mommy."

There were rings of what had to be thousands of dogs all around the house. All shapes and sizes and breeds. All staring down her house's warm, inviting windows. She could feel their desire. Their hunger. Far beyond them, millions more whirled about as if caught in a cyclone, aimless and adrift.

She sensed that, out of all these dogs, maybe only one or two would make it inside the house. It was even quite conceivable—probable—that none of them would ever make it inside.

"I want to pet the doggies," Troy said.

"No," Marilyn said. "Not now."

Troy pointed. "Can we swim in the river, then?"

"What river?"

Troy pointed. All at once, it came into view. How had she not noticed it before? The street by their house was now a stream, speckled by the glow of streetlamps.

"Stay here, sweetie," Marilyn said, ushering back toward the door. "Close the door and stay inside, okay?" Troy began to whine, and she turned and held up a stiff finger. "I mean it."

Her youngest son's face fell. He harrumphed with crossed arms, but obeyed.

"Good. I'll be back."

She stepped out. The night air was balmy. Unusually tropical. The dogs watched her, a constellation of awarenesses. Something about the void in each of their eyes told Marilyn that these creatures weren't dogs, not really. Something in her consciousness was building on a memory, one of Troy standing at the window, looking at a poor, stray dog that had squatted down on their yard once.

These dog-things weren't bad, either. They simply wanted what she had. A home.

A light.

A life.

•   •   •

When Marilyn awoke and made her way from the cove, dusk had fallen.

She dragged herself across the pond. The shadows and stars divided the world. Against the darkness, Marilyn's pale naked skin shone almost alabaster. She cupped her hands together, bent and scooped up water and drank more. She quivered with hunger.

She walked upon the bank, pressed the gravel into her bare feet. Blisters rang. Several muscles across her arms and legs twitched spastically, as if in protest.

(Tommy)

(Tammy)

(Troy)

A wave of defeat sent her to her knees.

As a freshly licensed teenager, she'd once taken the wrong turn and wound up cruising the streets of a strange neighborhood (Norwalk, she would now think with a laugh), toting a dead cell and no map and plenty of mounting panic. Will I ever see home again? she'd wondered.

Through a blurry film of tears, she peered up at the stars, the only sight right now that struck her as the least bit familiar. The least bit home.

3

Present Day

The jungle ushered them in. The stately banyans and jacarandas stood as elder residents of a population, branches spread wide. Bug and birdsong spoke excitedly.

Thunder rumbled toward the coastline. Clouds grayed the daylight.

Marilyn stayed just behind Vanessa, hyper-aware. Since they'd truly entered the jungle, Vanessa had been quiet, only minimally responsive to the shards of conversation Marilyn would fling her way and initiating nothing herself—something of a contrast to just an hour ago.

For a while Marilyn didn't really see or feel anything. The trail was noticeably fading. From the car they had taken a light footpath which had intersected with what looked like a fire road, which in turn had taken them through a high-grass clearing toward denser flora where the path became little more than strips of red clay, divided by weeds and braided with tire tracks.

And then, like a river reaching the sea, these weeds joined the untrammeled expanse of greenery. She tried to remember why she was even out there: these "Lofts" being the place where the Road Walker— might—be. The strange man she'd seen roadside, and by Pyramid Bay, who might just clarify anything of what was going on in those waters. Still, the threads were loose, the connections possibly specious.

It was all she had to go on.

"Hey," Marilyn said, as they strode over brush. "Do you know where we're going?"

Vanessa slowed to a stop. She remained quiet, peering into a section of jungle as if transfixed. Chills broke over Marilyn.

"Vanessa," she said, unable herself to totally discern the shape lurking in the bushes. "What's wrong?"

There's something there…

"I feel like we're being watched," Vanessa said. She glanced back. For a second, she appeared surprised, as if she'd forgotten Marilyn's company. A disconnected look filled her eyes.

Marilyn scoured the trees, feeling, sensing. Trying to make out some sense of form, the *shape* of the energy that stood out just slightly from the jungle, like a seam in a cloth. It was hard to locate.

"It's a shade," Marilyn said.

"Huh?"

She took several steps forward. To her mind, the jungle offered no obvious trail. If Vanessa had misremembered, or was now brainfarting, they would have to backtrack, which would only cost time.

It worried her, that she wasn't feeling much internal guidance. Had she lost some of her intuition? She had once felt directed, however ambiguously. But even her Other fingers seemed callused now, or like a thick glove that had been slipped over them.

A sudden wind picked up. Vanessa stiffened…

…then wrenched from Marilyn's side and bounded away, crashing away through the foliage.

"Vanessa!"

Agitated, Marilyn gave chase. Muddy earth splashed up her legs. Wide ferns slapped at her. Her shin caught an exposed root and she collapsed face first into a bed of vegetation. Pain burst across her face and ricocheted down her bones. She dabbed her nose—no blood.

"Vanessa!" she cried again. "*Stop!*"

A loud rustling ahead. An agonized cry.

By the time Marilyn was up, Vanessa's footfalls had ceased, the forest twittering and humming its innocence.

She walked forward. "Vanessa?"

Twenty or so yards of parted brush later and Vanessa was there, squatting on a ridgeline veined with roots of a koa tree. Her eyes were closed, her right leg stretched out. She clutched her ankle as she whimpered, rocking slightly back and forth.

"What happened?" Marilyn asked, pulse racing. Stars winked across her vision. "Are you okay?"

"I'm sorry," Vanessa said, her eyes shut tight. She exhaled, shuddering. "I don't know what that was. I just freaked. And I think—" She touched her foot, which was bent at an odd angle—"*ow*. I think I torqued my ankle pretty bad. Goddammit."

Marilyn reached out and touched her arm. Vanessa grasped her hand, digging dirt-lined nails into her skin though it didn't hurt. In a way, it was weirdly fulfilling.

"It's alright," Marilyn said. She knelt to scrutinize Vanessa's ankle. There was a bulge there and a pinkish tinge, both of which would probably worsen. Tommy had once twisted his ankle playing basketball. "You'll be okay."

Vanessa looked at her. A loopiness existed in her eyes, a thing detached and swirling.

"What did you say it was?" Vanessa asked.

"What?"

"Back—*ow*—there." She shifted her position. "Whatever it was. You said it was a 'shade'?"

Marilyn leaned back. Dark knowledge groped toward the light, ushered on by that one word, *shade*.

"Yes," she said.

Vanessa's eyes narrowed. "What did you mean?"

"Um. It's not a strictly physical thing."

"Like a ghost?"

"Kind of. Don't worry about that now."

Wincing, Vanessa glanced around. "Do you know where the trail is?"

"It's back that way, I think." Noticing the small panic in Vanessa's face at *I think*, she added, "We'll get our bearings."

Vanessa lowered her head. "I'm so sorry. I fucked up."

Marilyn stuck out her hand. After a second's hesitation, Vanessa took it and gingerly climbed to her feet, Marilyn lifting her all the way. She dusted herself off.

"Can you put weight on it?"

Like she was testing a pool's temperature, Vanessa carefully placed her foot forward.

"*Ouch.* Shit."

Marilyn rushed to grab her, clutching elbow and shoulder. "I'll help you."

"Thanks. I have a compass, I think." Moving with caution, Vanessa threw down her backpack.

"Want me to look?" Marilyn asked.

"Yes, please."

She dove in, unzipping, opening, rummaging. Thermos. Towel. Cliff bar. Umbrella. Flask. No sign of a compass.

Vanessa lowered her gaze. "Is it not in there?"

"I don't see anything."

"Must be in the car then. Shit. *Shit.* God I'm such a fucking *loser*."

"We'll figure it out," Marilyn said curtly.

Their phones: no signal whatsoever.

Marilyn helped Vanessa strap on her backpack as they slowly started walking. "Didn't we leave footprints?"

"It's hard to see with all the vegetation." Marilyn herself felt like a dolt. "And I wasn't looking."

"Fuck."

Thunder grumbled. Close. An electric hush fell over the forest. Marilyn's heart sped up. Drizzle began ticking gently down the leaves, across her shoulders.

"Rain," Vanessa said. She looked up. "Thanks, asshole."

Marilyn felt guilty for empathizing, but also empowered. They paused long enough for Marilyn to unzip Vanessa's backpack and pop open the umbrella.

They staggered on. Nothing appeared familiar. The trees had cinched closer together, pathways narrowing.

"Oh my *God*," Vanessa whimpered. "This isn't happening. How did we get so fucking turned around? We couldn't have been more than, what, twenty yards off the trail? I'm sorry. I'm so fucking sorry."

"The trail was already fading." Marilyn gritted her teeth, trying to swallow resentment. Yet she wasn't frightened. There was a familiarity to all this.

Thunder bellowed this time, so loud Marilyn stiffened.

The drizzle strengthened into rain.

•   •   •

They came across a small clearing ruled by a massive banyan tree. Marilyn slowed, overcome not by déjà vu, but by knowing-ness. She *knew* this tree. This area.

"Everything okay?" Vanessa asked.

More thunder. Rain pattered, the jungle trembling in thirsty dance. Before Marilyn could reply, she noticed a yawning enclave in the trunk—surely the nook was big enough for two people.

"We should take shelter there," Marilyn said, gesturing.

"Might be a good idea. Till the rain lets up."

"No. I mean for the night."

Vanessa looked at her as Marilyn brought them closer to the tree.

"We don't know how turned around we are, or how long it'll be raining." She caressed the nearest branch, on which she noticed clusters of bright red fruit, like small cherries. "I'd rather hole up here, then move out in the morning. Or, if necessary, you can stay here and I can look for the trail, go get help—"

"We are *not* splitting up."

Marilyn held up her hand defensively. "Okay. Don't worry. Just thinking off the cuff. You have a flashlight, right?"

"Yeah." Vanessa turned so Marilyn could dig through the backpack again. Once retrieved, she clicked the flashlight on.

Click. Click. Nothing.

"Not working?"

"No. No new batteries with you?"

"No. *Fuck.*"

Marilyn inhaled. "Then we're definitely staying here. For now."

She turned to the bright red fruit, plucked one and ate it. Ripe, mildly sour, fresh. Edible.

"Uh, do you know if those are safe?"

Marilyn picked a handful, held several out for Vanessa. "They're fine. I think they're berries. They grow up in higher elevation."

Vanessa's caution softened. She took one and popped it into her mouth. "Not bad."

Marilyn collected more. "Just in case. We can just put them in your backpack."

"How did you know about these?"

As she dumped the two handfuls into Vanessa's backpack, Marilyn offered a tiny shrug. "Guidebook, I suppose."

They set about lowering themselves into the tree, out of reach of the rain. Framed by the edges of the enclave, the jungle seemed momentarily at a remove, like a movie or a museum exhibit.

With a visibly withheld frown, Vanessa surveyed the space. Her ankle was swelling, the pinkish color darkening and spreading.

"I think I do have a blanket," Vanessa said. "But it's small. May be hard to share it."

"It looked more like a towel."

"That's because it basically is." She visibly trembled, shifted her foot. "Christ."

"Calm down," Marilyn said, surprised at her own assuredness. "We'll make it back." After an awkward second, she added, "I promise."

Vanessa fished out the blanket, which they used as a towel. In a wet, warm and pulsing moment that might've been divine or delirious, Marilyn knew a vivifying connection to sheer Element.

Wordless time passed. More thunder. Marilyn wanted to pray but something held her back. There was a feeling she'd be giving away something better kept. Something needed.

"I take it," Marilyn said, "you don't believe in God?"

"I do, actually. Basically. Why?"

"You said 'asshole' before."

"Oh. So? God *is* an asshole. Or can be." Vanessa blew a bug off her arm. "Same could be said for my ex-boyfriend. But he's still my best friend." Vanessa looked at her foot. "Gah, it's swollen and gross. I need ice."

Marilyn dug further into her backpack. "I didn't see any ice pack in there."

"Nope. But something that'll do in a pinch." Vanessa brought out the metal flask, unscrewed it and took a long gulp. Her pretty features scrunched. She swallowed loudly, then offered the flask to Marilyn.

"You're married, right?" Vanessa asked. "To that guy John?"

"Joe. Yeah." Unsure what to do or say, Marilyn took the flask in hand.

"Joe, sorry. How long?"

"About seven years."

"Whoa. Wait, how old are you?"

"Twenty-seven."

"Damn. You knew that fast?"

Marilyn's canned reply whenever something like this came up from so-called Gentiles—"God gave me big enough hints along the way"— struck her now as embarrassing. A disingenuous wad of cheese.

"We just knew," Marilyn said. "It's not always easy, of course. But we scratch and claw. And kiss, too. And hug."

"And fuck. Hopefully."

"That too."

"You thinking kids?"

"Already thought." She sniffed the flask. Definitely whiskey, or something pungent and hard. "We've got three."

"Holy hell. Are you Jehovah's Witnesses or something?"

"No." After a short lull, she said, "Kids can help with making the marriage work."

Looking at the open flask, Marilyn despaired. The faces of Tommy, Tamara and Troy haunted her thoughts, and she was overcome with a desire to see and to hold them. For a fraction of a second, Marilyn dared herself to imagine not seeing them again. And, by her never-explained disappearance, leaving them with perpetually open wounds.

"In a way, I admire you," said Vanessa. "You've gone and done it. You're on the other end of that adventure. I don't know if I'll ever really know about the having-kids thing."

"You won't regret having them, when they come. The love cancels everything else out."

"I'm sure. I mean, I'm also talking about big issues. I'm selfish. But I'm honestly wondering what the fuck kinda shape this planet is gonna be in just a few decades from now."

Marilyn listened.

"Apparently we're in the 'Anthropocene' period," Vanessa went on, "which means humans are steering shit. Seas are gonna swallow coastal cities. Wars are gonna break out over dwindling resources."

Marilyn nodded. "The Authoring."

"The what?"

She paused, not quite understanding where that word had come from. More like it had been burped up from her subconscious.

"We're authoring this era, I mean," Marilyn said. "For better or worse."

Part of her attention had gone to a series of hard, round shells scattered not far away. They, too, were edible, pending a hard enough rock to crack them open and reveal the nut within. Some of them looked aged, as well, which meant the nut would more likely be intact, less prone to crumbling.

Nature provides, she thought, wondering how she knew this.

"No shit," Vanessa said. "You know they're even saying the melting permafrost in the Arctic might expose some prehistoric superbugs? God only knows what kinda havoc *that'll* wreak."

"I try not to think about that stuff."

"How could you not, though? Isn't that irresponsible? No offense. Your kids are awesome, I'm sure. But everyone needs to vacuum up shit just to survive. Doesn't matter how good a person you are."

Marilyn lifted the flask to her lips. Sipped. Liquid flame flowed over her tongue and down her throat, but the burn was sweet, and strangely enlivening.

She took a bigger swallow.

"And how big's our number gonna go?" Vanessa went on. "Eight billion? Nine bil? Ten? Twenty?"

"I suppose," Marilyn said, wincing, "till our number's up."

•   •   •

The flask went back and forth several times, Vanessa imbibing the most before she decided to cap and put it away. "Can't get trashed," she said. "Party's still young."

Having taken about three cautious gulps, Marilyn awaited the stormrush of guilt. All she felt, though, was a certain buoyant lightness, the rinsing away of burdens. *This is how people get hooked*, said a voice. She deflected these thoughts, however. Exceptional situations called for exceptional actions—or coping mechanisms.

Vanessa turned to her. "You said 'kind of' before."

"Sorry?"

"When I asked if 'shades' were ghosts, you said 'kind of.' What did you mean?"

Marilyn's sigh broke into a chuckle. "Well, they're not quite ghosts. Not in my experience."

"What *are* they? Wraiths? Demons? I mean, can they hurt us?"

The word "demons" stuck in Marilyn. No, not demons, of course, not in the Dante or Exorcist way. Not even in the way the Mormon church believed. But just as there were evil people, so too were there entities that, in their single-minded malice or cruelly intelligent mischief, might well be called demonic.

A memory tried to get through, smeared with green, fringed with dread. She'd been utterly isolated in the jungle, hungry and stalked and—

"My whole life," Vanessa said, rubbing her temple, "I've only told one person about stuff I've felt. My grandma."

Marilyn's brain seized on the operative word: *felt*.

"Was your grandma sensitive, too?" Marilyn asked.

"She, um, never talked about it herself, so I dunno exactly how sensitive she was, but…let's just say she knew things about my dead cousin that no one else knew. That were confirmed later.

"I've never properly 'seen' anything," Vanessa continued. "But every once in a while, I know they're there. It's like if you're alone in a room and shut your ears and close your eyes, and someone else comes into the room. You still feel them."

"And they've felt human to you?"

"I think so. Weird thing is, they would never really scare me."

"What frightened you back there?"

With her index finger, Vanessa caressed her swollen ankle. "Um, for one it didn't feel like a ghost. It felt more, like, animal. I mean animals have souls, I think—"

"They do," Marilyn said.

"But the strangest thing," Vanessa went on, "is that, just now, it didn't feel like *me* freaking out."

Marilyn watched her. A feeling of dislocation crept through her. Her stomach tightened.

"It shot through me," Vanessa said. "It was like a full body version of a cat panicking on your shoulders, claws out."

"You might have felt its fear."

Vanessa frowned. "Why was *it* afraid? And what do you mean by 'it'? I'm confused."

The loopiness had returned to Vanessa's eyes, but had transformed into something less fearful than curious—a student supplicating a teacher.

An urge took hold of Marilyn. Like so many seeking, searching, wondering (and wandering) people, Vanessa was a listless ship in need of righting, of navigation. Not authoritatively, of course. Not dogmatically. Yet Marilyn sensed an opportunity to make known for someone what was normally unknown. And, what's more, to do it with the weight of true experience.

So she told Vanessa all of what she knew, or rather, what Marilyn *knew* she knew. She stripped out all stink of Maybe, too. Because right now, out here, where real nature, *Nature* nature, demanded unforgivingly, "Maybe" was a liability. Even deadly.

She told Vanessa of the Big Stranger. Of Baldy. Of all the things she'd told Joe. She alternately called them "elementals" or "earth-spirits". Or, for reasons that felt right but which weren't wholly clear to her, "potentials."

Vanessa stared at her, jaw unhinged slightly, eyes widening. At one point, she said, "You haven't really told me why you want to go to the Lofts."

The question frustrated Marilyn, if only because it highlighted how ambiguous her "lead" really was.

"There's something happening in Pyramid Bay," Marilyn said.

"Yeah, they said there might be toxins in the water."

Marilyn inhaled. "In a manner of speaking."

"I have…" Vanessa began.

"You've what?"

"I have, um, felt something, sometimes, in Pyramid Bay."

Marilyn leaned in. "Human?"

Vanessa nodded, tentatively. "Yeah. I think so. It's faint, and goes away quickly. Like a smell you're not sure you smelled. But it doesn't seem happy."

"Hm."

"It feels old. Maybe a native? I try not to focus on it."

"I understand." Though Marilyn was perplexed. She hadn't felt anything beyond the dark, decidedly non-human Presence in Pyramid Bay. Then again, as far as she knew, she'd never felt a human spirit. She didn't have that sensitivity.

"So," Vanessa said. "I mean, do the Lofts have to do with that?"

Another dislocated memory floated back to her: murky visions of Pyramid Rock, and a figure—a man, physical and human—standing next to it, about to do something wrong or stupid or dangerous, or all three. An ominous dusk filled Marilyn's soul. The large creature was drawing near. The thing she'd called the Presence.

She had jumped into the churning surf, kicking and flailing after the young man as he headed for that monstrous being. Yet right then, through the whizzing bubbles and gray-blue haze, she saw more: this massive creature edging further into the world, suspending her in a cold dark cauldron of alien sensation and emotion.

"Marilyn?"

•　　•　　•

Within an hour, the rain passed, and the clouds broke. Not much later, evening began coaxing out the shadows, which submerged the trees.

The two women shared the bright red berries and Vanessa's Cliff bar—peanut butter—then nestled down. Marilyn scrunched into a fetal position against Vanessa's back. Both seemed eager to lose themselves to unconsciousness for a while.

"Comfortable?" Vanessa asked.

"Much as I can be."

"Feel free to grope me if you're so inclined."

Knowing the tongue-in-cheek nature of the comment didn't stop the flush in Marilyn. "Thanks." Her mind raced for an appropriate reply. "I'll need something to hold onto if the flood comes."

This commitment to sleep—Night One—was the final relinquish that struck Marilyn hard in the middle of her breast: the searing reality that the jungle had swallowed them.

After hours of pushing it away, she allowed That Word to settle down into her mind, to fill the large, cratered groove her anxiousness had already carved for it.

Lost.

They were lost.

4

620 A.D.

...these trees, the little medieval homesteads and Bone Mountain beyond, shrouded in red clouds. Things once built of polygons and pixels had found their way around her, now. No longer isolated to a computer screen.

Her Myrulian Dwarf-Knight, former Queen of the Myrulia Dwarves, moved ahead of her, long braided red hair swaying across her armored back, the double-bladed axe held across her fists.

The world of Errowind contained her now. Running with her: Gally, the elvish warrior, Hermett, the aquatic Xoran prince, and Piro-Mar, the half-dragon, half-orc born in a mad wizard's lab.

The town of Krakeo was out in celebration: children hurried toward them, eager to join the women, men and elderly that were cheering and offering them sweets and wine.

The monstrous Zmurg was dead—and her Dwarf-Knight had struck the fatal blow.

Marilyn knew: this was that *night, that* campaign, *that* quest, *one of the most memorable in her Errowind career. The epic late-nighter when she and Jen from Seattle and Renee from Memphis and Stephen from the UK had saved this town—possibly this kingdom—from imminent destruction. When real time had vanished. When Joe, scowling, had peeked in on her on his way to a 2 AM pee, only to repeat the journey around four and, shocked to see her unmoved, walk in to yank off her headphones and hiss at her about taking Tommy to preschool in three hours, and stoking in Marilyn deep resentment because, well, look what we did, Joe!, Krakeo's all out and safe, and you're nagging me about school drop-offs and pack lunches—?*

In the sleep-deprived "hangover" the following morning, she'd decided to take a two-month hiatus from the game.

Right now, amidst the celebration, her Dwarf-Knight turned toward her.

I'm not controlling her—am I?

In this dream, she existed in the Kingdom of Errowind, but she was not the Dwarf-Knight and not exactly herself. At least she didn't think so. She was more like a spectator.

By the glint in the Dwarf-Knight's eye, it seemed her character knew she was there. And that she knew something Marilyn didn't.

"It's not safe here," said the Dwarf-Knight, looking directly at her.

What do you mean? It's safe now. We killed Zm—

"Look again at these people," said the knight. "Look closer."

Almost immediately, Marilyn noticed it. The crowd faces were longer than they should have been. Stretchy, like masks. A sameness existed across the eyes. All the varied, happier emotions had collapsed to some neutral craving.

The Dwarf-Knight, customized by her, companion in all her digital escapades, appeared to exist as a half-alive creature itself. It knew its creator, and sought to protect her. To fight as any worshipper would for their own god—or goddess.

"I can only do so much," said the Dwarf-Knight. "You are the Author."

• • •

When she awoke, Marilyn glimpsed a ring of figures around her—blurry blobs and forms against the sun. Dewy tropical heat settled over her.

She struggled to open her eyes further, but her eyelids were leaden and so was everything else.

Her Other ears, however, heard clicking, gasping, wooing, buzzing, muttering, delirious half-voices.

Her Other touch came away with scales, coarseness, slickness, hardness—sharpness— fuzziness.

And she saw them, too, in brief snatches. They were bird-like. Insectile. Humanoid. Bestial. Diminutive. Hairy. Scaly. Webbed. Multi-limbed. No-limbed. Many-eyed. Large-eyed. Beady-eyed. Spindly. Wide. They were so many things, a lava-lamp of would-be forms and there were truly alien ones, too, like Nature was showing off the unbounded breadth of her imagination.

She was succumbing to some terrible feeling of decoherence, where no part of her body could talk to any other part. Like she was being mentally dismembered.

More than any one voice, she understood the singular sensation behind them all.

Hunger.

What seconds ago had felt like ghostly brushes across her body became the feeling of many small hands clutching her feet, or thigh. Or the slithery dance of a thing without hands. Or the sharp prick on her chest, as if from the talons of a hawk, securing itself for better feeding.

"Get off me", she wanted to utter, "Get *away* from me", but her lips could barely part.

Then—focusing her inner voice, working her Other tongue, she cried:

—Get—OFF—ME—

The creatures stopped. Some recoiled. Their menacing closeness didn't cease, however, nor did the drain on her energy which she imagined as a hemorrhage of her, the beings bloodying themselves like ancient savages on all her days and hours, on her essence.

Though she struggled to resist, Marilyn slipped away again.

•　　•　　•

"Just in time."

She stood in a small, dark room. The Dwarf-Knight sat with its chainmailed back to Marilyn, turning a large whetstone and showering sparks into the gloom. Sharpening the double-bladed axe.

"I'm almost done with this," said the Dwarf-Knight. "Then I was going to offer it to you."

What's happening to me? Marilyn asked, not without a tinge of desperation.

The Dwarf-Knight regarded Marilyn sympathetically. "I'm going to let you in on a secret."

Marilyn was silent, in this face of what felt like a revelation.

"You control me," said the red-haired warrior. "And I can only control you as much as you allow me."

She chewed on this for all of a second. What kind of "secret" was that, after all?

"You are an Author," said the Dwarf-Knight. "Gifted with Authoring."

There was that word again, "author." And—"authoring"?

What does that mean? Marilyn asked.

The Dwarf-Knight pulled away from the whetstone. The sparks died, leaving only a few stragglers in the darkness. The Dwarf-Knight turned and held out the sharpened axe and Marilyn took it, her fingers closing around the coarse wooden handle.

"It means," said the Dwarf-Knight, "that you are a forger of Creation."

Something of the powerfulness she'd just known in the waterfall cove now returned to her. Marilyn felt heightened, privileged. Even magical.

In this space, emotions were instruments. In this space, she swam among all that she had felt, or imagined, or could feel or imagine. These things hovered in some timeless cloud, to be downloaded when she had the knowhow.

How many "authors" are there?

The Dwarf-Knight snorted. "I'd say—a goodly gazillion? I don't know."

What?

"Don't worry," the Dwarf-Knight said, turning her back to Marilyn and setting a sword upon the whetstone. "It's not everyone that can swing a mean axe."

A jolt of energy shot through her. It was her Other hands now clutching this axe—or, this idea of an axe. Her Other nose detected a scent of fear. Her Other ears picked up the anxious voices and footfalls of creatures now hurrying away.

Hurrying away from her.

Her Other body had coalesced into something. A form. A form with limbs that could unleash this axe, that could send its blade deep into the "flesh" of her attackers. Like the most badass warriors in all of Errowind. Or anywhere.

She swung it over and over, assaulting the dark and all its shades and shells and all things between or beyond—the spirits—cleaving them away with the double-edged madness of her mind.

The last cry faded into echo, and she—

•   •   •

—woke again.

The sun glared. Her hands, which she still could barely move, rang with the sensation of the axe handle. Her skin tingled with uncomfortable heat. She was probably sunburnt, and badly.

No voices. No figures. Birds sang obliviously in the surrounding jungle. A bug whizzed over her.

She was alone, but she might not be for long. *Move. Come on.* She tried to wrench herself into motion, to send more energy through her veins and faster, but the most she managed was turning on her side.

"P…please…"

She resisted a desire to close her eyes.

•   •   •

The sun had eased up, waning west. A large gray cloud blocked it for a while, even took pity on her with a few cooling drops of rain. Some found her tongue.

Three times now Marilyn had rolled herself over, toward the only passage into the jungle. Each time she'd had to wait maybe twenty minutes between each roll. The effort was taxing, pressing breath from her lungs, strength from her legs.

She didn't feel sick, exactly. The exhaustion reminded her less of the few times she'd been bedridden with the flu and more of the times she had woken up, usually before Joe, to stare out at a world she suddenly wanted no part of, her mind gnawed by that despicable (and thankfully temporary) thought: *Fifty more years of this?*

She'd been spoiled. So goddamn spoiled. Her kids and her husband were more rays of love than many millions of people received in their lives, and yet their main "crime" was that they'd distracted her from illusions, from stupid dreams and fake adventures with people she'd never met. They'd undermined her *her*-ness, even if she'd had no idea what "her" was.

Marilyn groaned. Her aloneness was a living thing in her, a cancer.

Tears blurred her vision.

Several beings had crept into the area. Whether they had been among the troop that had been "feasting" on her, Marilyn wasn't sure. Most just seemed curious, even reverential.

"Get away from me."

Summoning what strength she could, Marilyn placed her palm on the gravel bank. Waited. Inhaled. Then placed her other palm. Started pushing.

She was half-air.

Half-ghost.

Half-dead.

"…don't…"

Marilyn collapsed again. Her head cocked toward the jungle, where she could see the trees, backlit by the sun. There was a howling noise, too, like wind down a tunnel that, over the waterfall, was the last thing to reach her ears before she went under once more.

•   •   •

Night had fallen.

She had more energy. That was hopeful, at least. Her vitals and body parts were reconciling. Gears and motors turning again. Cold thawing.

Fundamentally, Marilyn realized, she was alive, and they—the beings—were not. That was the advantage she had over them. Her Dwarf-Knight had said she was an "Author". She could envision things. Yes. She could *make* things. Move and shake this world. She shared a kitchen with Mother Nature.

Marilyn crawled to the pond and dipped her cup in and drank. She felt chilled, energized.

Turning back, she saw motion in the darkness. Other beings were still, keeping their distance.

Forcing herself up, Marilyn fell instantly to her knees before clawing across the bank toward the jungle. Her teeth gritted, chest throbbing. Stars and spots flitted across her vision and her bones ached. She sucked in breath after breath, hastening with every lame step, lightning flickering down her limbs.

The jungle passage was thin, darker than the night—an Any dark.

Where she might lose herself.

And escape.

And return.

•   •   •

It was hours into this journey when Marilyn recognized her own strategy: follow the sun, as much as possible. She could use it as a guidepost to the shoreline, from which she could maybe navigate the perimeter and, eventually, return to Pyramid Bay.

Pyramid Bay. Why did she need to go back there? Because that was where it had started. Her whole presence on this island chain revolved around a mysterious purpose in those waters, and though Marilyn had no solid reason for it, she believed the bay could bring her back. Hiding behind this vast ancient mirage was her own time, her own "reality", where Joe waited for her, where Tommy and Tammy and Troy—

Stop.

Modest rain made its way through spaces sunlight could not reach. The coolness of it brought relief from her sweat and the humidity.

Beings lurked. Their intrigue, their fear, their desperate hunger, lingered heavy on the air. She tried to remain ever-watchful, her Other senses alert.

Behind a eucalyptus tree, something watched her that was shaped like a kangaroo, kind of. But leathery to the touch. Its eyes bulged black, like an insect's. Its mouth stretched wide in a joyless, big-toothed grin.

Marilyn halted, listening. There was a noise behind her. Though it couldn't have been what it sounded like.

It couldn't have been the *whoosh* of a passing car.

Marilyn whirled around and raced back, leaping over foliage and plowing past the vines until through the trees she saw the clearing— yes, definitely there, and not there before. And there was a metal pole holding up a sign, and—!

Bursting from the jungle, she had less than a second to take in the winding highway before it vanished. The vegetation swept over it once more, like an unseen artisan polishing an imperfection.

Sorrow crashed upon her, shattering her hope, one of the few outposts in her left to break. By contrast, the despair—the deep, visceral frustration—felt familiar, at a temperature even with her soul. God did not get his own universe, no. Had left it up to us to figure it out.

But then, a remarkable thing. That second passed, and the hope rebuilt itself, stronger and more vibrant than before.

She had been on that highway, after all. She recognized it. If she managed to press on in that general direction, she could get to Pyramid Bay. So maybe it wasn't a cosmic tease, she thought, thinking also of the sign that had pointed toward the waterfall, so much as a divine hint.

5

Present Day

When Marilyn awoke, the night felt much later, though she knew it probably wasn't.

She checked her phone. Only forty minutes since and Vanessa had laid down. By the breathing, it sounded like Vanessa was asleep.

She sat up, scooted forward and gazed through the canopy at the faint smudges of other galaxies, feeling simian fear mixed with a grand, invincible purpose.

I've been here before.

More uncertain memories trembled at the rim of her consciousness. How had she survived the jungle?

Thinking of Joe and the kids filled Marilyn with sadness and guilt. She was officially missing now, the news probably spreading through her family and friends. Maybe even to her online gaming friends.

But then, there were no helicopters. No bellowing search parties. That she could hear, anyway.

How would they know where to search?

Movement next to her. She thought it was Vanessa turning over, but it was something *on* Vanessa—a many-armed form, winding around her.

Cautiously, Marilyn sat up and peered closer.

The form held, but barely. The palest impression. It rose up, bobbing in and out of the shadows. The more Marilyn looked at it, the more it asserted definition: patterns, ridges, limbs.

Eyes.

The thing was scaly. As it swiveled toward her, its eyes shone the very color she herself had painted them.

Then there were the tentacles, blossoming out from its bottom half.

Marilyn gasped.

It was the Dractopus. Her drawing. Vanessa's tattoo. Risen, somehow, from the fleshly soil of Vanessa's leg.

She reached out. The Dractopus floated closer, like a pet seeking warmth and intimacy. Its existence was wobbly. Swimming in the blue light of its eyes was an unknowing delirium: the overstimulation of a newborn.

It was a spirit, she realized. Not a "shade." Because shades were just that: shadows. Ideas on the wind. Lighter. "Spirits" were a little more distinct, a little more touchable, able with enough effort to touch *back*. But they couldn't as much as…

Another word trickled back to Marilyn: *shells*.

At some point, she had formulated a crude science. That's what she'd called them. Shades, spirits, and shells. Like in *Errowind Tales*, only she'd added *spirits*, the more intermediary one. Shells were "closest" to us, wearing the finest, outermost layers of flesh. With enough effort, they could show themselves as visibly as any animal or person. Yet with the same effort, they could also cause as much trouble as any animal or person. Those poltergeist videos they showed on *Spooksters* (the real ones, anyway) were probably not angry human ghosts, but shells.

Marilyn also sensed in the Dractopus the dim signatures of many people—glimmers of those she didn't know who had, in their own way, affirmed its existence. She had put it online, after all. Instagram. DeviantArt. Facebook. Many minds upheld its proto reality.

Yet, she'd put up lots of characters and creatures. What was different about this one?

It was, she could only guess, that it had two "parents": she and Vanessa. That in their combined energies, they had pushed the creature that much closer to the physical world.

Wherever two or more are gathered in My name. Christ had been talking of prayer, of course. But was this kind of energy the same thing? A shaping of potential by invisible "Other" hands?

Another word came to her: *Authoring.* She'd used it earlier, and wasn't sure why. This energy, this creative force, had been called the Authoring.

Marilyn shuddered. She felt a rush. All at once, she straddled the great duality of the world, Earth and Spirit, could even reconcile them if she wanted. She felt like she could touch the foundations of the universe, that hiding in her all this time was Goddess energy: so explosively creative, so extraordinarily regenerative so as to, by necessity, have been long suppressed. By Joe. By motherhood. By the church. But now she had come to this intersection of time and space in which all of it, all such primal voltage, could be unleashed.

The Dractopus floated toward the forest, peeked out from the enclave. Fear emanated from the creature. It was hesitant, an infant bird undertaking first flight.

Vanessa had said: *It didn't feel like* me *freaking out.*

Maybe Vanessa's panic attack had come from the Dractopus, its fear at "awaking" in this world. Becoming any kind of a *thing.*

Marilyn walked out into the jungle. "Come on out," she said. "It's okay."

Maybe it wasn't, though. This creature could probably sense those other shades, spirits and shells lurking across those Other acres, where the hunger toward life was so strong it pressed into this world.

She crouched by the Dractopus. It was growing more ill-defined by the minute, dissolving like mist into the night.

"Marilyn?"

Vanessa's voice, from the darkness. But Marilyn couldn't move, couldn't speak.

"Where are you?"

She had an urge to explore. There was a reason she was out here. She had been summoned. *Chosen.* A mission. She had been called to some other time and place and it was all in preparation for—what?

"Are you okay?"

A stream of energy left her. She collapsed to her knees, overcome by sudden exhaustion. Newly nourished, the Dractopus zipped away through the jungle. Though she could barely see, she tried to follow its direction. It coiled around another tree, then moved off again. A crude path formed in her mind.

"Marilyn?"

•   •   •

She opened her eyes. Bewildered. Vanessa was leaning over her, rustling her awake. Birds chirped. The jungle was a dim gray, the sky touched by the faintest pre-dawn light.

Vanessa narrowed her eyes at her. "Why did you move out here? Did you sleepwalk or something?"

Fighting lethargy, Marilyn leaned up. The tree and its enclave were about twenty yards away. She'd been sleeping on weeds and leaves and mud. Stringy earth and clay clinging to her arms and shoulders, itching everywhere on her backside.

"I think," Marilyn said. "I guess, yeah."

"You scared the shit out of me. I thought you'd hoofed it outta here."

"I wouldn't do that."

Vanessa glanced about. "I know."

Marilyn rubbed her eyes. Though physically groggy, a heightened awareness now lived in her. She felt pulled in a certain direction, much as she had after visiting Shane that one time, when she'd sought the petroglyphs in that canyon. Except this feeling was even clearer. Stronger.

"How's your foot?" Marilyn asked.

Hesitantly, Vanessa showed her. Bulbous and purple. Some black.

"It still hurts like a motherfucker," she said. "But I don't think it's gotten worse."

"Good." Marilyn looked in the direction the Dractopus had gone in her dream. "I know where to go."

•   •   •

"And you're sure we're not just getting ourselves *loster*?" Vanessa said, hopping along at her side. "And yeah, I know that's not a word."

At times it was worse than walking on sand, trudging through beds of gnarled brush, Vanessa's arm around her shoulder and Marilyn's arm clutching Vanessa's waist. Sweat pooled in her tighter crevices. Periodically, she caught whiffs of her own ripe odor.

"I'm sure we're not," Marilyn said. But there was no way to convince Vanessa, or even her own more rational self. The knowledge lay deeper, in that Other part of her.

The sun rose higher, spearing young light into the wilds. Birds celebrated. Marilyn would stop every so often, close her eyes and feel the wordless voices, the shape of the jungle.

At one point, after she'd opened her eyes and moved on again, Vanessa spoke.

"Are you some, like, disguised guru?"

"Why 'disguised'?"

"Well, I mean, you're like my age, and, uh, blonde."

"I suppose if I were a crinkled hundred-and-two and hung with crystals, you'd think I was legit?"

"Not necessarily. You could be senile."

Vanessa tugged on a vine to test its sturdiness, then used it to help haul them over a log. "Don't get me wrong—*ow*—I believe you about what you told me before."

They came to the tree Marilyn had been seeking, one of many, brimming with the same familiarity as the one they'd slept in. She placed her hand on the trunk, caressed it. There were mountain apples growing on it, several yards up.

"Hold on," Marilyn said. She carefully relinquished Vanessa, then swiftly clambered up the tree, plucked three apples and hopped down. She bit into one and handed the other two to Vanessa.

"What if I told you I'm actually over a thousand years old?" Marilyn said.

"I would ask what you use to keep your skin so nice. Then I'd ask you the meaning of fucking life."

After finishing their apples, Marilyn reached for Vanessa's hand and clutched it, then clamped her other hand over both of theirs.

"Whoa, tingly," said Vanessa.

"You can feel that?"

"Um, a little. I think?"

"Close your eyes. Listen, Feel."

"I feel my foot, in pain."

Marilyn didn't respond. They stood a moment. She herself wasn't entirely certain what she wanted to accomplish with this. She just wanted some part of her inner universe to blend with another's.

"I hear something," Vanessa said. "Footsteps."

Marilyn opened her eyes. Vanessa's were already open and scanning the jungle. No doubt about it: footfalls crunching ahead, the source hidden by the branches and vines. It was too rhythmic to be a bird or rodent in a bush. Had to be larger. Far larger.

"Could be a wild goat, or pig," Vanessa said.

"I don't think it's either of those." Marilyn charged ahead. "C'mon."

She ran several yards ahead—

"Hey!" Vanessa called.

—where, through the thinning foliage, she glimpsed the shock of blonde hair against the dusky trunks. The frame of a person.

"Hello?" Marilyn cried, hopefully.

She regretted the greeting—*Don't know who this is*—except she did know who this was.

He was staring at them as they emerged.

The Road Walker.

This time, there was something else far more striking about him. As before, his eyes shone with a new light, yet now she knew that light, and instantly. All his other features cohered around it, revealing the impossible. The stunningly obvious.

Marilyn could barely get out the name of her son.

"*Troy*?"

6

620 A.D.

It was about an hour after dawn—some dawn, anyway—when Marilyn reached the coast, and another hour or so before she found her way back to Pyramid Bay.

Her snorkel and mask and fins lay roughly where she'd left them, at the base of a palm tree well out of reach of the tide. The sand on her soles proved comforting, a natural cushion compared to the mud and the rock and the ivy and the soil.

She planted herself by her swim gear, these items she'd initially resisted at SportFort but which now were the only things—and, maybe, Pyramid Rock itself—that gave her some unchanged connection to her own time.

Too afraid to assess the damage to her feet, Marilyn tried strapping on the fins. She quit almost instantly. Either her feet had swollen, or her fins had shrunk. Or they'd always been too goddamn tight to begin with. If she had a blade, she mused, she could cut off the clumsy "fin" parts and have makeshift sandals.

Moving on shaky legs, she cleaned her mask and snorkel in the surf, then stared out at the bay and the flat infinity beyond it. Everything inside her felt shriveled, half the thing it once was.

She closed her eyes. The creatures at the waterfall had reacted to her command. Kind of. She'd picked up glimmers of consciousness, but their "thoughts" were hard to isolate, running together like watercolor paints.

Can you hear me? she asked. Whatever lived in Pyramid Bay, it was older than many of the other spirit-beings she had encountered, more defined and yet, by the same token, *ill*-defined, somehow built of incongruities. Like it was still developing. Like, even though it was "old", it possessed the angry, confused mindset of a traumatized child.

Marilyn waited. The tideline groped closer.

No reply. None she could see, anyway.

She resolved to stay on the beach. There was no way something wouldn't present itself. Maybe the Pyramid Bay Presence would eventually communicate with her. Maybe those people she'd seen in the canoes, the Polynesians, would come rowing back here, though she didn't think that was much of a possibility.

Her swimsuit felt like a clingy, rubbery parasite. Marilyn stripped it off, trying not to feel too self-conscious out in the elements, and laid it on a nearby rock. Then, moving against her weakened state, she set about gathering what debris she could for any kind of shelter or campfire—even as she'd never so much as lit a campfire with a zippo.

She could catch crabs, perhaps. Or learn to spear-fish. Or crack a coconut. Or—

How the fuck am I going to do any *of that?*

It drummed over and over, the nagging terror and helplessness, speaking louder and louder the fact of her "modern", first world ignorance, that she hadn't the first fucking clue how to go about settling the hunger-shake in her limbs, or relieving her many aches.

Rage exploded in Marilyn. She tossed away the two palm fronds she'd been holding, turned toward the bay and screamed: "FUCK YOU!"

She knelt on the sand. For the first time since coming here, she let herself truly weep.

•　•　•

Armed with a rock and a sturdy piece of driftwood she'd found up the shoreline, Marilyn navigated the lava rock peninsula. The surf hissed and churned.

Between her pain, the crabs' quickness and the slickness of the rocks, she kept her pace slow and deliberate. The lava rock was sharp, precipitous, like whatever deity had carved these islands had left its blades here to crust over.

At one point she slipped and her abdomen struck a sharp, jagged edge, knocking the wind from her and leaving a stinging streak of blood across her belly.

After hours of effort, Marilyn managed to catch only two crabs. The process of bashing them nauseated her as much as the hunger itself. She hoped she might do them some justice by managing to spark a cookfire, but even after assembling the driest sticks she could find she was at a loss beyond rubbing them furiously together, harder and harder. She blistered her palm and cut two fingers before giving up.

She looked at the mangled crabs, imagined a thought behind their bulbous little eyes: *You killed us for this?*

Desperate to eat and desperate not to waste, Marilyn cracked them open and ate them raw. Probably it was a testament to her hunger that they weren't as disgusting as she anticipated. And at this point, food poisoning was almost welcomed. It might even kill her: a final, merciful push over the edge.

After dinner, she put together what she could of a shelter made of palm fronds, ivy and branches. It was hopelessly unsound, and still relied mostly on the natural cover of the nearby jungle, but it would have to do. For now.

•　　•　　•

"Psst."

Marilyn stirred, dimly aware of someone on the other side of her eyelids.

"You must see this."

She opened her eyes. The Dwarf-Knight stood over her, a mixture of alarm and reverence on its wide face. Clutched in its right hand was the double-bladed axe.

Beyond the knight's frayed red hair, Marilyn made out bedposts, a stone chamber and a thin sunlit window—the kind medieval archers might shoot out of.

An Errowind *castle.*

The Dwarf-Knight gestured toward the window. The sunlight leaking in struck her as ominous.

I can't, she said.

The Dwarf-Knight's expression fell. "Come see the Dragon."

Marilyn sat up. She had no sheets or blankets to pull off, and she was sleeping in her damp swimsuit. She rose and followed the Dwarf-Knight toward the window, stopping a few feet short.

"Go on."

Cautiously, Marilyn peered out the window, squinting against the tropical sunshine. The "castle" she was in overlooked a familiar green mountain, the one she and Joe had driven down at the base of which stretched Pyramid Bay.

She saw them instantly. Several humps rose in the bay, like small islands. A large, elongated tail snaked above the water, and lay coiled around Pyramid Rock.

The entity was massive, though it appeared less like a dragon than a lizard, a reptile-thing partially submerged and concealing its true scale.

And in the coarseness beneath her Other fingertips, in the rank, primordial odor invading her Other nose, Marilyn recognized it, much as those ancient Chumash muralists had when immortalizing its likeness on those cave walls:

The Dwarf-Knight held up its axe, looked at it resignedly. "I'm afraid…this is hardly going to be enough."

Marilyn noticed something else: pearly white spheres bunched on the beach. They were moving, too.

Hatching.

"Dragon eggs," said the Dwarf-Knight.

Marilyn watched as the eggs opened, revealing a blackness within each one. As they broke, the blackness spread, finding its kin and binding, becoming a single, many-limbed shadow that emerged and dragged itself down the sand toward the waves, where it slipped beneath the surf, where it grew one with the gloom of the sea.

An Offspring. Whatever lived in Pyramid Bay had been seeded by this massive reptile, this dragon-thing.

The Dwarf-Knight clutched her arm, eyes bulging.

"Wake—

• • •

—up.

She inhaled. And sucked in water.

Again. And the brine of the sea flooded her sinuses, her throat, her stomach. All was midnight liquid.

A laser show of terror went off in her. Marilyn convulsed. She was *underwater.* And not of her own volition—something had dragged her here in the dead of night. Her belly-scrape, once healing, rang again with pain.

She felt a clamp around her ankle, tugging with tentative strength. Reeling her.

Marilyn kicked and thrashed toward the surface. Spots filled her eyes, the lack of breath burning her lungs. Her body's every pipe and valve were cinching shut. Panic corroding everything.

And yet, she also felt the first warm ray of a calming light. The world softened. She thought she perceived a vortex above her, one made of all her memories—the days tiled with hours, years with days, decades with years. She was a fish swimming through a coral reef, a whole coral network snaking through spacetime, spilling into unknown ends.

And then Marilyn splashed up through the surface, gasping. She rasped, hacked. A coppery taste in her mouth which might've been blood. She spat it into the chop and swam for shore.

Everything was smeared, breaking down. Her stomach muscles clenched as salt infested the scrape on her belly. The water heaved. A haze settled over her consciousness. Blackness clouded the edge of her vision.

A wave rose, dipped. And she saw it.

The Huna'ia Resort!

She was *back*! Tourists sprinkled along the shore. Yellow lifeguard trucks. Faint whine of a jetski. How much earth and jungle had been scooped out to accommodate that place…how high and proud and dominant it stood.

"Hey!" she cried. "I'm *here*! Help!"

Another wave rose, lowered, and refreshed the scene.

The Huna'ia Resort was still there, but—destroyed. Broken. Cold. Emptied of people. Of life. Less than a colossal throne, it was suddenly a ruin. It almost looked like a bomb had gone off, the whole place abandoned, resigned to a slow, somber reconquering by the elements.

Another wave. Again, the scene changed—the shoreline returned, earth and rock and jungle and her pathetic little camp and all.

She was back, alright.

"No!"

Marilyn scrambled to land and collapsed. Her fists closed around clumps of sand. Her toes wiggled, scratchy. The ground was there. Yes, it was.

She lay still, panting. Any moment, a pair of lifeguard arms would grasp her and help her up. Right? Please, Christ, yes, *fucking right?*

Joe. Where was Joe? Would he still be there, looking for her? Would the kids have come? Were they all in danger?

Something is going to happen. To the resort.

Those dual visions of the Huna'ia Resort…in seeing them, Marilyn realized, she had not actually believed she was back in her own time. Both had felt like apparitions.

Both had felt like things *waiting to be*.

When her normal senses caught up to her, she smelled smoke. Her heart skipped. Was there a campfire somewhere?

Marilyn sat up, glanced around. The bay now looked strangely calm. Over the mountains, thunder grumbled. Except it wasn't a coming storm that had given ominous color to the night sky.

She rose to her feet and staggered along the tree line. Through her dizziness, she kept watch out. She crossed an intersection of sand and lava rock, attended only by her footprints and the small gray particles twirling down and stippling her skin. She wiped them off, leaving charcoal smears.

Ash.

Marilyn rounded a bend, where the eastern horizon spread across her vision. She gasped.

The horizon had exploded.

By comparison, the smoke in the San Francisco bombing had been a bonfire. Yet much as she had with the parade (was it accurate to still say four years ago?), Marilyn had trouble processing the sight.

Even islands away, it was audible: the deep, earthen grumble. Enormous black plumes spread across the reddening sky, some volcanic Hell portal bursting up to corrupt Heaven. Threatening to flip the overworld into the under.

7

Present Day

Bad water. What Troy had said before, when Joe and Marilyn had been Skyping with him and Kevin and Margie and the other kids. And he had said it again over the phone.

Daddy there's bad water you should leave.

Sitting in the hammock, inches above the manicured grass, Joe had just stared out at the endless ocean, phone to ear. He felt like he had passed through a membrane into another reality.

"What do you mean, Troyasaur? Why is it bad?"

A pause. Then:

"It doesn't like people."

"The water itself doesn't like people?"

"Yeah."

"Why doesn't it like people?"

Another pause, during which he chastised himself for even asking his son these questions. For putting him *four*-year-old on the spot like this.

"Because," Troy said, his tone detached, "people're stealing Creation."

The answer chilled him, if only for the slight distance in his son's tone, as if Troy didn't know himself what he was saying.

"I'm not sure what you mean, bud."

Further pause.

"When are you coming back, Daddy?"

What am I doing? Consulting a four-year-old on woo-woo. Then again, he had to give himself a break. Marilyn had become a thinner, wild-type woman in the span of minutes, and Pyramid Bay was becoming a mysterious stew of animal carcasses. And she had told him all those things, about Gordon Lake, about everything.

Joe did not remember much about the rest of the conversation with Troy. He had made sure to say "I love you," he knew that. But Troy's words and Joe's own thoughts had combined into a thick smog of distraction. For the last few seconds, a baffled Kevin had come on the line, chuckle-asking what was *that* all about, and Joe did not remember how he'd replied—only that, five minutes later, he was headed back to the Tiki hut bar, where he ordered four more beers and became the most intoxicated he'd ever been in his life.

Every morsel of his anger was now justified. Everyone who had arbitrarily decided to turn their sharp ends on him—Marilyn, his boss at WaveSystems, his brother-in-law Shane, even God—owed him a lengthy amends.

The tears were manageable at the bar. By the time Joe returned to the hotel room, however, they ran hard and wrenching and messy. The most he'd cried in years, probably since high school or maybe even earlier. With every sob he brought up more of it, convulsing it across the coffee table from where he sat on the couch.

Where was Marilyn going? The "Lofts", she'd said. With some hippie stranger she'd meet when she'd snuck out one night. Like some flighty teenager. Why was there so often a specter of resentment hovering around her?

Don't come back, Mare. Have fun. Have all the woo-woo fun you want. Except she wasn't having fun, right? She was convinced she could play a part in solving something to do with this "bad water." Call up the *Spooksters* team! Whip them out here, up your Insta followers, hashtag your way to celebrity heaven. That's all you're really after, right?

The beer had unleashed a windstorm of emotion, and Joe let it all come. It felt good. Cathartic. But it was also tiring, and he was addled and spent. He lay down on the couch, listening to the rumble-hush of activity below, recognized the ominous absence of the happy, light voices and shouts from the beach. No cliff jumpers. No mothers idly calling for children to be re-sunscreened. No excited cries from snorkelers or surfers, or the carefree buzz of jetskis.

Joe bent his head back, so he was looking upside-down out the sliding glass door. Gray clouds amassed, traced by meager reminders of the sun.

Then, feeling emptied, plagued by dizziness and snotty congestion, Joe sank into blackness.

•   •   •

When he awoke, the blackness held. The only noise was the same testy murmur of the tide.

Joe blinked, leaned up and struck his head on the dull corner of a hangover. The second one he'd ever had. Shame ripped through him. He could barely bring himself to sit up.

The leather of the couch croaked loudly in the dark. Joe peered across the room at the only pinprick of light: the digital clock on the microwave.

9:13.

He bolted to his feet, headache now miles away. Tripping over one of the coffee table's legs, Joe bumbled toward the couchside lamp and switched it on.

"Marilyn?" he called.

He swept through the suite; no sign of her. Next to the humiliating image of her coming back and finding him passed out in a scent of beer and mucus was another of her simply choosing not to come back at all. Or…

Calm down. Check your phone.

He retrieved his phone. Only one new message: Thank you for your auto-payment of…

He'd slept for about six hours, waking only briefly and blearily, enough to be aware that, at some point, rain had fallen. It seemed to have cleared up by now. Breezes rustled the palms. Had Marilyn been out hiking in the rain?

Why hasn't she called or texted?

Every paranoid thought now came coalescing back into him. Who knew anything about that hippie guitar woman, or these "Lofts"?

He called her. Straight to voicemail.

He texted her. Waited.

Failed to send.

Joe inhaled a long breath. He went to the sink, washed his face, then hurried out into the hallway and down to the elevator. He had no patience to wait and so took the stairs, all eight floors, his footfalls in lonely cement echo.

VI

1

620 A.D.

In that space between water and shore, Kaimi found himself afloat in what could have been the very top or the very bottom of the world.

Likely it was some place beyond, occupied only by him and that most astonishing of beings, the Reptile, the apparition he had followed as it made its way to the sea, leaving behind the erupting mountain. Kaimi sensed it had had something to do with the eruption, too.

The Reptile was the Earth made manifest. *Mana* collected, like seawater in a tidepool. Its eyes, burning like stars, nonetheless shone from realms beyond. Its coiled tail like a vortex—a passage to Elsewhere.

He thought: *We came and we disturbed you. Forgive us. Forgive the wayfinders. Forgive Chief Haunani. Forgive Makui.*

Forgive me.

Even with his sea-honed stamina, with his adequate skills of navigation, his intuition, the folly and the chaos of that night had overtaken him. He did not regret the motivation: he was a seer, of sorts, meant for greater things. The Reptile-eyes had confirmed his destiny.

Yet he had been rash.

Kaimi awoke with a mouthful of gravel. He crunched it between his teeth, just to center his realness. He was wet, trembling and clouded with the mothersmell of the sea.

Ashen taste between his lips. Blinking, he saw the death-gray color that had blanketed much of the beach. Though it was daylight, the sky was dark, the sun a pale blind eye through the haze.

No sign of his canoe. With each determined stab of his oar, he had hauled himself far across the waves, across the night. As the volcano erupted, the Reptile had entered the ocean, its head lifting to the sky. Kaimi had been perhaps several hundred yards from it. The Reptile's eyes had dimmed like embers, its body bleeding into nightwaters. Kaimi remembered being able to see the stars through it, and the smoky band across the sky: the home of Rangi, the Sky Father.

Of the Reptile, he had thought: *It spent itself, unleashing the volcano. Now it must rest.*

Presently, Kaimi glanced around. High red bluffs crowned with jungle and mist. He had been tossed upon the greenest of the islands, the one they had first passed.

He rose wearily to his feet. Taking stock of his surroundings and his person, Kaimi realized how empty-handed he was. No blade, no adze, no spear, no rations and no instruments. A fever of mind and spirit had possessed him, and he had launched himself upon the sea toward what he thought might be the very shores of transcendence—only to be pushed back into the elements, with little to start over.

Yet Kaimi had to admit the dizzying swell of liberation, of opportunity and possibility. This island was now his own.

And it was not an insignificant thing—couldn't have been, anyway—that he'd been cast back to the very place they had first passed in that final stretch of the Great Voyage. Where their canoes had been overturned by that formless shadow-being. Where they had seen the woman-creature with the sun-gold hair.

Not far down the beach lay a large green sea turtle. Kaimi walked toward it. Its eyes were closed. His grandfather had once told him that his father, Kaimi's great grandfather, had spun lighthearted tales of turtles being the animals closest to stone, the first to soften to the notion of life.

Kaimi knelt, staring at the turtle, deliberating. It would be an easy kill, certainly easier than others, and more nourishing than scrounging for tidal clams, seaweed or berries. He could start a fire, prepare the meat and have enough to sustain him for the first couple days.

Approaching closer, Kaimi took notice of the patterns in the sand around the turtle, the almost artful swirls she had created in her trek ashore. They ignited something in his mind.

Those visions of the mysterious spiral symbol, the one he'd encountered at sea chasing the Reptile, and…when he'd been underwater in that bay, when gazing upon the shadow-being after it'd flipped over his canoe…

Was the shadow-being in that bay connected to the Reptile?

Was the woman-creature?

He had to find out. Even if it meant a journey across the island.

•   •   •

If she were honest with herself, there was a big part of Marilyn that understood she might never make it back toward the beach—to say nothing of her own time. Her purpose here, her Grand Mission, lingered aimless on the wind and the tide.

Suns and moons would float by, taking with them further layers of meat from her bones and scattering yet more thoughts amid a dizziness that was becoming disorientation that, in weeks or even days' time, Marilyn sensed would become outright delirium—a place of no return.

That morning, she had awoken surprisingly refreshed. However, Marilyn quickly noticed change in the texture of her surroundings. She was also standing, which, unless she'd caught herself sleepwalking, she wasn't sure how—

That's when she saw it.

Her body, her *own* body. Tanned, burnt, peeling and thin. So thin, lying motionless by the bank of the pond.

The waterfall's murmur carried on, as if in eulogy.

She had little time to even begin processing what was happening when she noticed the creatures up the nearby trees, and the two smaller ones just under the surface of the pond—spirits—and more flitting by. Many had the same hungry hyena energy she'd encountered before. Others were simply curious.

This time, however, none encroached on her. All seemed afraid.

Then she returned to her body, and the aches, the hunger, the exhaustion, the pain, all pounced on her once more.

• • •

Sometimes, Marilyn thought she could feel or even see death, looming at the end of every thought. Slowly, it was creeping up, claiming more of her. Her memory grew worse, unless that was just because she tried to snatch upon certain memories and obsessed over how accurate they were. Notions that seemed rational were quickly exposed as anything but.

Increasingly, her strongest nourishment came from inhabiting her Other senses, which grew stronger. Marilyn imagined it like super-hearing on blind people, a kind of compensation; though it also occurred to her that, in peeling away her attachment to her physical body, she was maybe allowing herself more "room" in the Other space. More flexibility to hang those Other senses on forms of her own imagining.

In dreams, and dream-like visions, her Myrulian Dwarf-Knight visited her, scolding her not to leave her body. Not now. *Why not?* Marilyn asked. There was so much beyond, so much potential to explore.

The Dwarf-Knight's eyes burned with something like incredulity. Where do you think any such potential draws its power? Her body, of course. Her body of flesh and blood, which allowed her to participate in the ongoing creation of the world, to "Author" it. Her mortal body was the horse, potential the carriage.

She still had power to give the world, said the red-bearded knight.

To even save the world.

After managing several mouthfuls of water, Marilyn closed her eyes. Could she *will* herself out of here? Not physically—but, mentally? *Other*-ly?

Marilyn held her breath, closed her eyes, and focused—on home.

Home.

First, the house: the weedy front yard, where Troy's play-car sat not far from the coiled garden hose under the hedge, the white stucco walls and the rough, patched-brown roof and the chimney connected to a fireplace rarely used (mostly because of Joe) and the barred windows and rickety automatic garage door and then…

She went further, mentally carving into place the many corners, angles, colors, patterns and senses of her house, even deciding on her ideal LA weather—cloudy and cool-fresh, a day after rain—and she went down the sideyard (can't forget the tarp-covered barbecue grill they'd used only once in six summers, with the spiderweb by the wheel) and into the backyard and then she turned attention to the interior of the house, leaving messes and stains where they should be, like the weird gray blotches on the living room carpet by the TV, and changing nothing of any arrangement or upholstery she'd always disagreed with, and the hallway long and sprouted with the bedrooms of her children and the bathroom where all of them had learned to potty and splashed with nervous excitement through their first bath, and all along she exerted great effort to hold these thoughts together, to not allow the kitchen, say, to crumble into oblivion as she worked on recreating the linen closet.

Her breathing, her pulse, her dizziness and the waterfall noise all became distant things.

Marilyn laid on the living room couch and wrapped herself in the blanket with the cartoon octopuses stamped on it. It was her nest, her favorite place to nap.

She had carved out her own niche in this Other Realm, maybe even a place that would receive her when she was unable to prevent her tired soul from leaving her body.

But she would be alone.

And yet—she did feel a presence. Not particularly close, but it was strong and even vaguely familiar.

Human.

The sudden, new presence was enough to make her sit up. Leaning toward the front window, she parted the shutters and gazed out toward the lawn's edge and the more tenuous backdrop of Turner Road and the neighborhood beyond, all humming with the energy she'd given them.

Someone was out there. In the neighborhood.

Hesitantly, she asked: *Are you—*

•   •   •

—there?

Kaimi awoke, the voice echoing in his mind. Except, he thought, it seemed to have come from another place, perhaps even outside him.

He was curled up in the groove of a banyan. His sleep had been long and restful, sinking him to bottoms where dreams might find ways beyond their dreamer.

He sat up, took in the dawn jungle around him. Much of his focus, though, was on recapturing—understanding—where he'd been in his dream.

There had been mountains in the distance, the only truly natural thing he'd recognized. The surrounding land had been carved into straight lines and shapes of stone and grass, and there were inordinately large, if impressive, dwellings all arrayed together. None had been inhabited—except for one across the way. The place where the voice came from.

It had been a woman's voice, desperate and high and the words (if they were words) had sounded like those of the sun-haired woman-creature in the water.

However, this time he could understand her. Perhaps because this had been a deeper, dream place, one where language blended with pure thought.

Kaimi retrieved his hastily woven vine pouch from where he'd hung it and fished out three mountain apples, berries and bird eggs. He regretted not taking the time to harvest seaweed, but greater hungers had pressed him toward the strange bay.

With some food in his belly, Kaimi concentrated again on that strange place that had visited him: the blocky grass areas there, the stone paths, the cold geometry of the dwellings. He tried to walk in the direction from which he thought he'd heard the woman's voice.

"I am here," he said.

As soon as the words left his lips, however, he knew it was not right. He had spoken his own language, through the crudeness of his throat and tongue. He needed to speak deeper.

To speak, perhaps, in a spirit-tongue.

He focused.

I am here, he said.

Yet his voice did not feel resonant. It was, he imagined, like the throat of an infant hoping to sing like a storyteller.

Kaimi decided to experiment. The image and the sound of the woman-creature bobbing in that bay had been burned onto his memory. He recalled her now, and anything he could of that moment, all its many edges, the fear, the rain-scented winds, the stormclouds, the woman's exotic beauty and the soft heaving of the sea.

I am here.

• • •

She had been in Tommy's room when she smelled it—the faint, wispy smell of the sea, and a strong flavor of salt on her tongue. She had the disorienting sensation of being in the ocean.

Marilyn walked down the hallway to the shared space between the dining and living rooms, where the much stronger sea odor made her stop.

As did the tiny waves of water lapping in under the front and back doors, flooding respectively across the carpet and linoleum. Slivers of kelp lay like green snakes in the shag.

Faintly, she heard:

—am—here—

She rushed to the front door and pulled it open. The yard was a surreal waltz between weeds and water. The neighborhood beyond had been largely absorbed into an image of the Kauai jungle, house-windows and slanted roofs and lamp posts jutting between tangled trees and ferns.

Like the tide upon the shore, another vision was wearing away her own. Still, Marilyn could not see any other presence.

Follow me, she said. She focused on the sound of the waterfall, inviting the presence toward this space. *Follow me and follow the waterfall I will not hurt you I will not I—*

·   ·   ·

—need help.

Kaimi was almost certain now that the voice came from the woman-creature. Who else here would have such a strong presence?

The spirit-creatures were here, lurking as they had on the previous island, but those here felt fainter than expected. As if they were cautious, maintaining their distance.

As if something had frightened them, and word had spread.

His whole life, Kaimi had heard stories that instructed him in navigation by the stars, by flight patterns of birds, by the swells of the ocean and the turning of the wind. But now he was being summoned toward a new mode of direction, an instinct-beyond-instinct that opened pathways in the wild, that perhaps allowed like-beings, those of like-*mana*, to find one another—invisible connections such as those that shaped constellations.

He was being summoned to engage those spirit-senses, which, in relating them to bodily senses, he saw as the fishing spear to one's fingers—where the latter's reach was limited, the former could penetrate farther, and more resolutely.

And so he walked.

•   •   •

He was two days into his journey when he heard the waterfall, and when he found her.

Kaimi had trouble believing it was the same woman-creature, but he had no doubt it was. If the sight of her malnourished body had tried to dissuade him, the *mana* he'd felt through the trees, even before laying eyes on her, was more than enough to convince him.

If anything, her mana had only grown starker, like sunlight spreading through newly vacant spaces in canopy.

She was dying.

When he broke the tree line, her back was to him, her golden hair sullied and matted and darker than it had been out on the bay, much as her blistered, sun-browned skin. The shiny black rubber-cloth she'd worn was torn and dirtied, beneath which ran a pronounced spine.

Kaimi stood still, caught between pity and guardedness—a flicker of paranoia that this might be some crafty illusion to lower his defenses. It did not seem so, of course. Strange as she looked, this creature was as much a woman as Akamu or his own mother had been.

Slowly, she rolled over and opened her eyes. A quiet gasp escaped her lips, and she struggled to sit up but almost immediately lost her balance as she began sobbing.

Her *mana* radiated. Kaimi sensed relief, but it was not, as far as he could tell, relief at possibly surviving. It was the relief of company. Of a solitude broken.

Kaimi made his way to her.

Marilyn saw only the person-like outline, blended with the jungle dusk. In that very first moment, she wasn't sure that someone was actually, physically there, or if it was some mental projection. Or a death-angel had come.

In truth, she didn't care. The sight of another human form was enough to shoot through her a thunderbolt of emotion.

But in that second moment, she knew. This was the presence she had felt in the vision of her neighborhood. They had shared an Other space.

They had found one another.

And in the third moment, it became clear: this was the same man with whom she'd met eyes days (weeks ago?) when floating out in Pyramid Bay. The one man among all others across those dozen canoes whose eyes and energy seemed softer. More understanding.

Marilyn collapsed back onto the ground, where she stared up at the canopy and sun quietly shredding one another, until all of it was eclipsed by the wonder-eyed moon of the man's head.

She asked: *You can hear me, can't you?*

His face twitched. He stepped back. While familiar with his own Other senses, it was clear that Marilyn was using them in a way he had not, or had not thought possible. She had only her desperate situation to thank for this, the harsh, wind-lashed world that had blown her closer and closer to its borders.

I c—, said the man, his voice fragmented, *—understand.*

He pulled open a pouch stitched with vines, then plucked out a greenish-red fruit shaped like a pear and held it toward her.

Quivering, Marilyn reached up and took it. Her fingers brushed his palm.

My name is Marilyn, she said.

He appeared to process this. To chew on the syllables.

Then, what sounded like a name brushed her Other ear:

—Kaimi—

Marilyn put the fruit to her lips, and bit. Her teeth hurt; she didn't even want to imagine what they might look like now, how yellow, or how red her gums must be. The coppery flavor of blood had been consistent in her mouth for the last several days. When she would awake, she would be terribly queasy, sometimes throwing up the water she drank.

The fruit was crunchy and sour-sweet, not unlike an apple. She didn't remember coming across these in her attempts at foraging. Though, in the paranoia of her own ignorance, she had not really allowed herself to partake of much.

Carefully, she ate.

•　　•　　•

Feeling marginally less weak with several items in her stomach, Marilyn thought back on the scant bits of Hawaiian history she'd picked up, most of which pivoted on the names Captain Cook, King Kamehameha and George Q. Cannon, the Mormon missionary. She thought, at most, they had been only a few hundred years back, but didn't trust her grasp of historical time, let alone of a land and a culture about which she knew so little.

Then, she remembered the glass case of human bones in the lobby of the Huna'ia Resort. To her mild surprise, the kiosk's listed date had stuck with her: 1500 A.D.

To Kaimi, she said: *Fifteen-hundred years?*

•　　•　　•

Seated a short distance from "Marilyn", Kaimi took in this uncertain revelation with a long breath. It was amusing and peculiar, to think that such acres of time—fifteen-hundred years—would, when referring to the past, seem not that long. Ancestors could reach millennia. But in speaking of the future, it was a daunting, tidal wave of time.

Kaimi said, *Do you come from the same place as the spirit-beings?*

No. Her spirit-tongue was crisp and forceful, markedly more confident than his own.

Kaimi picked up a stone from the bank. He scouted for a relatively smooth mix of soil and gravel, in which he drew—

—a spiral.

Marilyn's eyes widened. She curled her lips inward.

—*the bay,* Kaimi said. *The—*

—*Reptile,* Marilyn said, picking up on Kaimi's next thought.

I've seen it, she said.

A light warm rain began to fall, ticking across the trees.

Do you know what it is? Marilyn asked.

Kaimi frowned.

As best as she could, Marilyn conveyed her dream-vision: those eggs on the beach that broke open with shadow, forming the dark presence there, the Offspring. And the giant Reptile-thing, its tail curled around Pyramid Rock and the same being draped dormant over Shane's neighborhood in Los Angeles and the Chumash rendition of it, crawling endlessly up that cave wall.

Kaimi appeared to hesitate. A brief, out-of-body picture wafted through Marilyn's head—this blonde woman from 21st century Los Angeles sitting across from an ancient Polynesian sharing the same soil. It was so improbable as to almost feel probable.

How often had something like this happened? They couldn't have been the only ones. The world's law made exceptions; and, maybe, in unique circumstances, it exercised strange authority to unite its children.

Kaimi asked: —*Reptile—sleeps?*

She was about to reply when more images came to her. They were loose and runny, but Marilyn knew they had come from Kaimi. His feelings and memories filled in the more ambiguous gaps.

Through his eyes, she saw the Reptile in the darkness, astride a volcanic ridge. Its glowing eyes were markedly distinguishable from the night sky, as well as the brightening magma behind it. She saw it out at sea, its tail curled in that spiral, and felt what Kaimi did: that it knew of him, and knew of his awareness of it.

By what Marilyn could glean, he also seemed to think it was responsible for the eruption of the volcano. That the Reptile was in deep communion with the forces of the earth.

Marilyn wasn't sure of any of this, of course, but based on what she had come to know, to feel, some dots, possibly connectable, began to form.

It could be resting now, she said. *Like it sleeps for years and years, then—*

—summons earth-power, Kaimi broke in, *and—*

—needs to rest again.

It also became clear to her that Kaimi held the volcano erupting in no uncertain coincidence.

Our arrival, he said, meaning his village, *disrupted—*

His voice became "garbled."

Disrupted what? Marilyn pressed.

A few seconds later:

—mana—the mana—*of these lands.*

That word, "mana", had circled his thoughts. Marilyn recognized the meaning of it the second Kaimi gave it a name. As far as she could tell, it meant life energy. Life-ness.

Had the Reptile responded to the arrival of Kaimi's people? Had it lain across that volcano, dormant and absorbing what sheer energy it could—spring-loaded to unleash it all at some cataclysmic moment of its choosing?

If so, Marilyn thought with a chill, what did that mean for other places in the future?

•　　•　　•

Kaimi tried to remember Grandfather in the field that day, speaking to him in idle speculation of "dreamfruit", how all mankind partook, how all mankind knew ultimately the same flavor, how its juices might be the source of all our *mana*. That just as a demigod once brought fire to man, the fruit of this tree (which Grandfather had simply made up) had snuck into the darkness of our souls the capacity to imagine, to create alongside Nature.

He had never felt another's dream before, mingling with his own. It was like the smell of another's cooking, wafting into one's home. It could be sweet, enticing, disruptive. Beyond her pale skin and yellow hair, there was doubtlessly something "other" about Marilyn: a closer union between the plane of *Rangi*, heaven, and that of *Papa*, the earth.

Though there was clearly something "other" about him, too. And with every word and image she put in him, and invited from him, that passage within Kaimi seemed to grow wider. It also grew noisier, as the voices of the jungle reached him deeper and louder.

One dream-image of Marilyn's he focused on: the Reptile, submerged in the bay, its cluster of eggs cracking open, the shadows oozing out and amassing and moving on their own. She had called the shadow-being "the Offspring."

The shadow-being in the bay, Kaimi said, *is the offspring of the Reptile?*

There was a pause.

I think so, Marilyn said. *And I think we're here because of it.*

Why had he felt so strongly that the Reptile had summoned him? That he was the exception in his village?

He could see and feel it, of course, and other spirit-creatures. By far, it was the largest spirit-creature he'd ever encountered. But, Kaimi mused, he also understood its plight. Perhaps there were very few in this endless world with such insight, or sensitivity, and so that was why Marilyn—gifted even more than he—had been summoned here, too: they were to be the guardians of the child of the Reptile. To protect it.

Perhaps, he thought, to warn away other travelers.

Perhaps, to preserve something of the natural *mana* of these lands, and these waters.

•   •   •

The nibbles and the chunks of food became multiple bites, some of which made Marilyn queasy. Yet she closed her eyes and pushed past it as best she could, figuring her stomach had grown weak and temperamental and needed a chance to adjust. To unknot itself from these weeks of isolation, disorienting terror, anger, dread and giving up.

More than simply rebalancing blood sugar, what brought her back was the presence of another; more, one who *knew*. Kaimi's presence injected into her a new feeling of purpose. Maybe she'd not been crazy to assume some "mission" lay before her.

By virtue of appearing, of sharing this Other frequency, of knowing of the spirit-beings, Kaimi had cracked through her entombing malaise, sent upon her a ray of hope.

A glimmer, even, of faith.

It surprised her, too, how quickly her physical body returned to her once she started moving; indeed, once she had a *reason* to move. Twice now Kaimi had foraged for food in the jungle, bringing back in his pouch a number of fruits, eggs and some kind of hard-shelled nuts he warned her not to eat too much of (miming what she could only imagine was diarrhea, which made them both laugh). Though he was far more adept at surviving here than she, it was clear that even Kaimi was adjusting to this environment, that several if not many things here, on this island much later called Kauai, differed from his homeland.

With awe, she thought: There was no one here before Kaimi's people. He was among the first.

When time came for the third foraging excursion, Marilyn accompanied him. With every hour, a vital springtime bloomed in her bones, her limbs refilling with an excess of energy. They gathered what dry wood they could for fire, as well as any sharp rocks which could be used to whittle torchstands or spears. Marilyn found herself climbing more trees than she ever had, the vines and varied branches offering many hand and foot holds. Her body displayed a wiry flexibility she'd never known before.

At one point, as they returned to their "camp" by the waterfall, Marilyn asked: *What does your homeland look like?*

—no longer have—home.

She hesitated. *What* did *it look like?*

As soon as the images began filling her mind, Marilyn knew she was unprepared. Tension gripped her—a dueling set of memories rocked about her mind, as if Kaimi struggled to convey only one but the other was simply too strong to be ignored.

She saw him and another young boy, playing about surf-lashed rocks. A woman called to them, and the name 'Makui' floated into her mind. Then, this boy was suddenly far older and standing blood-spattered over a dead body, his once-mischievous eyes burning with vanquish, with vengeance and even lunacy.

Then there were fields where crops were growing, and an elderly man was there, speaking to Kaimi with exuberant love and wisdom that was quickly lost in the roaring memory of village-consuming flames, and the death-screams and silhouettes of loved ones scrambling for their lives as faceless hostiles pursued them, all the smoke in enviable eddy from the chaos, and accompanied by God knew how many slain souls.

The visions convulsed in Marilyn. Tears sprang to her eyes. It was a shot of some concentrated tragedy. Of incalculable loss.

She put her hand over her eyes. From Kaimi came a sentiment that was something like an apology, but she put out her hand and sniffed and tried to assure him that, no, it was alright. And she realized the callous shortsightedness in her thinking that she wouldn't be impacted as much by him as he had her.

Please, she said, *show me—*

—more.

He hesitated. Marilyn wanted to be shown further visions of his home, the "Old Land", as Chief Haunani had called it. Why? He sensed a thirst for what was to her uncommon experience, to know something utterly foreign. But he didn't want to dwell any longer on the old world, on the loves lost, the shores of his upbringing blood-streaked and charred by warflame and madness.

All of it pained him. And, by their connection, it clearly pained Marilyn, too.

He remembered those moments late into the night, miles from the ravaged village, when Chief Haunani had spoken to them of far-flung lands, a half-mystical place he believed was not unreachable. These lands were "clean of the stain of man," Haunani had said, prompting Kaimi to wonder why they themselves should seek to upend that purity. Because in that long starry stretch of night, Haunani had quite exercised his gift of gold-tongued inspiration, dabbing their wounded hearts with hope and the balm of *possibility*—the sense that the world was enormous, perhaps endless, and that it alone was their home, sure to offer a new corner of itself where they might thrive.

The sense of *possibility* circled his mind, stronger now than ever. It was what had driven them upon the open seas, what had driven him after the Reptile and what, ultimately, had driven him here.

• • •

Not counting Hawaii, Marilyn had only been to three places her entire life: Oregon, Los Angeles, Nevada and Utah—and Nevada was just a blurred passage to Utah. For the rest of the world, she had only Google Images, magazines and documentaries.

Nevertheless, Kaimi seemed curious to know more of her world. And so, after uncertainty about where to start, Marilyn began showing Kaimi things like highways, cars, computers, skyscrapers, movie theaters and airplanes. In doing so, though, she found herself less proud than ambivalent about it all.

Kaimi's reaction was more confused than anything else. He saw in Marilyn's pictures a variety of people—indeed, a stunning variety—but so many were enclosed, not unlike poultry in pens. Their world had retreated from the boundless to the bound.

Yet—the further he and Marilyn meshed, the more their shared Other space grew, well beyond Marilyn's neighborhood or Kaimi's village.

Stories churned between them, the Israelites and Eden and the demigods and the planes of *Rangi*, heaven, and *Papa*, the earth. There were untouched forests and vast deserts and creatures exotic and prehistoric and then there were things from *Errowind Tales*, too, and as they moved deeper into the chaos of one another they also, in a way, moved farther from the existing shells of known ideas into wholly virgin places no one had ever gone prior, worlds dusted over distant stars and worlds divorced from our laws and worlds beyond the dark. Both Kaimi and Marilyn felt in themselves and in the other the almost carefree zest of children scampering about a playground, only this was their own, an Other sandbox whose every grain they might shape by the force of their will, this force of "Authoring."

As these memories and imaginings blossomed between them, Marilyn and Kaimi felt as though they had run headfirst into a fecund garden of the other, a place where sky melted into sea, present into potential, ideas into infinity.

They were unleashing something in themselves, and in one another—the glow of some fundamental animating furnace.

A new vision opened between them, as if some external dream had elbowed into their space.

They saw an ocean roiling below a giant thunderstorm. Lightning gave brief form to massive black clouds. No life here. No life *could* be here. Not yet. Ashen odor on the primordial wind.

This is Earth, Marilyn thought. Earth before life.

Another kind of cloud descended on this young world, except this cloudbank contained beings. Forms. Shades. Silhouettes. Spirits. Shells. Beings of fleeting existence, if you could call it existence. A tide of beings, beings Yet To Be…attracted to the growing, life-giving beacon of this new Earth.

The beings pushed aggressively across the empty sea and land. Weaving, mingling, stretching, overtaking one another. Spectral and silent as these things were, still they pulsed with a violence and a hunger as brutal as any carnivore pursuing prey.

It was all a sort of Grand Auditioning. A proto nature. A wilderness before life, in fact a wilderness vying and fighting and eating *toward* life.

Potential, seeking greater potential.

• • •

In their return to their usual faculties, neither Marilyn nor Kaimi could make out definitions in anything: all was formless.

But then, everything began to resolve, and to solidify: Kaimi and Marilyn, the waterfall and the trees and…

…except, some things remained cloudy. Marilyn was reminded of her experience at the Kekepania Falls, how the many spirit-beings had surrounded her. They had been hungry.

Now, in sensing them all about the jungle, creeping toward them, she felt another energy from them—rapture. Wonder.

Kaimi saw them, too, of course. The spirit-creatures between the shadows, some more present than others. He thought he could make out the hovering orbs of their eyes.

They were amassing, like animals to a watering hole. The waters of potential, he thought. *Mana*-waters. Water was all things, all shapes. Water no less than god.

He and Marilyn, through their Immersion, had perhaps tapped into a deep reservoir, and flooded this place, inviting, by the purest scent of Being, all those that Could Be.

• • •

Kaimi could taste the salt and the kelp on the air, could make out, by ear, the shape of every wave.

He awoke on the beach. No sign of Marilyn nearby.

His thoughts returned to the night of Makui's uprising, the volcano and the Reptile, how in a blink he had moved a mile into the jungle without recollection. Like he was being summoned.

Just past dawn, and the sun was pushing up east, slowly draining color from the clouds. He must have traveled down here during the night.

Kaimi closed his eyes.

Marilyn? he said.

Kaimi rose and faced the surf. He closed his eyes again. Being with Marilyn had elevated his spirit-senses and, not without some hesitation, he reached out spirit-fingers into the bay.

Something was clear: the Offspring of the Reptile was frightened. It possessed otherworldly power, but did not seem to truly recognize that.

Was it his duty to awaken this power, and to protect it?

Again, that familiar spiral symbol flashed through Kaimi's mind. There were feelings of confusion and contempt around it.

The spiral symbol felt almost like the "cry" of a lost child, seeking its parent across untold Other acres. Was it calling out for the Reptile?

He himself knew loneliness, and isolation. As did Marilyn.

We are here, Kaimi said, making steps toward the bay.

I am here.

•   •   •

She had started counting the days she'd been here using rocks and sticks and leaves, but had abandoned the effort so many eons ago. Or so it felt.

Now, time had collapsed into one blob, gradated with light and dark, and the occasional splash of storm. Marilyn had no real idea how long it'd been since she'd last been to Pyramid Bay. It could have been a week as much as a month.

Kaimi, she said, her desperation mounting as she navigated the trees. Hopefully she was going the right way.

She heard no response, so she called, "Kaimi!"

Only wind.

Marilyn had awakened that morning, tense from a dream of waves and shadows, Pyramid Rock standing among them.

He's gone to Pyramid Bay, she had thought with a shudder.

Encompassed by jungle, with the sea appearing in the small crevices between the trees, Marilyn called out again.

Kaimi—

Walking farther, then:

—Mari—

She heard him, yes, barely. It was nearly drowned out by other noises, noises like language but incoherent to her.

Though her body protested, Marilyn pushed herself through the foliage, struggling to ignore the spirit-creatures around her and to fix her 'scent' on Kaimi. She received only snatches of his voice. Mostly it was frenetic visuals of sea-lashed rocks, and a large form just under the surface of the water, drawing closer.

And then the trees began inching away from one another, the jungle leveled off and the beach spread before her. Marilyn stumbled into sun and sand, where she saw Pyramid Rock jutting against the horizon.

And, standing just next to the black spire, gazing into the water—

"Kaimi!"

Marilyn scrambled toward the rocks, nearly slipping. Clouds had gathered farther out at sea, the wind just starting to whip the waves and water into a mild storm frenzy.

Kaimi looked up. He stood, knees bent, poised on a rock dripping with foam. When he met Marilyn's eyes, his shoulders lowered, and his knees straightened.

He gestured toward the water.

What are you doing? she asked, clambering across the slick rocks.

Even at this distance, his Other voice was broken. Marilyn sensed something about fate in his reply.

Then, as if timed, a large wave surged up behind him. Kaimi saw none of it, however: with a graceful folding of his body, he dove straight into the sea.

Marilyn cried out. Halfway across the peninsula of rocks, she tried to watch for him. The ocean roiled, hissed. Maneuvering as carefully as she could, she tried to gain better foothold but slipped and tumbled down to the bottom of the peninsula where she tried to hang onto a moss-slicked rock but the sea was greedy and insistent, and a strong rill of water rushed upon her and pushed her back into the bay.

Kaimi—

Seawater went down her throat, up her nose. She struggled to orient herself, to flail her way toward where she thought Kaimi might be. Bubbles rioted across her vision. In hasty motions Marilyn surfaced to breathe, taking in little air as well as mucus and water.

She felt detached. The sea sloshed.

Can you hear me Kaimi where are you—?

Marilyn thought she heard a response but couldn't make it out. Splinters of emotion she couldn't identify.

The texture of the water almost felt spongey, like a pliable thing that could be stretched, manipulated, bored through. As the bubbles zipped around her, Marilyn thought she glimpsed pictures in them, colorful, psychedelic flashes of people.

People she knew.

Her lungs burned for breath. The oceanworld before her was warping. Drawing away. There was a spinning motion around her, like a slow whirlpool forming—or a vortex.

A vortex rimmed with bubbles, she realized, all the bubbles of her life's moments—where Mom cooed over her. Where she was baptized. Where Dad lifted her by her wrists like it was nothing. Where Uncle Steve covertly read to her her first comic book. Where in sophomore year she'd had her only non-Joe kiss.

And then there was Tommy and Tamara and Troy, and the heat of all these memories warmed the ocean-cold, like they were draping themselves over her skin and her soul, re-seeking her, and then Marilyn reached out to one moment near her and thought, in the back of her mind, that, no, in spite of what everyone might assume, the universe had *not* made up its mind about what it was or what it could be, that it was still soft, that still there were pockets of All Possibilities, of timelessness, of ill-defined laws. Pockets like this very bay.

Kaimi no where are—

The water warmed considerably. The sky brightened.

And then Marilyn was surfacing, gasping. She felt like her face had melted. For several turgid seconds she forgot who she was, even her name.

Instinctively, she turned toward shore. People were there, dozens and dozens of them. So were buildings, tall and glittering in the sun.

There were others in the water, also, splashing to reach shore. Panic in their movement. The word "shark" fluttered on the wind.

Something had happened to her, she knew that. Did it have anything to do with a shark? She saw nothing around her.

No.

What had she been doing? She'd been snorkeling, separate from Joe. But something else.

Some*one* else.

She was among the last to emerge from the waves. She walked forward, collapsed, crawled several yards. Beachgoers looked at her, eyes wide. Several motherly hands whipped to cover their children's eyes.

The realization crashed down on her: she was naked. In public. At the Huna'ia Resort.

I'm back. But where had she gone?

Nearby, a trotting lifeguard—"Ma'am, are you okay?"—to whom she held up a hand as she rose to her feet, and then…

"Marilyn?"

Joe, coming toward her.

"Oh my God," he said, face pale. "Marilyn, what's going on?"

Slowly, lamely, she lifted her arms to cover herself as best she could, the waves pushing and pulling at her feet.

•　　•　　•

On one of the islands between they discovered Kaimi's canoe, sea-tossed and lying upside down in the surf. Makui had insisted they search for a while and call for him, even if no one, including himself, thought Kaimi would be anywhere nearby.

Makui read in the eyes of his brothers what they were all too afraid to express. However, overcoming his own anxious instincts, he said, "Kaimi was too adept an oarsman for the ocean to have taken him. We must keep looking."

Two outriggers strong, they continued rowing about the islands, circumnavigating each one. They bellowed the conch shells, especially at night, when they would also light the torches as the stars gleamed down upon their lone lights.

•　　•　　•

Makui was the first to spot the dark figure prostrate on the beach. He ordered their direction, aware all the while of the others' fear—for he felt it, too—in heading for the strange bay where weeks ago they'd been overturned by that strange wave, where they had encountered that "seal" shaped like a woman with sun-colored hair and extremely light skin.

"Kaimi!" he cried, as the canoes drifted closer. He blew into a conch shell.

No movement. A cold weight swelled in Makui's gut. Whatever conflicts they had suffered, Kaimi *was* his older brother, the only immediate sibling to escape the warfare that had driven them to these islands in the first place. Kaimi also had access to a hidden world, possessed vision and understanding that surpassed that of any chief or priest they had known.

Kaimi had been afraid of his own power. Now, Makui thought glumly, as the outrigger rode the waves toward the beach, whatever passage was open in Kaimi had sealed shut forever.

Makui was the first to disembark. He carried a sharktooth blade, in case of any ambush from Haunani's sympathizers. The solitude here was palpable, though. His elder sibling was the only human being these shores had seen.

Maybe.

Kaimi lay on his stomach, head turned in perpetual gaze upon the sea. It struck Makui, the apparent freshness of the body. Wet and stippled with sand, the flesh bore only a hint of gray. The eyes held a remarkable echo of life, so much so that Makui wouldn't have been completely surprised if his brother's mouth moved. Some *mana* remained in the dark of Kaimi's vessel. Even the death-stench wasn't too offensive.

"Are you still there, Kaimi?" he said.

Only the wind and waves answered. It was difficult to make out the emotion frozen on Kaimi's face. It could have been awe as much as terror.

Working quickly, they buried him farther inland, beyond the reach of the tide. The whole time Makui felt watched, and a growing compulsion to leave. He wondered if the "spirit-beings" Kaimi had spoken of when they were younger—before he restricted himself from speaking of them—had gathered about as they put him in the soil. Maybe they were perched up the surrounding trees, peering in from other realms.

As they returned to the outriggers, Makui stopped.

—help help—

It was as if the wind had whispered in his ear.

He looked upon the bay. Though it might have been his imagination, the color of the water had darkened. A strong wave crashed ashore, reaching farther than others and pushing petulantly against the outriggers.

—help Makui help—

"Kaimi?"

He stiffened. He considered exhuming his brother and taking him away from here. Perhaps Kaimi's soul was still tethered to his body. Perhaps removing his body might liberate his soul.

The others studied Makui. They feared him, certainly. And though he wished no harm upon them, Makui wanted to maintain that fear. It kept matters sustainable, and easy. And one of the best ways to maintain such fear was to not show it himself.

In moments, they were pushing back out upon the sea, passing the tall, spearhead formation of lava rock that marked the terminus of that cursed bay.

2

Present Day

"Who's 'Troy'?"

She barely heard Vanessa's question, as they stood there in the jungle before the Road Walker.

The man looked on Marilyn with a fog of uncertainty she'd not seen before in him. The name (which, with a mother's conviction, she was positive was correct) did not seem to stoke any recognition in him.

But he's there.

How had she not seen it before? Another new-ness in his eyes, completing the image of her son's impossibly matured features and form.

Marilyn stepped closer, arms out to cup his face, or embrace him.

"Troy, is that you?" she said. "How is that *you*?"

And then, several step away from this man that might be her son, she saw that fog in his eyes pass. Another awareness peered out from those sockets, dimming the glow of her youngest.

She stepped back. The new eyes studied her with far more interest. The Troy-man lurched forward, his mouth working back and forth like it was unhinged, strange half-word grunts surging up his throat.

"Marilyn, what the hell?" Vanessa said behind the trees. "What's going on?"

The sheer bewilderment in the Troy-man's eyes broke something in Marilyn. She felt like she'd betrayed her son. Failed him, even.

Vanessa stumbled and fell into view. Marilyn hurried to help her up, holding both arms.

"Who the fuck *are* you?" Vanessa said to the Troy-man.

All three stood still for a moment, Marilyn and Vanessa watching the Troy-man who watched them with that confused, working expression.

Then, another light came to the man's eyes.

"I'm s—suh—sorry," he said. "Not all of us are ac-c-ccustomed."

Marilyn and Vanessa looked at one another.

"Accustomed?" Marilyn asked. "To what?"

"H-h-harbors."

"What does that mean?" Vanessa pressed.

His eyes rolled up into his head for a second, then came back down. He patted his arm, his shoulder, his hip—crudely sculpting his container. Marilyn thought she understood.

Bodies.

He means bodies.

•   •   •

Per Vanessa's photo, the Lofts were a small cluster of treehouses built across several banyans. Up close, the lack of any real maintenance was clear. Much of the wood looked rotted or askew, several of the dark windows were broken or altogether shattered and the sagging bridges and staircases seemed two heavy steps away from collapse. Squinting, one might not be faulted for thinking its host trees had grown right-angled tumors. A certain grandeur had retreated here, ideals in ruin and fading gracefully back into the nature that had inspired them.

Toward the other end of the village sat an old pick-up truck, parked by the overgrown remains of a road.

Vanessa pointed. "Does that truck still work?"

The Troy-man stopped. "I d-do not know."

"Would you mind if I tinkered with it?" Vanessa said. "If you'll notice, I can't exactly run out of here."

Between her wariness and her limping, Vanessa's confidence came across forced, though the possibility of a ride out did give Marilyn a little hope. She also wondered: if people had once lived here, and those like the Troy-man could walk out of here and back, they must not be *too* isolated.

"W-we d-d-do not drive," Troy-man said.

Marilyn was positive, too, that she had been here before, not in these exact Lofts but in this area of the jungle. And she hadn't been alone. Forest-growth had since edged into different patterns and spaces, and much more recent habitation lingered on the air, but there were still signatures of far older energies, and older passions.

Second by second, minute by minute, Marilyn felt the awakening of her Other senses, bringing back a current of memories.

She felt…him. She saw that face, the hard features, the sun-dried skin, the soft, distantly understanding eyes, and with it the name— *Kaimi*—returned to her among an avalanche of knowing from that hidden time. She tingled. It was like everything about Kaimi came back to her, filled her, even. Everything, save the man himself.

In returning to her own century, her circuits had been scrambled, her memory fragmented. But even so, how could she have forgotten? How could any part of her have relinquished that strange kinship with Kaimi, the mutual comprehension that had fused their spirits quicker and deeper than anything she'd experienced with Joe? Or, really, with anyone.

"It's more dilapidated than I thought," Vanessa said, looking at the treehouses.

Voices scurried through Marilyn's head, unknown languages though she did pick up smatterings of English. She sensed Other touches of rough skin, of hair, of slick, slimy textures. Smelled Other whiffs of rank, wild odors. All of what she sensed seemed near, though less distinct than she might have expected.

Then, they appeared.

Some came from the nearby jungle, or stepped out from behind the banyans, or appeared in the broken windows where they gazed out like ghosts from a Gothic manor.

All were thin, and all wore torn or dirty clothes. Marilyn noticed men, women and children, as well as multiple ages and ethnicities though most looked to be younger—twenties or thirties—and white, native Hawaiian or Asian. Those with lighter skin had been tanned years beyond their age.

Vanessa's hand clamped Marilyn's shoulder. "Um."

"It's okay," Marilyn said to her.

"They look different," Vanessa muttered. "They all look different."

Marilyn, of course, saw it too. The different-ness lay not in their age, race or sex. It lay in that fluid dance of…essences?…across the eyes of these people.

These bodies harbored spirit-beings. They were walking hostels.

We won't hurt you, Marilyn said.

A rustling of replies. The Troy-man put up his hand, and they all stopped. He turned to her. His eyes remained those of the being that had taken over after the brief, wrenching moment when Troy had shone through.

We know, he said.

Vanessa fidgeted. "Are they cool with us?"

"I think so."

"Do they have food?"

"Fffffoo-ooo—ood," echoed an elderly man, his pitch riding what sounded like several voices.

To the Troy-man, Marilyn said, *Do you know who I am?*

The Troy-man just stared at her. No reply.

Do you know the…harbor you're using? It pained her too much to say "body", like he was a dead, ventriloquist's dummy. She was glad for their strange euphemism.

Finally, he said, *We know little. Beyond what memories remained.*

Her stomach knotted.

He added, *There are very few.*

She swallowed. *What are—*

Having barely just asked the question, her mind was suddenly assaulted with disjointed images: dark crashing sea swells, sharp lava rock and a passing flicker of Pyramid Rock, the surf, the beach.

And hovering behind it all were the echoes of an impassioned ache. A thirst to know.

Marilyn stumbled back, sobs catching in her throat. "Oh God."

"What's wrong?" Vanessa asked.

Marilyn wiped her eyes, her nose. In a moment of perverse release, in which all things were naught in one great, malicious joke, she gestured to the Troy-man. "I think…he's my son."

"*Huh?*"

"Not right now. But—"

You let the cat outta the bag, she thought.

"Marilyn, what are you—"

"Not right *now*," she almost screamed.

Vanessa recoiled. Working through the distorted lens of her thoughts and emotions, Marilyn's imagination assembled a picture of what might have happened. In some very possible future, she had never returned from that time with Kaimi. Over the years, Troy, the most sensitive of her children, had fallen prey to the bizarre enigma of her disappearance.

And, when old enough, he had traveled here, only to meet with an accident, maybe a time-slip like she'd had. One that hurled him not to the distant past, but to now. Maybe he had been brain-dead, or comatose, or gravely wounded. In any case, an accommodating vessel.

Why were you in Pyramid Bay? Marilyn asked the Troy-man.

After a bloated pause, in which he surveyed the rest of the community, the Troy-man's eyes changed, and, in a different voice, replied:

The Offspring.

She said: *The creature in Pyramid Bay.*

The Offspring, said the Troy-man, *has sustained for centuries.*

There was bewilderment, even envy, in his tone.

"Can I help you?" Vanessa said abruptly.

Marilyn turned to see a young Asian woman approaching Vanessa, slightly crouched, her eyes cycling excitedly with different reactions, different ideas. Curiously, she reached out her hand—toward Vanessa's Dractopus tattoo.

"It's okay, Vanessa."

Marilyn glanced back at the Troy-man. These people, these beings-in-people, stood at that ever-fluctuating tideline between the elemental and the ethereal. They were vulnerable, easily worn away or, with a strong enough push, swept out to oblivion.

She said: *You fade, don't you? All of you. You fade over time.*

Marilyn figured this was the reason for the envy in the Troy-man's tone: somehow, the Offspring had defied death, had not faded, had perhaps settled like a permanent, simmering storm in Pyramid Bay.

And these bodies, these "harbors"—hey weren't so much walking hostels, she thought.

They were convalescent homes.

•   •   •

The Troy-man led them on a sturdier path, a staircase up the southernmost banyan tree that led to a platform sagging with rot. They trod carefully, Marilyn still clutching a hobbled Vanessa. The other denizens gathered behind them, some remaining on the ground, others following them up.

"Is there anything I can use to wrap my foot?" Vanessa asked, as they made it to the treehouse.

The Troy-man looked at her. He paused, caught in the moment, as if everyone (thing) behind his eyes were conferring on how best to answer that question.

Finally, he stammered, "W-w-we h—sss—hh—"

Multiple voices appeared to tumble over one another. Marilyn picked up what he was trying to say and played translator: "They have supplies."

They entered the first treehouse, not unlike what Marilyn might have expected from the outside. Cobwebs and dust had settled over a once-busy space. There was a corner of old tools and a pile of unframed, mildewed paintings, vividly abstract.

Toward the far wall stood an emaciated older man, shirtless and sporting a long ashen beard. With careful, deliberate gestures, he was dabbing red paint on a hung map of Kauai. In its entirety, the map was stippled with childlike finger-paintings of basic figures, triangular peaks, flames, clouds and other, more ambiguous geometric shapes scattered around the island. Only a few colors were represented, though most of them were one shade of red.

"I think that's him," Vanessa said, half-whispering to Marilyn and gesturing to the painter. "The guy that watched me and Tatiana surf the other day."

Vanessa lowered herself onto the corner of an old, detached cupboard, where she studied her injury. Several other denizens appeared in the entryway. One of them, an older Asian woman, fought to control violent twitching in her face and arms.

"You all live here?" Vanessa said, with a wrinkle of her nose.

"Ye-yyyyeeees," said one of the women, contorting her mouth.

The painter paused in his duties and turned to them, his milky eyes staring everywhere.

On a decrepit shelf, Marilyn found black-and-white photos of young men and women, all unshaven and nude and cuddling in hammocks or bunk beds. Scrawled in crayon on the back of one photo: *Aug '68.* She was taken aback. The man appearing most commonly in the photos was a younger version of the painter. Some hippie-turned-harbor.

What are you painting? she asked him.

Though the old man didn't respond, he did step slightly aside, as if inviting Marilyn to look closer.

Over Pyramid Bay on the map, he'd painted a red spiral.

What is happening there? she asked.

It was hard to tell if the ensuing silence and expressions were one of dumbfounded ignorance, or disturbed knowing. She sensed a mixture of both.

Animals are dying, she said. *People could be dying. Please. What's going to happen? What's the Offspring going to do?*

Multiple voices answered at once, but the reply was uniform enough that Marilyn could understand.

It wish-wishes—violence—

She had a flash of memory, one that felt like a dream but true, a premonition of the Huna'ia Resort broken and shattered and sitting in ruin.

She asked: *Violence…on the resort?*

More images returned to her: the dream of "dragon eggs", cracking open their shadow-yolk on that beach, the strange mass hatching and slipping into the waters of Pyramid Bay. The lizard-like petroglyph in that painted Chumash cave. The enormous Reptile being—the "dragon" itself—that Kaimi had spoken of, that drank Earth-energy and spat it back. That, according to him, had stirred the eruption of the volcano.

Vanessa pushed herself up from her seat and limped over to the corner filled with old tools. Slowly, she knelt and began sifting through them.

"I wonder if I can't get that truck started down there," she said. Looking up sternly at Marilyn, she added, "We should bunk there, by the way."

"In the truck?"

She threw furtive glances at their company. "Yes."

Marilyn turned back to the Troy-man.

It was left in the bay, wasn't it? she said. *The Offspring.*

Yes, said the Troy-man. *It holds a captive light.*

Before she could ask further, he added:

A human light.

• • •

"Marilyn," Vanessa said, as they approached the truck. She carried a box of tools scrounged from the treehouse. "Tell me right now: who exactly are they? *What* are they?"

Her mind raced. To Marilyn, the rational and irrational had reconciled. What she suspected of these "people", their bizarre nature, made sense to her on an intuitive—perhaps Other—level.

"Think of them," Marilyn said, "as hosts."

Reaching the truck, Vanessa pulled the passenger's handle and the door popped open. "They're fucking possessed. Is that it? Is that what's going on?"

The wildness in Vanessa's eyes, the whiff of contempt and defeat in her tone, made it seem like she was on the verge of forfeiting all expectation of the world being explicable, or even good.

"Yes," Marilyn said. "And no."

The truck didn't look terribly old, and the interior wasn't as bad as Marilyn might have expected. The upholstery was torn, but mostly intact, and the tightness of the space, in the sprawl of the wilderness, did seem inviting.

She watched a spider scuttle across the dashboard. It slowed halfway to the steering wheel, as if suddenly aware it had outside spectators for the first time in its existence.

Marilyn closed her eyes. "I'll back up."

"Okay."

"There's the physical universe. Us. All this."

Vanessa snorted, hobbling her way to the front of the truck. "I got that. And a spiritual universe."

"Well, yes. But…"

Vanessa popped the hood. "But?"

"For all the billions of life forms on Earth," Marilyn said, "I'm pretty sure there are countless more who never made the jump. To life, I mean."

"Yeah. So?"

"But—they still exist. As potentials."

"Wait." Vanessa leaned on the engine compartment. "So, like, all the creatures that *could* have been are actually somewhere?"

"And the closer they've gotten to becoming," Marilyn said, "the more they're able to interact with us."

"Interact in what way?"

"Think poltergeists. Think doors opening by themselves. Dolls moving."

Vanessa hung her head, shook it quickly like a dog bucking off water.

"But," Marilyn continued, "they need a lot of *mana* to be able to do the kinds of things we can do everyday: move things, make things…"

"What's 'mana'?"

Marilyn hadn't even realized she'd said the word. "The stuff of us, and everything," she said, after a second's reflection. "The life-force, basically. They seek it. They want to become part of it all. If they don't, they fade into unlikelihood. Into oblivion."

"So, hold on, they want to become part of—"

"Creation," Marilyn said. "If this world is the page, and people and everything else in it are the 'authors,' then think of the pen as *mana*, the instrument of 'authoring'. Of creating more, well, creation."

Vanessa scrunched her face. "Okay."

Marilyn reached into the truck and put her index finger under the spider. When it crawled on her hand, she brought it out into the open. It inched timidly to the end of her finger, where it froze.

"You could say," Marilyn remarked, "that this little guy is an author, too. Any living part of this world. But he doesn't have as big a grip on the pen as we do."

"I think we're taking over the pen," Vanessa said. "And the whole fucking story."

Marilyn set the spider down on the forest floor, watched it scuttle into the shadows.

Vanessa peered down into the automotive pit of pipes, tubes, and nozzles. "Then—what are *these* people? You said one of them was your son?"

"I was wrong. I was seeing things." Marilyn glanced back toward the Lofts. Three of the denizens were playing clumsy catch with a stone, one man was getting inordinate recreation out of peeing in the bushes, and one couple—both young-ish—were playing what looked to be an adult game of doctor.

"They are children," she said, idly.

Or, perhaps more accurately: strangers in a strange land, seeking all avenue of touchable discovery.

•   •   •

Toward evening, the residents made their way into the jungle behind the Lofts. Some of them carried containers of fruit and vegetables. Some walked with hands or arms linked while others rode piggyback. Many of them consciously touched, grazed, or held every object that delighted their fancy, which was almost everything. A woman stared acres into a single blade of grass. A middle-aged man and woman chased birds. A younger man tried to "poke" every gnat in a cloud of them that danced amid thinning shafts of sunlight.

Still others began relishing the fruit and vegetables. From what Marilyn could observe, though, it was difficult to classify it as true relish—the act of eating prompted a spark of initial joy, followed often by twitches, jerky gestures, or what looked like mild seizures. She could only imagine what might be happening: that the spirit-beings within were clamoring and competing to be the first at that rush of taste.

She took some of the picked fruit back to Vanessa, who continued fussing over the truck, using a flashlight she'd found among the tools. Vanessa's demeanor was irritable, insistent, at times a quivering word or two away from tears. She scarcely made eye contact and was doggedly focused on the task at hand. Marilyn figured it wasn't just a desire to make it back home but also a defense mechanism, a way of blurring into the background the questions and strangeness crowding her mind.

"Are you sure you can get it running?" Marilyn asked her.

"I have to," she said, without looking up. "I have to."

As Marilyn followed the others into the jungle, she asked the Troy-man: *Where is everyone going?*

Three voices answered, one for each word:

To—the—waters—

The trees closed in on them. Shadows grew to meet the night. Growing louder: the hush of a waterfall. All individual paths through the jungle converged at a clearing, which Marilyn could feel before she could see.

Watching them approach the clearing, she realized this was some kind of ritual. Maybe even a religious event. There was no formal gathering, no songs, no chant, no specific ceremony beyond a filling of the space with awed whisperings—a wordless mantra of gratitude and wonder and reveling. A soaking-up.

This is where the First Two, said the Troy-man, *opened the higher light.*

And it hit her. It was like walking into an electrical cloud. Marilyn's whole being hummed with light and memory.

She knew where she was.

A waterfall formed the centerpiece of the clearing, lacy white streams down to a shallow pond where the Troy-man and others waded, or splashed playfully and fell awkwardly backward into the water. Some cupped their hands and drank, or showered and bathed themselves in ways that looked like a self-baptismal.

The water was sacred to them.

Water is evidence of god, Mom had once said. But maybe water—renouncing all shape, crucial to life—*was* god.

Marilyn reached the pond. Stepped in. Tingles shot up her legs. She walked in deeper, maneuvering around the bathing denizens, and put out a hand to the trickling lullaby of the waterfall. A sob rose in her throat.

The falls had looked like the calligraphy of an unknown language, an endless story somehow told in one, neat sentence. She'd been part of it, lying there starving and weakening and helpless.

In that moment, she felt herself in this water. She felt Kaimi.

In that moment, she felt the power they had shared, that meshing of *mana*, of whatever inner magic lay in them. That explosive force that could both imagine and make worlds, maybe even Universes. It had been an untapping of a geyser.

An eruption of Potential.

In that moment, she remembered the ring of spirit-beings had gathered around them.

In that moment, her Other senses were bombarded by the energies she and Kaimi had thrust upon this place.

In that moment, that sense of Gaia energy returned to her, and Marilyn knew what she could do—indeed, knew what she *had* to do.

She had to take this power with her to Pyramid Bay. Had to confront the Offspring, before it carried out in full whatever it sought to inflict upon those shores.

•   •   •

This time, she was high, so high she thought she could see the slightest curvature of the earth. The land spread below, a mix of dense forest and desert with several mountains bunched near its center.

Was this Errowind? Or Hawaii? She couldn't tell. Somehow, it felt like both, even if it didn't quite look like either.

What was she? She was no longer a spectator, like she'd been with her Dwarf-Knight. That was clear. She was something.

Something large.

And—she was flying! The wind and clouds whistled past her. She angled down toward the forest.

She pumped her—wings?

Twisted her—long neck?

Whipped her—tentacles?

Shouts and movement erupted from the woodland as she soared low over the canopy. She took in the sights much as she had when cruising over the coral while snorkeling, the strange denizens below scattering like so many frightened fish.

And there were many easy pickings, morsels prime for plucking by any of her appendages. Swelling through her limbs was the power of great, prehistoric beasts, of gods, of myth, of mind. Of the very merging of creator, and creation.

She was the Dractopus, *and she could—*

—rooooooowwwwwwwOOOAAARRR—!

Marilyn wrenched awake. The nearby bellow echoed through the jungle.

"Yes!" shouted a voice. "The Frankenstein touch! Never fails! Ow!"

She sat up, feeling antsy. Like a surplus of energy had filled her.

She heard a metallic rattling. Clanking. The truck's hood was up, the driver's side door open. It took a second for her to orient herself. She was in the passenger's seat of the old pickup truck, of course, and it was trembling, growling.

Running.

Vanessa shut the hood and hobbled over to the passenger's window, where she met Marilyn's eyes with a cautiously proud grin.

"I got it going," she said. "But I'll need you to drive."

Marilyn wasn't sure how to respond. Her gaze drifted beyond Vanessa toward the treehouses. In the dawn stillness, they'd assumed an even stronger specter of ruin. She saw no movement in the windows or entries, no visible reaction to the sudden engine noise.

"Do you want to say goodbye or something?" Vanessa said. "I just want to get out of here. It looks like there's enough of a road we can follow."

Marilyn took a breath.

"No," she said. "We need to go."

•   •   •

Half a mile in, the violent shuddering and diesel smell were making them both sick. Several times they stopped with an ominous *crunch,* every jam bringing with it the prospect of being lost yet again. With a strong enough push, though, the truck kept on.

Vanessa pulled down the window and threw up. She kept her head hung outside, despite the invasive sweep of the foliage.

"Sorry," she said, wiping her mouth with the back of her hand. "Apparently I haven't logged enough hours on a jetski to accustom my gut to trucking through the jungle."

Marilyn placed a hand on Vanessa's thigh, intending no more than comfort, the way she might have done with any of her kids. Vanessa covered her hand with her own.

Eventually the old road began asserting itself a little more, two tracks scarring the green which took them down to the more well-traversed road closer to the base of the mountain. The bouncing lessened and Marilyn's stomach began to settle. Her hope rose—though any light in her had not far to shine before dread rose to meet it.

"There's a road," Vanessa said.

Passing a bend, they could see through the trees the strip of highway below. Marilyn punched the truck. It growled back. By now, smoke was leaking out but she didn't mind as much. They had a direction. They were back.

"We shouldn't drive this on the highway," Marilyn said.

Vanessa squirmed in her seat. "We can hitch."

"As in, hitchhike?"

"What other option is there? I sure as hell'm not regular-hiking back."

About fifty yards from the highway, Marilyn eased the truck alongside the dirt road and killed the ignition, almost convinced she'd done so the moment it'd decided to die on its own. She climbed out and gathered Vanessa's gear from the bed and helped her disembark, clutching her waist as Vanessa leaned on her shoulders. They limped together like conjoined twins toward the highway, where the first car passed blithely by.

There were no more visible cars either way. The hills dwelled in their ancient, mist-swept meditation. Marilyn thought she could hear a constant, murmuring rush, like running water only far more expansive.

Vanessa examined her ankle: swollen and purple, dark vessels snaking out.

"We'll have whoever drop us off at the medical clinic," Marilyn said. Then—a car.

A white sedan, though it was going in the opposite direction towards Lihue. Vanessa held out her thumb anyway, as did Marilyn. Right now, *any* civilization, any proper care or shelter, sounded ideal.

Remarkably, the sedan slowed and pulled off toward the side of the road. The gratitude and relief in Marilyn right then was enough to forgive all of humankind's sins. For now.

Still holding Vanessa, she ambled across the highway as the driver's side window came down, revealing the kind-but-weary eyes of an older man with white hair.

"Are you girls okay?"

"Mostly," Marilyn said. "We got lost hiking. She needs a doctor."

"Looks like you both could use a doctor. Where're you going?"

"Pyramid Bay," Marilyn said, gesturing. "The Hun—"

The man's face fell, his eyes retreating. "I just came from that direction. Road's closed."

Marilyn felt like someone had just partially unscrewed all her limbs, so that any movement might just collapse her to the pavement.

"No one's getting in," the man added. "It's a bad scene."

3

Two officers came by the lobby and spoke with Joe, receiving basic details and asking basic questions—*Did you have a fight? Has she done this kind of thing before?* He wasn't sure what to say. It had been a fight, kind of. And she had tendency to do things within this ballpark: wondering off in San Fran, for one, or sneaking out of the hotel room after hours. But not like this.

Neither of the officers had heard of a place called "the Lofts". Google searches proved strangely unhelpful, as well.

Sleep, of course, would be a stranger that night. Joe knew this, but it was not the primary reason he avoided returning to the room. Unseen, the room would become a reservoir of hope and potential, a place that in any given moment could play host to her return, so long as he, the observer, stayed away.

Kauai—and most of Hawaii, as he recalled—shut down early, so a lot of the Tiki bars and cafes were dark. One of the hotel bars was still an hour from closing, though, and Joe stopped by and ordered a red wine which he finished in four burning gulps.

He put a tenner on the bar and pushed off toward the beach, passing through mazes of lounge chairs and rain-slicked pavement, past the iridescent glow of the main pool and the idle chatter of people engulfed in jacuzzi steam.

A makeshift chain-link fence had been erected across the beach sand, complemented by ubiquitous signage and caution tape. Even though they'd underdone a large, coordinated effort to remove the carcasses, a rank hint of death still hung on the wind.

As always, the waves rolled in, rolled out. The tropical breezes carried a sudden slight chill.

"Sir!" called a voice.

Joe turned. A burly officer strolled from the gloom. The resort seemed to be taking no chances.

"I'm not going any further," Joe said. "Don't worry."

The officer nodded.

"Any idea what's going on?" Joe asked.

The officer shrugged. "They're running tests. That's all I really know."

Wandering away, Joe came to the same hammock from earlier. This time he laid all the way down and stared up at the clouds as they quietly ruptured, revealing the scattered stars in their midst.

•   •   •

Somehow, sometime, Joe fell asleep again. A strong warm wind brushed him awake. The patchy clouds had since come together in a gray film over the dawn. Birds whipped across the sky, soaring hurriedly inland.

Disoriented, Joe winced as he pushed himself up in the hammock. The few micro-seconds of forgetfulness gave way—Marilyn was missing, he was desperate and depressed and his mouth, unwashed and haunted by liquor, tasted positively rancid. And, for the first time in his life, he'd slept outside. Like an actual beach bum.

He shifted himself off the hammock, rubbed his face. His scalp itched and he went nuclear on the scratching, his fingertips coming back with faint smears of red.

Shouting. Down by the beach. The wind grew stronger, whistling out toward sea as more birds flew in the opposite direction over the resort's main building. Across the rolling lawn, several mice scurried inland.

Something ancient inside him began humming with dread.

Joe rose to his feet, walked over and peered toward what he could see of the bay. Was the tideline always that far out? Then it struck him.

It was *still going.* Receding. The ocean inhaling a big breath of itself.

Sirens sounded, long, protracted air-raid wails. Over and over. The whole energy of Pyramid Bay was like an animal roused violently awake, startled into mortal combat.

Bad water.

The wind strengthened, the sound of the gathering wave louder like a cacophonous wet groan. Someone near shouted "Get *away*! Get *high*!" Though he'd no idea if the person were addressing him, Joe didn't need the starter—he was off and running, pushing against the wind, following the rodents and the birds who were now suddenly much smarter than he.

—water's ALIVE—

Others scrambled through the courtyard, most of them older. An elderly man tripped over a lounge chair and without thinking Joe rushed to help just as the man's wife and another couple did the same and soon the man was on his feet again and hobbling, Joe at his elbow while he breathed an unbelieving "thank you" and no one answered, plied so violently as they were by the instinct to help and the growing instinct to save themselves as the hissing roaring crashing surged behind them.

"Keep going!" Joe cried. "Don't look back just keep *going*!"

Even as he said this, Joe had to fight his own furtive glances at the chaos where everything appeared flung from the earth, to be broken and rendered indistinguishable from all other debris.

—doesn't like people—

The resort lobby was only minutes away, but in a second of dreadful clarity Joe knew that none of them would make it. The cosmic film reel slowed its spin, and Joe saw those final acres frame by frame, a whole body of sensory detail breaking open that he'd never been aware of, the secrets of his own awareness hidden between moments like items lost between couch cushions. So much of himself and the world denied, forgotten, dismissed.

Why had God made so much of it inaccessible?

Showers of salt-spray across their backs. Screams. Pleas. Thundering mayhem, ungodly pillaging and wrenching as the wave uprooted all in its path with the casual ease of one ripping up weeds. Fingers of soapy surf reached them, splashing up their legs and sweeping them off their feet and separating Joe from all else and the water swelled and tossed him backward and for the first time he saw it: the horizon rushing upon them, carrying life and non-life, like some rogue element scraping up ingredients for a new mad concoction and then the resort's glass entrances shattered and the seas charged and bellowed and flipped and rammed and saltwater flooded Joe's sinuses and lungs and eyes and he coughed and convulsed and struggled to grab anything God *anything*, his vision blurred though he noticed something with a dorsal fin floating beneath a chandelier and thought with playful delirium: *There's a shark in the lobby.*

He saw another thing, too, though in all the chaos it may well have been a hallucination— something rose beyond the wave, a Creature, something horrific and unknown, standing there as a conductor before an orchestra, overseeing this insurgency of some blasphemous new Nature upon the old.

4

"Hello, this is Joseph Toomey. I'm clearly unavailable right now, so—"

She clicked off the phone. With the amount of text messages, she was well into double digits. The signal wasn't very great, either, but she managed to update her social media status as "Safe from the Huna'ia tsunami", and to send personal updates to everyone who immediately mattered: Mom, Dad, her siblings—except Shane—and Kevin and Margie, so that they might tell the kids.

When the driver, Hank, offered them his USB phone cord, Marilyn had asked Vanessa if she wanted to charge her phone first.

"Go ahead," Vanessa said, gazing out the window. Her expression was difficult to read. There was something of relief in there, and sadness, but, more than anything, a sense of shutting down. Marilyn thought about asking how Will or Tatiana or the other "firepit" friends might have made out, but kept quiet.

She waited the interminable minute for the dead phone to boot up. She closed her eyes, unable to control the small bursts of helpless terror detonating across her body. Her hands were cold.

According to Hank, and to the bits of news from the radio they heard before Marilyn asked that he switch it off, the thing was being described as a "freak tidal wave." Caused, perhaps, by unknown shifts deep in the ocean. A climactic domino in a series of unknown, geophysical triggers.

In a past life, Marilyn would have been one of the many watching such a tragedy unfold on TV, or across online news feeds. She would offer frowny emojis, or empathetic mutterings, while a good third or more of her attention would still be sunk in a drawing, or dealing with her kids, or trekking through *Errowind*. She would defer to The Experts, those exercising their jaws with theories, and would, somewhere along the line, quietly try and square the tragedy with her belief in a divine plan.

Now, she felt like the only person who knew anything. Who knew that, sometimes, purpose *did* lurk beneath the random, but nothing of it was divine. Who knew something of the nature that wore this nature as its mask. Who knew, right now, two truths—one, what had truly happened. And two, why.

It was because she had failed.

Yes. She had failed. Completely. She had been brought here to stop the tsunami. It had been up to her to figure it out, to uncover her fate, to employ the talents and wisdom with which she had been both innately blessed and, through hardship, won.

Failed.

It would not be productive to flagellate herself, though Marilyn couldn't help it. If only because such judgment was animated by another awful thought she could not bury, the one that, in all the words bubbling up in the face of Joe's possible death, stood out against the tragic, the despairing, the dark.

Liberation.

• • •

Hank dropped them off at the ER in Lihue, and Marilyn helped Vanessa inside. In the waiting room Vanessa scratched out paperwork, as they and those around them—all ailing in their own right—kept a grim shocked vigil before the TV, and the garish graphics of the cable news cycle turning over and over upon the catastrophe.

"…no warning…"

"…experts believe…"

"…tens of millions of dollars…"

"…untold body count…"

"…rescue teams…"

"…reports of strange animals…"

In the seat next to her, spoken at a decibel low enough that Marilyn thought maybe she'd just imagined it, Vanessa muttered, "Is that thing really there?"

Marilyn half-turned toward her, not making eye contact. "Yeah."

"And that spirit-thing caused this?" she asked, in a slightly higher voice. "You really think it caused this?"

Though it might've just been her anxious imagination, a few nearby people glanced in their direction.

Marilyn nodded.

"How?"

Not now, Marilyn wanted to say, but felt obliged.

"The animals," she said, in a low voice. "You know the dead animals in the bay?"

"Uh huh…"

"It was sucking their life force." She almost said *mana*. "Juicing up."

"To cause a tsunami?"

Again, Marilyn nodded, slowly. What Baldy had done to her cat Tardis—and, a little, to Troy—the Offspring had done across dozens of species, over multiple seasons. Stealing life. Building its arsenal. Its muscle. Prying its way into some god-like power.

Which meant, too, that it was spent. That right now it might be the weakest it'd been in quite some time.

Unless, said a voice, *it has more up its sleeve.*

How many had the Reptile borne? All over the world? Were they like troops deployed, awaiting incursion, ready to do what they could to charge up the arsenal of Nature and deploy it on us as we blithely built and blazed and ate our way across more of this world?

After Vanessa was carted off in a wheelchair, Marilyn kept watch of the TV. CNN began playing a video, shot by someone driving in the hills above Pyramid Bay: shaky footage of the shoreline far below, the few mite-sized people scrambling as the bay waters receded, exposing all the rock and coral she'd once swam over.

It was the pulling-back of an archer on a bowstring. The piercing shot imminent.

Then—the wave, all concentrated element crashing down upon the resort village like watery crocodilian jaws stretching and reaching in hungry savor. Except for the higher floors of the Huna'ia Resort, everything became a churning stew of mad ocean.

Marilyn lowered her head upon clasped hands and closed her eyes. She tried to settle her stomach.

She opened one tentative eye, glanced at the TV. Live chopper feed now. Pyramid Bay and the resort village were still mostly submerged. The damage looked immense.

Counting what she could of the Huna'ia Resort's floors gave her some comfort. The water rose only to about the second floor. Their suite had been on the eighth. 812. More—the tsunami had happened in the early morning, which meant Joe was likely in their room, and still in bed.

Likely.

Still—wouldn't he have woken up?

Wouldn't he have called her by now?

•   •   •

From the ER they took a sullen, quiet Uber to Vanessa's place, a rental backhouse on the outskirts of Lihue. In noticing Vanessa's crutches and wrapped ankle, the driver remarked that they'd gotten to the hospital just in time, before the hospitals and medical facilities would be ablaze with caring for tsunami victims as they were found and flown in. Honolulu stood on alert, too, ready to receive who they could.

Marilyn followed Vanessa down a canvas-shaded sideyard next to a slightly shabby, one-story home. Chicken and roosters clucked and stuttered about the backyard. "Hey girls," Vanessa said to the birds, all of whom maneuvered in her direction. "I know, I know. I'm back."

The inside of Vanessa's backhouse proved cozier—and cleaner—than expected, consisting of little more than a central living room with a couch (no TV), kitchen extension, bedroom and bathroom.

"Obviously, you can crash here however long you need to, or not," Vanessa said. "The couch is surprisingly comfy."

"Thank you, Vanessa. Thank you so much."

Vanessa leaned her crutches against the kitchen counter and sat at the small, two-person table there. She carried a hint of dismissiveness toward the crutches, as though having them was nothing new. She pulled out her phone and began texting.

"Could I take a shower?" Marilyn asked.

"Sure. I don't really have too many proper towels, but you can rummage in the closet."

"Thanks." Marilyn stepped forward, then halted. "Do you have clothes I can borrow?"

"Uh huh. Hold on. I'll get some out for you."

"Thanks again."

Marilyn went and opened the closet. She noticed instantly the wetsuit hanging on the back of the door. Then, the single scuba tank and fins stored in the corner, under a bathrobe. On one of the shelves was a mask, far more heavy duty-looking than those Joe had bought at SportFort.

"Do you scuba dive?" Marilyn asked.

"Yeah. I haven't in months, though."

Marilyn grabbed a towel, closed the closet door and made for the shower.

•   •   •

How long had it been since an actual shower? Standing under the warm water, her tears joining every drop from her nose and chin, Marilyn tried in vain to drive such thoughts away.

At the waterfall, the Troy-man had said: *This is where the First Two opened the higher light.*

Had she and Kaimi been those beings' own Adam and Eve? The catalysts for them reaching some higher awareness? The thought made her shiver, though not with fear.

In a cloud of steam, Marilyn emerged wrapped in a towel but could find Vanessa nowhere, only the gym shorts and Yamaha jetski tank top draped over the couch for her.

"Vanessa?"

She heard soft snoring. She followed the sound and peeked through the only bedroom door, where she spied Vanessa curled up on her bed, asleep. The sight of her uncorked a deeper exhaustion in Marilyn. She could do with rest, too.

If she could sleep.

She dressed and laid down on the couch. Kevin and Margie had texted about Zooming with Tommy, Tammy and Troy, but Marilyn had used the then-legitimate excuse of a weak signal. Though it was no longer legit, with Joe up in the air she didn't want to see their faces or hear their voices, or field the questions. She wanted to deliver an answer, however awful it might be.

•　　•　　•

The ocean found every pore. It was noticeably colder, too, as if much of the heat had been sucked from the bay. She floated in this blue vacuum, sunlight winking just meters below the surface before giving way to the darkness below.

And the darkness stirred.

She was swimming, too, furiously, scanning every which way for—

Kaimi, *she called.* Where are you?

He was here. He'd just been here. He had jumped into the ocean.

Marilyn—

Kaimi…

—help—

This moment had been the last thing she remembered, before the space around her had distorted, and she found herself bursting up into her own time, her own world.

But something else had happened. There was that darkness, the unfolding, shadowed bulk of the Offspring. And drifting toward it…yes, something limp, something—

Someone.

It was human-shaped.

Marilyn surfaced, took multiple gasping breaths. Her lungs unclenched, a little. Swells splashed over her.

She realized: it was Kaimi down there.

Gulping another breath, she dove below. The pressure grew in her ears, her eyes. The Offspring had become more visible. It groped for Kaimi's motionless body, enveloped him like a burglar's gloved hand might a small jewel.

No!

She'd been told: It holds a captive light. A human light.

—help—

Was Kaimi still alive? She didn't hold out hope. It seemed like their connection was waning, that he was calling to her from a place increasingly distant—much as the cry of someone caught in a riptide, moving farther toward eternity.

• • •

"Hey."

A tap on her foot.

"Hey."

Another tap. Stronger.

Marilyn opened her eyes. Vanessa sat on the arm of the chair, her face pale, holding a glass of amber liquid on ice. She gestured to another such glass on the coffee table.

"I gave you more ice," she said. "I figure you aren't really the hard liquor type. But it's all I got at the moment."

Marilyn sat up. Her head pounded, especially the area behind her eyes.

Though she was grateful for Vanessa's hospitality, Marilyn found herself resentful of the woman's abrupt, almost invasive presence. Not to mention the presumption of throwing alcohol in her face, though in all honesty being drunk didn't sound half-bad.

"Is this something to celebrate?" Marilyn asked.

"Are you fucking kidding me? How about being *alive*?" Vanessa swirled ice in her glass. "Plus, drinking isn't just for celebrations. It's for the other end of the spectrum, too."

Marilyn took the glass in hand. "Thanks."

"I've been checking the updates," Vanessa said. "As far as I can tell, they haven't released any names. It's all still chaos right now."

Marilyn exhaled. "And you're sure it's okay I'm here for the time being?"

"Of course." Her gaze fell to her glass and held there, as though she were trying to make out a bug in it. "Could be good for me to have a roommate, anyway."

Roommate. The word frightened Marilyn beyond all reason. It meant longevity. It meant limbo.

Marilyn picked up her glass and gulped a mouthful. Felt the slightest loosening of oppressive bonds.

"Vanessa," she said.

"Hm?"

"How difficult is it to scuba dive?"

•   •   •

"What do you think you can *do* down there?" Vanessa asked. Loopy with three drinks, her eyes were a minor tempest of terror and incredulity. She lay on her bed, her bandaged foot propped up on a pillow, the wrap covering the bottom half of her Dractopus tattoo.

Marilyn sat cross-legged beside her, now two drinks in. Though her head spun, there was a clarity to her thoughts—aided by contempt, by mourning, by something like vengefulness—that defied the alcohol. She also found herself aroused by the idle way Vanessa sometimes shifted her legs. The feeling was not outrightly sexual, though, so much as a craving for bodily comfort, to be embraced by another set of limbs.

"I can make it right," Marilyn said.

"How?"

She took another sip. "That's for me to worry about."

"Not anymore. Not if you want me to jetski you back toward Pyramid Bay, so you can swim in what is probably really dirty-ass water. I mean, you know that, right? You'll be swimming through shit. Sometimes literally. *Shit.* You could get sick."

"I gather."

Vanessa fidgeted, pushed herself up with her elbows. "Is this creature-thing going to keep causing tidal waves, you think? Why? I mean, is it some supernatural terrorist, or something?"

Yes. But, of course, she couldn't be sure.

"I can find out," Marilyn said. "I can find out and I can make it stop."

"Marilyn, you still haven't told me *how.*"

"It's weak right now," she said, more in a blurting-out fashion than actual reasoning.

"You mean—"

"The creature. Yes. It's used up a lot of its energy to make the tsunami. It's vulnerable."

How can you be so sure?

"And you're going to, what, fight it?"

"If I can."

More pressing to Marilyn, but which she found herself less capable of articulating, was that her combat mission had become more of a rescue one. She was almost certain Kaimi—or his spirit—was still down there somewhere. Imprisoned by the Offspring.

"Vanessa, believe me, I know this is a crazy ask…"

She snorted into her glass. "Yeah."

"Would it even be possible to jetski there? How long would that take?"

She sipped a mouthful. "Well, we can go to Point Hoaloha, which is northeast of here and about halfway around the island. There's a resort there and one of the jetski instructors used to work at Huna'ia. From there it'd be about an hour in, I guess, an hour back? The tanks usually get about two and a half hours."

"What about your foot?"

"You accelerate with the handle. I'd have to take it careful going over the waves, the bumps. But honestly I'd be way more worried about whatever you're doing. Have you even gone scuba diving before?"

Thoughtlessly, Marilyn said, "Yes. Once."

"You remember how?"

Marilyn hesitated. "It would probably help to have a refresher."

Vanessa eyed her, as if sensing the lie but neglecting to say anything. "My neighbor up the road has a pool. Maybe we can practice in the morning." She downed the rest of her drink. "Christ."

Marilyn considered that the primary (if not sole) reason for Vanessa's agreeableness came from the woman's warped spontaneity: the impulse that had thrust her into the ocean to night-swim after whales.

"I can pay you, you know," Marilyn said. "At this point I don't care. Name a price."

Vanessa's manner softened. "Don't worry about it," she said. "For now."

5

All time, all light, had fallen to waste.

Bound with the shadow-being, Kaimi had only a few available memories of his own, to help anchor what remained of himself. He tried not to dwell on the inevitable: that, like the last of an island chain sinking below rising depths, even those memories would fade in time.

There was his grandfather, seen through Kaimi's child-eyes, when the man was more virile. With a bone club, he beat several breadfruit to a pulp, then recruited Kaimi to delicately wrap them in hibiscus leaves for storage and fermenting. Days later, that first taste of the fermented paste, the savor…

…and there was him and Makui, so thin and on the eve of manhood and sneaking after dark into a canoe and paddling it round the bend of the reef, where something large nearly capsized them, and Makui's looking back at him, eyes all agleam in the night, the innocent thrill…

…and Akami and Kahal'i, freshly born, their *mana* so vibrant and unsullied, their little limbs grasping at what they could, their cries echoing with the loss of some forgotten bliss before…

…and the sight of his home shores, the "Old Land", as Chief Haunani had come to quickly call it, burning on the horizon—the last Kaimi would ever see of it as the Great Voyage entered its first mile…

….and there was the woman called Marilyn, of course, what he'd first seen of her and how alien she had looked floating in the water, how further alien she appeared when he encountered her by the waterfall, barely alive, and how within what seemed seconds in his memory they had entangled themselves in spirit, merged what she called their Other bodies…

But he had been drawn to the mystery of the shadow-being, the Offspring of the Reptile. Foolishly, he had pursued it. Sometimes, Kaimi thought he'd been deceived, but that was wrong: it was his own hunger that had imprisoned him.

And, like one clinging to torchflame in cold dark, it was the memory of Marilyn that Kaimi clung to strongest.

Especially as the Offspring had nourished itself on all that stolen life.

As it reveled in all it had taken.

As its essence trembled with grand, violent purpose.

As it summoned the surrounding waters, making the seas its plaything.

Its weapon.

Kaimi had ceased to fully comprehend "when" or "where" he now existed. But if Marilyn was still out there somewhere, seeking him, wondering of him, he thought he could perhaps reach her by the connection they had shared. His cry for help might reach her on the wind—in the depth of dreams, through some open passage in her soul.

When the Offspring had unleashed its assault, when it was spent of all it had gathered, Kaimi had known an opportunity. A chance to, weak as he was, call out that much louder.

And he felt her, too. He was sure he did. Though it might have been delusional hope, in the wake of the Offspring's attack it seemed as though his memories of Marilyn had been enlivened.

As if she were close, maybe even drawing closer.

Kaimi worried, however, that she too might fall prey to the Offspring. It had drained him, sustained itself like a giant parasite on his *mana* which it had used as a beacon to summon forth all manner of life. In vague glimpses, Kaimi had seen sharks, manta rays, turtles, even small whales—creatures whose *mana*, too, the Offspring preyed upon.

This struck Kaimi, as there were times when he could feel the consciousness of the Offspring, and sensed that it was the seas, after all, that it sought to protect. That it wished to preserve Nature's creation. And yet, it was using what energy it could to defend its territory against encroachment.

What exactly that encroachment was, Kaimi couldn't be sure. But he knew it involved people. The *mana* of Man.

The spiral—the symbol of the Reptile—represented a purity that did not include men, or their creations.

In truth, it sought to destroy their creations.

•　•　•

Far enough out, with Point Hoaloha roughly half a mile behind them, Vanessa revved the jetski to full speed. Marilyn bristled. She tightened her grip on Vanessa's waist, certain with each wave's spraying *hiss-bump* that she was going to be bucked right off. The scuba tank weighed her back. The wetsuit felt like a membrane clinging to her skin.

As they zoomed on, the ride smoothed. She softened her hold, clutched the sides of Vanessa's life jacket. To their left stretched the Kauai coastline, where fog touched down on verdant cliffs and valleys.

Marilyn sucked in breath, her stomach knotting tighter. She turned to vomit, but not much came out.

"Doing okay?" Vanessa shouted.

"Yeah."

"I think we're about ten minutes out."

They rounded another point, and that's when it came into view—Pyramid Rock. Even without the visual marker, Marilyn knew they were approaching. An oppressive smog hung over Pyramid Bay now, its whole aura cratered with darkness and violence.

Boats appeared, of varying size. Coast Guard, probably. Police. Search and rescue and clean-up operations. A helicopter thundered away over the hills.

Vanessa slowed the jetski. They soon came to a bobbing stop about a thousand yards from the bay.

"Ow, ow," Vanessa said, reaching down and gingerly touching her bandaging.

"Are you okay?"

"Yeah, just some of those jolts…" She looked up. Not without a hint of relief in her voice, she said, "Listen, I don't think we can get any closer."

"Really?"

As if to validate her point, a single-note siren blared behind them. Both Marilyn and Vanessa craned their necks to find a boat approaching, churning up water.

Marilyn's stomach sank.

"Do *not* approach any closer!" shouted an officious male voice, crackling through the horn. "For your safety, and to avoid incident, turn back now."

"Shit." Vanessa stiffened her posture, revved the jetski.

By then, however, Marilyn had plunged in.

She kicked as fast as she could. It was an odd exhilaration to take seamless breaths underwater. To defy a planet's worth of an element.

Somewhere above, the garbled whine of engines. Who knew what awaited her on the other end of this? Giant fine? Jail? Maybe an infection, from all the sewage they'd said had been loosed into the water.

All that, though, felt like a distant future.

Marilyn slowed. The ocean blue closed in on her. Flashes of silver not far away. Long. Big. A school of barracuda.

She couldn't turn back. Not now. She kicked on, checking her breath gauge as Vanessa had taught her in the swimming pool session. Little under an hour to go. The sea floor a yellowish haze below. Fish darting, oblivious to all the awful Bigness. Jellyfish—the "janitors of the sea," she randomly remembered—pulsed along like disembodied hearts, unaware they were bodiless.

She tried to moderate her breath. With every inhale's hissing, metallic *rip*, she was reminded of her single tank.

Was she going the right way? She didn't want to surface and see, not with boats around. But she also didn't need her eyes. Not her physical eyes, anyway. She could follow the foul, pulpy death-texture of the bay.

More and more, her Other ears picked up that crackling buzz, the death-hum of Pyramid Bay. Like flies over a carcass.

Looming about a hundred yards to her left was an incline of sharp, greenish rocks. The peninsula? Marilyn paused, felt the energy of it. So many scattered pictures of all the history that had passed through Pyramid Rock.

She was close.

The water grew murkier, sludgy. Random plastics, wood and objects like shattered chairs, palm fronds, nails, umbrellas and bags grew visible in the green-brown gloom. Inanimate things filling the void of the animate. Articles of clothing floated by, as though their wearers had dissolved into the ocean.

She checked her gauge: about 4900psi. Twenty feet.

In shallower water, and with measured pace, Marilyn allowed herself to drift to the sea floor. Pressure grew in her skull. Bearable. The descent took slightly longer than expected, but soon her fins touched down in a soft plume of sand.

Eighty feet.

Energy-wise, it was quieter down here. This is the way, she thought, that most life had known the world.

Something popped out at her. Snatches of a voice, barely audible, like a distorted signal. It did not speak English, but she didn't need the surface language: Marilyn could feel the meaning behind the words, the intention and the reaching.

The fear.

And she knew, right then, that it had not been God that had called her here.

It was Kaimi. He *was* here, *still here*, his presence nearly as strong as when he'd been swimming out in front of her.

Through this bottom twilight, she called out.

Kaimi?

She pushed forward, sensing. To the best of her knowledge, Marilyn had never felt an actual human spirit before, and was struck by its different-ness. It was like a shell, just more electric. Not a ghost of what could be, but an echo of what was, still aglow with some of its worldly power.

But the more she reached out to Kaimi, the more she sensed the darkness around him.

Entombing him.

A familiar darkness, too. She had a vision of the Offspring, still the massive multi-limbed, multi-eyed shadow she had first seen. Yet the shadow now harbored a light, and it was from this light that she received an image of Kaimi: hopelessly cocooned, his every effort to escape only further feeding his captor.

Marilyn's chest tightened.

Kaimi—I'm so sorry.

Breath gauge: 3500psi. Little over thirty minutes.

She knew now what she had to do.

Several yards farther and the temperature plummeted to a sharp cold. There was a dust-up of sand, gravel, trash. Something big and hard grazed her leg—a lounge chair from the pool area.

The Offspring was there, hovering not far from her. Wearing sandclouds. Wearing waterdusk. Marilyn felt the full press of its attention. A militant sense of duty burned in the thing.

Chaos swept through Marilyn's mind, overloading her mental senses. There was a loud kind of chirp-buzzing, pulsing in terrible rhythm, forming almost a cyclonic pattern in her imagination. She felt suffocated, caught by the force, a vortex:

And dwelling at the bottom of this vortex, like one caught in a pit of quicksand: Kaimi. Blinking desperately up at her.

Marilyn's throat closed. She was certain she peed her wetsuit. She was four years old again, floating and hyperventilating out on Gordon Lake. Again, she was scrambling through the crowds of San Francisco, smelling smoke and terror and death—

Breath gauge: 3100psi.

She concentrated. She had to disengage from her body, rise higher, toward that realm of Other-ness. What did her metaphysical anatomy look like, if it could be mapped out?

She could be anything imagined, or some form of *all* such things. As well as the changing-ness between them.

Much as he could, Kaimi reached out. Marilyn was here. He felt her, knew the spirit-touch, the scent, the sound of her Other-voice and the shape of her thoughts.

A sense of alarm shivered through him, though it wasn't from him. It was from the Offspring. It seemed more frightened than he'd felt before, probably because it was more vulnerable. Evacuated of the *mana* it had stolen.

Marilyn, he called. Stronger: *Marilyn*.

Kaimi, I'm so sorry.

Can you hear me?

She might have replied, but it was little more than a buzz. The Offspring shifted, perhaps aware of their communication and hoping to stifle it.

Kaimi turned over in his mind the scattered few memories he'd managed to keep. There was still power in them, *mana*. Life-ness which the Offspring had not completely taken for itself. He could draw from them and, with Marilyn's presence and Marilyn's aid, use that last reservoir to try and reach out for her, to break through his own powerlessness.

The Offspring moaned. Its "voices", its cries, bellows, hisses, growls and things once inaudible to the human ear, now filled Kaimi's mind like a swarm of insects, obscuring what he could sense of Marilyn.

…Kaimi…

He pressed. Resisted.

…fight…

He was. He *was*. He struggled to fixate on her. Very quickly, though, Kaimi glimpsed a different picture. Marilyn appeared to be transforming, becoming something else in his mind's eye.

Her feminine contours fell away, expanded into something far larger. She sprouted what resembled massive wings that rose up like those of some bat-demon, and blinked open eyes that gleamed yellow, and bore teeth and a snout like the largest lizards and, even more strikingly, she grew a great bottom-half of thick, writhing tentacles.

She was fighting the way she knew how. With Other-ness.

And he had to help any way he knew.

She lashed with her many arms, roared from her fang-lined mouth and stared from her yellow dragon's eyes. Inhabiting this idea of the Dractopus, Marilyn tried to plunge through, toward that space where Kaimi hung, ensnared.

His spirit was the Offspring's power source. Its heart. She had to rip him out.

Voices filled her head, like static.

Then, in a coronal burst of energy, the Offspring showed itself. Long tendrils, some like giant squid and some much thinner like jellyfish. Head long, narrow. Mouth lined with enormous barbed teeth. Body the sleek girth of a whale. Shells lining its bulbous crustacean back. Other appendages indescribable, impossible. A mad phantasmagoria of form, snatches of stolen life packed upon shadow.

And though it had no obvious eyes, its gaze radiated heat and consciousness.

Breath gauge: 1300psi. Less than twenty minutes.

She tried to focus, locking with the Offspring. Phantom arms entwined. A clash of claw and conceit. She sucked up more air—a hissing, rasping storm in her ears.

On the battlefield of the Other, blades locked.

Her physical vision spotted with black dots, which grew. Her muscles steeled and her whole body felt like it was going a thousand miles a minute, pressure-cooked to explode at any point.

Marilyn I am here I am HERE—

Kaimi drew closer to her. She could feel his spirit, his edges but it was difficult for her to secure him with whatever grasp she could. The Offspring lashed out, sunk its teeth into the notion of the Dractopus. It wavered. She wavered. Grew exhausted. Dizzy.

Breath gauge: 600psi. Less than ten minutes.

Kaimi was waning, faster and faster. Marilyn swirled and clashed with the Offspring, a heightening, vibrating, lightning storm of pure thought and capacity. In its own savage desperation, the Offspring began taking yet more of him.

The *rest* of him, in fact. Kaimi could feel the draining of those last few memories, the reaping of their energies. He knew a falling back. A shrinking.

Yet he fought, like one mired in a sinkhole. Though the distance between him and Marilyn was short, they could not touch one another. The Offspring continued to separate them.

Disturbingly, she appeared to be waning, as well.

...Mari...

He reached.

...lyn...

Suddenly, she didn't seem to be reaching back. Nor did he glimpse anything of the monstrous image she had projected.

Darkness closed about him. Kaimi focused on that final, blurry silhouette of Marilyn, floating in the void of the sea.

She wasn't moving.

The strength of the Dractopus had retreated, or at least retreated from her. Her body, whether physical or Other, was exhausted. Marilyn sensed power in the Dractopus, like it was an idea bigger than she, yet it was not a power she alone could uphold. It was not wielding an axe on weaker beings. It was helming a warship against a sea monster.

She was tempted to give up. Her psi needle trembled dangerously low, her air felt thin and her lungs clawed for each breath and her body was overtaxed and her heart raced, as if eager to make a quick end.

She could feel Kaimi slipping away.

Marilyn blinked, and the blink lasted longer than expected.

Then, all at once, there was a new presence. Strong, heated with life—or recent life. Her Other ears picked up rapid chittering. A voice unaccustomed to its new throat.

—*Mare-Mare-Mare*—

It took a second.

Joe?

He appeared to her, far at first but drifting closer. Fuzzy, ill-defined. His arm outstretched.

—*hand-my-hand-hand-my*—

It didn't register with Marilyn right away, the significance of what was happening. For the last eight or nine years of her life Joe had been a staple, a constant familiar, and having him here—even with this craziness—felt logical. Why *wouldn't* he be here? He was her husband, vowed before God, the father of her children. He was, and always would be, in her life.

But he was here, and that could only mean…

Why weren't you safe? Marilyn cried. *Where were you, what—?*

This time, his answer came more in sentiment than words: "Don't worry about it." He could sense she was locked in strange combat, in ways and for reasons he might not totally comprehend, yet he wanted her to be okay, to return to herself and to be *Marilyn* again.

He reached.

No, she said. *I can't go with you, Joe, not going, not now I'm sorry not now—*

—just-just-take-take-take—

She began to understand that he wasn't trying to take her, or guide her. She lifted her head, grazed his fingertips and knew instant, revitalizing warmth.

—don't   know—help—needed—what's-what's—could   use— happening—

Joe's words were jumbled, erratic. An infant Other tongue. His spirit soft, raw. The layers of her husband's years, judgments, biases, anxieties, had thinned considerably. With a surge of heartache, Marilyn realized she was seeing Joe perhaps as she'd never seen him before, that, in a sense, she was meeting him for the first time.

Life-ness empowered her. Joe was giving her whatever *mana* he could.

She opened her eyes. The Offspring was faint, far fainter than she had thought a moment ago—or had that been an illusion? A trick on its part?

Kaimi was reachable.

—careful—more-more—love—be—you-you—

Joe get out of here. She was not intending to be callous, more concerned for his safety. The Offspring might leech upon him, use him as a fresh power source.

—Mare-Mare—

Kaimi come on—Joe please—

The Offspring's shadowy tentacles surrounded her. There was intrigue about Joe, but its attention was on her.

With renewed strength, Marilyn focused on the image of her Dwarf-Knight's axe, sharpening it in her mind. Gripping it in her Other hands, she cut forth, chopping, swinging, reaping toward Kaimi.

He lunged for her.

Success!

When she thought she had enough of a hold, Marilyn clutched him. Pulled. The sensation of Kaimi's spirit coming away, collapsing in her arms, was perhaps much like the moment they'd met in person, when it had been she, collapsing under the weight of exhaustion.

Kaimi's full image appeared clearly to her. He looked pale, sallow. Drained.

She embraced him.

The Offspring thrashed, buzzed, gnawed. It was weakening, fast. All these centuries, it had been using Kaimi's spirit like a battery. That was how the Offspring had sustained itself. How it had drawn so much life to these waters to absorb, and to exploit.

She kicked her fins backward. In swimming again, Marilyn realized how tense her muscles had been. They now throbbed, everywhere. Like she'd just wrenched herself from a year-long spell of paralysis.

Kaimi—can you understand me?

A pause, then: *I …yes…*

—Mare-Mare-Marilyn-Mare—

Grief escaped her in a stream of bubbles and shudders.

Joe…

She swam steadily upward. Somewhere above: the growing whir of an engine. Below, the Offspring had fallen away into formlessness, as though dissolved into all the murk and the mess it had wrought.

Joe, too, was receding. Fading.

Joe I'm so sorry, she said. *I love you.*

The surface glowing above. Closer.

She sensed nothing else. Heard nothing else.

The eternity with the Offspring had become just that. It was almost as if Kaimi had never been touched by anything else, in fact had never *known* anything else.

And so, this was a rebirth. A liberation. He sat cradled by the woman whose energy he understood instantly and intimately, who had reached her hand across the void to meet his own, their *mana* conjoining—a show of light, to drive back the dark.

Kaimi could feel the surrounding ocean, but at a remove. The cold tingled, sweet and invigorating but not "cold". Not affecting him as it might have flesh. He was grateful for it.

He asked: *Marilyn, who was that?*

There was a pause. He felt her grief, which was like needles.

My husband.

Kaimi wished he had the capacity to physically comfort her. *I am sorry.*

No reply.

His journey, he said, hoping to bring solace, *is now mine.*

They rose now through a brightening ocean dusk. He watched the surface, shifting with light. And as they drew closer, the cold retreated entirely, as did Marilyn's soft embrace which, like cupped hands clutching a bird, now opened to liberate him higher. He kicked off and joined those spirit-winds which took him from daylight to a yet greater light, a *mana* light…the brightest, most nourishing he had ever seen, and against which he could perceive figures.

Again, he reached.

This time, several hands broke the surface to reach back. To pull. He felt them.

Akamu…Kaha'i…Eloni…

…Haumea…Ewelani…

…his grandfather, who had told him of *dreamfruit*…

…Chief Haunani…

And somewhere in there was Makui, too, waiting with a grin unburdened as any since they were children, frolicking on the shores of the Old Land.

VII

1

10 Years Later

"You know, you can come in and actually listen," Marilyn said, popping open the passenger side door. "And watch. *And* meet them. Just sayin'."

The energy inside the car curdled a little. Troy, fourteen, with a pimply expressionless face and buzzcut, sat quietly with the game console in his hand. He offered the briefest of smirks and threw a deferring gaze to Tom, now three months from graduation and hunched behind the wheel of the idling car.

"Yeah, mom, we know," said Tom. "But look at the generation you're talking to."

Marilyn snorted. "Whatever that means."

"We're anti-social, and we wanna hear you in real-time, online. As most people are gonna hear you."

Marilyn shrugged. "Okay." She leaned over and kissed Tom on the forehead, then turned to Troy. "Make sure he drives safe."

"I will," Troy said, smirk lifting again, his focus still primarily on the tinny digital action in his hands.

Marilyn watched him for a second. Perhaps it was for no other reason than him being the youngest, but with Troy she felt like she was fumbling in the dark. Some definitions had formed around Tom and Tamara: Tom the budding drummer, the D&Der, the "quasi-jock" (his words) with his track and field, and Tamara the staunch churchgoer, all her pep and fire igniting her faith to a temperature decidedly higher than Marilyn's, at her most pious, had ever been. But there was a shapelessness about Troy that, while periodically frustrating, part of Marilyn also relished.

Troy's gaze flicked away for a second from the console toward the window. Marilyn reached over and playfully clawed his knee.

"Everything okay?"

"Uh-huh."

Dr. Warren, the grade school psychologist, had been the first third party to suggest that Troy was neurodivergent. Truthfully, she and Joe had touched on that possibility when he was only three.

Sucking in a breath, she turned to finally climb from the car and walk up the huge driveway to the home-slash-studio, where she was to be interviewed (*interviewed* live, in audio, not just in print), when Tom abruptly touched her arm.

"Remember," said her eldest son. "Bowman offers drinks to his guests. Take the gin—"

"I don't like gin—"

"Eh, gotta find the right one."

"And how would *you* know, Mr. Four-Years-From-Legal-Age?"

"Just, whatever," said Tom. "Take the drink. Calm your nerves. And remember: you're just speaking into a mic. And to him. Just a conversation."

"Yes. A conversation that gets a million ears."

"You deserve it," Troy chimed from the back.

Both she and Tom turned, surprised. Troy's eyes had not left his game.

•   •   •

The closer she approached the front door, the more she could hear the murmur of activity inside. She knocked, softly at first, then harsher.

Cut the timid bullshit. You've met with city councilmen, with the mayor.

Plus, she was here on their invite, the fruit of a chance meeting between the comedian-podcaster-activist Steve Bowman and her online friend, Jen—originally her *Errowind* companion from Seattle—at this year's *Realms of Magic* convention.

A young man with a ball cap and headset popped open the door.

"Marilyn?" he said, smiling. Before Marilyn could even say anything, he waved her inside, his attention on his phone.

"Indeed," she said.

The young guy gestured. "Have a seat in the lobby. Help yourself to anything there."

She walked in. The house was spacious but largely empty and functional, like a warehouse. Any area that might once have been filled with Hollywood ostentation was filled instead by various camera, lighting or recording equipment. The lobby toward which the young man directed her appeared to be the only furnished room, complete with two leather couches and several chairs and a coffee table.

A middle-aged man sat alone at the end of one of the couches, staring light-years into the far wall. He looked faintly familiar.

Marilyn sat on one of the chairs. She caught the eye of the middle-aged man and smiled, following it with an involuntary snort.

"Are you the first to go on," she asked, "or is it me?"

"I think it's me," he said. "But I could be wrong."

She slouched a little, exhaled. "I'll just stay here until someone tells me to do something, then." She turned to the man. "I'm assuming you're the famous one? Though I'm sorry I can't place the name."

He chuckled. "Arthur. And I wouldn't say *famous*."

Just then, Marilyn noticed the book on his lap: *Glory to the Glitch*, by Dr. Arthur Moore.

"Oh." The name rang a bell. Her brother Shane had read a few of his books—or at least, she'd seen them out and about his place. *The Unholy Ghost* had been one she often noticed, the verbal blade thrust at all things religion and spirituality.

She pointed at the book. "Is that you?"

"That's me. Steve wanted a signed copy. Like usual."

"My brother's a big fan of yours."

"That's nice." Arthur leaned forward and picked up a Styrofoam cup of coffee. He looked vaguely hurt, perhaps wondering why Marilyn herself wasn't a fan. "Would he like a signed copy, too? I've got a few more in the car."

Marilyn paused. The "big fan" thing was a stretch, or might've been. Honestly, she wasn't sure. Having spoken to Shane so little over the years, as he receded from much contact after his stepdaughter Barbara had moved away and he'd joined some weird, atheist circle-jerk social club that Jeannie half-joked was Masonic, Marilyn nowadays knew precious little about her younger brother. He deserved no gift from her.

"A signed copy would be awesome," she said. "Maybe give it to me after the show?"

Arthur finished a gulp of coffee. "You got it."

Another early twentysomething, this time a punkish, tattooed girl, emerged from the hallway carrying a clipboard.

"Marilyn!" said the young woman, like she knew her. "I was just talking to Steve, and it looks like we're gonna switch you two on the line-up. So, Marilyn, you'll be going first, and Dr. Moore, you'll be second."

"Call me Art."

"Got it." With that, she left.

A whole new system of nerves flared up in Marilyn. Her leg trembled. For the umpteenth time, she glanced at her notes and the questions they'd sent her of material they wanted to cover.

Question: You co-founded an organization, Effect, that promotes scientific literacy, specifically—

Marilyn closed her eyes. Words written about her, no matter how true, always felt like fraudulent realities attributed to her. Even as she knew every financial hurdle, every bureaucratic mishap, every meeting, every moment harsh or hopeful that these past three crazy years had brought.

—related to environmental policy, and an interdisciplinary understanding of the natural world. And yet you yourself have no science

background. In fact, you've noted that your background is much the opposite, and that gives you a unique perspective. How so?

She shuffled the paper back into the folder, then offered another tepid smile to Arthur.

"I think my late husband would hate that title," she said, pointing to the book.

"What? 'Glory to the Glitch'?"

"Yeah. He was a computer engineer. Glitches were the bane of his existence."

"Makes sense. We need them, though." Arthur idly speed-flipped through his book. "It's not computer glitches I'm referring to, though the principle still stands. Programmers are always looking for a glitch, to strengthen the program, right?"

"Essentially."

"So the basic idea is that we should be doing that with everything— every argument, belief, theory, every institution. There's always a glitch." Arthur raised his hands theatrically. "Some little hole through which we can feel the winds of confusion, ignorance, and discovery. It's a good thing."

"That's gotta be a line from your book, right?" Marilyn said. "That 'winds' thing?"

Arthur blinked. "Of course it is. I'm just that pretentious."

She laughed. The punkish woman with the clipboard returned.

"Marilyn," she said. "Let's get you set up."

2

She almost never remembered her dreams anymore, if she even had them. Marilyn wasn't sure why, if it was a product of getting older, or that her creative output had waned or that she didn't game as much. With all the legwork and outreach demanded by Effect, her brain now marinated in the abstract, living mostly in the future.

Which wasn't to say she slept well, necessarily. Marilyn tried to ignore the discolored bags under her eyes, and would periodically marvel how for the first thirty years of her life she'd functioned without several espressos during the day.

Almost 8:30. She'd overslept. Or, rather, over-lounged. Vanessa, her business partner, had texted her about a few forthcoming events, mostly at schools or festivals. "You're on kid-watch," Vanessa had once said. "You can deal with the little stinkers way better than me."

Another text from Tommy, telling her he and Troy had left for school.

Just as she fished her bagel from the toaster oven, Marilyn's phone rang. It was Jeannie, her sister-in-law.

Marilyn answered, put it on speaker. "Hey, Jeannie."

"Marilyn, thank God." There was a disturbed tenor to her voice. "Are you home?"

"Um, I am."

A moment of hesitation. "We may need a place to stay. For the time being."

"What? What's going on?"

Shane's voice mumbled something in the background. She could hear sirens. Traffic. It sounded like they were in the car.

With a tone that almost sounded insulted, Jeannie said, "Look out the window."

Marilyn hurried to the window, peeled back the curtain. Breath caught in her throat. A gigantic column of smoke loomed over the distant hills. Definitely in the direction of Chatsworth. In its cataclysmic grandeur, the smoke carried the aspirations of another, even greater atrocity that Marilyn had once seen, a destruction that had swallowed cloud, moon and sun into ashen oblivion.

•　•　•

Twenty or so minutes after the phone call, Marilyn took the stairs down to the sidewalk where she stood and waited, preferring to see Shane and Jeannie coming.

She fought down the dread, tried to diminish self-pity by watching that giant plume of smoke spreading across the sky. Homes destroyed. Families separated, homeless.

Didn't they have anyone *else* they could stay with? All she had was a two-bedroom apartment, after all, shared with Tommy and Troy. Marilyn hated herself for this thought, even as she couldn't shake it. That Jeannie had called her probably meant that this arrangement was not exactly Shane's ideal, either, even if, as he'd said years ago, Marilyn had "scored more points" with him for leaving the Mormon church.

"Welcome to the more erect stage of Australopithecus *rationalis*," Shane had added, with semi-glazed eyes and a hollow curl of a smile. "You're seeing farther."

No, they had nowhere to go. Because Shane, likely, had pushed away all other family and friends.

When she was sure it was their car rolling down the street, Marilyn waved. Jeannie reciprocated from the passenger's seat, her eyes far away. From what she could see of Shane, he looked neutral. Marilyn directed them into the driveway of her complex.

Jeannie lowered the window. "Hi Marilyn."

"Hey sis," Shane said, just beyond her.

Marilyn leaned down. "Hey guys. So, you know I have a tandem parking spot, if you want me to just get in and direct you."

"That'll be great." Jeannie reached out and clutched her forearm with the haste of someone tipping backward. "Thank you again, Marilyn, so, *so* much."

"Of course. I'm just glad you're both okay."

"Do you think Tommy and Troy will be okay with this?"

Marilyn hesitated. "We'll do our best."

She proceeded to open the gate for them, then slipped into the backseat. The car lurched forward into the winding narrow driveway tracing her complex.

"Do they have any idea what caused the fire?" Marilyn asked.

Her gaze met Shane's in the rearview mirror. She sensed it instantly, the strongest in years: the whiff of menace, the scaly texture of his energy.

"No idea, right now," Shane said. "But obviously the drought's so bad and everything's so dry that all it takes is some careless smoker, or something."

"I just *pray* it doesn't get our house," Jeannie said.

Shane glanced at his wife. Marilyn thought he might remark on the P-word, but he kept silent, zooming through the driveway at nearly twice the posted speed limit.

"Hey Nascar, slow down," Marilyn said. "Kids and cats live here."

Another cold flicker of eyes across the rearview mirror. The car slowed. As they bounced over a speed bump, Marilyn noticed a tattoo on the back of Shane's neck that she'd never seen before:

• • •

Though she'd fought herself on the idea, Marilyn wound up giving them her bedroom. Whether the remnants of her Mormon conditioning or guilt for having effectively written them off these past few years (not that Shane or Jeannie had done much to reach out themselves) that tipped the scales, she wasn't sure. Marilyn offered, they mumbled surprised gratitude, and she wound up piling a pillow and blankets for herself on the living room couch.

She found a moment and texted Tommy and Troy: *Your uncle Shane and aunt Jeannie were displaced by the big fire. I am letting them stay with us for a little while. Just to warn.*

"How close is the fire to you?" Marilyn asked Jeannie, pouring her sister-in-law a glass of red wine. Shane was in the shower.

Jeannie took the glass with relish. Marilyn wondered whether to pour one for herself. Yeah, it was still before noon. But suddenly putting up Shane was the social and emotional equivalent to a flash flood. She was knee-deep. Maybe higher.

She poured her own glass.

"I don't know," Jeannie said. "We could see the flames from our balcony. Our neighborhood is like some post-apocalyptic hellscape. It wasn't burned when we left, of course," she sipped her wine, "but I'm fortifying myself with pictures of nothing but a giant barbecue when we get back. If we get back."

"Of course you'll get back," Marilyn said.

Jeannie shrugged. She held up her wine glass. "Sorry to ask, but you got anything stronger?"

"I have tequila and margarita mix. And vodka, I'm pretty sure."

"Tequila's fine."

"No mix?"

Jeannie shook her head. "No mix."

Marilyn set out a glass and the tequila bottle. With well-practiced movement, Jeannie knocked out two quick shots in a row before pouring a tall glass.

"You want ice? Or a lime or anything?"

"No, I'm okay." Jeannie's hand trembled slightly as she lifted the glass to her lips.

Marilyn came over and sat a cushion away from Jeannie. Down the hall, shower water crackled. Even in the thick of a drought, which had fostered a wildfire that may well be destroying his house, Shane still held to his long showers.

"Jeannie," Marilyn said in a lowered voice. "What the hell is it that Shane's gotten into? What's that spiral tattoo on the back of his neck?"

Still looking dazed, Jeannie nodded. There was a cold inevitability to the motion. "The Serpent's Tongue," she said.

"That's the group he's in, right?"

"Uh huh. The 'men's club.' He doesn't like it when I call it that, because women are allowed, but the few times I've been around them I've never seen any women."

"But you told me before you thought it was, like, Masonic. Freemasons, or something."

Jeannie's eyes narrowed. "I don't remember saying that. It was probably a joke. Maybe they are. I don't know."

She raised her glass of tequila again, but Marilyn placed a firm hand on her sister-in-law's wrist and brought the glass back down calmly to her knee.

"What's with their name?" Marilyn asked.

Jeannie threw a glance toward the hall. "The biblical serpent, I think."

"Satan?"

"Well, yeah, technically. But they don't see it as, you know, SATAN. It's more philosophical. Devil's advocate. The questioning of religion. That kinda thing."

So it *is* like Masonry, Marilyn thought.

"You know he's always been ra-ra atheism, since he left your church," Jeannie said. "I know it's not 'your' church anymore. But…I thought you knew all this."

"Sort of."

"You haven't been around, I know."

Marilyn blinked. "I haven't been around?"

"Yeah. We always invite you to dinners and things, and you never respond."

Marilyn chuckled, and there was a gasp in it. "I've *never* gotten a dinner invite from you or Shane. The last time we saw each other it was because *I* reached out. Two years ago, when Mom and Dad were in town."

Jeannie snickered. "Okay, whatever." She drank, then said, "Doesn't matter anyway. Our house is now a fucking ash heap."

Setting the tequila down, Jeannie closed her eyes and inhaled. Exhaled. Marilyn wanted to touch her, but something held her back.

"Do you know exactly what they do at Serpent's Tongue?" Marilyn asked. "And how often they do it?"

"He's out with them like twice a week, usually."

"And you're—"

"Can we fucking *drop* this? Please?"

Almost immediately, the shower knob squealed, the water shut off. Marilyn watched Jeannie as she drained the rest of the tequila and staggered to her feet. "I'm gonna take a nap," she said. "Thanks again for the room, Mare."

•　　•　　•

In truth, they *had* invited Marilyn for dinner—once. And while she'd accepted, she wound up sputtering her way out in a series of half-true excuses. Jeannie called the next day and Marilyn had ignored it, watching it become a missed call. No voicemail. She never called back, and they'd never set up a new date. Just as well.

That had been almost two years ago.

Marilyn lay in the open darkness of the living room. It was October, a little over a month away from Thanksgiving and yet the lingering heat forced her to sleep without blankets. Had it not been for her company, she would have forsaken her pajama pants, too.

She listened to the night breathing.

Something else is here.

Over the years, the beings and the Other-ness had receded. Which is not to say some didn't manage to get through: there was periodic movement in the corners of her eye, or the heatwave-like shimmers that reminded her of the *Predator* when he was cloaked. Her "Other senses", she figured, were pretty much atrophied.

The Reptile, however, remained one of the stronger presences, able to penetrate the years of conscious disuse. Since Hawaii, she had only been to Shane's neighborhood a handful of times. There was a reason she'd not followed up that dinner invite.

Her brain and body abuzz, Marilyn sat up on the edge of the couch and listened to the stillness. The hallway before her drew away long and deep, night concentrated there.

She closed her eyes. Her Other body was still there, just dulled. For the first time in quite a while, she doubted the choices she had made, not only for herself but for Troy. An excessive, overreaching imagination, she'd said. Certain dreams insisting beyond their time and place. Not to be ignored, necessarily, but to be diminished, and, soon, when the crust of Western skepticism had formed around the mind, dismissed *de facto*.

But, yes, there was something still leeching off Shane. By what she remembered of that first evening she'd glimpsed it, it had grown stronger. Among the times she'd encountered her younger brother over the decade since Hawaii, that scent of the Reptile in him had, in fact, lessened; whether because Marilyn was by then consciously detoxing from her "talents", or the thing knew better how to lie low, she wasn't sure. It didn't matter. Maybe, with the fires, with Shane's involvement in Serpent's Tongue, it had emerged closer to the fore, polluting his eyes once again.

She deliberated. With her under-used abilities, she might not get a lock on the thing in Shane during the hustle of daylight hours. But here lay her brother now, just ten feet away, the first time in twenty or so years they'd slept under the same roof.

She pushed herself up and walked toward the hallway, where the darkness only seemed to thicken.

With one final, creaky step, Marilyn stood outside her bedroom door. She held her breath, pressed her tongue against the roof of her mouth and tried to calm the drum-bangs of her heartbeat. For a second she thought she might pass out.

Thankfully, she knew her door—pulling it toward her, and turning the handle at a certain pace, would not make much noise.

The door opened. More smothering blackness, but for the haziest whisper of light from the open, uncurtained window.

A slight rustling of sheets. A low, unintelligible murmur.

For a fraction of a second, Marilyn froze. Then she hurriedly closed the door behind her and felt her way to the chair she kept by the dresser, mere feet away.

She sat. Shut her eyes again, tried to listen, to feel, past the sounds of her own body.

A slight tingle.

Is something here?

The silence, the stillness and the dark all kept mum.

Is anything here?

The shadows were quiet.

Moments later, Marilyn caught a hint of a familiar, primordial "smell", one she could also taste, and the brush of a rugged, moving thing that was fast and elusive, and which she was certain watched her from some Other perch.

By the time she made it back to the couch, over and hour and a half had passed. If Shane and Jeannie had noticed her presence, they had not reacted at all.

She would try again the following night.

3

"This might sound weird," Shane said, looking at Marilyn across the table. He rolled the mouthful of pizza from cheek to cheek. "But were you by any chance in our room last night?"

"Uhh, what?" Tommy said, with the faintest smirk. Troy's attention remained buried in his own pizza.

Jeannie set down her beer. "What're you talking about?"

"I know it's not 'our' room," Shane said. "You know what I mean, though."

Marilyn kept her eyes on her own slice. All day she'd been consistently aware of one thing: *Shane keeps avoiding eye contact.*

"No," she said. She forced a smile. "Not unless I was sleepwalking."

"Did you *see* someone come in?" Jeannie asked Shane. She was now three wine glasses in.

"Nevermind. It was a dream."

"Or an optical illusion," Marilyn ventured.

Shane shrugged, kept chewing. The pizza sat between them, their meat half largely massacred, Marilyn's veggie half still holding strong.

Eager to change subjects, Marilyn said, "Kevin texted me earlier, by the way."

"Who?" Shane asked.

"Joe's brother."

"Oh. He's the one Tamara's living with, right?"

Marilyn nodded. That he even had to reconfirm this saddened her, but didn't surprise her. "He and Margie are thinking of organizing a beach day next week if you two want to come."

"With who?" Jeannie asked. "Who else, I mean?"

Marilyn snickered. "Tammy. Their son, Calvin. Maybe one or two others. I'm not sure."

"We could do that," Jeannie said. She looked at Shane. "As much as I know you hate the beach."

Again, Shane shrugged. "It's fine."

He doesn't look much at Jeannie, either.

When they'd finished, she rose and bussed their dishes. At the sink Marilyn stood, watching through the window the sunset's ominously rosy beauty drain away from the long stretch of fireclouds.

•   •   •

Four nights later, the bedroom door stood slightly ajar. An eerie sense of invitation.

Marilyn walked in as before, sat in the same chair. The moon shone full, slipping more light through the window. She could barely make out her brother and sister-in-law's features. As before, they appeared to lie away from one another. Both were dark lumps on the bed.

Shane cleared his throat.

But it didn't come from the bed.

On the other side of the dresser to Marilyn's immediate right, the toilet flushed. The bathroom door opened. Marilyn watched, breathless, as Shane shuffled out, sniffing and mumbling before returning to bed.

The dark lump on Shane's side of the bed didn't move, as her brother settled back in under the sheets.

Jeannie stirred a little. Shane grew instantly motionless, his soft wet snores rising in the darkness. He remained turned away.

Marilyn's pulse filled the room, the apartment.

Again, she reached out her Other fingers. Still creaky. Still rusty. This time, however, something was there.

If you can hear me at all, she thought, not wanting to risk speaking aloud. *Get the fuck out. Get away from my brother. Get away from* here.

The command rang lame to her. Unsurprisingly, there was no response, nothing she felt, anyway. Only the hush of late-night traffic.

I know what you want.

Waited again.

Nothing.

Marilyn tried to ignore the notion that, whatever this energy or entity was, it had merged so intimately with Shane that the two had effectively become one.

Very quietly, she muttered, "Get out."

Jeannie groaned in her sleep. Marilyn steeled, rose partway from her chair. She felt lightheaded. She tiptoed the few feet to the door and walked out into the hall, clicking the door shut behind her.

She made her way to the kitchen, where she poured herself a glass of red wine. Leaning elbows on the counter, she took a swift, hearty gulp, then buried her face in her hands. Shane, she decided, was lost a long time ago.

Marilyn tried to remember what she could of her time with Kaimi, on the island. The entire episode in her memory ran like a largely out-of-focus film, the emotions and sensations like a soundtrack played separately from the blurry imagery. Nevertheless, she had made sure to nurture some of the clearer moments, to think over them and to polish them in her mind so that they might keep.

There was a *click*. Marilyn leaned up from the counter. Listened. Shuffling, down the hall.

Coming closer.

She darted forward and threw on the kitchen light, recoiling as Shane stood in the archway, half-clothed and staring at her. His eyes were decidedly not Shane's. They were far deader, unencumbered by any barrier of humane notion, regret, opinion, idea. Or conscience.

Stormwind whistled from her brother's gaze. Shane's jaw worked back and forth. Twitches flared in his neck.

He said, "What is it that I want?"

"You want to destroy," she said.

Shane made a strange hiccupping noise, body convulsing in kind. The dead expression held. She wasn't sure if the noise was a laugh.

"We oversee," he said. "We Correct."

He walked over to the kitchen table and lowered himself into a chair. Marilyn could think of no better word for his gait that "fitful," the awkward effort of every step. A thing unaccustomed to its costume, like some residents of the Lofts.

They met gazes. For the first time, Marilyn saw the rawness of that primal light burning in her brother's eyes. The smell was there, musky and aged and animal, and the sense of coarse, rugged contours— scales—grew against her Other fingertips.

"I don't know what you're talking about," she said.

"Yes, you do."

Marilyn swallowed. "Did you cause that fire?"

Shane reached for a nearby pen. He popped the cap and pressed the tip into the wood of the table and began drawing, carving, circling round and round.

"Hey—" Marilyn leaned forward.

He'd carved a spiral into the table.

"Correction will destroy people," he said. "Unless they relinquish."

"Relinquish what?"

But she knew. The Authoring.

Shane leaned back, stared at her. "You are the children. We are the guardian."

Suddenly Shane reached out, snatched her wrist and forced her hand onto the table, her palm smack on the center of his crude spiral. Her knuckles rang with pain, but it was the shock of the action that made Marilyn gasp.

In her mind's eye, she saw it—the Reptile, lying across the canyonlands near Shane's house. The thing appeared as physical as any prehistoric creature that might have once inhabited these lands, heaving with breath, great eyes shut and tail spiraling down across the sandstone and scattered residences.

We oversee.

We Correct.

In this vision, the Reptile was simply dormant. Resting. Gathering its power. It would find a spot to its liking, a place exuding some great geophysical energy like a volcano or fault-line, and it would lay itself down, absorb itself into the Earth from which it drew fuel, like a vehicle from a pump. For centuries or even millennia it would sleep, creating a dark pull upon the land that attracted confused or violent souls, those wondering and wandering, those heated by visions of reshaping and of upheaval.

Marilyn wrenched her hand away. "When will it wake up?" A thought struck. "Or is it waking up now?"

"We will wake when ready," he said.

"What's going to happen?"

"What's going to happen," he said, "is what has been happening."

Shane's eyes bored into hers. Beginning to understand the totality of the Reptile's project, she knew revulsion and sadness but also a kind of perverse sympathy.

"There are too many of us," Marilyn said. "What are you going to do? The whole world? How do you plan to 'correct'?"

Unless there were many Offspring, laid across many a shore, hatching or growing or becoming, waiting to unleash their own kind of destruction like the one in Pyramid Bay.

With some hesitation, Marilyn closed her eyes. She felt dizzy, as though she were falling. She half-opened her eyes again and Shane remained seated and unmoving, still staring at her.

"You will not meet resistance," he said, "if you seek to remove me."

Whether accurate or not, Marilyn took that as a skeptical challenge. She closed her eyes again, breathed, if only to control her heartrate. The darkness had texture. Just visiting the sleeping Shane these last few nights, the conscious effort of reconnecting, had sent some new life pulsing through those "Other" limbs. They were still there, just rusty. She could—

Yes, she could *lift* them.

Marilyn briefly opened her eyes. Shane's gaze and position unchanged. She sucked in more breath.

Closing her eyes once more, she reached out with those Other arms and grazed the thing dwelling in Shane. It was cool, rugged to the touch. It felt old, but not as old as she remembered the Offspring feeling.

Her Other arms fastened about its shape. Indeed, she met no resistance.

Marilyn walked forward and took Shane by the wrist. She pulled him up and walked him slowly down the hall and back to the bedroom, pushing open the door and shuffling inside. Halfway to the bed, Jeannie's voice issued quietly in the dark, "Everything okay?", to which Marilyn whispered, "Yes, it's okay," expecting Jeannie to say more though she never did.

Shane kept silent throughout, going along like a confused elder guided by his caretaker. For the first time, Marilyn noticed how warm and clammy his skin was. Almost feverish. She laid him down on his side of the bed, above the sheets. He stared at her. Somewhere deep in the recesses of that stare ten-year-old Shane looked out, reduced to an elusive flicker.

Marilyn stood back, concentrated again. The last stretch. As best as she could tell, her Other arms felt secure about the thing inside him. She pulled, and it came away easily, like tender meat falling from the bone that was Shane's soul.

She hung there, eyes closed, clutching this thing now clarifying in her mind's eye. It was no more than a coiled snake, patterned with colorful blotches and glittering, celestial scales. Its mouth was stretched in a human-like grimace.

It said: *We give eyes to stone. Ears to the wind.*

The grimace held.

We give mind, it added, *to the Earth.*

With the mental equivalent of a torquing motion, Marilyn relinquished the creature. She felt its scaly consistency leave her grasp. Its presence smoothed out, like choppy surf into placid waters.

Shane was now snoring softly.

•   •   •

Marilyn awoke on her couch and knew instantly she'd slept in later than she had in years. She smelled bacon.

Jeannie stood at the stove, scraping a spatula about two frying pans and a column of breakfast-scented smoke. Troy sat on the couch, head in a game.

"Oh," said Marilyn.

Jeannie startled a little, turned. "Welcome back to Earth, sis. Thought I'd take it upon myself to make—" she checked the microwave clock "—well, brunch, now, I guess."

Through a yawn, Marilyn said, "Wow. Thank you."

"Tom went out to get soda," Jeannie said. "Also, you'll have to help me with the coffeemaker, though. If it's broken, I don't want to break it even more."

Marilyn rose to her feet. "It can be fussy. Feel free to wake me when I'm zonked out, by the way. I hate sleeping in too late."

"Don't feel guilty." Jeannie lowered the flame on the bacon. "Shane's a log, too. Woke up like thirty minutes ago and I think he's slowly getting dressed. I don't think any of us slept well."

"You didn't have to do this—"

"Whatever. It's a distraction. Something to do. And a wee bit of thank-you for putting us up. And for putting *up* with us. That goes to you, too, Troy!"

"Huh?" he said, looking up from his game.

Marilyn started to head off down the hallway when she paused and pointed toward the stove. "You got that from my freezer, I assume?"

"The bacon? I did."

"You know it's veggie, right?"

"Ah. That explains a couple things."

Marilyn continued down the hall. The door to her bedroom stood ajar. She stopped, pulse accelerating. All at once, she was unsure if last night had been real.

She dribbled a knock. "Shane?"

"All's clear," he said.

Pushing open the door, Marilyn saw her brother sitting shirtless on the edge of the bed, thumbing through his phone.

"Any updates?" Marilyn asked.

He flipped the phone screen toward her, displaying a map with a big red-colored region. It looked like an open wound.

"Fire's grown by several thousand acres," he said. "So there's that."

"Shit. I'm so sorry."

For a moment she stood still, arms crossed, watching him as he scrolled through what was probably social media or news.

"Should I not ask what it was you were doing in here last night?" Shane asked, without looking up. "Or what was going on?"

Marilyn froze. Her first instinct was to deny, but figured that was pointless. She remained silent and Shane regarded her. His eyes remained hard, but it was a familiar hardness, typical of her younger brother—gruff, often-inappropriate sarcasm, forever simmering.

He looked back down at his phone. "I appreciate you not waking Jean."

Marilyn auditioned a thousand ways to elaborate. To explain. Instead she replied, "I have children. I know how to sneak-check."

Shane snickered quietly. "I'm assuming ignorance is bliss."

Still at a loss for a proper response, Marilyn started to turn away. "Jeanie's got breakfast going."

●　　●　　●

"They're here," Marilyn said.

"Are they coming up?" Jeannie asked.

"We'll just meet 'em down there."

"Shane," Jeannie called from her seat at the kitchen table, where she stared at her laptop. "We're about to head out."

Marilyn finished lathering sunscreen on Troy's back. Tommy stood holding his surfboard, browsing his phone.

Addressing Jeannie, Marilyn said, "You know, you two don't *have* to go." The curious flash of hurt in Jeannie's eyes prompted her to qualify: "I just don't want you feeling obligated. I know Shane's not a big beach guy."

Jeannie shrugged. "Forget him. It's family."

Marilyn smirked. "So we can't forget him, entirely."

Shane emerged in shorts and a workout shirt. "Alright, I'm set." He pointed to the collapsible beach chair leaned next to the front door. "You have more than one chair, right?"

"I don't, no," Marilyn said. "Kevin does. I'm sure he brought them."

They readied to leave. Marilyn tried to suppress the flutter of nerves that never really went away around Kevin, Margie and Tammy, to say nothing of having them together. And *especially* to say nothing of this unique situation in which she was carpooling with them *and* Shane and Jeannie. She might wind up being something of an intermediary. Even, God forbid, a referee.

As they made their way outside, though, Marilyn observed the huge gray smear of smoke over the hills, a tenacious staple of the past few days, and hoped the tragedy of the fire might level any tensions.

Kevin and Tamara stood waiting by Kevin's SUV, smiling as they approached though that might've been partly due to noon glare. Tamara wore a yellow sundress that Marilyn had gotten for her two Christmases ago. The way her wide-brimmed straw hat and garish shades hid her pretty face, she resembled an elusive movie star. Hell, maybe someday she would be. She'd become active in her high school drama club, somewhat to Kevin's concern though he vowed to "lay off" until he spotted, quote, "something." Initially, that "something" had been Tamara dying her hair red. Marilyn had just laughed, for once becoming the "nice" parent when it came to Tammy.

"Hey folks," Kevin said, outstretching his hand toward Shane. "How you holding up?"

"By the power of bipedal evolution," Shane said, "and not boozing myself into a fetal ball."

"I'm so sorry about your guys' home," Tammy said. "Seriously, been praying for you. Like every night."

"Thank you," Jeannie said.

"No Margie?" Marilyn asked.

"She had a work emergency, sadly."

Greetings went around. Marilyn embraced Kevin, who regarded her with the same distinct melancholy she'd come to realize would never fully disappear. She had not seen him in a couple weeks and was surprised to find several new lines on his face.

Marilyn hugged Tamara. "Hi, Tam-Jam."

"Hi, mom."

•   •   •

Nestled into her beach chair, Marilyn dug herself ankle-deep into the sand. The prickly, stinging heat was cathartic. Nearby, Kevin lathered himself with suntan lotion—particularly his scalp, after a questionable brown spot had been removed two years ago—then unfolded a chair of his own. She offered him a smile and he returned one in kind, though it proved as brief as his eye contact.

"You okay?" Marilyn asked him.

"Yeah," he said, slumping down in his chair. "I'm okay."

"What job-thing called Margie away?"

"Eh, best not talk about now. It's a long story."

Marilyn dropped the subject. She let Kevin be, and watched the others: Shane and Jeannie, sitting hunched on towels and talking amongst themselves, Shane repeatedly rubbing the back of his neck; Tom, paddling past the third breaker on his surfboard; Tamara, walking barefoot with Troy across the wet sand and helping him scope out shells and sand crabs, something he'd not tired of doing since he was younger.

Marilyn's heart swelled. In that moment, any disagreements with Tammy—some of which had resulted in red-faced blow-ups, and weeks of silence—became immaterial, and Marilyn was in awe of the goodness in her daughter. And not just in her, but in all her children. These were opinionated little forces of nature, cosmoses unto themselves that had somehow tumbled out of her. They were now gathering their own momentum to pinball unique paths across this world, and the moments in which she might behold them all in one gaze were growing rarer, to say nothing of the moments in which a slight head-turn would also include their uncles and aunts.

Her family was here.

A sizeable wave crested before Tom, and he turned on his board. It swept toward him, doubling up, and he paddled furiously and rode it a second or two before rising shakily to his feet with forced confidence that to Marilyn was obvious but maybe not so to the two admiring girls several yards away.

She cringed as the wave made short work of Tom's budding surfing skills, left him bobbing in the chop before splashing ashore on its billion years of inexhaustible fuel. Marilyn exhaled, curled her toes in the sand. The distant smoke darkened the edge of her vision. She wondered, idly, if they were sitting beyond the reach of high tide.

ABOUT THE AUTHOR

Author Photo by Kristi Barron

Born and raised in Los Angeles, Mike Robinson has been writing since age six, and professionally since nineteen. He is the award-winning author of multiple novels and dozens of short stories, and has received honors from Writers of the Future, Publishers Weekly's BookLife Contest, the Next Generation Indie Book Awards, Maxy Awards, and others. As a seasoned editor and coach, he's also helped shape multiple award-winning books, and for six years was the managing editor of the online magazine *Literary Landscapes* for GLAWS, or The Greater Los Angeles Writers Society.

Growing up in L.A. put him well within the gravitational pull of Hollywood, and he's been an active screenwriter and producer for nearly a decade. In between, he swims, draws, and hikes, often with his two dogs.

NOTE FROM MIKE ROBINSON

Word-of-mouth is crucial for any author to succeed. If you enjoyed *Ancient Tides Ashore*, please leave a review online—anywhere you are able. Even if it's just a sentence or two. It would make all the difference and would be very much appreciated.

Thanks!
Mike Robinson

We hope you enjoyed reading this title from:

www.blackrosewriting.com

Subscribe to our mailing list – *The Rosevine* – and receive **FREE** books, daily
deals, and stay current with news about upcoming
releases and our hottest authors.
Scan the QR code below to sign up.

Already a subscriber? Please accept a sincere thank you for being a fan of
Black Rose Writing authors.

View other Black Rose Writing titles at
www.blackrosewriting.com/books and use promo code
PRINT to receive a **20% discount** when purchasing.